PRECISION KILL!

Wyatt put the nose down.

The desert rolled through his HUD, speeding quickly beneath him. He could see six targets in the immediate path of his search radar. Four, in apparent disarray, were closing on him. The fifth was headed east, and the sixth was streaking across the screen on a perpendicular course to the north at almost double Mach.

Then he saw the missile launch.

He had a solid lock-on tone from his first Sidewinder, then the words "LOCK-ON" appeared in his HUD. The targets became visible, black dots against the terrain.

Depressing the release stud, Wyatt closed his eyes for a second to avoid the exhaust glare, ignited and shot. Kicking in left rudder, he saw his missile was streaming vapor toward the enemy MiG.

He fired off two more Sidewinders in fast sequence, then eased the rudder and aileron.

Number two impacted the MiG on his far left side.

A bright yellow-orange blossom burst into bloom, spewing segments of shrapnel out of its center.

"One down," Wyatt said, hauling back the throttles to avoid the head-on rush.

PHANTOM STRIKE

WILLIAM H. LOVEJOY

ZEBRA BOOKS
KENSINGTON PUBLISHING CORP.

DEDICATION

The State of Nebraska does have some positive traits, and the most positive is its people.

This novel is dedicated to some extremely nice and talented Nebraska people: Doug Bereuter, Rich Bringelson, Anne Campbell, Chris Christofferson, Bill Colwell, Jim Exon, Roger Flanders, Dorset Graves, Chuck Harrington, Murl Mauser, Ed Nelson, Ward Reesman, Larry Tangeman, Gerry Vasholz, Dave Wagaman, Bob Walker, Jerry Warner.

And in memoriam, Henry Ley and George Rebensdorf.

I consider myself fortunate to have been associated with, and to learn from, all of them at one period in my life.

Resurrection

One

From a half-mile away, the birds still looked proud, sleek, and capable. The mid-morning Arizona sun glanced white-hot off shiny aluminum and titanium panels and stabbed the eyes of observers. Wavery heat made the earth quiver in the far distance.

In the lead Jeep, Andy Wyatt backhanded the sweat from his forehead and fished his sunglasses from the breast pocket of his tan, knit sport shirt. The Polaroids killed the glare and gave him a more dismal view.

As they approached the first group of aircraft, Air Force Captain Owen Dinning, who was driving, slowed the Jeep to thirty miles an hour. Dinning was a fair-haired, smiley young man who displayed easy deference to his visitors. In the real, nonmilitary world, he would have a business address on Madison Avenue. He was following one of the asphalt roads that crisscrossed the aircraft park and delineated half-mile-long checkerboard squares. Within the squares, the sagebrush and weeds had been killed off with some defoliant, leaving sun-baked soil that was the color of spilled tea.

Behind them, a flight of F-15s took off from the air base with a roar that rumbled forever across the flat desert. Wyatt's eyes followed the two fighters as they banked away toward the Saguaro National Monument, then nosed upward and climbed steeply to the north.

Live airplanes interested Andy Wyatt far more than did dead ones.

He gazed solemnly at the aircraft they were passing. They appeared frozen to the earth, and he was certain that many of them should have been entombed.

The amiable Captain Dinning flipped a thumb at the behemoths broiling in the sun on their left. "Sure you don't want a BUFF, Mr. Wyatt?"

BUFF. Big, Ugly, Fat Fucker. The scourge of Hanoi. In the course of the war games in Southeast Asia, the B-52s had dropped more ordnance tonnage on North Vietnam than was expended in all of World War II. The daily pounding of the capital city was enough to drive any nation into mania and submission, but something was wrong with the strategy.

Hanoi won.

Viewed from up close, these B-52s saddened Wyatt. There were over a hundred of them parked in long rows. They were forlorn and neglected. Paint and insignia were peeling; metal skin was tarnished; tires were flattened; control surfaces were missing; Plexiglas was grazed and cracked. Most of them had empty engine nacelles, their turbojets scavenged for other uses. He knew that most of them would have had their radar and avionics stripped out. Stacks of debris—drop tanks, pylons, access panels—littered the ground beneath the wings. In the second row over, a blue pickup was parked in the shade of one of the giant swept wings, and two technicians were busy performing a surgical removal of something somebody somewhere needed on one of the forty-year-old bombers.

The design was forty years old, but the B-52 was still one of the mainstays of the Air Force, with 165 G- and H-model aircraft in active service. It said something subtle but powerful about the design.

"I think I'll pass," Wyatt told his driver.

"You don't look too happy, sir."

"If I were running this air force, I'd strip the damned things, then melt them down."

"Maybe we'll need them again?" the captain suggested.

"It'd cost more to rebuild one today than Boeing billed the taxpayer originally, Captain."

"That's true, sir."

Andrew Wyatt did not like viewing the mothball fleet at Davis-Monthan Air Force Base. Supposedly, the thousands of aircraft were being held in reserve, but realistically, most would never fly again. The skeletons neatly scattered over this sandy acreage were a highly visible tribute to obsolescence, an expensive symbol of American waste, Air Force style.

Dinning slowed, downshifted, and spun the wheel to the right at the next intersection. They passed ghettos of Lockheed C-121 Constellations, P-2 Neptunes, a few Electras, some Martin B-57 Night Intruders, Grumman Albatross amphibians, and F-101 Super Sabres. On a faraway plot, Wyatt saw a few golden oldies: B-17s, B-36s, a crippled Mustang.

Wyatt looked behind him. The other Jeep was keeping pace. Bucky Barr waved at him, his big, horsey teeth revealing his glee. Barr got a kick out of almost anything, but his exuberance did not pass to Wyatt. It was not only this traipse through avian tombstones that depressed him. The coming weeks carried the very real possibility that he would be buying memorial markers for some people he liked.

Captain Dinning dropped to second gear, bounced off the hard surface of the asphalt, and raced between the first two rows of what had to be over two hundred F-4 Phantoms. The second Jeep pulled up alongside them, to get out of the mini-cloud of dust Dinning raised.

Wyatt's guide found his clipboard in the space between the seats, checked the top sheet, and began to scan the tail numbers of the fighters. Halfway down the first row, he braked to a stop, and the tech sergeant driving the other vehicle skidded to a stop next to them.

"Here's the first one, Mr. Cowan."

"E model?" Wyatt asked, responding to the name he was using.

"Yes, sir. One of the dozen we've got. Most of the retirements here are B, C, and D models. Anything later is still in service, usually with the air reserves. A lot of them, all models, have been sold to friendly governments."

Wyatt swung his legs out of the footwell and stood up. The desert dust immediately coated the spit-shine of his Wellington boots. His chino slacks had had a crease in them at seven o'clock when he pulled them on in his motel room, but the crease was blurred now by heat and perspiration. His shirt felt sticky. Wyatt had big, muscled shoulders and arms, and the damp shirt acted as if it were part of his skin, another dermal layer.

Barr, Demion, and Kriswell slipped out of the other Jeep, and joined him in front of the Phantom's snout. They were dressed casually also, fighting the dry heat with jeans, sport shirts, and running shoes. The tech sergeant was in wilted fatigues, and Dinning, in summer Class As, was the only one who appeared fresh.

In his Air Force days, Wyatt had known commanders like Dinning, who seemed immune to the elements.

The six of them stood there silently for a moment and looked at the airplane.

"I don't see any dents," Bucky Barr noted.

"Maybe they used bondo on it?" Jim Demion said.

"Whatever they used, it's still pretty," Kriswell told them.

Despite the technological advances made with Eagles, Tomcats, and Hornets, the F-4 was still a lethal-looking airplane. It was also a reliable craft, Wyatt knew. Over five thousand had been built, one of the highest production records ever for a fighter aircraft. Only the MiG-21 could boast the same numbers. The Phantom first flew in 1958, and its combat record in Vietnam, flown by the Air Force, the Navy, and the Marines, was commendable.

The huge, ovoid air intakes on each side of the fuselage gave the craft added mass from the head-on view. The outer wing panels were canted upward in a dihedral angle, a counterpoint to the steep, twenty-three-degree anhedral droop of the rear tailplanes. This Phantom was missing its external fuel tanks, and the two wing-mounted weapons pylons which normally sprouted four Sidewinder missiles were bare, The underside was finished in dull white paint, and the fuselage and top surfaces were coated in the most recent scheme of matte olive, green, and tan camouflage colors. The ID was for the 32nd Tactical Fighter Squadron which, as far as Wyatt knew, was still operating out of Europe.

"Want to kick the tires, Mr. B?" Wyatt asked, being careful to avoid true names, deceiving his country, and as far as that went, his air force.

13

Barr grinned at him. "Hell, yes. I'm a tire-kicker from way back. Salesmen hate me."

"That's because you flatten the tires when you kick them," Kriswell said.

Nelson Buckingham Barr, III, was a solid chunk of a man, his physique akin to that of many boulders Wyatt had seen alongside Rocky Mountain highways. It had always seemed to Wyatt that someone had invented a giant shoehorn solely for the purpose of wedging Barr into fighter cockpits. He was five-feet, nine-inches tall, but his breadth gave him solidity.

Tom Kriswell, the electronics engineer/magician, was a foot taller than Barr and half as wide. He spoke to Dinning. "When was it brought in, Captain?"

Dinning checked his clipboard. "Three months ago, on April seventh."

"Flown in? Not transported?"

"Under her own power, sir."

"Suppose it's still got electrical power?"

"If they haven't pulled the batteries yet, we can give it a try," Dinning told him.

Dinning, Kriswell, and Jim Demion, Wyatt's aeronautical engineer, approached the side of the plane. Kriswell found the recessed control for the forward canopy and played with it. With a reluctant slurp of the rubber seals, the canopy began to raise. It was a slow process, attesting to the depleted condition of the batteries.

The tech sergeant got a ladder from the back of Dinning's Jeep, brought it over, and hooked it over the cockpit coaming. Kriswell scampered up the rungs with agility surprising in such a long and lean body, checked the safety pin on the ejection seat, swung his skinny legs inboard, and dropped into the seat.

Jim Demion began a circuit of the aircraft, sticking his head up into landing gear retraction wells, testing control surfaces, peering up the tail pipes of the twin J79-GE-17 turbojets. He popped the Dzus fasteners on access hatches, swung them open, and poked around in the innards. He came around to the front of the airplane and removed the protective covers on the air intakes.

Bucky Barr kicked the port side tire.

Kriswell tossed Wyatt the aircraft maintenance log, which had been stored in the cockpit.

"What have you got up there, Tom?" Wyatt asked.

"Not much. I've got power on the instrument panel, but not enough amperage to check radios or radar."

Wyatt took the log back to the Jeep. He sat on the passenger's seat and slowly read through it, making his own notes in the black leather notebook he carried in his hip pocket. This Phantom had been built in 1975 and had therefore missed the Vietnam festivities. The airframe had over forty thousand hours on it, but both of the General Electric turbojets had been changed out and now had eleven thousand hours on them. They would have to be rebuilt to achieve the reliability he wanted. The craft sported a Tiseo zoom-lens video system which enhanced the pilot's visual target-tracking. None of the F-4s featured Head Up Displays, but this machine did have the advanced sight system. It was computer-based and made interception and air or ground weapons delivery more accurate. The newer APQ-120 fire control radar was installed, as well as the additional fuel cell in the rear fuselage. That gave it a sixteen-hundred-mile ferry range.

Jim Demion sauntered back to the Jeep and waited for his turn at the log.

Their inspection took forty minutes.

When they were done, standing in a half-circle around the forlorn airplane, Wyatt asked, "Anybody have questions for the captain?"

There were none, but then the captain was not an airman, anyway.

"Okay," Wyatt said, "let's take a look at the next one, Captain Dinning."

At the next Phantom, Wyatt pulled Demion aside, out of earshot of Dinning and the tech sergeant. "What do you think, Jim? Are these old bastards going to work for us?"

"It's the best thing we've got going, Andy."

"That doesn't answer the question. We're going up against damned sophisticated weapons systems. I don't want bodies all over the landscape when it's over."

"We talking our bodies?"

"They're the ones uppermost in my mind, Jim."

"Go back to what we talked about before, Andy. The opposition's systems may be state-of-the-art, but keep telling yourself about the people behind them. They're assholes, remember?"

"Maybe. But assholes are conditioned to react instinctively."

"Just be cool, boss. When Kriswell and I are done, those aero-fucking-planes will be things of beauty. Venus de Milo, step aside."

"I don't give a good goddamn what they look like," Wyatt told him.

"But Bucky does," Kriswell said.

Barr had demanded, and received, responsibility for cosmetic changes. It would, he said, keep him out of the innards where he was all thumbs, anyway.

In four hours, the team looked over the three F-4Es, four F-4Ds, and one C model. By one o'clock, the sun was delivering temperatures above one hundred degrees, and probably much more than that on the barren surfaces of Davis-Monthan Air Force Base's "Boneyard."

"I'm hungry," Barr said.

"That doesn't tell us anything," Kriswell said. "You're always hungry."

"I'm tired of kicking tires. Let's play airplane tomorrow, and go back to the motel now."

"If you start walking now," Wyatt grinned at him, "you'll make Tucson by the time we're done."

"Shit. How come I always get hooked up with a bunch of workaholics?"

"Do you want to see a couple more, Mr. Cowan?" Dinning asked.

"We're about Phantomed out, I think. Let's look at that 130F now."

They all got back in the blue Air Force Jeeps and drove about three miles to where a C-130 Hercules was parked. The Lockheed C-130 transports, born in 1951, were operational airplanes still in production and utilized globally by a dozen governments and some private enterprises. It was a competent workhorse, and Wyatt already owned one that he had committed to this project.

This single Hercules condemned to mothballs was a one of a kind, designated a KC-130F. It had been an experiment in converting the Hercules to the role of aerial tanker in the normal, designated way of military contracts and design, though Wyatt had heard stories about jury-rigged C-130 tankers created on the spot in Vietnam. By the Marines, probably, since they were expert at Rube Goldberg devices. Apparently, the Air Force had decided to stick with their larger, jet-engined tankers because this aircraft log showed very little time on the four Allison turboprops. After a short reconnaissance trip around, and inside, the aircraft, both Demion and Kriswell appeared satisfied.

Back on the main grounds of the base at three o'clock, Captain Dinning lost the tech sergeant and took them into the officer's club for a sandwich and a beer.

"Jesus! Air-conditioning. I'd forgotten what it was like." Barr picked at his yellow Izod shirt with thumb and forefingers like a dainty dilettante, tugging it away from a chest as hairy as a brown bear's. He took off his Pebble Beach golf cap and wrung it out.

"Your upbringing left something to be desired," Demion told him.

"Like what?"

"Like upbringing."

"I was a deprived youth," Barr explained.

Barr was one of three sons of a noted and *Mayflower*-linked New Hampshire family. Lacking one physical trait that identified him with the Barr clan, he had evolved as the black sheep. While he had a Yale education, Bucky Barr took delight in being good-naturedly boorish. He also had a multimillion dollar trust fund that paid him a quarter-million dollars every January 2.

They pushed two tables together to give themselves some elbow room and spent an hour with French fries, hamburgers, Heineken, and their respective notes. The debate involved the perceived condition of subsystems, mostly.

Captain Dinning kept the coffee cups filled and the beer cans rolling, and listened to them with what Wyatt thought was growing suspicion. The captain appeared to have a growing distrust of their apparent cover story,

18

which had not been fully detailed for him. Wyatt did not worry too much about their guide, but from time to time, he threw in a statement intended to support the cover. "On 3387, what's the result if we re-rivet with the new countersunk rivets?"

Demion said, "Much cleaner. It's worth maybe point-one Mach."

At four o'clock, the four of them agreed on a list, and Wyatt jotted down the tail numbers. At the bottom of the page, he wrote in a phone number with a 202 area code. He ripped the page out of his notebook and handed it to Dinning.

"That's the roster, Captain, providing, of course, that each of them still carries an airworthiness certificate."

The captain, who was a public relations specialist rather than a pilot, looked over the list carefully. "I'll double-check the certificates for you and get the paperwork started, Mr. Cowan."

"We need drop tanks installed on that first F-4E," Demion pointed out.

"Also," Kriswell added, "we need to rob a couple planes for two drag chutes, a replacement IFF for 1502, and a rear canopy for 925."

"Of course. It's not a problem." Dinning turned his head toward Wyatt. "Do you mind my asking what you're going to do with these planes?"

"Not at all. Back in '61, the Phantom held some world records for speed at Mach 2.6 and for altitude at ninety-eight thousand feet. It's still a good airplane, Captain, and we're going to modify these for racing and endurance trials, as well as taking them on the air show circuit."

"I see. I wish you luck, but do you need all of these electronics?"

"Hell, if I'm buying them, I might as well get what comes with them, right?"

The set of Dinning's mouth suggested he thought otherwise. "Yes. I suppose so."

"Thanks. Now, I'd appreciate it if you could get them all towed in in the morning and checked out. We won't worry too much about avionics at this point, but we do need batteries installed on almost all of them, and battery charges and fluid levels will have to be up to par. I'd like to have everything fueled and ready to go by the day after tomorrow."

The captain straightened up in his chair, his face apologetic. "On Thursday? I'm afraid that won't be possible, Mr. Cowan."

"The aircraft we selected shouldn't pose many problems, Captain."

"Not on the flight readiness, no, sir. However, before surplus aircraft can be sold to civilians, we are required to have our ground crews remove a number of weapons-related systems: the ordnance pylons, the cannon, threat warning devices, jammers, chaff dispensers, attack radar, and the like. I'm sure you understand, sir. None of that would be necessary for your objectives, anyway."

While Dinning was explaining his problem, Wyatt got out his wallet and withdrew a certified check for $225,000. The check was identified as issued in favor of Noble Enterprises, Inc., of Phoenix, Arizona. He placed it on the table and slid it across to Dinning.

"What's this, sir?"

"That's payment for seven aircraft, Captain. And I'll give you another check for the fuel and whatever maintenance is required."

From the look on his public relations face, Dinning

apparently did not think that some twenty million dollars worth of aircraft should be surplused to some civilian at a penny to the dollar.

"Well, sir, I think the surplus material people will want to negotiate a little further."

"The price has already been approved by the Department of Defense," Wyatt explained to him.

"Oh. I didn't know that, Mr. Cowan."

"And the price includes all equipment now aboard the airplanes. We get them as is."

Dinning stood up, the resolution to prevent civilians access to sophisticated, and possibly still classified, military weapons clearly revealed on his face. "I'm going to have to check on that, Mr. Cowan."

"I know. That's why I gave you the phone number."

Two

Andrew Michael Wyatt's hair was full over the ears, tapered above his neck, and fell across his forehead in a casual swoop. With the deep tan of his face, he might have been a Malibu Beach or Honolulu surf bum in appearance. The deep etching at the corners of his ice-blue eyes and his firm mouth suggested otherwise. He did not smile very often, and his closest friends sometimes found him short on humor. What really killed the leisurely image was the iron gray color of his hair.

Though he was only in his mid-forties, Wyatt impressed people as being a little older and a little wiser, maybe fifty. He had lived with the overly mature image for twenty years, having gone prematurely gray at twenty-four. He could, in fact, pinpoint the date when the silver began to appear in previously dark locks.

It was April 17, 1970, a few hours before April 18.

It was a night mission over Haiphong, and he was flying an F-111A swing-wing fighter bomber under development by General Dynamics. Wyatt was assigned to the 428th Tactical Fighter Squadron out of Ubom in Thailand, and the squadron had been given six F-111's for operational trials over North Vietnam. The early version of the aircraft was disappointing for they lost half of their complement within a month.

His was one of them.

Armed with two 750-pound bombs, Wyatt's airplane had been given a dock and warehouse in the harbor as primary targets. Military intelligence had determined that both the dock and the warehouse were supposed to be military targets rather than civilian. Targets were very specific in that war, approved by the White House inner circle—all of whom considered themselves military experts, and anything not adorned with some kind of NVA insignia, whatever that might be, was off-limits.

He and his wingman, a second lieutenant named Ruskin, approached the harbor low from the west, riding the hilly terrain as low as possible in order to avoid radar detection. They were accompanied by a flight of four Marine F-4s flying cover. As they neared the city, Wyatt and Ruskin climbed to five thousand feet and spread a quarter-mile apart in search of their mission objectives on the far side of the anchorage. His Weapons System Officer, Miles Adair, in the seat next to him, had his head buried in the radar boot.

Wyatt never reached, nor saw, either of his own targets. Five miles before reaching the harbor, the radar screen lit up with the blips of Fan Song target-seeking radars. Adair counted off six surface-to-air missile launches. Most of the Fan Songs went passive as the missile-carrying F-4 fighters launched retaliatory strikes against the radar installations. As the harbor finally burst into view, the dark skies were peppered with bright pinpricks of light: exploding SAMs and erupting antiaircraft shells from the quad-barreled ZSU-23 batteries surrounding Hanoi and Haiphong.

Some brave communist radar operator kept his set

active in order to guide his missile, and Wyatt's earphones sang with the pitched tone of the threat warning and Adair's verbal additions to it.

"Lock-on, Andy! Break right!"

Checking his rearview mirror, he saw the flare of rocket exhaust circling the dark hole of the missile body, and he jinked the plane hard to the right, climbing, but could not lose his deadly pursuer.

The missile went right up his starboard tail pipe.

And did not detonate. It was a Soviet Union version of a dud.

The aerial collision still disintegrated his right Pratt and Whitney TF30, shredding the fuselage and wing with snapped turbine blades. The F-111 skidded and bucked, then started vibrating violently. Red warning lights lit up the instrument panel like the Las Vegas Strip. He killed power on the right engine. A quick stab at the transmit button told him he had lost his radios. Vital electrical and hydraulic arteries had been severed.

Wyatt jettisoned his bomb load and his drop tanks in the middle of the harbor and retarded the port throttle, which eased the vibration. Making a slow 180-degree turn, he limped the airplane back to the west as far as Laos. Ruskin stayed with him all the way and circled when Wyatt could no longer keep the F-111 airborne, and he and Adair ejected over a rice paddy. They were picked up by helicopter within an hour, and Wyatt woke up the next morning with the first strands of gray showing at his temples.

He was fully gray-headed by the end of 176 missions and his third tour.

On Thursday morning, he was up by five-thirty to run through his twenty minute regimen of sit-ups, push-ups, and deep-knee bends. Wyatt's six-foot frame of hard muscle was probably in better shape than it had been twenty years before, but it took increased effort to keep it at the level he wanted. After exercising, he showered, washed his hair, and shaved. It took him five minutes to dress in slacks and a blue sport shirt and to pack his single carry-on bag. Wyatt carried the small bag and the larger one containing his flight gear down to the Holiday Inn's desk and checked out, paying in cash. Everyone was supposed to pay in cash. He bought a copy of the *Phoenix Gazette* and went looking for breakfast.

Barr was already in the coffee shop, working away at four eggs and two breakfast steaks. He grinned as Wyatt took the chair opposite him. "Morning, boss."

Wyatt poured himself a cup of coffee from the insulated plastic pot on the table. "You look amazingly alive. How was Nogales?"

Bucky Barr and two of the others had crossed the border the night before to analyze the current level of Mexican revelry.

He reported, "In a world of change, Nogo doesn't. Same varieties of debauchery."

Wyatt ordered an omelet guaranteed to contain extra *jalapeno* peppers and read the paper while he waited for the rest of his team. From Tokyo to Beirut to Washington, the world was in typical disarray. A little greed, a little power-grabbing, a lot of fanaticism.

By six-thirty, they had all stacked their soft-sided luggage in the lobby and were gathered at two tables, urging their beleaguered waitress to greater speed. In addition to Barr, Demion, and Kriswell, there were four more faces. Norm Hackley, Dave Zimmerman, Cliff Jordan, and Karl Gettman had flown in commercially from Albuquerque the previous afternoon. Hackley and

Gettman were the two Barr had cajoled into joining him for his Mexican spree. Both were droopy-eyed this morning and particularly fond of ice water and orange juice.

Zimmerman, a clean-cut, sandy-haired man of twenty-eight, was the youngest pilot in Wyatt's group. He had been an F-15 Eagle jockey for the USAF until eighteen months before. He leaned toward Wyatt's table and said, "Beats the hell out of me, Andy, why these old fossils, who are supposed to be wise veterans of life, can't grasp some simple truths. I've learned that there's a direct correlation between the night before and the morning after."

"Go flub a duck, Davie boy," Gettman muttered.

Barr, who was never affected by mornings-after, said, "The truth, Dave, is that the night before is worth the morning after."

"Selfish bastard," Gettman told Barr. "You always speak for yourself."

"I knew there was a truth in there, somewhere," Norm Hackley said, "but I think it's only a half-truth."

"Do you guys realize you all sound incoherent?" Wyatt asked.

"Now, there's a truth," Zimmerman said.

"You should have heard them last night, you want incoherence," Barr said.

"I especially don't want incoherence today. I want bright-eyed and bushy-tailed."

He got nods in response, but some of them seemed halfhearted.

Wyatt folded his paper and surveyed his group. All of them were employees of his Aeroconsultants, Incorporated, and he was fond of them all. Except for Zimmerman and a few of the technicians back in

26

Albuquerque, he had served Air Force time, somewhere in the world, with all of his people.

After the waitress had brought yet two more coffeepots, Wyatt briefed them. "Bucky, Cliff, and I will take the F-4Es. Jim, you get the Herc, and Tom will ride in the right seat for you."

Demion had multiengine and jet ratings on his private license, though he had never flown for the military except as a peripheral activity in consulting for them. His interest was secondary to his profession of aeronautical engineering.

Kriswell was not a pilot. He had abandoned pursuit of a flying license after his first landing on his first solo flight in a Cessna 182. He had managed to leave part of the propeller and the landing gear a few hundred yards away from where the airplane finally came to rest.

"You get to handle the Thermos, Tom," Demion said. "No touching the yoke."

"Can I play with the throttles?"

"If you're real good," Demion promised.

"The rest of us are here to sightsee?" Hackley asked.

"Nope," Wyatt told him. "I only pay you to work. I've got a couple F-4Ds for Dave and Karl. Norm, you get a C model."

"Shit. The slowest one of the bunch, no doubt. Anybody want to flip a coin?"

"No trades. The hydraulics are a little iffy on your bird, Norm, and if there are any problems, I want your experience in the cockpit."

Mollified, Hackley—who had F-4 combat hours—shrugged and said, "Ho-kay."

"Our destination is Ainsworth." Wyatt had not mentioned that to any of them before.

"What the hell's an Ainsworth?" Barr asked.

"And where in the hell is it?" Hackley added.

"It's in north central Nebraska. Just under a thousand miles, and we can make it in one hop."

"Nebraska in mid-July?" Barr complained. "You've got to be shitting us, Andy."

"The sandhill cranes like it."

"Yeah, but I'll bet the crane population is composed of two genders," Barr said.

After the last of the coffee was drained from their cups, the group made last pit stops and then carried all of the luggage out into the dry heat of morning and dumped it into the trunks of two taxicabs. Thirty minutes later, they hauled it into the operations office at Davis-Monthan and stacked it against a wall opposite the counter.

Wyatt figured that all of the right telephone calls had been made and most of the objections overcome because he could see his seven aircraft lined up on the tarmac about a quarter-mile away. A fuel truck, three start carts, several pickups, and a dozen men were clustered around them.

They waited, milling around, hitting the Coke machine.

Captain Dinning arrived at eight-fifteen wearing a haggard smile and carrying a four-inch-thick folder. He dropped it on the counter and said, "You don't know what I've been through in the last twenty-four hours, Mr. Cowan."

"I've got a fair idea, Captain. And all of it in quadruplicate, too."

Bucky Barr asked, "Did we get all of the tail numbers we asked for?"

"That's correct."

"I'll get a couple of the guys, and we'll start filling out flight plans. Jim went off to get the weather info."

"Good. I want the Hercules to go first, followed by a flight of the 4Ds and the C model. The rest of us will fly out last."

"And get in first, no doubt," Barr said.

Barr, Gettman, and Hackley went to the end of the counter and began to fill out forms.

Dinning opened his folder and, one by one, began laying multipart forms in front of Wyatt. He saw that ownership had been vested in Noble Enterprises, Phoenix, Arizona, as requested. With his ballpoint pen, Wyatt dated and signed each form as Roger A. Cowan, President, Noble Enterprises. He was given copies of receipts, temporary registrations, temporary FAA certifications, and, on the F-4E fighters, temporary registrations for the M61A1 twenty-millimeter multibarreled cannons.

"The understanding is that you're to contact the Treasury Department's firearms division and arrange for a hearing on those," Dinning said.

"You bet," Wyatt said, but did not think he could fit it into his schedule.

"That's what caused the most trouble," Dinning told him. "Even the base commander got involved."

And lost, Dinning guessed.

"And finally agreed, if the M61s were disabled."

"How was that accomplished?"

"The fire control black boxes have been removed," the captain told him.

"Where are they?"

"On board the C-130."

"Okay. That's safe enough."

29

"One other thing," the captain said. "With those radios. You're supposed to stay off military frequencies."

"I don't like to listen to Eagle pilots, anyway," Wyatt assured him. He signed a sheet promising just that.

"Then, we have this."

Wyatt took the statement from Maintenance and Operations and went over the entries. Two tires had been replaced. Four sets of brakes were new. The avionics and basic instruments had been superficially examined and temporarily okayed. There were labor charges for installing a rear canopy on 925. Every engine had been started and run for fifteen minutes, but there were no guarantees. Fuel tanks, including external tanks, had been topped off. He had been charged for nearly eighty gallons of lubricants and hydraulic fluids.

The billing came to $34,292.67.

His guess had been close to right. Wyatt produced another certified check for thirty thousand, and wrote out a company check for the balance. Both checks were written against Noble Enterprise's Phoenix account. It was an account that would cease to exist as soon as this last check cleared.

"Does that make us even, Captain?"

"I believe it does, Mr. Cowan. Happy racing."

The captain did not believe the racing angle for a minute, Wyatt thought. "Thanks. And thanks for your help."

"Anytime, sir." Dinning turned and left.

Barr came over to him. "We're all filed. You need to sign your flight plan."

After he signed off on a flight plan that hinted at a destination in Montana, Wyatt led his team down to a dressing room, and they changed into flight gear. Their flight suits were identical, dove gray in color, with their first names stitched in red over the right breast pockets. Across the back of each garment, red letters advertised, "NOBLE ENTERPRISES-AVIATION DIVISION."

Demion and Kriswell left their matching helmets and their parachute harnesses in their duffel bags, but the rest of them hoisted chutes over their shoulders and carried their helmets, G suits, personal oxygen masks, duffel bags, and overnighters. In a group, they left operations and crossed the hot concrete of the apron toward the parked aircraft. The short walk resulted in sweat-darkened armpits. Wyatt could feel the perspiration dripping down his back.

"Don't you feel like Wyatt Earp and Doc Holliday, heading down the main drag in Tombstone?" Barr asked.

"As a matter of fact, no," Wyatt told him.

"We've got to work on your imagination, Andy."

The excess luggage was stowed in the crew compartment behind the cockpit of the Hercules.

Everyone found his airplane and spent the next hour going over it with the crew chief who had worked on it. When each of the pilots had expressed to Wyatt his relative satisfaction, Wyatt said, "Looks like a go, then. Jim, you and Tom can fire up."

Demion and Kriswell climbed through the crew door on the forward, port side of the C-130 and locked it after them. One by one, the four turboprops came to life, then the big transport moved out of line toward the taxiway. Half an hour later, the plane was a black smudge on the wavery horizon.

Hackley, Zimmerman, and Gettman took off next, Gettman's Phantom dragging what Wyatt thought was an overly thick kerosene vapor trail, though the Phantom was known for its identifiable exhaust signature.

Ten minutes after that, Wyatt slipped into his pressure suit, buckled on his parachute, climbed the ladder, checked the safety pins on the ejection seat, slid into the cockpit, and settled into the seat of the Phantom numbered 3387. It felt good to be back, he thought, as he locked in the seat and shoulder harness. The crew chief came up the ladder to help him connect oxygen and pressure suit fittings. He settled the helmet on his head, snapped the oxygen mask in place—letting it hang to one side, then hooked into the radio system.

"All set, sir?"

"Ready to go, Sergeant. Thanks for your help."

"I'm just happy to see 'em flying again, sir." Even if by a civilian, he thought.

"Let's light her up."

The crew chief scampered down the ladder and took it away.

Wyatt ran through his never-forgotten check list, powering up the panel and radios. The inertial navigation system gyros had been activated earlier, using the Auxiliary Power Unit, since they took a while to spin up. He punched in the Davis-Monthan coordinates. He went through the start sequence, setting ignition toggles, and then gave a thumbs-up to the man tending the start cart. The airman signaled back, and Wyatt started turning the turbine. When the RPMs reached thirty-five percent, he lifted the flap and hit the port ignition. The turbojet whined as the turbine built up speed, then whooshed as it took hold on its own. The starboard engine fired a few seconds later. All of the pertinent instruments read in the green.

Lifting a thumb-and-forefinger okay to the crewmen on the ground, Wyatt released the brakes and rolled forward. When he reached the taxiway, he braked for a right turn, lined up on the yellow guiding line, then braked to a stop.

Barr and Jordan fell into line behind him.

Wyatt adjusted the barometric pressure on the altimeter for the setting Demion had gotten during his weather check, dialled in the local ground frequency on the NavComs, then thumbed the transmit button. "Davis Ground Control, Phantom three-three-eight-seven."

"Go ahead, eight-seven."

"Davis, eight-seven has a flight of three near Hangar B. Requesting permission to taxi."

"Phantom eight-seven, you're cleared for taxi to Runway two-seven right. Switch to Air Control."

"Phantom eight-seven, wilco."

The three aircraft rolled along at thirty miles an hour as they headed for the assigned runway. In his rearview mirror, Wyatt checked the planes behind him. The forward canopies were still raised, capturing the hot breeze. It made him think of the takeoff lines he had waited in at Ton Son Nhut Air Base.

Redialling the radios to the air control frequency, Wyatt got immediate takeoff clearance, and the three Phantoms turned onto the runway, Barr and Jordan lining up in echelon off his right wing. Wyatt snapped his oxygen mask into place.

On the interaircraft frequency they had agreed on, Wyatt asked, "You two ready?"

"Yo, Major," Jordan replied.

"Can we use afterburner?" Barr begged.

"No afterburners. We're not showing off just yet. Let's hit it."

Wyatt ran his throttles forward, released the brakes, and felt nearly thirty thousand pounds of thrust immediately. It shoved him back satisfyingly in his seat. By the time he passed the operations tower, his airspeed was showing 160 knots. A quick glance to his right confirmed that Barr and Jordan were right with him, demonstrating the discipline and ability taught them by seven thousand hours of flight time.

He eased the stick back a notch and the long, narrow nose ahead of him rose. He felt the lift take over, and, a minute later, the wheels quit rumbling. The Phantoms crossed the Davis-Monthan boundary fence at a thousand feet of altitude and banked into a right turn.

Wyatt retracted flaps and landing gear and got green lights.

"Phantom eight-seven, Davis Air Control."

"Go ahead, Davis."

"Eight-seven, you are cleared to thirty thousand feet, heading zero-zero-five."

"Roger, Davis, confirm angels thirty, zero-zero-five. Eight-seven out."

Barr's baritone sounded in his earphones. "Now?"

"Now, Bucky."

Wyatt shoved his throttles outboard and past the detents into afterburner, pulling back on the stick at the same time.

The three Phantoms leapt upward, climbing almost vertically, airspeed reaching past the five hundred-knot mark, looking for the rarified freedom of thirty thousand feet.

Jesus, I love this.

The Excelsior Hotel on Bath Road was convenient to Heathrow Airport for the German, or Formsby would

34

not have agreed to it as a meeting place. He did not like to hold such meetings in ostentatious surroundings.

Neil Formsby got out of his cab in front of the main entrance to the hotel at 6:30 P.M. in the evening. He tipped the doorman just enough to remain unremarkable and pushed his way into the ornate lobby. He stood inside the doors for a moment and looked around.

Formsby was in evening dress for he had to meet Pamela at D'Artagnan in Regent's Park immediately after seeing the man from Bonn. In fact, Muenster's telephone call had almost upset his entire evening. He did not care for unexpected disruptions in his schedule.

He was a tall man at six-feet, two-inches and always tailored in the latest of immaculate fashion. His dark blond hair was crisply styled to his aristocratic head. Set widely on either side of an aquiline nose, his eyes were hazel and very direct. People who spoke with Formsby thought he was either extremely interested in them or obnoxiously intrusive. Those who thought him impolite also thought that his wide shoulders were padded and his slim torso girdled. They were incorrect.

Spotting the man who must be his quarry standing near the entrance to the bar, Formsby crossed the deep pile carpet of the lobby toward him. He walked with an obvious limp. The bones of his left ankle were nearly solidified with aluminum pins, and there was almost no flexibility left in the joint.

"Herr Ernst Muenster?"

"Yes. Mr. Carrington-Smyth?" The German spoke almost unaccented English.

"Correct. Shall we?" Formsby lifted a hand toward the lounge.

"By all means."

Seated at a table near the back, after ordering a

cognac for the German and a single malt scotch for himself, Formsby said, "I appreciate your responding so quickly, Herr Muenster."

"Please. It is Ernst."

"And Malcolm, if you will. Do you frequently conduct your business face-to-face?"

"Always. It assures that I will do more business."

Formsby nodded, but remained silent as their drinks were delivered and placed in front of them with a flourish.

Muenster spent the diversion examining Formsby closely, but then that was the very point of the personal meeting, Formsby thought.

Muenster appeared to be nearly sixty years of age. What was left of his hair—a fringe that was trimmed close to his skull—was snowy white. His jowls sagged some, an accompaniment to his massive girth. Formsby guessed that he would tip the scales at better than three hundred pounds. His tailors had much to work with, but performed a credible job. The man wore a summer-weight wool worth a thousand U.S. dollars. He also wore a constant half-smile, as if the circumstances he found himself in bordered on the humorous.

He was not in an amusing business. Herr Ernst Muenster was an arms dealer, but to be honest, an arms dealer of the highest caliber and reputation. Formsby managed to keep the pun to himself.

When the waiter moved away, Formsby raised his glass, and his eyebrow, in a toast. "To the point?"

Muenster sipped from his crystal glass, then ran his tongue lightly across his upper lip. "I appreciate a man who comes right to the point."

"Very well." Formsby withdrew the single sheet of

yellow notepaper from his inside breast pocket and passed it across the table.

The German scanned it, his eyes hesitating over a couple of the entries. He nodded. "It can be done."

"I am encouraged."

"Delivery included?"

"Please."

"And End-User Certificates?"

Formsby shrugged. "Quite up to you, I'm sure."

Muenster nodded. "Expensive, but manageable. The destination will have a bearing. Might I know where that will be?"

"To be determined at a later date, but certainly on the African continent."

"Yes. I see."

"How about a price?" Formsby asked.

"To be determined at a later date," the German told him with a slight increase in the grin. "I will need to check on several items. Demand and supply, you understand?"

"I do understand. I will ring you the first of the week next." Lacking a true name and a telephone number for Formsby, the German could not telephone Formsby.

"Thursday may be a better day," Muenster said. "I will have to travel some."

"Thursday it is," Formsby agreed.

They finished their drinks, and Formsby got up and made his way back across the lobby and out the entrance. While the doorman whistled a cab forward, he reviewed the meeting and thought that it had gone well.

Soon, he would be armed again.

* * *

The brown and tan Nebraska plains stretched from one horizon to the other, seemingly endless at Wyatt's altitude of fifteen thousand feet, about 12,500 feet AGL—above ground level—at Ainsworth. A few blue dots that were the remains of lakes in July were scattered about. Fifty miles ahead was the Rosebud Indian Reservation in South Dakota.

"Trees seem to be in short supply," Barr told him over the radio.

"We don't have to build a homestead."

Cliff Jordan broke in, "Tally ho, there we go. Eleven o'clock."

Wyatt saw the airfield just as Jordan reported it. The long, straight runways broke up the terrain.

"My God!" Barr said. "What's that doing here?"

Turning slightly left to align himself with the airport, Wyatt touched the transmit button and said, "It was a bomber training base during War Two, Bucky."

"Well, it was a big son of a bitch."

The concrete runways were wide enough that small aircraft could take off crosswise. Each of the three runways looked to be about ten thousand feet long. Spaced along the north side of the field was a row of massive hangars, their corrugated roofs streaky with rust and dirt. From two miles away, it looked deserted.

Jordan clicked on, "Can you imagine that place with B-17s, B-25s, and B-36s lining the aprons?"

"Yeah, Cliff, I sure as hell can," Barr said, his voice a little awed. He had a soft spot for 1940's era warbirds.

Wyatt took them down to five thousand feet and made a pass down the northern runway so they could check conditions. One corner of one hangar, near the dilapidated tower, contained a local flight service. A couple Aeronicas, a Mooney, a Cessna light-twin, and

38

a Beechcraft were parked in a row out in front. In the middle of all that concrete, they looked like exquisite miniatures. A wind sock high on the hangar hung limp. As the three Phantoms shot down the runway in formation, seven or eight figures abruptly burst out of the flight service and peered up at them.

The runways appeared to be in good repair, though clumps of weeds grew in the cracks between slabs. Some of the outer edges had crumbled, but it was nothing worrisome. There were no painted centerlines.

Wyatt banked left to circle around and begin his approach. By the time they reached the eastern end of the approach leg, the other three Phantoms appeared from the southwest. Wyatt's flight of F-4Es had passed them up a hundred miles back. The C-130 tanker was much further behind, making the trip at a cruise speed of 330 knots compared to the 550 the Phantoms had been averaging.

Gettman's voice came over the air. "Is that our home, Andy?"

"Sweet home," Wyatt told him.

"You don't suppose there's someone in, say, L.A., who'd adopt me?" Gettman asked.

"You've been kicked out of every home you've been in," Barr said. "Remember last night?"

Norm Hackley cut in, "The chart says there's no airport operations."

"True," Wyatt said. "The flight service has a base radio, if you feel like you need to talk to someone."

Wyatt retarded his throttles, dropped his landing gear, and set forty degrees of flap. The Phantom floated in, trailed closely by its identical sisters. The tires squealed as they touched down on hot pavement. He had completed his rundown and turned right onto the taxi strip as Hackley's flight of three passed overhead behind them, performing their own examinations of the airstrip.

The flight had taken less than two hours, though they had lost an hour crossing the time zone.

Rolling down the taxiway, Wyatt raised the canopy. After the dry heat of Arizona, the humidity here was like a slap in the face with a barber's hot towel. Immediately, the sweat popped on his forehead. The chalky white concrete reflected the sun, and the stillness trapped the superheated air.

Hangars Four and Five had been leased by Noble Enterprises. The structures were tall, built to allow clearance for the vertical stabilizers of now-antique bombers. Weeds as high as six feet crowded against the sidewalls. Faded, barely legible numbers on the front corners identified the two for which he was looking. Wyatt toed the left brake and turned toward Five just as the giant doors on the hangar began to rumble open.

Thirty yards from the building, Wyatt stopped, set the brakes, and killed the engines. He was disconnected from his electrical and environmental systems by the time Barr and Jordan parked next to him in a neat row. Wyatt stood up in the cockpit, leaned forward against the windscreen, and looked around.

Half a mile away, down at the flight service, people were piling into two pickup trucks. They just had to come visiting the tourists.

Behind him, the engines of Hackley's flight lost their high pitch as the landing aircraft whistled by.

Ahead of him, five men stood grinning at him in the open doors of the hangar. Behind them, parked in the cool-looking depths, was a Cessna Citation business jet and a Lockheed C-130 Hercules. The Citation was painted the color of cream and the Hercules was in pristine plain aluminum, and both carried the thin blue fuselage stripe which was the signature of Aeroconsultants, Inc.

But the red-trimmed logos on the tails identified them as property of Noble Enterprises.

Three

Ace had a white amulet in the middle of his chest and a white circle of fur around one yellow eye, but was otherwise a solid smoke gray. He was about three feet long, from his nose to the tip of his broken tail, and after a round of betting by the technicians, had been weighed in at nineteen pounds. He had wandered into the shop area one morning, a month after Aeroconsultants opened its doors for business, and had hung around since then, four years now. He liked to sit on top of things (tool chests, airplanes, the computer terminal in Kramer's office) and survey his world. Ace was not big on affection. About the only one who was allowed to pet him was Janice Kramer. Anyone, however, could feed him, and Ace went through cans of 9-Lives in lionish fashion. His food bill was a major draw on petty cash.

After his lunch on Thursday, Ace stretched out on the desk next to the computer terminal and cleaned himself up while Jan Kramer instructed the machine to print out the monthly statements. When he was done with his bath, Ace laid his chin on the telephone and went to sleep. Every once in a while, she reached over and ran her fingers through his thick coat.

Liz Jordan, Cliff Jordan's wife and the company's secretary/receptionist/bookkeeper, normally ran the billings, but Kramer liked to operate the computer now and then. In fact, only Kramer, Andy Wyatt, and Bucky Barr could access certain of the data files stored on the hard disk. Anyone trying to get into the files without the proper access codes would only find gibberish when they got there. The files were programmed to self-destruct at the first hint of unauthorized entry.

Kramer had been with the company from just before the beginning. Freshly out of work and frantically near the end of her savings, she had been submitting resumes to almost anything that appeared in the paper, even the skimpy, blind ads. She had been highly skeptical when one of those submissions brought her a phone call. One of the strange things about the interview with Andy Wyatt was that she had not gone to him. He had flown to Seattle and interviewed her in the lounge at Sea-Tac Airport at five in the afternoon.

He was a very presentable man in a good suit and conservative tie, with a few hard edges to him, and a no-nonsense, let's-not-waste-time approach.

Kramer had worn her best skirted business suit—a creamy beige—with a green silk blouse that complemented her deep green eyes and contrasted nicely with her heavy, dark red hair. The suit dampened some of the more daring curves of her figure and gave her a professional appearance, she thought. She was not yet desperate enough for a job to use her femininity as a drawing card.

However, as far as she could tell, Wyatt did not even notice. Half the time, he was turned sideways to her, watching the air traffic on the runways and apparently only partially interested in the interview, though his questions were sharply directed.

He went right to the first, hurtful point. "You got fired from Boeing?"

"Along with many others, Mr. Wyatt. There was a major cutback in the division."

He tapped her resume. "This says you got your law degree from UCLA. Third in your class?"

"That's correct. If you feel it's necessary, I can get the transcripts for you."

"You tell many lies?"

"What! Of course not."

"Then I don't need the transcripts, do I?"

"Oh. No, you don't."

"Can you tell a lie if you need to?"

She had to think about that one. This was not an interview like any she had ever read about or experienced. "I don't know. Are you talking about legal matters?"

"If the security of your nation were involved?"

"That's what Fawn Hall thought."

"If Baghdad was going to poison Seattle's water supply?"

She hesitated once again. "I suppose I could, if the rationales were justifiable."

"You're up-to-date on aviation law?"

"Very much so."

"How about office administration?"

"I think I could handle that. I worked in my father's accounting office through high school and while I was attending college at the University of Washington."

"And you're divorced?" Wyatt asked, his blue eyes holding hers, being just a little obtrusive.

That was not on her resume. Wyatt had run some background checks on her before showing up. That indicated he was more thorough than her first impression had suggested.

"I don't know what bearing that has on. . . ."

"This position would require that you move to a new city, Miss Kramer. It's easier for a single person."

"The divorce was finalized over two years ago."

"You mind if I call you Janice?"

"I go by Jan."

"And you don't object to moving?" He went back to staring at the airplanes.

"Probably not," she said. "Mr. Wyatt, your ad simply asked for, 'Attorney, aviation law and contracts.' I don't know anything about your company. For instance, for starters, where is it located?"

Wyatt turned his head and grinned at her. "It isn't. It's not even formed yet, which is the first reason I need a lawyer. But I'm leaning toward Albuquerque as the base of operations at the moment. Do you like Albuquerque?"

"I've never been there."

No wonder it was a blind ad. The whole thing was beginning to sound like a fly-by-night scheme. Without really meaning to do it, Kramer started to reverse the procedure of the interview. She became the interviewer.

"What kind of business are you starting, Mr. Wyatt?"

"We'll be consulting professionals in aviation matters," he said. "Anything from efficiency studies to route management to federal aviation applications to customizing and rebuilding very sophisticated aircraft for clients."

"And you have the background for that?"

Again, she got the half-grin, as if he was amused at

the course of the conversation. "I just got out of the Air Force, Miss Kramer."

"You were a pilot?"

"Of just about every aircraft type they have."

"And you retired?"

"No. I left a couple years early."

And gave up his pension? No way. He was probably kicked out of the service. She was becoming very skittish. "Mr. Wyatt, I'm not sure I'm the one. . . ."

"You haven't asked about salary."

"All right. What salary are you offering?"

"We'd start you at seventy thousand."

Well, now.

"If it works out for you, and for us, we'll boost that steadily and throw in stock bonuses and stock options."

"You say 'us,' Mr. Wyatt."

"There are some friends of mine who will be joining the company."

It sounded a little more interesting to Kramer, being in on the start-up of a new enterprise. Still, there were no guarantees.

"You seem assured that this venture will be successful," she said.

"It will be." He spoke with absolute confidence. "I already have four contracts lined up. Of course, my attorney will have to check them over before I sign them."

"It sounds like a fair opportunity," she said, attempting to be nice, "but I guess I'm also looking for some degree of security."

His grin widened. "Well, Jan. At the moment, I could guarantee your salary for a couple hundred years. I've got ten million in capitalization."

"My God! Where do you get money like that?"

"That's one of those little secrets we have to rationalize. Think of it as Seattle's water supply."

Shady. All she could think was that this was on the shady side.

"I don't know about you," he said while looking at his watch, "but your questions have convinced me. Do you want to go to dinner with a new boss?"

"You're offering me the job?"

"If you could pack tonight, you can fly to Albuquerque with me in the morning."

The whole thing was preposterous, of course. She couldn't just fly away to some vaporous destination with a stranger she had just met.

But she did.

And her father was furious with her.

In four years, Andy Wyatt had never been bossy. And after four years, Janice Kramer was vice president, treasurer, and general manager of the company and making $100,000 plus bonuses annually. She did not get the really impressive bonuses some of the others did, but then she did not take the same risks they did. Wyatt appreciated her, though. He hated administrative details and left all of the day-to-day decisioning and the standard contracting to her. Only on general policy questions and special contracts did she get together with Wyatt and Barr and argue the merits. She had learned to love and trust both of them. She thought the feelings were reciprocal, though Wyatt wasn't the effusive type, and Bucky Barr was so outgoing he loved everyone.

And her relationship with Wyatt had taken a course with more curves in it than the Rio Grande. She wasn't quite certain how she had allowed herself to become so involved—enthralled?—with a man whose attention was so easily diverted by high risk.

The phone rang and Liz Jordan answered it, then swivelled her chair toward her, "Andy's on Line One, Jan."

"Thanks." Gently moving Ace's massive head from the telephone console, she picked up the receiver. "Are you on-site?"

Whenever this kind of operation was under way, they used extreme caution on the telephone.

"On site and schedule," Wyatt told her.

"Good."

"Have you heard from Neil?"

"He called last night," she said. "He made the first contact, even though it interfered with a fabulous dinner he had planned."

"How did it go?"

"The dinner? He didn't say."

"No, damn it."

"The contact looks promising. He thinks it will pan out, but he won't know for certain until the end of next week."

"All right, then. We may put this together yet."

"You didn't have problems in Arizona?" she asked.

"Only a good one. We were able to obtain the full complement of equipment. If we're going to stay on schedule, I need a couple more bodies."

Of Aeroconsultants' thirty-eight employees, only sixteen, including herself, had been cleared by Wyatt and Barr for special contracts. "You've used them up, Andy. All we've got left is Fox, and I've got him out in Riyadh."

"I know. What do you think about bringing in Harris and Gering?"

Lefty Harris and Arnie Gering were engine techs. "You've got power plant problems?"

"We're going to rebuild them all, but no, not real problems. They can handle some of the other chores, like everyone else is doing. Painting, for one."

"How long would you need them?" she asked, feeling suddenly protective of her schedule. "I've already got a backlog of projects for them here."

"A week."

"Andy."

"Ten days, maybe."

"You think they're ready for this?"

"They won't know the whole operation. I'll meet them in Lincoln, first, and work them through it."

"Okay," she said with some misgivings.

Jan Kramer did not like risking her whole future on unexpected developments.

Nelson Buckingham Barr had been married once, while he was stationed at Nellis Air Force Base in Nevada. Raylene Delehanty Barr was a statuesque blonde who stood four inches taller than Barr. Her physique had matched the strict requirements for showgirls at the Tropicana, and Barr had thought at the time that everything about her was flawless. It was not the first time he had been wrong, but it was the most expensive time. The excitement went out of the marriage in about thirty days, and the passion followed a couple months after that. It had cost him a $200,000 settlement to get unmarried.

The episode still stung, whenever he thought about it. Despite his outward demeanor, Barr was not careless with money. He was not materially acquisitive. Back in Albuquerque, he owned a small two-bedroom condominium, an eight-year-old Ferrari 308GT, and an antique Bell Model 47 helicopter that dated from the Korean War. He and Wyatt shared ownership of a restored P-40 Warhawk.

Since his twenty-fifth birthday, when he started receiving $250,000 a year from the trust set up by his father, he had learned that he could get along pretty well on his Air Force pay. He had set up a budget then that he still followed today. A large chunk of the trust payment was set aside to meet taxes, five or six thousand dollars was dumped into his checking account for play purposes, and the balance was invested. Barr's stock, bond, money market, and Certificate of Deposit portfolio was currently valued at close to seven million. He owned fifteen per cent of Aeroconsultants, Inc., and was listed on the private corporation's paperwork as vice president and secretary. The position paid him $100,000 a year, plus an occasional bonus. Sometimes the bonuses matched the salary, but every time he received one, he doled out chunks of it to the Red Cross, the American Heart Association, AIDS research, and/or his favorite educational foundation.

Mostly, what he did for his salary was fly, which was his first and true love.

He also talked about flying a lot when he and his friends gathered around a table.

The Rancher's Cafe and Lounge was going to be their kitchen for the next few weeks, and the whole group arrived there at eight o'clock in the evening, parking the three Jeep Wagoneers rented in Lincoln at the curb. It was a nice small-town establishment. Formica-topped tables and new linoleum on the floor. Big glass windows gave them a view of the main drag and the half-dozen cars and pickups cruising it. Barr had high hopes for the food.

There were ten diners in the place when they arrived, and the seventeen-year-old waitress behind the counter straightened up to her maximum of five-five when the thirteen men trooped through the door.

Wyatt crossed the room directly to her. "Is the manager around?"

"Yes, sir. The owner. I'll get him."

She turned and went to the doorway behind her, calling, "Dad!"

The man came out of the kitchen, wiping his hands on a towel. He was in his forties, dressed in an apron.

"Mr. Jorgenson?"

"Yes. What can I do for you?"

"My name's Cowan. I'm with Noble Enterprises."

Which was obvious, Barr thought. All of them wore either shirts or jackets with the company name tastefully displayed. It was part of the act. Class act, he thought, since he had designed the logos and the clothing.

"I understand you prepare the best food in town, Mr. Jorgenson."

"We are proud of our reputation," the man agreed.

"I tell you what," Wyatt said, digging a roll of bills out of his pocket and beginning to peel them off. "We're going to be hanging around for a few weeks. We'll need breakfast every morning and dinner every night. I'd like to have you make up lunch boxes daily. If I give you five thousand dollars now, would you just run a tab for me?"

The economy of Ainsworth just took a giant leap, and it showed in Jorgenson's face. "I'd be happy to do that, Mr. Cowan."

"You just let me know when the tab catches up with the deposit. Let's start off with a case of Budweiser."

"I'll get the beer, Julie, while you put four tables together."

Barr went over and helped Julie shift tables and chairs around in a back corner, then plopped himself down. Julie was a quiet girl, but developing quite nicely. She seemed uncomfortable with Barr's innocuous questions. When Barr looked up at Wyatt, the boss gave him a stern look.

The others gathered around the tables, many of them wiping away the sweat of the day, preparing for the air-conditioning of the cafe. Dennis Maal sat next to Barr. He was a company pilot, too, the one who had flown the C-130 in the day before. Next to him was Winfield Potter, the company's best technician. He was also a rated pilot and had flown the Citation. The other specialists in ordnance, electronics, and jet engines were Ben Borman, Sam Vrdla, and Henry Cavanaugh.

"Where's Lucas?" Barr asked, realizing they were missing Littlefield, their airframe technician.

Potter responded. "I expect him late tonight. I sent him to Lincoln to rent a ten thousand-gallon tanker and buy a few buckets of JP-4."

Jorgenson started placing bottles of Bud around the table. Barr downed his in three gulps. "Mr. Jorgenson, I'm ready for another."

The man smiled happily. "Be right back. And call me Max, please."

Hackley asked, "Hey, Andy, were there enough motel rooms in this burg for us?"

"Winnie took care of it," Wyatt said.

"Got us fourteen rooms at the Sandy Inn," Potter said. "Nothing but the best. And I was damned lucky. We're at the height of the tourist season."

"You're shittin' us," Demion said. "What tourists?"

Potter whipped his thumb toward the east. "Hey, if you're over thataway, and you want to go thisaway, you got to go through Ainsworth."

"What's over thisaway?" Barr pointed toward the west.

"Black Hills. Mount Rushmore. You wanta see where the cavalry cut down Chief Crazy Horse, you got to go to Fort Robinson. That's over west of Chadron."

"Chadron."

"Bucky, there's a bunch of history in this part of the country."

"I think I'd rather read about it, or fly over it," Barr told him.

Julie got their orders in sequence, her eyes going wide at the quantity in some cases. Barr gave her his best, most polite smile and ordered two chicken-fried steaks.

They lived up to his expectations.

Major Ahmed al-Qati had a fetish about cleanliness, perhaps because he recalled his Bedouin youth as one of dirt and sand. He bathed daily or more often, and he dressed himself in a fresh khaki uniform each morning. Though his closet contained traditional Arabic garb, he was most comfortable in a short-sleeved uniform shirt and knife-edge creased slacks bloused into combat boots in the paratrooper fashion.

In his mid-fifties, al-Qati was lean and as hard as the desert from which he had emerged. His forearms below his shirt sleeves and his face were burned into bronze from the sun. He was meticulous about the trim of his dark hair—which was tightly curled and contained a bald spot at the back of his head—and the smoothness of his cheeks. His eyes were almost black, peering through a permanent squint. The lines of his face deepened with each passing year, spreading outward from his eyes and vertically down his cheeks from the base of his wide and proudly humped nose.

Al-Qati commanded a motorized infantry battalion—including a company of special forces soldiers, and he commanded it well. He had learned the finer points of his trade as a foreign officer visiting the Ranger training center at Fort Benning, Georgia, thirty years before. The foundation of that education as a professional soldier had instilled in him a discipline that he was certain could be found nowhere else in the Libyan military.

He was aware that most of the men in his command did not like him. They respected him, however, and that was far better. His men worked harder, drilled more frequently, and engaged in realistic training exercises on an accelerated schedule. They did not like him, no, but they took pride in themselves, and al-Qati was certain that many would die for him if called upon to do so. The men in his companies and platoons were qualified as parachutists, as airborne assault infantry, and as members of a rapid deployment force. The majority were cross-trained in at least two combat specialties.

The four hundred soldiers in his battalion had more morale, more *esprit de corps,* than could be found in the balance of the Libyan armed forces. Of that, al-Qati was certain. He knew that other commanders were jealous of him, and though he offered advice when asked, it was never acted upon. Ahmed al-Qati considered most of his brothers in the officer corps to be elitest and lazy, and that kind of leadership manifested itself in sloppy, mistake-prone combat units.

The Leader, naturally, recognized al-Qati's abilities,

for al-Qati was often called upon to deliver lectures at various military workshops.

Which was why, he assumed, he was now at the Tripoli barracks, ordered away from his battalion which was garrisoned at El Bardi, adjacent to the Egyptian border on the Mediterranean Sea.

Though he was irritated at his sudden recall, al-Qati did not reveal it as he attended the briefing on the morning after his return to Tripoli. The briefing was held in a cramped conference room on the first floor of the wood-sheathed and air-conditioned administration building and was attended by only al-Qati and a uniformed air force lieutenant. The lieutenant did not provide his name, and al-Qati did not ask for it.

"I am to give you an overview of an aircraft, Major."

Al-Qati did not know why, but he said, "Then let us get on with it, Lieutenant."

The lieutenant turned down the lights in the room and switched on a projector. On the large wall screen appeared the silver and gray form of a late-model airplane that had been built in the former Soviet Union. "This is the Sukhoi Su-24 fighter bomber."

Al-Qati had seen it before.

Another slide flashed on the screen. It was a drawing of the airplane with cutaway sections allowing internal views. Lines and arrows and crisp Arabic lettering identified various parts of the anatomy. In many cases, where the Arabic was insufficient for the technology involved, the original Russian words were utilized.

"The NATO forces have given the Su-24 the name Fencer."

Al-Qati knew that also. He was already bored.

"The aircraft matches the American FB-111A in capability. It is a two-seat, all-weather craft that can fly at speeds of Mach 1.2. It is extremely accurate, Major, delivering its ordnance within fifty-five meters of the target. The D model, with which I understand you will be concerned, was put into production in 1983."

The lieutenant seemed to know more about al-Qati's assignment status than he did, and that irritated him further.

"The D model has been enhanced with an in-flight refuelling system obtained from the French. It carries one thirty-millimeter, six-barrel cannon and up to eleven thousand kilograms of ground attack weapons. These can range from heavy, free-dropped ordnance to air-to-ground AS-7 high-explosive missiles, laser-guided AS-10 missiles, and AS-14 missiles. The most advanced electronics are used for navigation and attack radar. There is also terrain avoidance radar employed. Targeting methods can be either laser rangefinder or marked target seeker."

Most of it was gibberish to al-Qati. He was more concerned with motorized infantry tactics and the capabilities of his armored cars and personnel carriers.

The lieutenant moved to the front of the room, next to the screen, and with a long metal pointer, began to take al-Qati on a sight-seeing trip of the cutaway drawing. To familiarize al-Qati with the nomenclature, he identified everything in the drawing, from flaps to sensors to chaff dispensers.

"Do you have any questions at this point?"

"No, Lieutenant. I have no questions."

"Nothing at all?"

"Do I have to fly in this bloody thing?"

"I do not believe so."

"Then I know all that I have ever wanted to know."

With a skeptical look on his face, the lieutenant said, "Then you are to report to Colonel Ghazi."

Al-Qati did not bother thanking his instructor. He got up, left the conference room, and went to wait in the anteroom to Ghazi's office. After twenty minutes, a man al-Qati did not know emerged from the office, and the male secretary told al-Qati that he could enter.

For the man who commanded Libyan ground forces, the colonel did not possess a large office. He had made it comfortable, though, with wool carpeting, several antique office furnishings reupholstered in new gray leather, and pastoral paintings hung on the panelled walls. The paintings focused on Neva River scenes outside of Leningrad where Ghazi had once been trained by the Soviets.

Ghazi got up and came around the desk to give al-Qati a hug. He was bearish in appearance. a typical Arab prototype stuffed with Western foods, which he adored. His body was square and broad, his face the same. He had heavy dark eyebrows shading dark caverns for eyes.

"Ahmed al-Qati, you appear fit."

"Thank you, Colonel. I have been active. And you are well?"

Ghazi smiled, "Very well. How is El Bardi?"

"It still awaits me. I have an important exercise under way."

The colonel circled the big desk back to his chair. "I know. I am afraid, however, that it must fall to your deputy. Please, Ahmed, sit."

Al-Qati sat in one of the two leather straight chairs. This meeting with his superior was not starting well. Al-Qati had never left any operation incomplete before.

Ghazi was, however, his superior, and al-Qati would not be allowed many negotiating points.

"You have had the briefing on the Sukhoi bomber?"

"Yes. It seems to me to be well within the province of the air force."

The colonel was not interested in al-Qati's opinion. "Until a few years ago, the Su-24 was not deployed outside the Soviet Union. The powers-that-be, or were, at Red Army headquarters did not want to risk making the secret electronics accessible to outsiders."

Al-Qati nodded. He knew what was coming.

"You know, of course, that twelve of these fine fighter bombers have been provided to our air force?"

"I know this, Colonel."

"And with the demise of the Soviet Union, the bombers have become a permanent part of our inventory?"

He nodded again.

"And do you also know that the bombers are assigned to Colonel Ibrahim Ramad?"

"That I did not know," al-Qati said.

"Do you know Ramad?"

"I know him, Colonel."

"He is a worthless bastard."

Al-Qati smiled for the first time in two days. "That is an optimistic assessment of his character."

Ghazi inclined his head in agreement. "The Leader felt it imperative that we monitor Ramad's program, as well as integrate it with current ground forces strategies. You are to be the liaison between Ramad's project and my office."

This was not likely to be a fruitful assignment.

"What is the nature of this project?" al-Qati asked.

"It is, of course, a bombing program. What we want,

58

what Ramad suggests, is that his bombers could be utilized in close infantry support. You are to evaluate the methodology, make any suggestions you like, and report the results to me."

"And I am to watch Ramad?"

"Of course, but that is between you and me."

There was something to be gained here, al-Qati thought. "It would be quite difficult, Colonel."

The commander frowned. "Why is that?"

"Ramad outranks me. I should have more stature."

The frown evolved into a lopsided grin. "You are blackmailing me, Ahmed al-Qati."

"Not at all, Colonel. Certainly, I am due."

The colonel nodded slowly. "Very well. I will talk to the Leader about it."

Despite the promise of a long-delayed promotion, al-Qati was still extremely disappointed. He did not want to be stuck in the middle of some hot, barren airfield with an aggressive and ambitious bomber commander. He wanted to be back on the beaches of the Mediterranean, where he had established his headquarters. He wanted to be involved in the action and movement of his BMPs and BMVDs as they wheeled across the desert, securing the border from Egyptian invasion.

Which was not going to happen, anyway.

But it was well to be prepared.

Al-Qati believed in preparation.

He also believed in the promising young lady he had met in Tobruk two months before.

Martin Church hit his intercom button and said, "Okay, Sally. Send him in."

Church was Deputy Director for Operations of the

Central Intelligence Agency. He had fifteen years of field experience backing him up, experience that had thinned his brown hair and etched deep wrinkles across his forehead and at the outer edges of his nose. His face was lightly scarred from acne.

In addition to holding an excellent reputation for his field work, Church was a competent administrator. He had a multitracked mind capable of following dozens of current operations. He synthesized concepts well and kept the Deputy Director of Central Intelligence and the Executive Director abreast of developing operations and shifting intelligence estimates. He also attempted to keep his office out of media trouble, which was a primary responsibility of the DDO's office. Church would never be faulted for his dedication to country and duty.

George Embry entered the office through the wide door and plopped in a chair on the other side of the desk. Protocol was not one of Embry's major priorities. Embry, who ran the North African Division, and who usually made some jealous comment about the DDO's view of the Virginia countryside, skipped the comment today.

"You look pissed, George."

"I am pissed."

"Do I get to know about it?"

"Marianne Cummings?" Embry said.

Church had to think for five seconds. "We've got her undercover somewhere. On the Med."

"Right, in Tobruk. She's been there seven weeks, and she just about had Ahmed al-Qati roped in."

"Okay. I've got it placed."

"Tripoli just recalled al-Qati."

"Goddamn it!" Church exclaimed.

"I already said that myself, Marty. Now we have to start all over, and we have to convince her to seduce someone else."

Four

After a group briefing in the morning—which was more of a conference than a briefing since everyone got a word or two in—Wyatt fired up the Citation and flew to Lincoln, Nebraska. They were using the Cessna as their air taxi. Popping into Lincoln with a C-130 or an F-4 was guaranteed to attract unwanted attention.

Before starting his approach to the airport, he made a wide circle of the city. The grid of the streets delineated blocks of heavy foliage; elms and shrubbery were profuse, fed by the high humidity. It was a pretty city in the summer, just as he remembered from his four years at the university. In midsummer, the plots of grass had the barest tinge of yellow. The State Capitol dominated the central part of the city, and traffic was heavy on the east-west O street which passed by the university's main campus.

Lincoln, and to the east, Omaha, had been wonders of metropolitan sophistication to Wyatt at one time. Raised on a farm close to Norfolk, in the northeastern part of the state, he had come to the university naive, and he had left it still naive, but with a degree in engineering and an Air Force ROTC commission.

His aerial tour of the city brought back memories of his parents. They had died when a tornado twisted their farmhouse from its foundation in 1972, the year of his last tour in Vietnam. By then, he had been committed to a career in the Air Force, and he had willingly turned over his interest in the 320-acre farm to his sister and her then-new husband. In the intervening years, he had occasionally considered how much simpler his life would have been if he had just gone back to Norfolk.

As he called air control for landing permission, Wyatt thought that there were only two things wrong with Lincoln, Nebraska. The hot, sticky summers and long, frigid winters were one. He much preferred the dry heat of New Mexico at five thousand feet of altitude. Secondly, they needed a professional football team. The Kansas City Chiefs were too far away, and in another state, to generate widespread loyalty, and without their own pro team to diffuse fan interest, the fans achieved near mania over Big Red. Wyatt didn't think it was healthy. He was biased, of course. He had tried out for the football team as a freshman and didn't make the first cut.

He parked the airplane in the general aviation section and ordered the tanks topped off, then crossed the blistering tarmac to the waiting room and pulled open the glass door. A frigid dollop of refrigerated air smacked him in the face.

After getting a Coke from the machine, Wyatt went to the public telephone hanging on the wall and used his secondary credit card number—he never saw the bills, but they always got paid—to call Washington.

He reached the recording he expected: "No changes at this time."

Hanging up, he carried his Coke to one of the

couches and sprawled out on it to wait for Gering and Harris.

The girl behind the counter, restocking aviator paraphernalia in the glass case, glanced surreptitiously his way from time to time, but Wyatt only smiled at her. In his go-to-hell-or-bust days, he'd have been leaning on this side of the counter in two seconds. There had been a lot of such adventures, and misadventures, in his early hot-shit pilot years. Like Barr, he had been married once, but Tracey had found solace in a bottle and another pilot while Wyatt had been detached from Homestead Air Force Base for special duty in Grenada. The divorce wasn't good for his career; the Air Force preferred stable families, at least superficially stable.

He had finished his Coke by the time he saw the United 737 touching down, then taxiing toward the commercial terminal. Forty minutes later, Gering and Harris tumbled out of a taxi and into the waiting room, hauling overnight bags.

"Jesus, boss!" Gering said. "I thought it was hot in Albuquerque."

Arnie Gering was twenty-seven years old, fair-haired, and red-skinned. He had prominent freckles on his cheeks. He had graduated with high grades from several specialized aviation schools, and he was a wiz with hand tools, machine tools, and diagnostic electronics. He was overtly ambitious, and he wasn't afraid to ask Jan Kramer for raises in his pay, which he did regularly.

Wyatt pointed to one of the air-conditioning outlets. "Enjoy it while you can, Arnie. It gets warmer at the next stop. Why so sour, Lefty?"

"I hate flying commercial," Harris said. "Don't like leavin' the drivin' to somebody I don't know."

Harris was close to fifty, gray-haired, and with a gray

tinge to his skin. He too was a master engine mechanic, but he had been around airplanes so long that he was proficient, though not certified, in a number of other specialties.

"Come on over here, guys," Wyatt said, leading them to a group of chairs stuck in the corner.

They sat down, leaning toward each other, and Wyatt asked, "What did Jan tell you?"

"Just to get on the airplane," Harris said. "That you'd give us the word once we got here."

"Here's the word," Wyatt said, "Mum."

"Mum?" Gering asked.

"That's right. What we've got here is a classified project, and if you don't think you can keep it to yourselves—I mean, Arnie, not even your girlfriend, and Lefty, not your wife, we'll get you a return plane ticket."

The two of them knew, of course, that some of Aeroconsultants' pilots and technicians disappeared sporadically to resurface days or weeks later with no explanations. Wyatt wasn't about to enumerate or amplify on any of the company's history with secret projects.

Harris asked, "Is it illegal, Andy?"

"Get right to the point, don't you, Lefty? Let's just say that anything you'll be doing is not illegal. You might, however, see some things that skirt the boundaries in a civilian sense. I won't elaborate beyond that."

"Who are we working for?" Gering asked.

"You don't want to even speculate about that, Arnie. Not with anyone."

"Are some of the other guys working on this?" Harris asked.

"Yes. And we work strictly on a need-to-know basis.

65

Some people will know more than you, and they know less than others. But no one talks about it."

"I don't suppose there's some kind of overtime pay involved?" Gering asked.

Wyatt grinned at him. "We're looking at about four weeks work, Arnie, but I'll only need the two of you for around ten or twelve days. For that, you get a flat two thousand dollar bonus, and you can't talk about that, either, because people might want to know how you earned it."

"I'm in," Gering said.

"This wouldn't be considered hazardous duty pay, would it?" Harris asked. He had served in Vietnam as a Marine.

"No, Lefty. Just the same risks you take working around volatile fuels and fluids normally. We take the same precautions as we ever do."

"Well, I've got to call my wife and tell her something."

"The cover story we're using is the salvage and rebuild of a corporate jet that belly-landed in North Dakota. We're not close to telephones."

"I'd better call Jackie, then," Gering said. "She'd be too happy to think I ran off with some new chick. Come to think of it, she'll probably worry about the farmer's daughter. They have farms in North Dakota, Andy?"

"A few. But tell her the closest one is seventy miles away."

"That'll do it."

Las Vegas looked dusty and washed-out under the

midday sun; the glare was subdued, but it always was from fifteen thousand feet.

Barr made a wide, left-hand circle of the city, losing altitude and coming back to the east. Ahead of them, Lake Mead was a shimmering mirror dropped on the beige earth.

Cliff Jordan was in the copilot's seat. He was a compact man at five-eight, with steady hazel eyes and a ruddy complexion marred by a three-inch scar on his left cheek. There were more scars on his left arm and torso, the result of pancaking his F-14 Tomcat onto the deck of the *America*. The crash occurred after a sortie over Baghdad when he had taken some triple-A hits in the aft end of the plane. Until he slammed the fighter into the arresting cable, he didn't know the landing hook had been damaged. The Tomcat hit the wire, hesitated, then broke free, slewing sideways, collapsing the landing gear, and then rolling up on its left wing. The plane didn't go over the side of the carrier, but it tore up Jordan and his backseater.

After the Iraqi war, and as the Navy downsized, Lieutenant Commander Jordan opted for an early retirement arranged by some shadowy people who knew Andy Wyatt.

Barr heard himself called on the radio. "Lockheed two-nine, you have a Continental seven-six-seven coming out of McCarran. Hold your present altitude for one minute and give him about five thousand."

"Roger, Nellis. Two-nine copies," Jordan said as Barr eased the throttles forward.

Barr leaned forward to peer downward through the windscreen. He found the Boeing 767 as it cleared the outer markers of the civilian airport. As he continued his turn, the passenger liner passed beneath.

"Lockheed two-nine, you are cleared for descent and landing."

"Two-nine, Nellis. Roger."

Barr scanned the instruments, then turned his head and looked back at the flight engineer's station and checked the readouts there.

"Hey, Cliff, we forgot the engineer."

"Little late to worry about it, don't you think?"

"Problem with our air force, it's not fully staffed."

"I agree. The Navy was so much more efficient."

"More efficient than what?"

"Than Congress, for one."

"You got a point."

Barr kept backing off the throttles and losing altitude. The C-130 came around to a northerly heading and he leveled the wings.

"Think we ought to use the landing gear, Cliff?" Barr asked.

"I'm all for it. Maybe some flaps, too."

"If you insist, and whenever you're ready."

Jordan deployed the gear and flaps, and Barr felt the big transport bounce upward with the added lift. He drained off more power with the throttle levers.

The wide, straight runway of Nellis Air Force Base aligned itself with the C-130.

"Outer markers," Jordan called off. "One-two-five AGL, two-eight-zero knots. You going to use the whole damned runway?"

"You want to do the flying?"

"Yes."

"Tell them we're down, and go to Ground Control instead."

"We're not down yet."

"Details."

A quarter-mile beyond the end of the runway, Barr flared the C-130, idled the big turboprops, and settled easily onto the concrete. The main gear rumbled and vibrated through the fuselage.

"I'll bet they don't often see a Herc with decorative stripes putting down here," Barr said.

"Let's just hope they don't go checking tail numbers, Bucky."

Like the phony Noble Enterprises logo, the Hercules transport also carried a tail number that had arisen from someone's imagination.

As the speed bled off, Jordan switched to the Ground Control frequency.

"Nellis Ground Control, Lockheed two-nine checking in."

"Two-nine, Nellis. I've got your plan here. You're not staying with us for long."

"Roger that."

"Ah, two-nine, take the second turnoff to the left, go right on the taxiway and straight to the end of the taxiway."

"Two-nine, wilco," Jordan said.

Barr eased in his brakes, and reversed the prop pitch to slow his forward speed, then turned off the runway.

Jordan shed his headset, unbuckled his harness, and crawled out of his seat.

"This chickenshit outfit even has Navy commanders doing loadmaster duties," he said.

Barr grinned up at him. "How many loadmasters get the same pay?"

"There are compensations," Jordan said, then went back and dropped down the ladder from the flight deck.

As Barr neared the end of the taxiway, he saw the ramp down indicator flash on as Jordan started to lower it. Ahead, off to one side, were two Jeeps with canvas-covered trailers. After he passed them, he toed in the left brake, goosed the starboard throttles, swung the transport around 180 degrees, then idled his way back to the Jeeps and set the brakes.

Both Jeeps, with one driver each, started their engines and drove out of his view toward the rear of the aircraft. He felt the slight jar as Jordan dropped the ramp the rest of the way to the ground.

The fuselage tilted a little as each of the Jeeps backed their trailers into the cargo bay, unhitched, and drove out again. Loading both trailers took less than four minutes, then the Jeeps departed.

On the intercom, Jordan told him, "Ramp's coming up. I've still got to chain these babies down, but if you drive real slow, I can do it on the move."

"Oh, Ainsworth, here we come," Barr sang, "right back where we started from. . . ."

"And don't sing," Jordan ordered.

Except for Ace the Wonder Cat, Janice Kramer was alone in the office. It was after ten o'clock, and outside the window, the lamps in the parking lot lit up only half-a-dozen cars, her Buick Riviera among them.

The hangar was locked up and darkened. The only light in the office spilled from the desk lamp under which Ace rested and from the screen of her computer.

Ace got up, turned end-for-end, flopped down again, and tucked his head under his forepaw.

Kramer finished her last paragraph and saved everything to disk.

"That, Ace, is a magnificent piece of writing. Creative writing."

Ace didn't say anything.

She picked up the phone and dialled the number of the Sandy Inn.

It rang only once.

"Wyatt."

"Andy, are you hooked up?"

"Just a second, Jan."

While she waited for him to connect the modem of his portable computer, she called up the communications program and selected the files she would send.

"Okay, darlin'."

"Coming your way."

She zipped the data off to Nebraska, then waited while he read it on the screen of his computer.

"Looks good," he said. "You do wonderful things."

"I can't believe that I, a member in relatively good standing of the New Mexico Bar, wile away my nights creating illegal documents."

"You're not doing it," Wyatt said. "Somebody else will. Somebody who's probably also a member of the bar."

"How about the roster?"

"It's still the same. Go ahead and send it all to the number."

"What if I'm ever asked to testify against you, Andy?"

"We'll just have to get married."

"You said you weren't ever getting married again."

"It's better than jail," he said.

But not much better, from his point of view, she knew. He was perfectly happy with their relationship, roaming when he wanted to roam, or had a contract to chase, and spending as much time in her condo as he did in his own. She had thought that it would work for her, also, but sneaky bits of doubt had been creeping into her mind in the last few months.

Maybe she wasn't truly a '90's woman.

"When do I see you again?" she said.

"I'll try to get back in the next couple of days."

"I miss you."

"Me, too."

She hung up, then used the computer to dial the 202 area code number. When she had the connection, she began sending each of the files to the Washington computer.

There was a file for each man taking part in the operation. In addition to a passport photograph, the file provided a short biography of the man along with his vital statistics, address, phone, and occupation.

The photo and statistics were correct, but everything else was the product of her imagination.

The last file provided a detailed cover story, what the spooks called a legend. From all of the information, whoever was the expert in this sort of thing would develop the necessary documents: passports, credit cards, driver's licenses, Social Security cards, purchase orders, aircraft paperwork, insurance coverage, and probably even matchbook covers that agreed with particular hometowns.

Kramer had done this ten or eleven times before, but never on such a scale. Usually, it was a team of two or three. She had the distinct impression that the larger the operation was, the greater were the odds of something going wrong.

This one didn't feel good.

Somebody wasn't coming back.

And she loved them all.

Especially Andy.

Formsby wore a pale blue Oxford broadcloth shirt of soft cotton, khaki slacks, and a khaki Safari jacket. His low-cut leather boots had cost him ninety pounds Sterling, but then his footwear was always expensive, handmade so that the left shoe or boot supported his ankle adequately.

He thought he was dressed appropriately for Rabat. Later he would prowl the marketplaces for souvenirs or perhaps even something useful. In the afternoon, he would stroll the waterfront, taking in the sights, and adding to his knowledge. He wished he had time to go to Casablanca, simply because he had never been there before.

If Formsby had a stated goal in life now, it was to go where he had never been before. At one time, the objective had been to fly anything and everything with a wing and a power plant. That was no longer to be, and he was fairly successful at erasing the desire from his mind.

His travel goals were well supported by his salary, and he was grateful for that. On top of which, his job did not interfere unduly with his life.

Today, he had two tasks.

He approached the first by sitting on the edge of his bed in his hotel room, picking up the telephone, and asking the operator to place a call for him.

Fifteen minutes ticked by before the connection was made. The telephone rang, and the operator told him in broken English that he might proceed.

"Hello?" the voice on the other end asked.

"Carrington-Smyth here."

"Ah, yes. How are you?" Muenster asked.

"Quite well, thank you. I'm calling to see if the pieces have fallen into place."

"Finally, yes. A couple of the pieces were difficult to find, but I have succeeded."

"And the paperwork?"

"Is all but complete," Muenster said.

"It is trustworthy?"

"To the highest scrutiny."

"And the cost?"

"It will come to one-point-eight. American, of course."

"Of course. However. . . ." Formsby let his voice trail off.

"Ah," the German laughed, "there is always a 'however.' Did you have another figure in mind?"

"I did indeed. My mind was firmly set at one-point-two."

"That is, I am afraid, quite impossible."

They haggled for a quarter hour before arriving at one-and-a-half million dollars. Muenster gave him a long number that Formsby recognized as a Swiss bank account number. He knew also that it would be only a receiving account, and the funds would be immediately transferred out of it, floating off to an account whose number was far more secret.

"Half-and-half," Formsby said.

"That is agreeable. And the destination?"

"The location will be forwarded along with the first payment."

"Excellent, Mr. Carrington-Smyth. It has been a pleasure."

"Quite," Formsby said and hung up.

He stood and straightened the hem of his jacket.

Now, he would walk the bazaars in search of something useful.

Perhaps one hundred thousand liters of JP-4 petrol for jet engines.

And tanker trucks to haul it.

And someone to drive the trucks several thousand miles into the desert.

It was not an insurmountable problem.

He had solved similar ones in the past, and as Director of Logistics for—whatever it was this time, Noble Enterprises?—he had no doubt whatsoever that he would find that for which he was searching.

Newly promoted Lieutenant Colonel Ahmed al-Qati bought some new uniforms before he left Tripoli. He had left almost everything he owned in El Bardi, and he did not want to get caught somewhere in the desert without a change of uniform.

He thought about calling Sophia, the Italian girl he had met in Tobruk, then decided against it. She seemed to him to be very sophisticated, and he did not want to appear too eager.

Al-Qati had a military truck take him to the airport in time to catch a ride on the weekly Aeritalia G222 transport to Marada. It was over six hundred kilometers away, and the flight took two hours. At the small airfield in Marada, he was met by a driver with another truck, and they drove for another two hours to the northwest over roads that were barely defined from the surrounding desert.

Twice, he saw mounted Bedouins topping dunes on their camels and was reminded of his heritage, now withered and gone, if not forgotten.

The Marada Base, which was actually 120 kilometers from Marada, was difficult to pick out as they neared it. The only visible signs were the small concrete bunkers containing antiaircraft guns, surface-to-air missiles, and radar and radio antenna complexes, along with the single wide and long runway. The runway was finished in camouflage colors that matched the desert surrounding it, but al-Qati was certain that America and Europe knew exactly where it was as a result of their satellite surveillance.

The base was not hidden, but it was protected.

Marada Base was underground.

From the runway, the taxiways led to slanted ramps that allowed the aircraft to descend some twenty meters below ground level. They were parked in caverns protected by blast-resistant doors and hardened steel-and-concrete roofs covered with many kilotons of sand.

Al-Qati had toured the facility once, and he knew that the Libyan Republic Air Force had deployed to the base its twelve Sukhoi bombers, as well as two squadrons of MiG-23 interceptors and MiG-27 strike aircraft.

His driver pulled directly onto a taxiway, scooted across it, and followed the ramp downward to pass through the huge doorway created by the shunting aside of the thick steel sliding doors.

He braked to a stop next to what, after his briefing, al-Qati now very well knew was a Sukhoi bomber. The driver pointed to a doorway in a concrete wall.

"The headquarters is through that door, Colonel."

"Thank you."

He climbed down from the truck, taking his canvas carryall with him. Compared to being in the direct sun on the desert floor, it felt relatively cool inside the hangar. Banks of fluorescent lights bathed the bunker in nonglare light. A large contingent of specialists of one kind or another moved among the four fighter-bombers in this hangar, performing maintenance chores.

Moving to the steel-clad door, he pulled it open and entered a hallway. There was a rudimentary air-conditioning system in use, and the corridor was perhaps ten degrees cooler than the hangar.

Halfway down the hallway, he found the operations room, peopled with air controllers and radar operators. Next to it, set off by a window wall, was Ramad's office. Al-Qati left his bag in the hall, crossed the operations center, and knocked on the glass door.

Colonel Ibrahim Ramad was at his desk, his head bent low over the papers spread across it. Al-Qati thought the man was probably a bit nearsighted, but too vain to acknowledge the deficiency. He was, to be kind, portly. His waist approximated his chest in circumference. His uniform, though crisp, did not seem to fit him well.

Ramad's face was moon-shaped, and he wore a mustache and goatee in the attempt to elongate it. The hair on his face and on his head was thin and brown. His nose was hooked and dominant, and his eyes were brown, but in the right light, appeared to flame with redness and lack of sleep.

Upon hearing his knock, Ramad looked up, smiled, and waved him in. He stood up to come around his desk and embraced al-Qati as if they were long-lost brethren. Or even friends.

"Ahmed, it is good to see you."

"As it is to see you, Colonel."

"Nonsense! I congratulate you on your well-earned promotion, and you must call me Ibrahim."

Al-Qati nodded his thanks.

"I have, naturally, been notified that we will work together to coordinate air and ground movements, and I am excited at the prospects."

"As am I," al-Qati lied.

"Come. I must show you what we have, and then we will find a room for you. Tonight, you will meet my staff officers at dinner."

Ramad led him back out of the operations room, back down the corridor, and back into the hangar. Crossing the floor between the aircraft, they reached yet another steel door—this one some two meters wide—in the back of the hangar.

On the other side of it was another corridor. It was five meters wide and four meters tall. On the right, it was dead-ended. Spaced along the opposite wall were more doors. On al-Qati's left, it seemed to go on forever, the walls narrowing with perspective, and the end a pinpoint never to be reached.

"This leads to the factory," Ramad said, "twenty kilometers away."

"An amazing achievement," al-Qati said and meant.

"All open excavation work was accomplished at night, so that surveillance satellites would not detect the activity. I am very proud of what we have accomplished."

"As well you should be, Ibrahim. Why did you make it so large?"

"We have electric-powered transports, and the tunnel had to be wide enough to allow them to pass each other. Otherwise, we would get bottlenecks."

"I understand. It is well-done."

"Come."

Ramad crossed the tunnel to another wide steel door

imprinted with Arabic lettering: "Entrance denied to nonauthorized persons."

He produced a key and unlocked one of the double doors.

They stepped inside.

Ramad turned on overhead lights.

It was a large room, dismal in its concrete finish. The air carried a sour odor.

Around its perimeter, resting on wheeled cradles, were dome-nosed cannisters.

Al-Qati recognized the yellow skull-and-crossbones symbol stenciled on them.

He stepped close to the nearest canister and read the legend: "Poison Gaseous Elements. Extremely Hazardous. Move with Extreme Caution."

"Are they not lovely?" Ramad asked him.

Five

After five days, they were settled into the routine that was necessary to accomplish the job, They were up by five, had breakfasted at the Rancher's Cafe and Lounge on pork sausages, bacon, eggs, pancakes, waffles, wheat toast, muffins, hash browns, orange juice, and gallons of coffee, and carrying their large boxes of lunch, were ensconced in the hangars by six. At seven or eight o'clock at night, they trooped back into the Rancher's Cafe to order stacks of hamburgers, or steaks, or chicken, or veal cutlets surrounded by baked potatoes, homemade fries, and Texas toast. Not many in Wyatt's work force were fans of green peas, corn, or broccoli. Max Jorgenson doubled his order with the Budweiser route delivery truck. When they came in at night, they were sweaty and tired and ragged, and most ambitions were aimed at showers and clean sheets.

Bucky Barr was getting to know Julie Jorgenson well. She wasn't nervous around him anymore, and after they had eaten, she would sit with him and talk about her life in Ainsworth, her hopes, and her dreams. Barr was a good listener.

Out at the old bomber base, the locals who hung

around the airport office had become accustomed to having them down the way, and if they were still curious, were polite enough to not press inquiries into the activities at Hangars Four and Five.

The Cessna Citation and the Aeroconsultants C-130 were parked in front of the hangars, and their thin blue fuselage stripes had disappeared, replaced by two parallel and wider, bright scarlet stripes that zipped along the fuselages, then swooped at a steep angle up the vertical stabilizer. The Noble Enterprises logos on the tails were also in red. The Hercules tanker was parked next to them, but it still wore its Air Force uniform.

Bucky Barr was in charge of decorations for this party, and he had made certain that the red stripes and logos, on adhesive-backed tape, were perfectly aligned and straight.

And after five days, the six F-4 Phantoms were simply shells parked in Hangar Four. Norm Hackley, Karl Gettman, Ben Borman, and Lucas Littlefield had climbed through and around them with air-powered die grinders, attacking any serial number they came across, burnishing it into near-oblivion. A number of fuselage and wing panels had been removed, also, in order to access hidden numbers identified by Demion as requiring obliteration. Exposing the interior ribs also gave Demion a chance to evaluate the structural members. Because of the high hours on all of the airframes, there were a few stress fractures, and Demion and the airframe technicians designed reinforcement repairs.

While their method of eradicating serial numbers wouldn't stand up to the latest developments in forensic examinations, where high-powered X rays and computers and acid-washes might raise an old serial number, it was sufficient for standard replacement parts not particular to an airplane. For those parts that might be traceable by serial number to a specific aircraft—an oleo strut, a Martin-Baker ejection seat—the area around the former serial number was heated with an acetylene torch to make the molecules dance around and perhaps totally eradicate an important number or two.

Almost all of the removed panels had now been re-attached in their proper locations.

When Barr slipped through the Judas door into the hangar at noon, he found the two pilots and two technicians sprawled in one corner, sucking on soft drinks and munching on thick chicken salad sandwiches built on homemade bread. He figured the heat inside the hangar was in the low nineties, a welcome relief from the heat on the tarmac. The five-gallon jug of iced tea parked against one wall was about half empty.

"You guys taking another break?" he asked.

Norm Hackley flipped him a finger. Hackley, who was short and dark and had flown F-4s in one Vietnam tour, was closing on fifty years of age. His light eyes were as sharp as ever, and Barr estimated he had lost fifteen pounds in the last week, which he wouldn't miss.

Karl Gettman also had F-4 time, though he was too young for Vietnam. Gettman had been a weapons system operator, the GIB—Guy in the backseat. In his mid-thirties now and certified as a pilot in a dozen jet types, he was black as night, with a mini-Afro, and a ready smile.

"You want to break something, Bucky," Gettman said, "take a walk over by the airplanes. Better yet, take a run."

Barr turned to look at the planes. Two five-horse-power air compressors and a commercial wet/dry vacuum stood near them, and air hoses snaked around the floor. The concrete was littered with the fine, dry sand used in the sandblasters. The sand was vacuumed up to be used again. About half of the insignia and camouflage paint had been stripped from three of the planes, and the aluminum skin was shiny and virginal. He could smell the sour aroma of the liquid paint remover being utilized in addition to the sandblasting.

"You're not the neatest housekeeper I ever met, Karl," Barr said.

"Me? Lucas is in charge of floors."

Littlefield, a bulky man with huge hands and an impressively bald and large head, grinned. "Thing I like about this outfit, everybody gets to be in charge of something. I drew sand."

With eight years in the Air Force and another eight at Lockheed in California before that aerospace giant folded its West Coast operations and retreated to Georgia, Littlefield was a top-rated airframe technician. When he made a suggestion, the pilots yielded to it without complaint.

Ben Borman was another big man, with a Swedish heritage apparent in his coloring and blue eyes. He had put twenty years of his life into the Air Force before signing on with Aeroconsultants. His specialty had been ordnance, and he was now learning to be a fuel boom operator.

"What are you in charge of, Ben?" Barr asked.

"I'm in charge of Norm. He needs all the direction he can get."

Barr squatted in front of the group, resting his forearms on his thighs. "What's the schedule look like?"

"There's a schedule?" Gettman asked.

"We're damned near as close as we can be," Hackley said. "Day after tomorrow, we'll be ready for paint. Then, we'll take on the tanker."

"Thank God we only have to strip insignia off it," Littlefield said. "She's got about two acres of skin, and if she'd been painted, I'd go out to the highway and raise my thumb."

Barr grinned at him. "Before you go, you want to patch the holes in the E models?"

"Hey, guy, I already fabricated my pieces. I'm waiting on these slow bastards to get the paint off."

The early models of the F-4 had not had an internal gun, a design failing that had raised complaints from Vietnam-era pilots who, as far as Barr could figure, only wanted the guns to prove themselves as hot-shit pilots on their glorious way to ace status. Of course, Sidewinder air-to-air missiles hadn't been very effective at the time, either. The complaints had been met with gun pods slung beneath the centerline for the early models, then the internal M-61A rotary-barrel cannon mounted in the nose of the F-4E.

Barr had always been a firm believer in missile technology, engaging battles with about twenty miles between the hostile aircraft. If one had to use a cannon one was too damned close. After some serious reconsideration and discussion about their mission, he and Wyatt had elected to remove the twenty-millimeter cannons from the E models. It not only saved a great deal of weight, though it changed the center of gravity, it precluded pilots from relying on the gun for close combat. If one was out of missiles, the prudent course was to turn tail.

Littlefield had fashioned new fittings which would lock the gun port doors in the closed position.

Barr pushed himself back to his feet. "You need anything from Albuquerque?"

"You're going to Albuquerque?" Gettman asked. "I thought Andy was going."

"He's got another appointment."

"I need about ten more gallons of paint reducer and five quarts of catalytic hardener," Littlefield said.

Barr pulled his notebook from his shirt pocket and wrote it down. "How come? I thought we had it figured."

"We did, but we forgot about later."

"Gotcha. Anything else?"

"I'd ask you to call my girl," Gettman said, "but you'd probably go see her in person."

"I'll do that," Barr said.

"No, you won't."

Barr left the hangar, crossed the dry steam of the tarmac, and entered Hangar Five.

Here, too, the lunch break was underway. The pilots and technicians were gathered at the back of the hangar, around the old wooden workbenches. In front of the benches, in twelve maintenance cradles, were the engines from the Phantoms. The Hercules engines had been pronounced fit by Demion and Hank Cavanaugh, the primary engine specialist, though the nacelles had to be removed in order to grind off serial numbers.

Each of the F-4 turbojets, however, was being fully disassembled, examined, shorn of identifying numbers, and rebuilt with new seals, bearings, and subassemblies where necessary. That was the primary reason for Barr's trip, to pick up parts. It wasn't an unexpected development, he thought. It was one of the laws of mechanics. Whenever he started a mechanical restoration, he always had to run back to the store a dozen times for forgotten parts. And he wasn't alone, judging by the number of NAPA Auto Parts or Checker Auto Parts delivery trucks he saw running to the Ford and Chrysler and GM service centers in any city in the nation.

Scattered around the hangar were toolboxes on casters, small lifting cranes, air compressors, start carts, a small sheet-metal roller, an arc welder, and a couple oxygen/acetylene dollies. A big electronic diagnostics unit was shoved against the sidewall.

The two trailers he and Jordan had picked up at Nellis were parked in one corner, still covered with canvas and packed with cardboard boxes. The boxes contained all of the avionics and electronics, and they weren't yet ready to dig into that pile. Wyatt wasn't ready, though Tom Kriswell and Sam Vrdla, the electronics wizards, were itching to get their hands into those boxes.

Barr hiked the long trail to the back of the hangar, approaching Demion, Kriswell, and Wyatt.

"I think I've lost five pounds just walking around these damned hangars," he said.

"Doesn't show yet," Demion said.

"You sure you want to fly with me today, Jim?"

"But I have noticed your face seems thinner," Demion said. "Don't you think he's better-looking, guys?"

"Julie seems to think so," Kriswell said. "How you making out there, Bucky?"

"You know she's carrying a three-point-six grade average in high school? She's a smart kid. Debate, FHA, and thespians, too."

"I noticed she's carrying about, what, thirty-four, twenty-two, thirty-four?" Demion said.

Barr gave him a pained expression. "Get off it, James. She wants to go to Chadron State College and become an English teacher. There's nothing wrong with that."

"So she's a candidate?" Wyatt asked.

"Yeah, I think so. I'll know more in another week."

Only Demion, Kriswell, and Wyatt knew about Barr's foundation because they were on the board of directors, fulfilling the number required by the regulations governing tax-exempt corporations. Barr was the executive director and the screening committee and the entire unpaid staff. He poured some of his excess cash into the foundation each year, and each year he personally found one or two kids—usually girls—for whom the foundation provided college scholarships. The unadvertised educational foundation was currently supporting eleven college students. Barr didn't want every girl he met to grow up and become a money-grubbing Raylene Delehanty Barr.

"The guns on board the Herc?" Wyatt asked.

"We got guns," Barr said. "Captain Dinning will be a happy man when he see them come back."

Barr and Demion were making a stop at Davis-Monthan to return the M61-A cannons. Since they had decided against them for the mission, they had also decided to turn them in. It might lower the stress levels of the local Air Force types at Davis-Monthan, and it might preclude having the Treasury's Bureau of Firearms get excited, just in case some of that paperwork fell through the cracks and actually arrived at the Bureau.

"I've got my shopping list," Demion said.

"And I've got a couple things to add to it," Barr said, ripping the page out of his notebook.

"And I'll take off for Washington," Wyatt said.

"What do you suppose they want?" Kriswell asked.

"Who the hell knows?" Wyatt said. "They've probably decided to call it off."

"Personally," Barr said, "I think that'd be a real shame."

"You're just bloodthirsty," Demion said.

"That's me, the New Hampshire vampire."

"One-and-a-half million dollars," Martin Church said.

"A steal," George Embry, who was standing at Church's window enjoying the view, told him.

"From us, maybe. What do we get for it?"

"You really want to know?"

"Damned right," the DDO said.

The North African desk chief turned from the window and pushed his glasses up on his nose. "How come you get the best view in the house, Marty?"

"Come on."

Embry dug a ragged-edged piece of notepaper from his pocket and scanned it.

"Let's see. There's four ALQ-72 countermeasures pods. That presupposes some airborne resistance, you know?"

"I know. Wyatt's being overly cautious, maybe."

"Wyatt wants to get out of there with the same number of people he takes in," Embry said. "Can't say as I blame him."

"What else?"

"There's thirty-six Mark 84 five-hundred-pound bombs. That's the ground attack complement. For the fun stuff, we've got twenty-four AIM-9L Super Sidewinders. Like I said, a bargain."

"Do we need it all?"

"You're trying to save money?" Embry asked.

"It's a new era."

"You want to start a war, Marty, you got to pay for it. There'll be more bills coming in."

Church sat silently for a moment. He, and others, were committed to the operation, and he didn't know why he was quibbling over what amounted to peanuts in the total scheme of things. Perhaps because in the back of his mind was a ghastly image of the results.

"What about Cummings?" he asked, to shift the subject from dollars and cents.

"Marianne? She's spending a lot of time on the beach, enjoying herself. No further contacts with al-Qati."

"Why don't you have her make some calls? Maybe she can run him down somewhere."

"Marty."

"Yeah, I know. Okay, just have her cross her fingers."

"There is one little thing," Embry said.

"Which you've saved for last?"

"I always save the best for last, Marty."

"Well, damn it, tell me!"

"This is kind of third-hand, but then, since we're so short of assets there, everything we get out of Libya is third-hand. Cummings doesn't have corroboration yet."

"George."

"Ahmed al-Qati has been promoted to lieutenant colonel and attached to Ibrahim Ramad's command."

"This tells you what, George?"

"You remember Ramad? He's air force, and he disappeared from the Tripoli military staff when they got the Sukhoi bombers. The consensus at the time, though never substantiated, was that he'd been given responsibility for developing a long-range bombing program. That was reinforced when our French friends gave them the aerial refueling technology."

"Do we know where he's located?"

"We have a good idea that he's at Marada Base, the one they buried in the sand. That's where the bombers are flying from, anyway."

"So what's al-Qati got to do with Ramad?"

"Exactly!"

"Goddamn it, George."

"Ahmed al-Qati is a superb tactician and strategist in ground warfare. My people think that marrying the two of them means they're developing a coordinated air-and-ground attack scheme."

"So it's just good military planning," Church said. "Contingency planning."

"Except that we also know that Marada Base is located thirteen miles from what the Leader describes as his agricultural chemical plant."

Church thought about that for a moment, then said, "You want to send me the dossiers on those two people, George?"

"I thought you'd never ask."

Ibrahim Ramad glanced sideways at al-Qati who was sitting in the bombardier/navigator's seat next to him. With the helmet and the oxygen mask, very little of his face was visible. His eyes were unreadable; they stared straight ahead at the onrushing desert.

The undulating desert unrolled before them with amazing, dizzying speed. The velocity indicator stood at Mach 1.1. The aircraft bounced lightly upward and downward as the terrain-avoidance radar instructed the automatic pilot to maintain a one-hundred-meter ground clearance above the sand dunes and wadis. The E-Scope on the instrument panel, with its "ski-tip" line imposed over the computer-generated drawing of the terrain ahead, showed how close the Su-24 approached the tips of dunes. The Head Up Display currently displayed the symbol for the bomber in the center of the screen, the symbol rising and falling as the aircraft responded to commands from the computer to change its vertical position.

They were so low that the horizons had pulled in on them, making their world much smaller and more isolated. Ramad could see nothing outside the canopy that bespoke of life. Looking backward and down, he could see the snouts of the missiles on the outboard pylons. The wings were in their swept-back configuration, and the missiles were mounted on the pivoting pylons. The bombs were shorter and not visible from his position. They were attached to the inboard pylons, which were fixed to the solid, inner portion of the wing. Four more missiles were affixed to fuselage hardpoints.

As always in the cockpit of an airplane, Ramad was entirely comfortable. He rarely became nervous, and if he did, he never demonstrated the condition to observers. He knew that he exuded confidence, even arrogance in regard to his talents. That was as it should be. His talents had brought him the command of an entire air base at the tender age of thirty-five.

He was more than a little disappointed at al-Qati's reaction to supersonic, ground-hugging speed. Others from Tripoli, from military staff, who had taken the orientation flight with Ramad, had paled significantly and allowed the fear to cloud their eyes. Some had gallantly attempted to retain their previous meals for minutes before ripping off the oxygen masks and spilling vomit over their borrowed flight suits.

Ahmed al-Qati's hands rested lightly and unclenched in his lap. Not even his shoulders betrayed an elevated sense of tension. This was a man, Ramad decided, who filled the large cup of his reputation.

He was not to be underestimated.

But then, neither was Ibrahim Ramad to be underestimated.

He had no illusions about the reasons for al-Qati's presence at Marada Base.

Lieutenant Colonel Ahmed al-Qati was there to spy on him.

Ramad knew that Kamal Amjab, the Leader's closest advisor, and Colonel Ghazi, chief of the army, considered him brave but untrustworthy. He had never done anything to invoke their distrust, and he suspected that they were jealous of his rapid rise in rank and responsibility as well as envious of his abilities and his close relationship with Farouk Salmi, head of the air force. So they had sent an army man to watch over him, though not as a guardian angel.

It was all right; Ramad could adapt.

He began to ease back the throttles for the Lyulka turbojet engines. The velocity readout flickered, then the numbers began to descend.

"Twenty-two kilometers to target, Ahmed," he said over the internal communications system.

Al-Qati turned his head to look at him. "I trust that you do not expect me to operate this thing, Ibrahim." The infantry commander tapped the hood of the radar.

"Of course not," Ramad said. "We will concern ourselves less with accuracy than with demonstrating the concept."

The airframe shuddered as they came down through the sonic barrier.

Ramad reached out for the armaments panel and armed the two bombs. They were simulated bombs, of course, each filled with three-hundred kilograms of white powder and three kilograms of high explosive.

He switched the HUD display to Continuously Computed Impact Line.

The airspeed dropped to 450 knots.

Then four hundred knots.

Ramad checked the wings. The computer was slowly rotating them forward as the speed deteriorated.

Automation. He loved it, and he had, after many flying hours of doubting it, come to rely on it.

Al-Qati leaned toward him, to get a better view of the HUD.

"Do you understand it?" Ramad asked.

"No."

"The circle in the center is the estimated location of the target, data that I programmed into the computer earlier. The almost vertical dotted line leading toward it is the recommended flight path from our present position. Our current heading, one hundred and forty-two degrees is indicated at the bottom. The number to the right, minus fourteen, is the distance in kilometers to the target."

Al-Qati leaned back into his seat and retightened his harness. "We have similar targeting computers for our artillery."

"We may give thanks to Allah for his beneficence," Ramad said.

"Or to the Soviet Union," al-Qati said.

Ramad let his eyes go icy. The oxygen mask hid his scowl.

He forced himself back to the task at hand.

As they topped a line of high dunes, he assumed manual control of the aircraft. In the faraway, hazy distance, he saw the tiny white tent that had been erected in a geographical depression as his target. He utilized the electro-optical targeting system to verify its location and found it to be nearly a kilometer away from the position he had estimated for the computer. He punched the correction into the keypad and watched the HUD symbols shift minutely. With a little right rudder, he realigned the bomber on the target.

Assuming the bombardier's role, and with the small joystick located between his seat and the bombardier's seat that controlled the electro-optical targeting symbol—a set of red cross hairs inside a red circle, he shifted the target rose until it covered the target circle on the HUD. Then he depressed the stud that locked the attack computer onto the target.

He committed the attack by depressing the button on the head of the control stick.

No matter what he did with the airplane now within predetermined parameters, the computer would determine the optimum release point.

At six kilometers from the target, Ramad pulled the stick back and shoved the throttles into full afterburner. The immediate thrust from the turbojets pressed him back into his seat. The gravitation readout climbed to five Gs. He felt the skin around his eyes forced backward.

The Su-24 aimed its nose toward the blue sky. In seconds, the altimeter indicated two thousand meters of altitude.

He felt the bombs release.

And eased the stick forward, centering it into the vertical climb.

Altitude five thousand meters.

The gravitational forces eased.

He snap-rolled 180 degrees to the right, jerked the throttles back, then pulled the stick toward his crotch. The aircraft went inverted, and he looked up toward the earth, found the small white square that was his target.

The bombs had not reached it yet.

"Do you see, Ahmed?"

"Yes. I see."

By the tone of his voice, al-Qati seemed unimpressed by the precision flying that Ramad was performing for him. He certainly gave no indication that the aerobatics had upset his equilibrium or stomach.

The simulated bombs impacted in the sandy surface of the earth, their small explosive charges destroying the bomb cases and creating geysers of white powder. He estimated each to be within forty meters of the target, which would have been destroyed had the bombs not been dummies.

As he came out of the loop at near ground level, Ramad passed to the right of the target so that they had a clear view of the bomb impact.

"That was very well executed, Colonel," al-Qati said. The man sounded sincere.

"Thank you, Ahmed. The technology and the training of my pilots—and I say that proudly—will allow us to deliver . . . whatever it is we wish to deliver with similar ease and precision."

"And we are to develop the tactics which will coordinate your bombs with my ground advance?"

"Exactly! Just think, Ahmed, how we will complement each other. Would it not be better for your tanks and armored vehicles to arrive at a target site that has already been devastated."

"Infinitely better," al-Qati agreed.

Again, he advanced the throttles to afterburner and climbed toward the heavens, performing one victory roll during the ascent.

"Together, Ahmed, we will show the world what we are capable of accomplishing."

"I am certain that is true, Ibrahim."

"Allah akbar!"

Ibrahim Ramad was but the tool of Allah, to be used as necessary to achieve the goals of Islam.

He knew that.

He also knew what Allah had in mind.

Wyatt parked the Citation in the transient section at College Park Airport and ordered it refueled. He rented a Mercury Topaz, drove north to the Capitol Beltway, and jammed himself into the eastbound traffic. His fellow travellers were of the hunt-and-peck variety, searching for spaces in adjacent lanes and jumping into them, only to be disappointed by the lack of progress and jumping back to where they had been.

At the interchange with Georgia Avenue, he extricated himself from the lineup in the right lane and took Georgia north to the suburb of Wheaton. Wyatt found the Wheaton Plaza easily enough, and he found a place to park the Mercury in a crowded lot with just a little more difficulty. He got out, locked the car, and started looking for a place called the Pizza Joint.

He was half-an-hour ahead of the dinner hour rush and had a large number of open tables from which to choose. Wyatt picked a red Naugahyde booth in the back corner of the dining room and slid into it.

It was a family kind of place. There were red-and-white-checked tablecloths, red candles in heavy iron holders designed to keep the pizzas warm, and travel posters lining the empty walls above the booths. Most of the travel posters promoted countries on the northern side of the Mediterranean: Greece, Italy, France, Spain. The owners were promoting safe travel, no doubt. When he thought about it, though, he couldn't recall ever seeing posters that begged him to "Take the Sun in Syria," or "Ski Lebanon."

A young man with a mop of dark hair atop a band of short-cropped stubble that went clear around his head, wearing a short-sleeved shirt that matched the tablecloth, sidled up to him.

"What can I get you, sir?"

He looked at the platters hanging over the serving counter which defined the sizes available, then said, "Let's have the gigantic with pepperoni, Italian sausage, mushrooms, onions, and green pepper. And a very tall, very cold, root beer."

The boy didn't seem impressed by the size of his order. "Twenty minutes."

The pizza didn't come for twenty-five minutes, five minutes after Church and Embry arrived. They poked their heads inside the entrance, spotted him, and walked to the back.

Church was in his typically preppy uniform of chinos, blue buttoned-down cotton shirt, striped tie, and blue sport coat. The only wrinkles were in his forehead, and they seemed deeper than ever.

George Embry wore a gray suit that was two or three years past its prime and contained enough wrinkles to match Church's forehead. He was half-wearing a paisley tie loosened against the heat. Taking the side of the booth next to Wyatt, Embry slid in, then looked up at the menu posted next to the platters.

"Hi, Major. What looks good?"

"I don't know what you want, George, but you're getting pepperoni and sausage."

"No anchovy?"

"Nary a one."

"Good."

Church sat across from them.

"I didn't know you were coming along, Marty, or I'd have ordered more."

"I'm not much in the mood for pizza, anyway," Church told him.

"Used to be, we'd meet where we could get a decent steak or a lobster tail," Wyatt said.

"New austerity program," Embry said. "I'm not happy about it myself."

The pizza arrived, along with Wyatt's root beer. Embry and Church ordered more potent beer.

While waiting for the waiter to deliver two steins, Wyatt and Embry worked wedges out of the pizza. It tasted fine to Wyatt.

With apparent reluctance, Church scooped up a slice for himself.

"You guys asked me here," Wyatt said. "I suppose there was an important reason?"

"That's right," Church said, "very important."

"You're not calling it off?"

"We haven't aborted any mission we've ever given you, have we now?" Church asked.

Four years had passed since Martin Church had first

approached then-Major Andrew Wyatt in a meeting at the Sans Souci, where they had eaten lobster.

"How good are you at predicting the future, Major?"

"I haven't been keeping track, Mr. Church, but the record's probably not impressive."

"We're in the prediction business in my shop."

"And how's your record?" Wyatt asked.

"So-so. There are a couple things I'm sure of, however."

"Such as?"

"The military is going to be reducing its numbers in the next few years."

Wyatt had the same premonition. "And?"

"And you will probably be one of those numbers."

Wyatt raised an eyebrow. Was this a recruitment pitch? "You've talked to Air Force personnel?"

"Not directly, no. The problem is, you're not in the right career track. You've antagonized a few people who wear stars. You're divorced. You open your mouth at times when it would best remain closed."

Wyatt couldn't think of any counterarguments.

"You're a prime target for reduction in force, just a few years shy of the pension."

"I fly well," he said defensively and somewhat lamely.

"Which is why we're talking. You're certified in a dozen types of aircraft, and you're also an efficient manager. The latter quality isn't always recognized in the military."

Wyatt didn't ask how Church knew what he knew.

"My agency will also suffer some cutbacks, and I'm preparing for that lean future," Church said. "I need an organization that I can call on for special projects."

"An organization with airplanes?"

"Right."

"A modern-day Air America?"

"Much smaller in scope," Church said. "We're cutting back, remember. There won't be anyone on a payroll."

No recruitment.

"Contract players?" Wyatt asked.

"That's it."

"Maybe I want to take my chances on reaching for that pension."

"You could do that, but I think you'd rather fly."

Again, Wyatt didn't have an argument.

"So I'll give you ten million dollars to keep you flying."

"This is great lobster, Mr. Church."

"For one thing, I've got the ten million today. Next year, or the year after, Major, I probably won't have it."

"That's the kind of money" Wyatt said, "that buys a lot of risk. A lot of dead people."

"DOD's paying you forty thousand a year to take the same risks now."

"It's legal."

"You'd never be asked to do anything that isn't sanctioned at the highest levels, though I admit that the general public might not always see it in the best possible light."

Wyatt scraped the last meat from the shell and dipped it in the butter.

"The ten mil comes to you in the form of four contracts, fronted through various agencies or companies. Five of it is your start-up cash. Use it any way you want to set up your organization. Buy yourself a pension fund if you're that security conscious."

"Five million up front buys some other things," Wyatt said, chewing his lobster.

"That is correct. It buys your absolute loyalty and your willingness to perform on short notice well into the future."

"How far into the future?"

"Not determined. We see how it goes. But you get paid on each project."

"And the other five?"

"At the moment, we've got four quickie projects on the table . . ."

Wyatt couldn't complain about many of the projects he had been handed over the last four years. Usually, they were small: transporting sensitive cargo into sensitive geographical areas, assembling teams of aviation experts to conduct workshops, seminars, and training sessions for governments and nongovernments which needed the help. A couple of times, he and Barr had been asked to extract endangered agents from hostile territory. The particularly lucrative contracts had involved the use of live ordnance, but those had only come up three times before.

"The difference might be, Marty, that we've never had a mission on this large a scale," Wyatt said. "With the number of aircraft and people involved, we've become way too visible. The risk factor is high. And with the way the politics keep shifting, especially in the Middle East, I expect the go/no-go switch to be thrown on and off."

"It's definitely not off," Church said. "George can tell you why."

Wyatt scooped up another wedge of the pizza as he looked to Embry.

"We—that's me and my analysts—think that our fears have been realized. We think the chemical plant is now producing weapons in large quantities."

"We suspected that going in," Wyatt said. "That was the rationale for this operation."

"Yeah, Andy, but when we planned it, we were worried about a small stockpile of delicate weapons under the control of a less-than-delicate administration. Now, it gets worse."

"How so?"

"One of my people went back through overhead surveillance tapes and made some estimates of the amount of raw materials that have been shipped in to the plant. He also computed the estimated tonnage of fertilizer coming out."

"And it doesn't come out equal?" Wyatt asked.

"Not by a long damned shot. Over the last couple of years, we figure we've lost track of about four hundred tons of liquid and solid raw material. That's based on mathematical projections, since we naturally don't have all of the photographs we might want to have."

"So they're storing it inside the plant."

"But in what form, Andy? If it's one-hundred-pound artillery shells or missile warheads or wide-dispersal bombs, that adds up to eight thousand units."

"That's a bunch," Wyatt agreed.

"Plus, with our estimates of storage space inside the plant, we don't think there's enough room to store that many shells."

"So they may have moved them?"

"That's the worry. If we don't hit them soon, they

could spread that ordnance all over the country. As it is, we may miss some of it."

"How come you didn't do all this computing earlier?"

"Maybe it's because we're human," Embry said.

Six

It was nearly midnight when the Citation landed.

Janice Kramer was in the office with Ace the Wonder Cat, and she had been ignoring the paperwork stacked on her desk so she could keep an eye on the runway. The Aeroconsultants building was located on Clark Carr Loop, a circle of hangars and offices in the commercial section of the airport south of the east-west runway. From the side window of the single executive office, she had a view down the alley between buildings. It was a clipped view, revealing just a few hundred yards of the west end of the runway and the adobe-styled passenger terminal building on the north side of the runway. The current activity was limited to a few night-scheduled passenger liners. Kirtland Air Force Base, which shared the runway with Albuquerque International, appeared quiet tonight.

She was also monitoring Albuquerque Approach on the radio in the outer office, and she heard Wyatt call in, so she was ready when the Cessna flashed across her limited view of the runway. It slowed quickly, then turned onto the end taxiway and headed directly for the hangar.

Sometimes, she daydreamed about the way things could have been, or might be, and she found herself damning Andy Wyatt for what he was. And she damned herself for putting up with it and waiting feverishly for his plane to come in. She had waited too many nights.

Again and again.

When she pushed herself up out of her chair, Ace sat up on the desk and yawned.

"You can't be hungry again."

"Mee-yaw."

That was "yes" in feline-mongrel, so she went out to the storeroom off the hangar, found a can of 9-Lives tuna, and popped the top off it. She had scooped it into his dish by the time Ace got there. There was very little in Ace's world that required haste.

Ace never said thanks, either. He just went into a semi-squat and started to nibble.

Kramer went on to the back of the hangar, which abutted the tarmac. There were two business jets in the hangar, both in partial disassembly as they underwent alterations in their technology as well as refurbishing from merely luxurious to ultra-luxurious. One belonged to a Texas real estate developer, and the other was owned by a Hollywood producer. Both men had been referred to Aeroconsultants by a Saudi prince.

Aeroconsultants enjoyed a credible word-of-mouth advertising program. Currently, Kramer had a seven-month backlog of projects, and they were going to back up even further since Wyatt was draining off all of the manpower for the latest Agency contract.

There were only four dim night-lights on, but it was enough to find her way to the back door. She defeated the alarm system, unlocked the door, and pulled it open.

A soft warm breeze struck her face, carrying with it the aromas of diesel oil, hot metal, and jet fuel.

A pair of floodlights mounted on the hangar lit up several rows of single- and twin-engined airplanes. Some of them awaited their turns at the hands of Aero-consultants craftsmen, and some of them belonged to employees. Wyatt let them park their planes for free. Bucky Barr's pristinely restored Bell helicopter was parked at one end, its rotors tethered.

The twin jet braked to a stop in line with parked client aircraft, the nose bobbing lightly, then the engines whined down. When the door opened and Wyatt descended to the apron, Kramer picked up a set of wheel chocks resting nearby and began walking toward him.

Wyatt saw her coming. "Hey, my favorite ground crewman."

"Crew person," she said, handing him one linked pair of chocks.

"You just watch. Someday, I'm going to have all the gender-definitive terms down pat."

"I doubt it."

"Anyone else around?"

"Just me. If they aren't in Nebraska, they're home in bed."

Together, they chocked the wheels, then Wyatt locked the door. She waited, fingering the new red stripes on the fuselage.

"I thought you weren't going to show this logo around here."

"I wasn't, but if anyone notices, they'll just think it was a client."

They walked back to the hangar, and Kramer wrapped her fingers around his arm.

"How was Washington?"

"Near gridlock inside the Beltway."

"The traffic?"

"That, too. Mostly, the politics and the intellectual capabilities are close to standstill."

Inside the hangar, Kramer locked the door and reset the alarm. Wyatt walked over to the Texan's Mystere-Falcon and peeked inside the open door.

"Security systems in?" he asked.

In addition to the luxury upgrade, Aeroconsultants was installing antiterrorist detection and protection systems which included bomb detectors and infrared and radar threat sensors. More executives who flew internationally were becoming nervous about drug-toting maniacs with Stinger missiles. The pilots who flew for them were treated to two-week workshops in defensive and evasive flying tactics conducted by Wyatt, Barr, Hackley, and Zimmerman.

"They're mostly in," she said.

He climbed the airstair and slipped inside, turning on an overhead lighting strip.

She followed.

Much of the interior panelling had been replaced with laminated teak. The new carpeting had not yet been laid and the sofa and chairs—reupholstered in new, soft leather—had not been reinstalled as yet. Snugged up against the rear bulkhead, behind a fitted fiberglass door that folded to either side, was a full-sized bed.

"The bed work?" he asked.

"Hasn't been tested."

"Should it be?"

She moved in close and wrapped her arms around his waist. The heat of Washington was still on him, musky. She could feel the strength in his arms as he pulled her to him.

She tilted her head back to look up at him and said, "Around here, we double-test everything."

Wyatt woke at five-thirty.

He was in his own bed, which felt a little strange. The first early morning light was sliding into the bedroom through the large and undraped window which overlooked his backyard. The overgrown, dense shrubbery and trees which completely enclosed the yard made it private, even though it was small. The grass was also overgrown; the neighbor's boy was a day or two behind on his mowing.

Wyatt's house was forty or fifty years old, located in a quiet residential area of northeast Albuquerque. Since buying it, he had painted it inside and out, installed new carpet, then added air-conditioning. It was the first house he had ever owned, and after three years, he still wasn't certain how he felt about his ownership. His feet were still attuned to Air Force ways, ready to move on at any moment.

The queen-sized bed dominated the room, which was the largest of the two bedrooms, and left little space for the nightstands and dresser. The bedspread was crumpled in one corner, where he had tossed it at two o'clock.

He sat up, worked his way backward, and leaned against the headboard.

Jan opened one eye.

"Sorry," he said. "I didn't mean to wake you."

"I know. You like to watch the sun come up."

She opened her other eye, and both eyes came alive,

a vibrant green in the soft light. Slithering her way up beside him, the sheet fell away from her full breasts.

Wyatt raised his left arm and put it around her shoulders, tugging her close.

"You're worried, aren't you?" she asked.

"Who, me? Worry?" he said, but he was. He was putting a lot of lives on the line, more than ever before. And he found himself thinking about the people attached to those lives, the wives and the families.

"You don't have to do this."

"Yes, I do. I made a commitment."

"Make this the last one."

"The commitment is four years old."

She knew that. He had told her. Church had given him five million dollars as the fair price of having Wyatt on tap for undetermined years into the future. More than that, Church had known Wyatt better than he knew himself. Church had known that Wyatt lived up to his promises.

She turned slightly and put her hand on his chest. She locked her eyes on his. "The company is doing very well. We don't need the covert contracts any more."

"I also believe in what I'm doing, Jan."

That was true, also. There wasn't one operation he had performed for Church for which he felt any regret whatsoever. His actions—or Bucky's or Norm's or Karl's—were necessary in some degree toward maintaining stability in one part of the world or another. His people felt the same way, he thought.

Her dark red hair was tousled. There was an impressed line on her cheek from a wrinkle in the pillowcase. Her hand felt warm on his chest.

He slid his left hand along her upper arm.

"So," she said, "you're only going to make one commitment in your life? To God and country, but mostly country?"

"That's the pressing one right now, Jan."

She pulled away abruptly, spun around, and sat on the edge of the bed with her back to him.

He leaned toward her and put his hand on her shoulder.

She shrugged it off.

"You don't think I should fulfill my promises?"

"Maybe you should make more of them, Andy. Maybe you should think more about the company, about the people who work for you."

"Well, damn it! I am."

"Bullshit!"

She stood up, crossed to the dresser, and scooped up her clothing. Clutching them to her stomach, she turned toward him. Her breasts heaved, and he saw a tear in the corner of one eye.

"You need to rethink your priorities, Andy."

"Jan . . ."

When she went through the doorway, she slammed the door behind her.

Wyatt sighed, leaned back, and waited for her to come back.

She had had temper tantrums in the past, and she got over them quickly.

He waited three minutes.

Then heard the yelp of tires on his driveway.

He scrambled out of bed, jerked the door open, and trotted down the hall and into the living room. Through the front window, he saw his carefully tended and lovingly treated 1965 Corvette roadster in a four-wheel drift as it rounded the corner at the end of the block.

Then she gunned the 396 cubic-inch V8, and black smoke boiled off the rear tires.

"Are you married?" she asked.

"I was," Ahmed al-Qati told her. "My wife and two children were killed when the Americans bombed Tripoli."

She put her hand to her mouth. Her fingers were long and slim, expressive. They danced against her lips, which were lightly defined with pale pink. "I am so sorry."

"Many would say it was God's will. I do not know."

The waiter interrupted to pour more coffee, then backed away with tiny, servile bows. He was seeking a tip that would last him a month, no doubt. Foreigners with money still visited Libya, but not in the droves of previous decades. Tobruk was no longer a thriving and bustling resort city; most of the tourists who stayed here came for reasons other than simple relaxation. Foreigners rented the hotel rooms while they worked on government contracts. There were Russians, Frenchmen, Germans, Dutch, even a few Americans.

Sophia Gabratelli had her reasons. When al-Qati had first met her, almost three months before, she had told him simply that she was hiding out until her divorce was finalized. She had not elaborated, but al-Qati, ever the perfectionist when it came to information, had conducted his own inquiry through friends in Libyan intelligence.

He had learned that Sophia Gabratelli—her maiden name—was indeed awaiting a final divorce decree from a French court. She had established a residency in the south of France since the Italian courts would not ac-

111

knowledge her right to leave her husband of two years, a Sicilian named Aragone. Moreover, the husband was a known Mafia chieftain, and that fact alone explained her desire to lead a low-profile life in Tobruk.

Al-Qati had learned more than that, of course. He knew that she had a small appendectomy scar on her lower torso and that her small toe on the right foot had been broken once. He knew the names of her parents, who lived in northern Italy. He knew that she had once aspired to a career in filmmaking or modelling, a dream worthy of the classic, high-cheekboned lines of her face, the smouldering dark eyes beneath full lashes, the perfectly smooth, olive skin, and the straight, flashingly white teeth revealed by her ready smile. She was petite, and though she wore loose-fitting, non-revealing, and conservative dresses—perhaps in deference to the mores of the country—al-Qati was aware that the curves she attempted to disguise were abundant and lush. He had imagined them out of disguise more than once.

Ahmed al-Qati also knew that she had lied to him. She had told him she was twenty-nine years old when, in fact, she was thirty-three years old. That deceit was perfectly understandable in a Western or Continental woman. She had also told him that she had a modest sum put by, enough to live in relative comfort in the seedy Seaside Hotel overlooking the Mediterranean until her divorce decree was handed down. He knew to the contrary that she had escaped the mansion in Sicily with the equivalent of two-and-a-quarter million American dollars. Considering that the spurned Aragone was probably looking intently for that money, that lie was also understandable.

In one of his fantasies, which would never be lived out, al-Qati had given himself the role of protector of

Sophia Gabratelli and her fortune. By her upbringing, she was considerably more worldly and outspoken, and probably needed less defending, than any woman he had ever met. Still, she was tiny and likely susceptible to wily men. After the sixth time he had met her for dinner, he had let it be known quietly around the city, and through the police, that she enjoyed his protection. He had not told her this.

He forced his eyes from her face and stared over the railing at the smooth, darkening expanse of the sea. White rollers coasted up the sand of the beach. A dozen people walked in the surf's edge. Two swimmers were far out.

For the life of him, he could not recall his wife's face. Sophia had that effect on him.

"Does it make you bitter?" she asked.

"The American attack? Yes, it does."

"Do you seek vengeance?"

He smiled at her. "At one time, it was all I could think of. But no longer."

"You are at peace with yourself?"

"Not at peace, I think. But I have decided that the fates of nations are not up to me. I will do my part, and I will be prepared if it should ever happen again."

"Defensively? With your battalion?"

"Yes. That is, I believe my soldiers will conduct themselves with honor, should the Americans come again." After convincing Ramad of the need to check on his command, al-Qati had conducted a quick inspection at El Bardi, then headed directly for Tobruk.

"And you?"

"Myself, I now play games with the air force."

"And you do not think much of the air force?"

"I do not think much of the games," he said.

113

She smiled at him. "Enough of this. I tire quickly of war talk and coffee. Will you walk in the sea with me?"

He grinned. "I have not done that in many years."

"Then you will enjoy it all the more."

Al-Qati paid the bill, then the two of them walked down the steps from the veranda to the sand.

She stooped to free her feet from her sandals, and he noted that the small toe of her right foot was slightly bent. Nevertheless, all of her toes were delightfully carved.

When she straightened up, standing a full head shorter than he, she wrapped her hand around his forearm. Her skirt swished against his leg as they walked down to the sea.

Ahmed al-Qati had not felt as content in many years.

Jim Bennett had Liz Jordan and mechanic Slim Reddy witness Wyatt's signature, then had them sign their names at the bottom of the document.

For a lawyer, Bennett was only mildly ambitious, a trait that had encouraged Wyatt to retain him a couple years before for his personal needs. His personal requirements weren't all that extensive, but Jan Kramer had insisted that Wyatt use someone other than the company attorney. Bennett also took care of the legal niceties for Bucky Barr's educational foundation.

After they were left alone in the office Wyatt shared with Kramer and Barr, Bennett asked, "Where's Jan?"

"She took some vacation days, Jim."

He assumed she had. By the time Wyatt had gotten dressed, called for a cab, and arrived at the office, she had totally disappeared. His Corvette was sitting in the parking lot with the keys in the ashtray, but her Riviera was gone. She either wasn't at her condo, or she wasn't answering the phone. During the day, he had left five messages on her machine.

He ended up spending the day with Liz Jordan, paying the monthly statements, preparing bank deposits, and constructing last month's profit-and-loss report. Jan was right; they were doing okay.

The meeting with Jim Bennett—the primary reason he had returned to Albuquerque—took place at three in the afternoon. Together, they reviewed the final draft of his will, Wyatt asked some questions, Bennett answered them satisfactorily, and Wyatt signed off.

Wyatt shoved the document into its envelope, then got up and put it in the wall safe. Only he, Bucky, and Jan had access to the safe. He noted that Barr also had a more recently dated will stored in the safe. Apparently, neither of them were very confident about this operation.

Bennett snapped his briefcase shut. "You sure you don't want to get in some handball?"

"Can't do it, Jim. The work's stacking up on us."

"Next week, then? I'm going to go to potbelly if I don't spend more time on the court."

"Give me a call, but don't write anything solid on your calendar, Jim. I'm going to be in and out of town."

Bennett gave him a wave, then went to the outer office to hassle Liz for a couple minutes. She didn't want to play handball either.

Wyatt stood, looked around, couldn't think of anything else he needed. He started for the door.

Then stopped and went back to lean over the phone.

He punched the memory number labeled, "Kramer." It rang four times, then the answering machine kicked in.

He hung up.

Checking his watch, he decided he had better get airborne for Nebraska.

He checked the contents of his wallet. Four-thousand-two-hundred-and-eleven dollars. The roll in his left pocket contained eleven thousand. He figured it was enough to get him through the next couple of weeks.

Shutting off the lights, he stepped into the reception area and headed for the door to the hangar.

Time to go.

"Are you leaving already, Andy?" Jordan asked.

"In a little while, Liz," he said, altering course for the door to the parking lot.

The Corvette started right away, and he rolled down the windows for air. The heat was oppressive, but his Corvette didn't offer air-conditioning except for the forced-air kind. Pulling out of the lot, he took the access road to University Boulevard and got the roadster up to seventy before he came abreast of the passenger terminal. The traffic slowed him down then, and he drifted with it onto Gibson Boulevard and got into the lane for Interstate 25 north.

He managed seventy miles an hour on the freeway, staying with the flow of the traffic until he reached Lomas Boulevard and took it west.

Jan Kramer's condominium was in a four-story mini-tower just north of downtown Albuquerque. It was a newer building, following the architectural principles in evidence throughout much of the downtown region. The rounded corners and lodgepole projections of adobe construction predominated.

His wallet contained a plastic passcard for the underground parking garage, and he used it to gain access to a guest parking spot.

Jan's Riviera was parked squarely in her slot, and his hopes lifted a trifle.

Taking the elevator to the fourth floor, he got off and walked the carpeted hallway to the north end. Being circumspect, he knocked on the door.

No answer.

He unlocked it with his key.

She wasn't home.

Wyatt walked through the living room and peeked into the master bedroom. He checked the closets and found large gaps in the hanging clothes.

In the second bedroom, which she used primarily for storage, he found that her luggage was missing.

And that made him feel somewhat lonely.

Memorial

Seven

Ibrahim Ramad stood beside the podium at the head of the briefing room. The ventilation system was struggling with the haze of cigarette smoke that drifted near the ceiling. He could never figure out why pilots, who should strive to be in the best possible condition, smoked so much.

His bomber and interceptor wing commanders, along with their squadron commanders, were sprawled in desk-armed chairs around the room. To Ramad's right, slightly out of the mainstream of air force officers, sat Ahmed al-Qati and army Major Khalil Shummari, the commander of the helicopter company which supported al-Qati's airlift operations. The aviation company was composed of Mil Mi-8 troop transports carrying thirty-two soldiers, Mi-24 assault helicopters able to transport eight troops as well as deliver devastating firepower, and a squadron of Mi-28 attack helicopters utilized as escort ships.

Ramad waved a thick sheaf of paper at them, and the buzz of conversation dwindled away.

"The work that Lieutenant Colonel al-Qati and I have accomplished in the past ten days has come to fruition,

121

brothers. These orders from the Leader, countersigned by Colonels Ghazi and Salmi, allow us to now test the theoretical.

"Colonel al-Qati, you are to move your special forces company to Marada for these trials, and Major Shummari will provide the tactical airlift."

"How soon are we to begin?" al-Qati asked. He did not appear as excited about the prospects as Ramad thought he might have been.

"We will start as soon as possible. I would like to have your units in place by tomorrow night. Or is that too much to expect?"

Play on the man's vanity.

"We will be here," al-Qati said.

Khalil Shummari said, "Colonel, these exercises will utilize simulated ordnance?"

Ramad tapped the orders with his forefinger. "The first five in the series will be conducted with simulators, Major. Then there will be a grand finale utilizing live chemical agents."

Al-Qati frowned. "It seems to me, Colonel Ramad, that a live exercise could lead to a large number of casualties among my infantry as well as Major Shummari's helicopter crews."

"Nonsense," Ramad said. "Are you saying that your soldiers are unprepared for chemical warfare?"

"We regularly train in CW techniques," al-Qati said, "and we are well-trained. However, in any large operation, it is prudent to expect mistakes to be made. We do not necessarily need to assume the risk—the certainty, in fact—of losing lives merely to impress higher authorities."

"Ah, but it is not higher authorities we intend to impress," Ramad said.

122

The briefing room fell silent as its occupants mulled over Ramad's statement. He always enjoyed having that edge of surprise, of knowledge that others did not possess.

Captain Gamal Harisah, first squadron commander of the bomber wing, rose from his chair. He was a study in intensity: small, dark, sharply focused. He was also a fierce and fearless pilot.

"Colonel Ramad, are we to conduct these flights, these exercises, without regard to overhead surveillance?"

"That is correct, Captain. The satellites may watch what they will."

"And that is the reason for the live exercise, is it not?"

"That is quite right, Captain Harisah. The Leader is now prepared for the world to know for certain that we control an arsenal of chemical weapons."

It was, Ramad knew, a complete change in policy, and one for which he had pressed. Until now, the Leader had insisted to the world that the chemical plant constructed with German assistance was purely in support of agricultural aims. Ramad—and others, like Farouk Salmi—had argued that a chemical capability did little to deter aggression against them unless its existence was confirmed and the resolution to utilize it was proclaimed and demonstrated.

"The objective of this program," he continued, "is not only to hone our skills, but to also make clear to the warhawks in America and Israel that forays against our homeland will have devastating results for the Israeli populace. No longer will we allow raids within our borders to take place without retaliation."

One of those acts of aggression still stung him every

time he thought about it. Ramad had been commander of the MiG-23 squadron that lost two aircraft to Sixth Fleet F-14 Tomcats over the Gulf of Sidra. The Leader had attempted to persuade the world that Libyan territorial rights extended in a straight line across the Gulf, rather than following the indented curvature of the coast. The Americans had successfully tested the proclamation, and the imaginary line, and the Leader's resolve, along with Ramad's pilots, were found wanting.

"No," he continued, "it shall not happen again. Our tolerance levels finally have been achieved."

Ahmed al-Qati smiled a ghostly smile at that statement. Ramad knew well that the man had lost his family to the Tripoli attack.

"The political objective of this exercise is to give the Israelis second thoughts about our will, our skill, and our resources. It is also intended to suggest to Washington that an American attack could well result in retaliation against Israeli targets."

"We are certain," al-Qati asked, "that a single live demonstration of CW weapons will achieve that end?"

"Absolutely," Ramad assured him.

He could be confident of his assertion because Ramad, and in this room, only Ramad, knew how impressive the final demonstration would be. The lesson would be taught, and it was, after all, the will of Allah.

Bucky Barr was stripped to the waist, the sweat running through the thick hair on his chest and accumulating in the waistband of his khaki shorts, which were just about as wet as he was

He was seated on the concrete floor of the hangar, next to the left main landing gear of three-six, hauling back on a three-quarter-inch-drive digital torque wrench. Lucas Littlefield was on his knees next to him, holding a combination wrench in place, to keep the bolt from turning as Barr tightened the nut down.

He tugged the torque wrench, and the nut reluctantly turned a quarter-turn.

"Goddamn," Barr said. "you think we're about there, Lucas?"

"Keep going."

Barr reset the socket on the nut, then put his weight into the handle once again.

CLICK!

The torque wrench let him know he had reached 170 foot-pounds.

Barr sagged forward, slipped the socket from the nut, and dropped the wrench on the floor.

"Goddamn it!" Lucas yelped. "Don't treat my tools that way, Bucky."

Aeroconsultants had bought the tools, but Barr didn't debate the point.

"Sorry, chief."

He rolled onto his knees, then his feet, and crept out from under the wing.

All six F-4s were now in Hangar Four, three each staggered along each of the sidewalls, their twin canopies raised. The nose cones were also raised, revealing the mounts where the original radar scanners had been fixed. Each aircraft had its fully overhauled turbojet reinstalled, and Barr was proud of the new and sleek appearance. The lower fuselage and the underside of the wings and tail planes were finished in low-visibility gray. Topsides, the color was that selected as the corporate color of Noble Enterprises, a low-gloss cream. From the nose cone to the air intakes, dividing the cream and gray, a single, expanding red stripe had been taped in place. From the air intakes back along the fuselage, then swooping up the vertical stabilizer were twin red stripes. The N-numbers—all imaginary—and the Noble Enterprises logo were also red and were placed above the stripes on the fuselage sides.

The trailing edge of the wings, incorporating the ailerons and flaps, were also taped in two-foot-wide stripes, red on top and yellow on the bottom. The scheme was meant to identify for air show spectators whether or not a plane was inverted when it was flying several thousand feet above the crowd. The small plane pilots who hung around the fixed-base operator's office had seemed reassured when they saw the planes in their new livery. Stripped of weapons pylons and military insignia, the jets presented the appearance of an aerial demonstration team.

Which was exactly what they were supposed to represent.

Both of the Hercules aircraft followed the same theme, though they had not received the cream paint. The tanker had been sandblasted down to its original aluminum finish, matching the Aeroconsultants craft, then both had received the red fuselage striping, N-numbers, and logos.

Noble Enterprises looked like a going concern, but it was misleading. None of the F-4s were currently capable of flight. Almost all of the avionics had been stripped from each aircraft. Pilots and technicians swarmed over the six aircraft, working side by side, congenially complaining while they focused on their particular tasks.

Tom Kriswell and Sam Vrdla had finally been turned loose on the contents of the Jeep trailers. They had black boxes, cables, and diagnostic equipment spread all over the workbenches. Vrdla had one old radio connected to a battery and antenna, and a Lincoln radio station pumped out Garth Brooks, Vince Gill, Tanya Tucker, and an occasional Willie Nelson.

Barr walked over to seven-seven and climbed the ladder. The ejection seats had been removed, and Wyatt was on his back on the cockpit floor, his head stuck between the rudder pedals, working a ratchet on the back of the instrument panel.

"Hey, Andy."

Wyatt lowered his head against a pedal and peered up at him. "Yeah?"

"How long we been here?"

"We're one day short of two weeks."

"It seems like one week short of two years."

"You get that main gear reinstalled?"

"Damn betcha! We are now complete on the body work and mechanical shit."

"So you climbed up here to tell me it's worth celebrating," Wyatt said.

"Hell, yes! It's a milestone."

"Okay. Send somebody to town for beer."

Barr slid back down the ladder and crossed to where Littlefield was cleaning tools and putting them away in his stack of castered cabinets.

"You want to check out the hydraulics while we still got her on the jackstands, Bucky?"

"We'll do it in the morning, Lucas." Barr pulled his wallet from his hip pocket. The leather was streaked dark with moisture. He fumbled in the bill compartment and extracted five fifty dollar bills. "You want to take a break?"

"Hell, yes, but we ain't going to find any females in this burg."

Barr stuffed the bills into Littlefield's breast pocket. "Take one of the Wagoneers and go buy us a propane grill, about ten pounds of chopped sirloin, buns, pickles, chips, the works. Potato salad. Don't forget the potato salad. And baked beans."

"You forgot the beer."

"The beer goes without saying."

Littlefield dipped his hands into a plastic vat of waterless hand cleaner and started to smear it around.

Barr walked over to the workbenches at the back of the hangar.

The seeming confusion of wires, cables, instruments, and electronics boxes was actually organized. Kriswell and Vrdla had nearly identical groups of components arranged into six areas. As they probed each piece with digital and analog instruments, verifying the correct functions of integrated circuits and silicon chips and other mysteries Barr didn't care to know about, they tagged the components that passed with yellow tape.

"How's it going, Tom?" he asked.

"*Magnifico!* This is top-grade stuff, Bucky. All we've run into are some calibration problems."

"I wonder how much it cost Uncle?"

"Don't ask. We've got maybe ten million bucks on the bench."

Barr reached out for a six-inch-square box.

"And don't touch!"

"Hey."

"This is my office. Go sit in your own."

"Is it going to work?" Barr asked.

"Hell, I don't know."

"That's comforting as hell."

"Of course it'll work," Kriswell said, putting down a probe and digging his Marlboros out of his pocket. "I flat-out guarantee it."

"For how long?"

"Hundred hours good enough?" He stuck the unlit cigarette in his mouth. He didn't smoke anymore.

"Should be," Barr agreed.

He moved down the bench and bent over to peer into a Head Up Display screen resting there. It was blank, but he pictured targets showing all over the place.

The F-4 Phantom was designed as a two-seat fighter, with the radar operator placed in the rear seat. The philosophy had been not to overload the pilot with too many chores to accomplish, especially when the going got hectic in a combat situation. The philosophy was still in vogue for F-14 Tomcats and F-111 swing-wing bombers.

Noble Enterprises was converting the F-4 to single seat operation, utilizing avionics and controls designed primarily for the F-15 Eagle. It was an ambitious venture, but one that Demion, Kriswell, and Wyatt thought feasible. And if they did, so did Barr.

All he had to do was fly it, and he was looking forward to that.

At four-forty-five in the morning, the air was unmoving on the perimeter of the small airfield. Ahmed al-Qati expected it to start moving at any time.

To the northeast, the faint glimmer of dawn was beginning to wash the squat buildings of El Bardi. It was not light enough yet to define the sea beyond the town.

Behind him in the darkness were the eighty-five men of his First Special Forces Company. The four platoon leaders and the company commander, Captain Ibn Rahman, stood with him at the side of the runway, waiting.

Al-Qati and Khalil Shummari had flown back to El Bardi right after the briefing at Marada Base yesterday, and al-Qati had put his special forces officers to work immediately, recalling the men from the exercise underway and cajoling them into cleaning and preparing their equipment for this morning's deployment.

The grumbling had been widespread last night, and still this morning, though he could not discern the exact words, al-Qati heard the tone of discontent in the dozens of conversations taking place behind him.

He also sensed that his officers were displeased with him, not because of the unannounced deployment—for which they had not yet been fully briefed, but because he had shirked his own duties for three hours during the night.

The magnetic attraction of the Seaside Hotel in Tobruk was almost beyond his will to resist. At least, he did not mount a defensive strategy within his mind. Al-Qati could not believe, nor fathom, the fates that had brought Sophia Gabratelli to him so late in his life. Nor did he even try to understand why, after months of what he was certain was fruitless courting, she had taken him into her arms and her bed.

He harbored no illusions about himself. He had become newly aware of the bald spot expanding on the back of his head. His bold, hooked nose dominated a face ravaged by wind and weather and sun. To be truthful to himself, there were some positives. He was hard and fit. The muscles of his arms and legs and stomach were apparent and utile. Unlike many Arab men, he tried not to treat women as inferiors. He supposed that there might have been some mystique in his reputation as a professional warrior, if she were even aware of it. When they were together, he talked very little about himself or his past exploits. He was not a braggart. She was quite aware of world politics and tensions, and their conversations embraced those topics as well as soccer, for which they were both avid fans, the cinema, and music. She was far ahead of him in the realm of art and literature, but he enjoyed her analyses of both. She was an avid listener when he talked of what he had learned of military leadership and tactics.

And despite the physical change in their relationship in their last two meetings, Sophia remained something of an unattainable ideal for him. That such a woman would hold him close, that he might nuzzle the smooth, freshly scented aroma of her flesh made him more capable than at any time in his memory. She had called him a magnificent lover. . . .

"I hear them, Colonel," Rahman said, startling him out of his reverie.

"Yes." He heard the thrupp-thrupp of rotors.

Seconds later, the two Mi-8s and three Mi-24s—known by their NATO codenames as Hip and Hind—came hurtling out of the dark. Four Mi-28 assault helicopters—the Havoc—flew to the sides of the main group.

Two C-130H transport craft were due to arrive within the hour, to load the company's armored personnel carriers. Rahman had detailed six men to stay behind and accompany the mobile equipment.

"All right, Captain," al-Qati said. "Let's check them out and load them up."

Rahman nodded to the lieutenants, who spun around

131

and went in search of their platoons for last-minute inspections before embarking.

The rattle of weapons and creak of web gear behind him was obliterated by the noise of the helicopters as they hovered into place and then settled to the asphalt of the airstrip.

The First Platoon, known as the Strike Platoon and composed of his most elite soldiers, loaded first. Ahmed al-Qati stepped back and watched them file onto the runway. They were dressed in desert camouflage utilities, with steel helmets painted in sand and tan and gray. Each man carried a twenty-seven-kilogram backpack and had four one-liter canteens of water attached to his web gear. A large pouch, attached to the side of the packs, contained each man's CW kit. The primary weapon for the platoon was the Kalishnakov 5.45 millimeter AK-74 assault rifle. One 12.7 millimeter DShK-38 heavy machine gun was also assigned to the platoon, as were RPG-7 antitank rockets and SA-7 Grail missiles for air defense.

Despite their earlier complaints, these men carried themselves well—heads up, shoulders back, proud. Lieutenant Hakim, their commander, trotted to the head of the column and assigned the nineteen men to seats in the Mi-24 assault helicopters.

The other three platoons loaded quickly aboard the Mi-8 transports.

Al-Qati reached down and picked up his pack, slinging it over his shoulder. He carried his web gear and holstered 7.62 millimeter Tokarev automatic in his left hand and headed for the lead Mi-8. Looking around, to be certain nothing was left behind, he saw only the eight parked BMD fire support vehicles awaiting their transport. He counted six men tending to them.

Clambering into the helicopter's cabin, he found Major Shummari standing in the cabin, talking to someone over a headset.

The clatter of the twin Isotov turboshaft engines made conversation impossible. Shummari handed him a spare headset, and al-Qati removed his helmet and slipped it in place.

"All accounted for, Ahmed?" the major asked.

"I start with eighty-five, Khalil. How many will be left when we are done, do you suppose?"

In the expanding light of dawn and the red overhead light of the cabin, Shummari studied his face for several seconds before answering.

"Do you really want a response, Ahmed?"

"Please."

"Ninety percent would be a good number."

Al-Qati bent over to peer out the door as helicopters began taking off. Through the open portals of the cabins, he saw the men who trusted him to provide them with as much safety as was possible for professional soldiers.

He thought that Shummari was probably correct. Eight or nine of them would be carried home. it was an acceptable number in wartime, though not in peace.

He would argue his position against the live exercise yet again.

But he did not think that he would prevail.

By the evening of the following Wednesday, the first revitalized F-4 was complete. It was an E model, carrying the number N20677. If their luck held, nine-three would be finished by the next day.

While Wyatt agreed with Barr that the external appearance of the Phantoms was impressive, he was happier with what Demion and Kriswell had accomplished on the interior.

Behind the nose radome was a Hughes attack radar scanner. It fed the APG-63 pulsed-Doppler radar which had a search range of 120 miles. A network of sensors installed in various places on the fuselage and wings were coupled to an ALR-56 radar warning system. The ALQ-128 launch warning and Identify Friend or Foe system was installed. The internal countermeasures system from the F-15 was designated ALQ-135. To protect the tail, the pilot's blind spot, ALQ-154 radar warning and AAR-38 infrared warning systems had been added.

The black box containing the programmable signal-processing computer had been mounted on the rear bulkhead in the aft cockpit. That computer processed information from the radar, and possibly from data links with an Airborne Warning and Control aircraft, then displayed the filtered information on the HUD, now mounted on the top of the instrument panel. Radar echoes from aircraft flying at similar or higher altitudes were simple, but the computer was sophisticated enough to pick up the faint returns of aircraft near the ground, eliminate the ground return, and display only the targets on the HUD. Instead of continuously looking down to check a cluttered radar screen, a busy pilot scanning the skies around him for hostile aircraft and missiles had all the information he needed directly in his line-of-sight. The HUD reported the true position of a target, along with its range and closing speed. The display also prompted the pilot when the distance to target was safe for missile firing.

The cockpit had been substantially revised. Circuit breakers, armament and radio panels, and switches were in new positions. There were two eight-inch cathode ray tube (CRT) displays set into the instrument panel.

All sixteen of the Noble Enterprises team were gathered near the front hangar door admiring their work before locking up for the night.

Barr pulled a handful of half-dollars from his pocket. He was probably the only person in the nation with a ready supply of half-dollars. He liked the heft, he said.

Wyatt saw his move and said, "No, Bucky."

"Ah, shit, Andy! We at least ought to let the God of odds become involved."

"No way. I'll do the first test hop in the morning. You can fly chase with the Citation."

"How thrilling," Barr said.

"If you get the first trial, Andy," Hackley said, "that eliminates you from the next five."

"That's only fair," Gettman agreed.

Barr passed out coins. "Let's settle it now."

Kriswell grabbed a coin.

"Forget it, Tom," Barr told him. "You've got to land a Cessna with prop and gear intact first."

They flipped coins in odd-man-out until they had a roster for the test flights of the remaining five aircraft: Jordan, Zimmerman, Barr, Hackley, and Gettman.

With the priority of risks settled, Hank Cavanaugh shut off the lights and locked the door, and they all crawled into the Jeeps for the drive into Ainsworth.

The closer they got to completion of the aircraft, the more celebratory was the mood. Everyone was in good spirits when they filed into the Rancher's Cafe and Lounge and started to place orders. Barr engaged Julie Jorgenson in a discussion of educational priorities. He was insidiously leading her into the belief that every student should be able to write well before an English

135

teacher pounded Shakespeare and Dickens into them. She had become very easy with Barr, perhaps somewhat awed by his command of the pressing issues in education. He knew about test results and national comparisons of ability.

Wyatt twisted the top off a bottle of Budweiser and carried it to the short hallway between the dining room and the semidarkened lounge. There were two couples at tables and three single men at the bar. He lifted the receiver from the wall-mounted telephone and used his CIA-funded calling card to place his call.

There was no answer at Kramer's number. He didn't leave a message on the answering machine.

The machine answered at Aeroconsultants, but didn't tell him anything he didn't already know.

For the fifth time, he tried Kramer's father in Seattle.

"Mr. Kramer, this is Andy Wyatt."

"Good evening, Mr. Wyatt."

George Kramer had always been very formal with Wyatt, perhaps because from the first he had resented Wyatt taking his little girl away from Seattle. Or maybe because he knew more about Wyatt's relationship with his little girl than Wyatt thought he knew.

"Sorry to bother you again, Mr. Kramer, but I wondered if Jan had checked in with you?"

The first time he had called Seattle, Wyatt had had to use the excuse that Jan was on vacation and he needed to get in touch with her.

"Why yes, Mr. Wyatt, she sure did."

"Great! Is she there? Or do you know where I could reach her?"

"She doesn't want to talk to you."

George Kramer sounded positively gleeful.

Eight

The Director of Central intelligence was not only the chief executive of the Central intelligence Agency, but also head of the other agencies in the intelligence community—Defense Intelligence, the National Security Agency, the military and cabinet-level intelligence services. He split his time between offices at Langley and in the District. It kept him busy enough that Martin Church and the other three deputy directors—Intelligence, Science and Technology, and Administration—had little day-to-day contact with him, though they all got together for monthly staff meetings.

Church reported directly to the Executive Director who reported through the Deputy Director for Central Intelligence to the DCI. That process was all right with Church because he didn't particularly care for the director, a seemingly cold man with political in-fighting ability who could get stubborn about his own viewpoints.

The Executive Director called him in mid-afternoon. "You busy right now, Marty?"

"Nothing I can't toss in the drawer."

"The DCI would like to talk to you."

"Me? Alone?"

"Go on over to his office now."

The director's office suite was lavish and spacious, with its own conference and dining room. His two over-burdened secretaries were working feverishly at computer terminal keyboards and fielding constantly chiming telephones. He was pointed in the direction of the dining room.

He knocked on the door before opening it.

"Come on in, Martin."

The DCI was in the kitchenette making himself a cheese sandwich. He ate half-a-dozen times a day, probably because his caloric intake couldn't keep up with the frenetic pace he maintained.

"Do you want a sandwich?" he asked. "Or maybe a piece of apple pie?"

"No, sir. Thanks, anyway."

He came out of the kitchenette, swigging from a can of 7UP, and plopped in one of the soft, castered chairs at the big table.

"Sit down, Martin. I've got about ten minutes before I leave for the District."

Church sat across from him.

"I read the intelligence estimate you sent up this morning. The Libyan thing."

"Yes, sir."

"Any reservations about it? About the eight thousand figure for the warheads?"

"No," Church said. "Embry's playing it right down the middle of the road. They could well have a few more than we're projecting."

"Okay. I'm going to bring it up at the NSC meeting. Then, I'm going to spring the Icarus Project on them. What's Wyatt's state of preparation?"

Church managed to keep his face immobile, but his mind reeled as if he had been slugged. For the past two months, he had been proceeding with Wyatt's mission—codenamed Icarus—under the impression that the National Security Council had already signed off on it. The DCI was capable of that deception, though. He was fond of building up his pet projects in secrecy for weeks at a time while concurrently spiking conversations with hints about the future, then springing the projects on people. It made him appear as if he was always prepared for any eventuality. His reputation as a Boy Scout hadn't been tarnished since he took office.

"Uh, sir, it looks like about ten or twelve days," Church said.

The director flipped open his Daytimer. "August four at the earliest?"

"Yes, sir."

"Good. The President's going to be at this meeting, and I want the image of eight thousand warheads to have some impact. I'm going to show that video that Science and Technology put together, the one about toxic effects on humans. I think I can get closure on the project immediately. If I can swing an Executive Order, we can bypass the Congressional oversight committees until the mission's complete."

"Is there a chance they won't approve it?" Church asked.

"Very damned little, I think."

"What do I tell Wyatt?"

"You don't tell Wyatt a damned thing."

Lieutenant Colonel Ahmed al-Qati leaned between the two helicopter pilots and squinted at the horizon.

139

They were flying low, though high enough to avoid raising a dust cloud behind them, and the horizons were close. When he saw the miniature sandstorm erupt and the two Sukhoi-24 bombers begin their climbout, he tapped the pilot on the shoulder.

"Go now, Lieutenant," he said over the intercom.

The nose of the helicopter dipped as it picked up forward speed.

Through the right side window of the Mi-8, al-Qati saw the sister helicopter, some fifty meters away, also increase its speed.

He turned to the rear and studied the thirty infantrymen poised in their seats. They were already dressed in their shapeless chemical warfare clothing, their packs strapped to the outside of the protective parkas.

Al-Qati signalled the lieutenant watching him, and the officer passed the signal to his men. The steel helmets came off as gas masks were donned. They pulled their balaclava headwear, constructed of flexible vinyl and extremely hot and uncomfortable, on next, then replaced their helmets. The unwieldy vinyl gloves were next, then they regripped their weapons.

They looked like bug-eyed monsters from some poorly produced Japanese movie, al-Qati thought.

"Two kilometers, Colonel," the pilot said. "We'll be entering into the cloud in a few seconds."

"Prepare yourselves," al-Qati said, pulling the headset from his ears and unsnapping the gas mask case at his waist.

The pilots took turns adjusting their own masks while al-Qati snugged his into place, blew through his nose to exhaust the air and seal the soft rubber against his skin. As soon as he tugged the hood over his head, his skin erupted in perspiration.

He always felt as if the mask shortchanged him on air supply.

Leaning forward, he again peered through the windshield. The dust cloud from the exploding 300-kiloton bombs was settling, blowing off toward the east in a light wind. Still, the air was hazy and rippled as a result of the tear gas that saturated it. The exercise called for the use of tear gas in order to simulate near-reality. Ramad had feared that al-Qati's soldiers would pull off their masks as soon as they were out of sight of an officer. Ramad did not really understand discipline, or how to instill it, al-Qati thought.

Through the haze, he could see the small sign posts that had been erected. They read, "Radio Transmitter," or "Ordnance Depot," or "Fuel Storage." They were the objectives of his ground advance.

"Resistance is expected to be nil," Ramad had laughed at the morning briefing.

"Well-equipped and trained Israeli soldiers, as an example," al-Qati had retorted, "will be in their protective CW gear within seconds of the first blast. Resistance can be expected to be fierce. Additionally, civilians have been issued CW masks."

The Libyan government did not so equip its civilian populace.

"That is possible," Ramad had conceded.

"It is probable. Your bombs target civilians. Is that what we are rehearsing?"

Ramad had not answered the question.

The lieutenant gave another hand signal, and the soldiers slipped out of their seats, kneeling on one knee, facing the rear. Al-Qati could almost hear the clicks above the roar of the turbine engines as the safeties were released on the AK-74 assault rifles. The muzzles of the rifles were fitted with devices to force a buildup of gas pressure in the rifle barrels, which ejected the dummy rounds of ammunition and loaded the next dummy round. There was to be no live ammunition for these first exercises.

He grabbed a handhold as the Mi-8 flared, than thudded to a landing. The rear doors spread wide, and his soldiers leapt into action, tumbling out the rear, fanning out to either side of the helicopter.

He followed the lieutenant, dropped to the sandy earth, then jogged to the left and dropped on his stomach.

The helicopter lifted off, spraying sand in all directions, blanking out the sun.

The second helicopter, a hundred meters to his right, also took off.

As the rotor noises died away, al-Qati surveyed his position.

Typically in Libya, there was very little natural cover. On each end of his skirmish line, squads were digging shallow foxholes to site the heavy machine guns.

Officers and noncoms shouted orders.

The hot sand burned into him, and the perspiration gushed beneath the protective clothing. He had estimated in a report the year before that a soldier's fighting ability was reduced by almost forty percent when he was encased in chemical warfare clothing and mask.

When the machine guns were emplaced and test-fired, the recon squads moved out of the line, slithering up the dune on elbows and knees.

The air was pasty with tear gas mist.

His radio operator splashed into the sand next to him, shouting through his mask, "Second squad is closing on the radio transmitter, Colonel!"

Al-Qati nodded his approval and checked his watch. One minute and forty-five seconds from touchdown.

And alarmingly, he thought about how ridiculous this all was. Grown men playing in the sand.

He would much rather be in the Seaside Hotel, ensconced in clean sheets, holding Sophia's head to his shoulder, becoming intoxicated by her perfume, talking quietly in the night as the ceiling fan turned lazily.

He couldn't even remember what it was that they talked about, but it was unimportant compared to the peace and euphoria she brought him.

Ahmed al-Qati got his feet under him, and cursing into the privacy of his mask, scrambled up the hill, zigzagging.

The first squad of the Second Platoon leapt to their feet and came charging up the hill behind him.

"Think of her as a beautifully and expensively restored '57 T-Bird, Andy," Jim Demion said. "We don't want to scratch the paint, the first time out of the garage."

"You're taking an awfully damned proprietary interest," Wyatt said.

"Can't be helped. She's reborn under my hands."

In the early light of dawn—they had advanced their starting time by an hour to beat the locals to the airfield—the Phantom appeared sleek and fast and—with her weapons pylons removed—less deadly. She did have her outboard fuel tanks slung in place. In her new cream livery, she was sitting on the tarmac outside Hangar 4, her forward canopy raised as Sam Vrdla sat in the cockpit and made some last-minute adjustments.

Wyatt finished strapping on his G suit, then stood upright. "You ready, Bucky?"

"The heart's ready, Andy. The mind will wake up around nine."

Barr was flying the Citation as a chase plane, and he and Win Potter trundled off toward it.

"Who's going to handle the comm system on this end?" Wyatt asked.

"That's me," Kriswell said, "Old Jockey Joe. You want rock or country?"

"Something symphonic might be a better omen, Tom."

One of the other F-4s had been pushed partway out of the hangar, to clear her antennas of the steel roof. Kriswell would use the airplane's radios to maintain contact with Wyatt and pass on messages, if necessary, to Barr.

They were testing the radios as well as the aircraft.

In addition to the standard NavCom sets, each of the F-4s, and eventually both of the Hercules transports, was to be equipped with a pair of scrambled UHF radio sets. The supersecret black boxes digitally encoded voice transmissions and decoded voice reception as a defense against hostile eavesdropping. A third black box accepted and decoded scrambled datalink signals. In the cockpit, the radios were identified as Tactical One, Tactical Two, and Data One.

Wyatt and Kriswell agreed on frequency settings for both voice channels, then Wyatt walked out to the aircraft.

"Hey, Sam! When do I get my airplane?"

Vrdla peered over the cockpit coaming. "Just want to be sure, Andy."

"I'll let you know what needs to be fixed."

"It better not be anything," Vrdla said, climbing up onto the seat and swinging his legs out onto the ladder.

Wyatt snapped his small clipboard onto his right thigh, then let Dennis Maal help him into his parachute harness.

"This has a label on it, Andy. Says 'Don't open before Christmas.' "

"I'll try not to peek, Denny."

Maal was a medium-sized, nondescript man with blondish-gray hair and a matching mustache. He wasn't much of a worrier, and there weren't many lines in his face. Nearly fifty, he had put twenty-five years into the Air Force, most of them flying KC-135 Stratotankers. That took steady nerves, and as far as Wyatt could tell, he hadn't lost much composure since his retirement. His steady hands would be at the controls of the C-130F tanker, and the assignment hadn't bothered him a bit.

Wyatt climbed the ladder, and Maal followed him and helped strap him into the seat. By the time he got his helmet on and his communications and oxygen lines connected, the sun was half a red ball on the eastern horizon.

With the APU providing amperage, Wyatt powered up the panels and tested his Tac One radio. "Yucca Base, Yucca One."

Since they were exchanging one desert for another, they had elected to use a desert plant for their call sign.

"Five by five, One," Kriswell said. "I couldn't have done it any better if I'd really tried."

"Try the Tac Two channel, and let's see if your luck holds up."

The second scrambled radio also performed well.

"I just told Bucky he could leave," Kriswell reported.

The Citation passed in front of him, with Barr waving, as Wyatt went through the engine start procedures. Both turbojets fired easily, and he left them in the idle range for a few minutes.

Maal gave him a thumbs-up, slid down the ladder, and removed it.

Wyatt released the brakes and let the F-4 creep forward. Adding throttle, he picked up speed, turned onto the taxiway, and headed for the end of the runway.

The Citation lifted off before he reached the end of the taxiway.

He locked the brakes, lowered the canopy, and ran up the engines to max power, watching the instruments closely. The aircraft rocked and strained against the brakes. Tail pipe temperatures and pressures appeared perfect. He backed off the throttles, checked for airplanes in both directions, then rolled out onto the runway.

Without stopping, Wyatt turned onto what should have been a center stripe, and slapped the throttles forward.

Almost instantly, the acceleration pressed him back into the seat. At 160 knots indicated, he eased the throttles past the detents and into afterburner.

The Phantom leapt to the chase, hoisted her slim nose, and climbed for the stars, folding in her gear and flaps.

"Ah, Yucca One, you disappeared on us."

Wyatt read the pertinent information off the HUD. "Base, I'm climbing through angels two-five, making six-zero-zero."

"That's exactly what I thought you were doing," Kriswell said. "Tell me about it."

"The cockpit's a little disorienting," Wyatt admitted.

"Hell, I've got over a thousand hours in Eagles, and the HUD seems to read correctly. . . ."

"What do you mean, 'seems'? " Demion broke in.

"Give me a while, Jim. What's bothersome, it still feels like an F-4, and I automatically look down at the instrument panel, but the instruments aren't in the right places anymore. Christ, they're not even instruments."

The familiar round and octagonal gauges had been replaced by digital readouts and a pair of cathode ray tubes. Wyatt figured each of the pilots would need about ten hours of flight time to become accustomed to the new layout and to learn to rely on the HUD for important data.

He leveled out at thirty thousand feet on a northerly heading.

It felt good.

He eased the stick over and did two rolls.

"Yucca One, Bucky says cut that out."

Leaning to the right, he looked back and down and finally found the Citation flying several thousand feet below.

"She's flying just fine," Wyatt said.

"Follow the script," Kriswell ordered. "Damn it, you wrote the script."

For the next hour, Wyatt followed the script. With Barr monitoring him, he put the F-4 through a series of maneuvers that gradually increased the stress on key components. He finished up with two intentionally staged stalls, and pulled out of each one easily.

"Bucky says you pass, Yucca One."

"That's nice to know. I've got two pages of notes on my knee here."

"How bad?"

"Minor things. Adjustments on the stick. Rudder trim

147

is a little jerky. The starboard throttle has a sticking point at seventy percent."

"Hell," Kriswell said, "any kid can live with those. Don't be so damned picky."

"I apologize profusely."

"That's better. Let's try the navigation."

They tried the TACAN first, using radio stations in Rapid City and Omaha to set up the directions. Then Wyatt cut in the NavSat system which used three of the eighteen satellites in the Global Positioning System (GPS) to triangulate his position above the earth. Combined with the radar altimeter, the electronics could pinpoint him to within a few yards of longitude, latitude, and altitude. With the right CRT in the instrument panel switched to the navigation mode, his symbol was displayed in the center of the screen and superimposed grid lines gave him a graphic interpretation of his geographical position. At the top of the screen, his position was displayed numerically: 43-05-19N 98-45-57W.

The HUD readouts provided him with the crucial digital data. At the top, his heading was provided: 265. In a box at the right side, the altitude of 32,465 was shown. Along the bottom were his fuel state and his speed indication, currently 461 knots.

Through Kriswell, Wyatt learned that Barr, flying right alongside him, confirmed the navigational information.

"Let's go to video, Yucca One."

"Roger the video, Base."

The sophisticated camera mounted in the lower nose cone behind a small Plexiglas window could capture true video, enhanced night vision, and infrared imagery. He brought up the true mode on the left CRT, using the small control box added to the side of the throttle console.

There had not been space enough to give the camera lens rotational or vertical movement, and it was mounted solidly. The screen showed him blue sky, and Wyatt dipped the nose until he picked up a patch of earth surrounding a tiny blue lake. With the thumbwheel, he magnified the image. The lake zoomed up at him.

"Got myself a lake, Base."

"Integrate."

With one flip of a toggle switch, the computer copied the true video image and added a simulation of it to the HUD. On a clear day like he had, the simulated image matched what he was seeing through the HUD, anyway, but at night, or in heavy weather, the computer would provide him with an enhanced picture he would not normally have.

He used two adjustment knobs at the bottom of the HUD and shifted the computer image on the HUD until it matched his real view. If he shifted his head too far to the right or left, the superimposed image slid off the actual one.

"Looks good to me, Base."

"All right, Yucca, that's enough of that for today. Let's do the first pass on the search radar."

Barr peeled off and ran away toward the south to act as the quarry.

Wyatt raised his nose to regain some altitude, then coasted along, giving Barr time to hide. Jotted a note on his fuel consumption. Viewed the faraway surface of the earth, which had a beige tinge to it. Noted the cloud formations, stratocumulus and cirrus, building in the west. Thought about buzzing a couple cars on Highway Two, which cut catty-corner across the state, but decided against inducing any heart attacks.

After ten minutes, he switched his radar to active which, in a combat situation, provided the enemy with radar emissions which could help pinpoint himself as a target. Selecting the 120-mile search scan, he eased into a mile-wide orbit and made two circuits.

One target presented itself immediately, and judging by its course and altitude, he wrote it off as a commercial flight headed for Sioux City. He couldn't find the Citation.

Barr wouldn't make things easy, of course, and Wyatt didn't believe for a minute that he had maintained a southerly course after they had parted company.

The Citation had radar, primarily utilized for weather detection and anticollision, but it would be sufficient for spotting the F-4 if it got close enough.

In ten minutes, at their combined speeds, if he had continued south, Barr could be close to 150 miles away. And out of radar range.

Wyatt didn't think so.

He switched the radar to passive.

Below on his left was the town of O'Neill, with the Elkhorn River passing to the south of it. Wyatt dropped his right wing, brought the nose over, and spiraled downward, picking up speed to 640 knots and straightening out on a heading of two-hundred degrees.

After five minutes, he began a wide turn to the right and drained off speed. The radar altimeter reported the Phantom at twenty-six-hundred feet AGL. The town of Atkinson was several miles ahead on his right oblique.

The Elkhorn River was clearly delineated by the meandering greenage that passed from west to east. Wyatt reduced his throttle settings some more and began a right turn that would align him with the river.

Atkinson flashed past his left wingtip. A few cars had pulled to the side of the highway—Route 20—so their occupants could crane their necks up at him.

He dialled in a thirty-mile scan on the radar, then went active.

The back-and-forth sweep appeared on his right CRT, imposed on the navigation screen. There were no aerial targets there, nor any on the HUD.

He increased the scan to sixty miles.

Blip.

Target at ground level, forty-two miles ahead of him, moving east at 320 knots, following the river.

Wyatt could imagine that Barr had the Citation about twenty feet off the river surface and below the tops of the trees.

He switched in the attack radar mode, used the small joystick to center the target reticule over the symbol on the HUD, and locked it in. The radar would now keep track of that target while, in its search mode, it continued to seek additional targets.

Wyatt advanced the throttles, moving the speed up to four hundred knots while he continued to lose altitude. He stayed two hundred feet above the river since his speed didn't allow him to make the same course changes as the river.

The gap closed to thirty miles.

If he had had missiles aboard, he would soon have been able to lock a heat-seeker or a radar-homer on the target, then go on to find himself another target.

"Lock-on, Yucca Base."

"Roger, One." After a couple seconds, Kriswell came back with, "Bucky says 'bullshit.' "

151

"He's lucky I gave him a chance to say it."

Wyatt checked his fuel state. He had about fifteen minutes left.

He shoved the throttles into afterburner.

The HUD symbol zipped toward him.

A few moments later, the Citation appeared sharply in the video screen, dancing above the thin trickle of the river, dodging the trees leaning toward it from both sides.

Wyatt pulled the stick back and went vertical as soon as he passed over the business jet.

"One, Base. Bucky says you're a show-off."

"He's probably right," Wyatt said.

The pressure of the gravitational force pressing him into the seat was sobering and exhilarating, yet he didn't feel the same sense of clarity and elation he knew he would feel when his target was the real thing.

It wouldn't be as easy then, and the targets were capable of shooting back.

That's what got the adrenaline pumping.

Janice Kramer's United flight landed at Albuquerque at one in the morning, and she took a cab north to her condo.

After unlocking the door, she dropped her two pieces of luggage on the carpet inside, then went around turning on table lamps and checking the soil of her plants for moisture. They were all in good shape, so she suspected that Liz Jordan had stopped by.

Someone cared, anyway.

She didn't think Wyatt had been in.

While she stripped off the jacket of her travelling suit, then her blouse and skirt, she punched the replay for the answering machine. There were eleven messages, six of them from Wyatt. His missives were curt and to the point, as usual. "It's me again. Call, will you?"

She picked up the phone and called the Sandy Inn in Ainsworth. It rang eight times while some poor soul got out of bed to answer the switchboard. Whoever it was tried to be cheerful, though not quite successfully, when she asked for Cowan's room.

The room phone rang twice.

"Hello?"

"Mr. Cowan. This is Miss Manners."

"Jan? Where are you? I've been trying. . . ."

"I'm back on the old stomping grounds," she said.

"Great. Look. . . ."

Are you going to ask me where I've been?

"Look at what?" she asked.

"Where have you been?"

"Out."

"I see," he said. The sleep was going out of his voice, and the steady baritone sounded good to her.

"I called to tell you I'll be here until the present project is completed."

"What? What are you talking about, Jan?"

"Somebody has to man the shop until you're back, and that's me. So I came back."

"Thank you."

Just say you need me.

After a long silence, she said, "I talked to some law firms in L.A. I think I'll be getting some offers."

"I'm sorry to hear that," he said.

Just ask me to stay.

"If you need anything—letters of recommendation, a phone call or two. . . ."

She slammed the phone down.

Nine

"You woke me up, Bucky."

"Some mornings aren't so grand," Barr said. He hadn't felt good himself since the middle of breakfast, when Wyatt told him about Kramer. In fact, he had left his stack of pancakes in favor of the phone in the hallway next to the unlit and vacant bar area.

"What is it? What's wrong?" Kramer asked him, and Barr could hear the concern in her tone. "Did someone get hurt? Who?"

"Me," he said. "I'm hurt that you dropped this bullshit about leaving on us."

"It's not bullshit at all, Bucky. It's time for me to move on."

"That's always an excuse for some other reason."

He waited for her to say something about needing new challenges.

She said, "I need some new directions, Bucky. New challenges."

"As an associate in some stuffy law firm? Where's the thrill in that, Jan?"

"They're talking partnership."

"You're already a partner. Hey, you have enough cri-ses in a week to keep you going for a year. . . ."

"The money's good," she said.

"You want more money? We'll give it to you."

"That takes a vote of the board."

"You're on the board," he countered. "Hell, you can have my salary."

"I don't want your salary. I want to move on."

"Goddamn it! Do me one favor."

"What's that?"

"Don't make a commitment to anyone until I get back and talk to you."

"We've just talked," she said.

"Face-to-face."

She sighed. "All right, Bucky."

The Noble Enterprises bunch were up from their ta-bles and filing out the door to the Jeeps when Barr hung up.

Wyatt was standing a few feet away, looking at him.

"What'd she say?"

"You need a kick in the ass."

"She said that?"

"She might as well have."

Barr was going to add more to that statement, then decided to hold off. He brushed past Wyatt, crossed the cafe, and pulled open the glass door.

It was hot out, but that wasn't unusual.

Neil Formsby arrived in Quallene, Algeria, at three in the afternoon of the twenty-fifth of July. It was 119 degrees in the shade of the date palms, but there weren't enough palm trees to go around.

By his estimation, they were almost nine hundred

miles south of Algiers and eleven hundred miles from the western coast of the continent. From his point of view, that was just about right.

The overland route from Rabat, with detours around population centers, had added eighteen hundred miles to the tens of thousands already on the odometers of his rented and badly abused vehicles. There had been a dozen breakdowns en route, but he had planned for the possibility with a cache of extra parts, and each repair to carburetors, fuel pumps, alternators, and broken springs had been accomplished at the side of the road.

His convoy included seven tanker trucks, one flatbed semi-truck with an aged D-9 Caterpillar tractor on it, and the Land Rover that he was driving. There were seventeen men of just about as many nationalities and driver's licenses assisting him, and he suspected that all of them were wanted in one country or another for at least a single capital crime. He had let his beard grow, and he had allowed the grime to build up in his clothing, just to fit in with the crowd.

The arrival of his drivers increased the population of Quallene significantly. It was barely a wide spot in what the Algiers government probably defined as a road. A dozen decrepit buildings housed an unknown number of people who, being intelligent and non-British, were staying inside and hidden away from the midday sun.

He stuck his arm out the window and rotated it in big circles, signaling the truck drivers behind him to keep their units rolling.

He drove on through the village and picked up speed to nearly forty kilometers per hour. The speed was positively exhilarating after the twenty-five kilometer per hour average they had managed.

Twenty kilometers beyond the town, he veered off the road, which was not actually a courageous act. The road was quite similar to the non-road. It was composed of hard-packed earth, and the dried-out weeds and shrubbery—akin to miles and miles of skeletons—suggested that vehicles did not normally travel there. The region was hilly, if three- or four-meter-high mounds could be called hills.

Keeping an eye on his rearview mirror, so as not to lose any of his charges, Formsby wheeled the Land Rover several kilometers to the north, weaving around the mounds. When he found a place that was relatively flat and isolated from every other living thing on earth, he stopped and parked. Shutting off the engine, he got out and stretched.

The sun beat mercilessly on his head, and he reached back in the truck for his wide-brimmed safari hat. His physical movement felt restricted by the buildup of dirt that had stiffened his jacket and pants. His boots barely cracked the surface crust of the earth.

"This is it?" his companion asked, as he too exited the truck.

"I believe it may well be the place, Jacque."

Jacque—his only name—claimed to have served in the French Foreign Legion, and it may have been true. His appearance was disreputable enough that Formsby had kept his 9 millimeter Browning automatic holstered by his side for the entire trip. His sleep had come in gasps.

Jacque went off to guide the semi-trucks into a militarily rigid parking line, and Formsby took a long walk northward, stopping to urinate on a bush that begged for any kind of moisture.

After gauging the area in all directions with his sharp eyes, Formsby decided it would do, then walked back to the trucks.

"All right, Jacque, we can unload."

It took almost an hour for the men to unload and set up the canvas wall-tent, the single cot, the cooking table and propane grill, the propane-powered refrigerator, and the portable shower. He got his boxes of provisions and his M-16 rifle out of the Land Rover and put them inside the tent.

Formsby thought the shower a nice touch, and he was not worried about water. He had brought along ten thousand gallons of water, figuring the Central Intelligence Agency would not balk at the cost so long as they did not know about it.

When the campsite was finished, the single canvas tent appearing rather forlorn alongside the big trucks, Jacque approached him.

"I think that does it, Mr. Jones."

Formsby was going by the name of Nevada Jones, a superlative touch of *The Carpetbaggers* and *Indiana Jones,* he thought.

"I believe it does, Jacque."

He pulled the envelope from inside his shirt, and handed it to the former Legionnaire.

Jacque counted it. "Ten thousand American. That is correct, Mr. Jones."

He had arranged to pay Jacque in ten thousand dollar increments, at intervals of every five hundred miles. Jacque knew he had a money belt wrapped around his waist, but Jacque also knew he had the Browning automatic, and Formsby had refused to allow any of Jacque's colleagues to carry weapons on this journey.

"Very well," Formsby said. "Now, you may take the tractors and the Land Rover and go back to Quallene. On the seventh of August, when you return here, you will receive the final fifty thousand."

"Plus the water?"

"And whatever is left of the water."

While the men were unhitching the tractors from the trailers, Formsby went inside the tent, dug around in one of his cardboard boxes, and came up with four square plastic boxes. He also found ten fragmentation grenades.

When he emerged from the tent, Jacque studied him for a few minutes before asking, "What are those?"

"These are infrared beam and motion detectors. I shall put them on my perimeter, and anyone who gets close receives the gift of explosively propelled shrapnel."

"I see," said Jacque.

And Formsby was certain that he did. Their agreement was that Formsby would be left without a vehicle, to insure that he would be present on the seventh of August with the balance of the payment. Formsby was adding to that agreement by insuring that neither Jacque nor any of his seventeen friends came calling in the night prior to the seventh.

He was relieved when the truck tractors and the Land Rover finally departed. He had not slept well during the long days of the journey.

As soon as the last truck disappeared, Formsby went to the refrigerator standing next to the tent, unlocked it with a key, and unwrapped the air-bubble packaging from a bottle of Molson ale.

He drank it in three long swallows, then opened another bottle.

Just in case Jacque had doubled back to check on him, Formsby spent some time playing out his role of security manager by siting the motion detectors and grenades at four corners around his campsite. The detectors did not really set off the grenades, but their transmitters would alert him if intruders entered the area.

And he knew how to set off grenades on his own.

The shower was erected next to the water tanker, and Formsby connected a hose from the tanker's pump to the holding tank above the shower. He filled the tank with the gasoline-powered pump, then stripped off his clothes and took a shower that lasted twenty minutes and cost seventy gallons of a commodity very precious in the desert. Then he shaved and took another short shower.

Padding naked across the hot sand to the tent, he entered and dressed in fresh Levi's and a white sport shirt. He felt immensely better, recharged, and ready for action.

The action was confined to stripping the M-16, cleaning it, and priming it with one of twenty magazines he had with him. Then he cooked himself a dinner of brussels sprouts, mashed potatoes and brown gravy, and rare roast beef. He topped it off with a bottle of 1978 cru bourgeois red Bordeaux. The CIA had paid for it, and he enjoyed it.

On the twenty-sixth of July, Formsby emerged from the mosquito netting protecting his cot, made coffee and a poached egg for breakfast, then unchained the Caterpillar tractor and got it running after several false starts. He climbed down to lower the ramps from the flatbed trailer, then backed the bulldozer off and tested his rusty knowledge of the controls for both the tractor and the bulldozer blade.

While the Cat idled, he broke ice cubes from four of the trays in his refrigerator and made up a jug of iced tea. He refilled the trays with water, put them back in the freezer, then got his safari hat.

Formsby spent eleven hours driving the Cat east and west, then had liver and sauteed onions for dinner.

On the twenty-seventh, he devoted another seven hours to leveling a two-kilometer-long, thirty-meter-wide strip through the mounds of earth. To Formsby, the rough airstrip looked like a scar on a land that knew far too many scars. In a month, no one would ever know it had been there. When he was done, he parked the Cat back on its trailer and chained it down again. Formsby might not have been a superb craftsman, but he liked to put his tools back in their proper places.

He had particularly tender veal chops for dinner, accompanied with an excellent St. Emilion. After dinner, he set up his radio and connected it to an antenna he erected outside the tent. At midnight, he turned on the radio, tapped in a frequency on the digital keys, pressed the transmit button, and said, "Paper Doll, Degas. In position."

He did not expect, nor wait for, a reply. Punching a new frequency into the radio, he shut it off and considered that the next nine days were going to be full of one-sided conversations.

Though he was up early on the twenty-eighth of July, it was to be a day composed mostly of leisure. He ate a breakfast of eggs, bacon, waffles, and muffins, then showered for the first time that day. He was managing four showers a day.

He stayed in the tent for the morning, lounging on his cot, and reading Proust. He perspired a great deal.

At ten minutes past noon, the radio barked.

"Goya."

He rolled off the bunk and picked up the microphone. "Degas."

"'K, fella, gimme somethin' to home on."

Formsby held the transmit button down, so the pilot could use his direction finder.

When he lifted his thumb, the pilot said, "'K, guy, be there in about ten."

Formsby prepared by buckling his holster in place, then slinging the M-16 over his shoulder.

One never knew quite who was coming to lunch.

The airplane—a De Haviland DHC-5 Buffalo without any national or corporate markings—appeared low out of the east and made one pass over the primitive runway. The pilot was apparently happy enough with what he saw for he made one circle, then brought the cargo plane in.

It landed with two bounces and a short rundown, then turned toward the parked trailers.

Formsby waved merrily and pointed to a place next to the flatbed trailer. The pilot goosed the throttles, shot toward the spot, then whipped around in a tight 180-degree turn. The engines died with several burping backfires.

Walking across the hot soil toward the plane, Formsby felt his muscles tensing up.

The pilot and another man emerged from a side door. Formsby figured the rawboned, cowboy-hatted pilot for an American.

His muscles relaxed a trifle.

"You're Jones?" the pilot asked.

162

"Nevada Jones."

"Yeah, I read the book and saw the movie. What's with the rifle?"

"I've been told that there are many wild things in the desert," Formsby said.

"I guess there are. You want us to dump all of it right here?"

"I surely do."

Thirty minutes later, fourteen pallets had been floated down the rollers of the ramp and left in the dirt next to the flatbed. Each pallet was covered with a tarpaulin.

Formsby untied the tarps and inspected the contents of every pallet.

"That what you ordered, Jones?"

"Exactly, my good man, exactly."

"We try to please," the cowboy said.

"Could I offer you gentlemen luncheon?

The pilot looked up at the sky, around at the horizon, and then at his wristwatch. "Yeah, I don't see why not."

Formsby made a half-dozen thick ham sandwiches and got out a six-pack of ale.

They had changed the tires on all of the airplanes, substituting the widest, softest tires they could mount and still get into the retract wells. Nitrogen gas was used to inflate them.

All of the pylons for the F-4s, and a pair for the Hercules, had been refurbished, painted gray, and stored aboard the transport.

Wyatt held up his clipboard, with the checklist clamped onto it, toward Demion. "That's the last tick-off on my sheet, Jim."

Demion's eyes scanned his own list. "Mine, too.

There were a few times, Andy, when I didn't think we were going to get here."

"We're a day ahead of schedule."

"Except for the fuel and the training schedule," Demion said.

They had had to refill their rental tanker truck six times, to meet the requirements of the test and training flights and to fill the fuel cells of the C-130 tanker. Winfield Potter was in Lincoln once again for another load. The Noble Enterprises charge card for fuel was getting a workout, and Wyatt hoped that someone on the other end was paying the bills.

The two of them walked slowly through Hangar 5, watching the activity as tools and equipment were loaded aboard the Hercules transport. In the morning, the transport was making a quick turnaround trip to Albuquerque to return the equipment they weren't taking with them: engine cradles, compressors, extra tool sets.

Huge, hand-lettered signs were spread all over the place. "NO SMOKING" was the rule since the tanker had been fueled.

Wyatt spotted Arnie Gering and Lefty Harris and waved them to the sidewall.

"What's up, Andy?" Harris asked.

Wyatt had their envelopes prepared. He handed one to each of them. "You guys get to ride back to Albuquerque with the Herc in the morning. I want to tell you how much I appreciate your putting in the overtime."

Gering opened his envelope and counted the twenty one-hundred-dollar bills.

"Be careful how you spend it, Arnie. You don't want to attract any unnecessary attention."

Gering stuffed the envelope in his back pocket. "Yeah, Andy, thanks. You sure you don't need some more help wherever you're going?"

"We've got it covered," Wyatt said.

Gering looked to Demion, who nodded his agreement.

"Well, I can always use the extra bucks."

"There might be some other special projects in the future," Wyatt said.

"When?"

"We never know when they're going to come up," Demion told him. "We'll let you know."

Gering and Harris wandered back to the transport to help load boxes.

Both of the C-130 aircraft appeared nearly identical, except for the fuselage numbers. The tanker, numbered 61043, had a few feet of the retracted fuel line protruding from the trailing edge of her port wing. The transport, 54811, had several new antennas and a plastic bulge mounted on the top of the fuselage, connected to the interior console that had been installed three days before. The tactical coordinator's console had been stripped from a Grumman E-2 Hawkeye and refurbished by Kriswell and Vrdla. The sonar, armament, and sonobuoy deployment functions had been discarded since they didn't plan on hunting for subs where they were going. In place of the antisubmarine gear were enhanced radar, voice, and data communications, and electronic countermeasures controlling gear. While they didn't have the massive radome of the E-2, with the equipment Kriswell had rigged, they were going to have a limited early warning capability in the Hercules.

Wyatt and Demion climbed through the port side door and found Kriswell tinkering at the console, which had been bolted to the bulkhead in place of the two crew bunks.

"You seen Bucky, Tom?" Wyatt asked.

"He and Lucas went to town for party-makings. He's calling it a wrap-up party."

"We still have a few days of training to go."

"Yeah," Kriswell said, "but that's the fun part. The hard stuff's over."

Wyatt hoped it went that way.

Colonel Ibrahim Ramad flew his personal MiG-27 into Tripoli to meet with his superior. He landed at night, when it was relatively cool, and was picked up by a truck and taken to Farouk Salmi's office at base headquarters.

Salmi's aide, a captain by the name of Mufti, was the only other in attendance at the meeting.

"Ibrahim, it is good to see you," Salmi said.

"And you, my Colonel."

Salmi waved him to a seat in front of his desk. "How are your exercises proceeding?"

"Exceptionally well," Ramad boasted as he sat down.

"And al-Qati's soldiers?"

"I must admit, Colonel, that Colonel al-Qati's troops are well-conditioned and well-disciplined. They have adapted quickly."

"That is good to hear," Salmi said. "I had feared that al-Qati's reputation was as much smoke as substance."

"No, he lives up to it."

The air force commander lit a cigarette and relished his inhalation.

Ramad waited patiently.

Salmi asked, "Do you suppose that the good Colonel is also prepared to engage in Test Strike?"

Test Strike was the live exercise that Ramad had designed three months and eleven days before.

"Probably not, once he hears about it."

"He must be told by tomorrow morning," Salmi said.

Ramad let his lips broaden into a smile.

"Test Strike has been approved?"

"It has."

"That is wonderful," Ramad said. "However, as I said, al-Qati will drag his feet. We have discussed before what we think his true mission to be, spying on our operations at Marada Base for Ghazi. He will want to talk to Ghazi before he makes a commitment. And Ghazi will balk."

Salmi, whose pockmarked, narrow face rarely smiled, offered a yellow-toothed grin. "The concerns of Colonel Ghazi have been taken care of, Ibrahim."

"How can that be?"

"The Leader, advisor Amjab, and I met with Ghazi this morning, and he has been given his orders. He agreed to cooperate completely."

Rather than lose his command of ground forces, Ramad thought.

"And therefore," Salmi continued, "al-Qati's objections are curtailed even before he makes them."

Ramad hoped that he would be in a position to see al-Qati's face when the man learned that Colonel Ghazi could no longer protect him.

"Now," Salmi said, "it is your plan, and you must make the final decision. Your name alone will appear on the recommendation."

The documentation would be self-protective of higher authority. Ramad understood that.

"My decision was made, Colonel Salmi, when I prepared the proposal."

Salmi nodded, "Captain Mufti, if you would?"

Mufti pushed a cart containing a television and a videocassette recorder into position next to Salmi's desk. He turned both on.

The screen blossomed into a view of a cell. Concrete walls and a steel door could be seen. The camera angle was from high in one corner. A man in stained clothing sat on a small stool in the center of the cement floor.

The camera looked down on him, but he was apparently unaware of it, or he no longer cared. He sat with his head hung down, his lanky black hair falling forward, his elbows resting on his knees. He was dejected.

"The subject?" Ramad asked.

"All of the subjects are condemned persons. It does not matter how they die."

"And this test?"

"This one utilizes the psychological agent. PD-86, I believe," Salmi said.

Of the five types of chemical agents—incapacitating, defoliant, psychological, nerve, and toxin—they had not concerned themselves with the short-acting incapacitating agents such as tear gas, nor with defoliants.

PD-86, Ramad knew, was based on lysergic acid, the LSD of the American hippies.

On the screen, the cell began to mist. It was unobtrusive at first, just a slight blurriness to the environment. The prisoner seemed unaware of it.

Nothing else happened.

The man sat there for about five minutes.

Then began to laugh.

A little laugh at first, a smirk and giggle. Without effort, he was coming out of his depression.

168

Then an uproarious laugh.

He threw his shoulders back and his head snapped upright. His eyes appeared vivid.

He shook his head violently.

Laughing.

His arms flailed about.

He scratched his chest, his armpits, his crotch.

Laughing.

Insanely laughing.

The screen went blank.

"That went on for nearly forty minutes," Salmi explained. "PD-86 completely disoriented him. On a larger scale, I think we could expect that a hostile force would act similarly, unable to mount a defense."

"What are the aftereffects?" Ramad asked.

"We do not know. We took him out of his cell and shot him."

That was to be expected.

Salmi nodded at Mufti.

The captain started the video machine again. It was the same cell, Ramad supposed, but the prisoner was a different man, taller, thicker. And he was just as dejected as the first man. The stool was closer to the wall. He sat on the stool with his head leaning against the wall. Tears streamed down his face.

"Toxin this time," Salmi said.

"The botulism?"

"No, the Leader ruled that out, even though chemically based toxins do not create epidemics, as do the organically based compounds. The designation for this one is TR-11."

Ramad knew the nomenclature. This toxin acted similarly to a psychological agent, but created abject terror in those subjected to it.

The base of the cell suddenly spurted white fog from half-a-dozen jets.

The man noticed immediately, and his face turned up toward the camera. Ramad could see the pleading in his eyes.

The fog roiled around his legs, rising.

There was no sound, but Ramad saw the man's mouth working. Please. Oh, Allah, please.

He climbed up on the stool, attempting to stay above the fog.

The fog began to disperse, a white haze filling the room so that the prisoner's movements were difficult to follow.

From the video, Ramad could tell the man was no longer begging God for mercy.

He was screaming.

His eyes rolled in their sockets.

His body recoiled from nothing seen.

He fell off the stool, knocking it across the cell. He immediately rose to his knees, slithered into the corner, backed into it.

His balled-up fists struck out at something, anything, the wall. In minutes his knuckles were bloodied from striking the rough concrete walls.

The screen went blank.

"We waited forty minutes before shooting him," Salmi said. "He never came out of his acute terror."

Ramad nodded his head affirmatively.

"A consequence we had not considered," Salmi said, "was that, in his terror, he was difficult to control."

"I can understand that," Ramad said.

"It will be interesting to see how al-Qati's troops deal with three or four thousand people acting the same way."

Mufti started the video again.

This would be the nerve agent. The final formula had been labeled GB31, and it was a derivative of Sarin, an older agent that was almost removed from the stockpiles of other nations. The newer version was non-persistent, precluding the necessity for decontaminating an area where it had been used.

Again, the cell appeared on the screen, though it now contained a woman. She was a pretty woman, and she was naked, perhaps for the enjoyment of her jailers.

She was afraid, ignoring the stool to curl against the far wall, holding her arms and hands in front of her.

She was weeping, perhaps sadly, but quite definitely quietly.

There was no visible release of the gas.

The woman became aware that something was wrong with her, and she forgot her modesty.

She leapt to her feet, her small breasts bobbing, her head rotating from side to side as she sought to find whatever it was that alarmed her.

Ramad saw her cheeks twitching. A tic in one eye. Her arm jerked.

"This attacks the nerve centers very quickly, Ibrahim. Muscle control is lost rapidly."

Her legs went out from under her, and she crashed to the floor.

All of her limbs became spastic.

Jerking, twisting, out of control.

Her eyes were so large, the whites dominated. They seemed to spin. Her chest heaved as she fought to breathe.

On her back now, her head slamming back and forth on the cement floor.

"The brain is the last to go," Colonel Salmi said. "It is aware throughout that something unfathomable is happening to the rest of the body. We judge the terror quotient to be extremely high, though there is little problem of control. The terror aspect is high for spectators, also."

Ramad did feel a little twitch or two deep in his guts, observing this ritual.

Abruptly, she died.

"Less than four minutes," the air commander said. "It is very efficient."

Salmi was watching him closely, Ramad knew. This was as much a test of himself as it was an observation of results.

"Very efficient," Ramad agreed. His stomach still felt a little queasy, but that was because he was so close to the action.

He knew the woman. She was a second cousin he had not seen in several years. He wondered what her crime had been.

Perhaps simply that she knew him.

"Do you still wish to proceed?" Salmi asked.

"Absolutely."

"With which agent?"

"All three, I think, Colonel. It would be well to let our adversaries know the range of our choices."

Salmi smiled for the second time in years.

Ten

After the fifth and final simulated exercise, Ahmed al-Qati and his company commander, Captain Ibn Rahman, flew back to El Bardi to meet with the company commanders of his other three companies. They spent an afternoon planning continuing drills and approving requisitions for supplies. There were four disciplinary problems for the battalion commander to address, all of them involving men late for something—to work, to formation, back from leave.

Neither al-Qati nor Rahman described what they were doing at Marada Air Base, though he was certain that the three commanders he had left behind at El Bardi were nearly overcome with curiosity. They did not know how fortunate they were, not knowing. Al-Qati himself, as soon as Ramad had revealed the plan, had gone into a shock that was difficult to conceal. For hours, his body had seemed removed from his mind. The mind was divided, normal functions occurring by rote on one side, and the other side desensitized, three or four steps removed from reality.

He forced himself to attend to routine.

Then al-Qati took a long bath, shaved, and patted the

last of his last bottle of Aqua Velva over his face and neck. He dressed in a fresh uniform, commandeered a Volvo from the motor pool, and drove to Tobruk.

He parked in front of the Seaside Hotel and went into the lobby to call Sophia's room.

"Ahmed! You are here!"

"Only by a stroke of fortune, and only for tonight. I am inviting you to dinner. If you do not have other plans," he added lamely.

"But I am not hungry," she said, "except for your company. If you would like to come to my room now, we will find dinner later?"

He resisted the urge to skip his way across the lobby and up the stairs to her second-floor suite like some carefree youngster.

She was waiting behind the partially opened door, peering through the crack at him as he advanced down the hall. When he reached her room, she pulled the door wide. Her smile was like the radiant beam of searchlights.

Her hair was piled high and wrapped with a towel, as if she had just emerged from her bath. She was wearing . . . what was it? . . . a peignoir. Her full breasts thrust at the loose, almost sheer fabric, and he found the effect nearly as exciting as her total nudity.

"You are so beautiful," he said.

"Come to me, Ahmed."

She wrapped her arms around his waist, and drew him tightly to her. Leaning back to look up at his face, she raised up on her toes to kiss him.

"I missed you."

"And I you," he confessed.

"Are you really hungry?"

"My appetite seems to have vanished."

She reached behind him, to push the door shut, then led him toward her bed.

They made love, intense and perhaps a bit ineptly, for nearly an hour, then went downstairs for a dinner that became rushed toward the end of the entree. He was aware of the flush that climbed up her throat and spread over her cheeks. He was rattled enough that he could not even remember what entree he had ordered and consumed.

Al-Qati paid the bill, overtipping the effusive waiter, and they hurried back to her room and spent a leisurely two hours satisfying themselves yet again.

In the early hours of the morning, with the French doors to the balcony flung wide and the lazy circles of the overhead fan creating a wispy breeze that cooled his flesh, Ahmed al-Qati decided he was very much in love.

He told her so.

"I am glad to hear you say it, my darling, for I wanted you to be the first to speak. I, too, love you."

Al-Qati sighed deeply, as lazy and content as he had been in years.

"I worry about our future," Sophia told him.

"What? What is there to worry about?"

"My husband, my almost ex-husband, can be expected to be vindictive."

He smiled in the dark. "We will not concern ourselves with him. I will see to your protection."

"And I worry about you, Ahmed. From the little you have told me, I know you must do dangerous things."

"They are not so dangerous."

"You lie to make me feel better," she said.

"They are not so dangerous, most of the time. Usually, they are quite boring. After this operation, I will be back in El Bardi performing boring tasks, and then we will be together almost all of the time."

"What is it about this operation that makes it so perilous, Ahmed? Could you resign your position before it occurs?"

"Resign? No, I do not think so."

"I have some money," she said. "Money I have not told you about. You could quit."

There was so much concern in her trembling fingertips as they stroked the side of his neck, and his distaste for Ramad was so near the surface, that he told her.

"Before you say anything," Martin Church told George Embry, "sit down."

Embry sat in the chair facing Church's desk. "I received a message from Cummings."

"Well, forget it. The DCI couldn't convince the security council, and Icarus is history. Pull her out of Tobruk. I've got to call Wyatt and tell him to stand down."

Embry ignored him, saying, "It was a long message."

"Long," Church said absently. He was so incensed with the DCI and his petty and self-serving games that he couldn't focus properly.

"Yeah, a long, long message. You want to know what she said?"

"You're going to tell me, no matter what."

"Yup. She's in love with the subject."

"She what!" Martin Church yelped.

George Embry held up his left hand, palm out. "Careful, Marty. Remember your blood pressure."

"She can't be in love with him! Goddamn it! That's just not done."

"Hey," Embry said, "you've got to give her credit for telling us."

"How can one of our agents fall in love with a goddamned Libyan terrorist? Tell me that!"

The corners of Embry's mouth dipped. "He doesn't really fit the definition, Marty. Our army Rangers at Benning trained him, after all."

"And Cummings has fallen for the guy. Jesus! The whole damned world's going to hell."

"I don't think it affects her job," Embry said.

"Christ! If you believe that, you're nuts, too!"

Church climbed out of his chair and turned toward the window. The forest along the Potomac appeared excessively green, as if someone had been playing with the tint adjustment on his private view.

Then he remembered that Embry always saved the best, or the most shocking, for last.

He whirled around to stare at the man who handled the African desk.

Embry wasn't smiling.

"She's still doing her job, you say. What are you holding back, George?"

"Ramad has planned himself a little demonstration, Marty. He calls it Test Strike."

"Test Strike? What does it do?"

"It shows the Israelis, and us, I suppose, that the great Leader has balls. He's going to reveal his arsenal of chemical weapons."

"I don't suppose this will come in a press release, will it, George?"

"No. It's a practical demonstration of three different chemical agents. If she's got it right, they'll be psychological, toxic, and nerve agents. There won't be any announcements, but we're supposed to read between the lines, I think."

"How practical is the demonstration?"

"From their point of view, Marty? Very. They're going to attack three Ethiopian refugee camps simultaneously."

"Shit!"

"It's the truth, as far as we can tell."

Church collapsed back into his desk chair. "Refugee camps."

"I suppose the Leader feels that no one will complain unduly about the loss of a few thousand mouths to feed. I suppose also that he'll film the attacks for the benefit of the Israelis. Deliver the tapes by accident, as it were."

"My God!"

"He's going to show them how he can operate over long distances, with all of the logistics that involves, as well as deploy devastating ordnance."

Church was less stunned by the revelation than he was professing. He had seen too many examples of man's inhumanity, and he knew that Arabic extremist groups—which was not to condemn all Arabs—were the driving forces behind many of the examples in his archives.

"Damn it, George! Why do you always wait so long to spring these disasters on me?"

"That's not the worst part, Marty."

"Shit, again!"

"It happens on August second."

Wyatt thought that his people were going to be ready by their date of departure, August 4.

They had been getting almost five hours a day out of each Phantom during the training and shakeout phase. The first flights had resulted in a rash of small but important glitches in the weapons and electronic systems. Kriswell and Demion were at fever pitch, diagnosing problems, supervising corrections, and reprogramming software.

He stood in the wide-open door of Hangar 4 and watched as Barr brought three-six in for a perfect landing. The sleek jet whistled by, heading for the end of the runway.

"He's still not getting the correct hydraulic brake pressure," Demion said. "He's having to fight it a little on the roll-out."

"Is that analysis by your observation or by report, Jim?"

"Observation, but you can be damned sure he'll complain about it."

Barr's F-4 wheeled around and off the runway as Hackley passed him, lined up, and took off. The scream of turbojets had become almost a continual background noise. Down at the civilian end of the tarmac, no one had complained. Quite often, there were a few carloads of kids, and sometimes of adults, parked near the office so that Noble Enterprises had a spectator section.

Barr parked the F-4E in front of the hangar, popped the canopy, and clambered out when Hank Cavanaugh brought the ladder out to the plane. He shed his helmet and carried it in the crook of his elbow as he approached them.

"Hey, Jim, the brakes are squishy on the left side."

"What'd I tell you, Andy?" Demion went back into the hangar to find someone to work on the brake hydraulic system.

Barr stopped in front of Wyatt.

"I'm going to head for town and get a couple hours of nap time and make a phone call."

"Okay."

"You want to know who I'm going to call?"

"No."

"I'm going to call Jan-baby."

"Okay."

"I'm going to ask her to marry me," Barr said.

That got Wyatt's attention. "I don't think I caught that, Bucky."

"Sure you did. We've got to keep her somehow, and I guess it's up to me to do it."

"Bucky. . . ."

Barr turned and walked off to where two of the three Jeeps were parked. He tossed his helmet into the front seat, followed it, started the engine, and drove off.

Just as a pickup from the airport office came rattling up to Wyatt.

The airport manager poked his head out the window. "Hi, Mr. Cowan."

"Afternoon." Wyatt couldn't remember his name.

"You've got a long-distance call on my line. It must be important 'cause they said they'd hold while I came down here after you."

"Thanks. I'll follow you back down."

The manager took a good, close-up look at three-six and whistled his appreciation before engaging the clutch and making a U-turn.

Wyatt crawled into the last of their Jeep Wagoneers and followed him back to the office, skirting wide around a Piper Cherokee parked at the fuel pumps. Inside the office, in rather blessed air-conditioning, he picked up the telephone resting on the counter.

"Cowan."

"This is the East Coast calling. You know me?"

The voice belonged to Embry.

"I know you."

"We've got a little problem, if I lie a bit. It's a big one, actually."

"This is nothing new," Wyatt said.

"You know what today is?"

"The thirtieth of July."

"There's going to be a disaster of mega proportions on the second of August."

"The hell there is."

"You've got to get there first. That means you take off within the next couple hours."

"That can't be done."

Wyatt's mind raced over the schedule. The pilots still needed another ten hours, minimum, of seat time. They hadn't even attempted practicing bomb runs, even though Tom Kriswell was confident that they could get by without them.

His caller's next statement jerked his attention from the schedule.

"If we don't get you in place, about five thousand people, maybe more, are going to die," Embry said.

Wyatt digested that. "You're not just talking to hear yourself talk?"

"Not this time, buddy."

"Do I get some details?"

"I'll personally meet you at your stop in Maine, which I'm setting up now. You'll get everything you need when you get there."

"While we're speaking of needs, have you heard from my logistics agent?"

"That is affirmative. The coded signal was picked

up by satellite some fifteen hours ago. He's in place and ready to go."

Wyatt's mind reeled as he considered the implications. The whole thing might actually come together. "I'll have to leave here without picking up after myself."

"You go right ahead and do that. I'll send in a team by morning to clear out the motel and get rid of the vehicles and any other junk."

"You'll need to send someone who can fly my Citation back to Albuquerque."

"Will do. One other thing. I've had the National Security Agency set up a satellite relay and monitoring system for us." Embry gave him a UHF frequency.

"You don't mean that we're going to have an ongoing conversation during this operation?"

"We might. There's some other things going on that you don't know about."

Wyatt started to ask him just what those other things were, but Embry hung up.

Wyatt depressed the reset button and called the motel. He gave the girl on the desk the airport number and asked her to have Barr call him when he got in.

Sixteen minutes later, the phone rang and Wyatt waved off the airport guy, then picked up. He turned his back to the manager.

"What's up, Andy? You don't want me to call Jan?"

"Cliff's in his room somewhere, Bucky, catching some Zs. Get him up, hit every motel room, and toss everyone's clothes and baggage in the Jeeps, then get back here. Wait. Stop and settle up with Jorgenson on your way. Tip him big, huh?"

"Damn. What's going on?"

"We've got an early go signal. And we're going."

Wyatt hung up and went back out to his Wagoneer. He had the engine running when he changed his mind and shut it off. Back in the airport office, he asked to use the phone again, then put the long-distance call on his special card.

"Aeroconsultants. This is Liz."

"Hi, Liz. Is Jan around?"

"Hold on, Andy."

After two minutes, she came on the line.

"Hello, Andy."

"How's it going?"

"Fine. It's better with Gering and Harris back. We may catch up someday. I've landed a restoration job and another security contract."

"Wonderful," he said.

He was prodding himself, but just couldn't reach over the edge. Come on, Wyatt!

"Is that all you wanted?" Kramer asked.

"Uh, one thing. Our schedule's been moved up. We're taking off this afternoon."

A few moments of silence passed before she said, "I don't like that. Last-minute changes mean mistakes."

"We'll be okay."

"You haven't completed your full training schedule, have you?"

"We've got enough of it," he said.

"Uh huh, that's crap. No good. This has been bad from the start."

"It's all right, Jan. What do you mean, 'bad from the start?' "

"It's a feeling."

How did he deal with that?

"A few more days, and it'll be over. Hang in there," he said.

"I've got an offer. Full partner, upscale firm. Tell Bucky that I'm taking it."

"I don't want you to take it," he said.

Long pause on her end.

"You don't? Are you into suppressing the advancement of women, now?" she asked with a laugh, but the laugh sounded hollow.

"You know better than that." He felt a little defensive, but didn't think he needed to feel that way.

"Give me a better reason," she said.

"I need you right where you are."

"You do? You need me? And where is that?"

"With me. beside me."

"Oh, damn you, Andy!"

"I mean it."

"But you can't say it?"

"You know me, hon. I'm not good with the words, but there's no one else." His own laugh sounded hollow. "Bucky said he was going to propose to you this morning, but I want to get my bid in first."

"Jesus Christ! This is fodder for the afternoon soaps."

"I don't watch them."

"Good damned thing."

"I love you, Jan."

"Finally, you ass! Oh, my God, I love you, too. More than you'll ever know."

"You'll be there when I get back?"

"Yes."

"Are you sure?"

"I don't know how I'm going to break this to my father. We are getting married, aren't we? I'm not sure I heard you mention the word."

"We're getting married."

Her tone changed abruptly. "Don't go."

"Got to, hon."

She sighed. "I know. Be very careful, Andy."

For some reason, he felt a great deal better on the drive back to the hangar.

The C-130 transport was parked out on the apron, being used as a radio base station for the training flights. Wyatt pulled up next to it, got out, and went to lean inside the hatchway.

Winfield Potter was on the radio.

"Hey, Win!"

He shoved his headset back from his right ear and turned to Wyatt. "Yo, boss?"

"Call all the planes in and start fueling them up."

"No shit?"

"We're on the way."

Potter started calling aircraft.

Wyatt walked over to the hangar and found Demion and Kriswell debating some point.

"Okay, guys, we're moving out."

They both turned to him.

"We've got some kind of deadline to meet. I'll give you the details later."

"Well, hell," Kriswell said, "I guess I'd just as soon be surprised as wait for another five or six days."

Demion held up his clipboard. "We've still got a stack of bugs to work on, Andy."

"But nothing that would ground an airplane?"

"No."

"Make up a schedule and hit the priority items any time we get a couple hours on the ground."

"Got it."

"We should have all planes on the ground in about fifteen minutes. I want a briefing with all pilots. Every-

185

one else turns out to refuel and preflight aircraft. We want external tanks in place."

"I'll see to that," Kriswell said.

Wyatt checked his watch. "It's one-twenty now. Wheels up by three."

The word spread fast through Demion and Kriswell, and Wyatt's team shifted into action. They all seemed to know what to do, and the standard bickering turned into good-natured repartee.

It was times like these when Wyatt appreciated the people who worked for him. With him.

Kriswell and the ground personnel began fueling operations from the tanker truck as well as loading the transport with tools, equipment, and spares still in the hangar. Castered pallets of oil, hydraulic fluid, and engine parts were nudged out to the lowered ramp of the Hercules with a tow tractor, then winched aboard. They were taking along one small tow tractor, miniature crane, and several ordnance carts. One pallet contained gear for quick encampment: tents, cots, sleeping bags, jerry cans of water, and Meals Ready to Eat (MREs).

Barr and Jordan arrived in two Jeeps and parked near the rear of the C-130. They had stripped the motel rooms without regard to filling suitcases.

Wyatt went out to meet them and helped carry the personal items aboard.

"You're not much of a packer, Bucky."

Barr dropped his load of clothing in a pile, and Jordan dumped his load on top.

"They're going to have plenty of time in the air to sort it out," Barr said.

"The Navy would never allow this kind of mess," Jordan said.

"Yeah, but the Navy takes ten days to deploy," Barr countered.

Wyatt went back to the first Jeep, grabbed a suitcase from the back, and tossed it to Barr, who heaved it on to Jordan in the cargo bay.

By the time they finished, Zimmerman had returned with the last F-4, and Wyatt called the pilots into one corner of the hangar.

Everyone was dripping sweat.

"I'm not going to miss this humidity," Gettman said.

"Assignments," Wyatt said.

They all had a pretty good idea of which seats they were getting, but Wyatt had not yet finalized them. Since equipment or personnel problems, or losses, might have forced changes, they had all been training in several different roles.

"I'm Yucca One," Wyatt said. "Barr is Two, Hackley is Three, and Gettman is Four. Zimmerman and Jordan get Five and Six."

"Damn," Zimmerman said.

"Sorry, Dave, but you and Cliff have the most back-seat experience. Those are the skills we'll need from you."

"And I get the Herc," Demion said.

"Right, Jim. Your call sign will be Wizard."

Dennis Maal, with his background in KC-135 Stratotankers, had always known he would fly the C-130F. "Do I get to come up with my own call sign?"

"Sure," Wyatt said.

"I'm going to be Thirsty."

"Thirsty?"

"I always wanted to be Thirsty. The guy from the comic strip?"

"Okay, you're Thirsty. And Borman will fly with you

187

as boom operator. We'll put Hank Cavanaugh in your right seat, acting as copilot. He's not rated, but I think he could get it on the ground."

"Does it count, in how many pieces?" Gettman asked.

"No scoring here," Wyatt said. "We'll make Vrdla your flight engineer."

Maal nodded his approval.

Wyatt turned back to Demion. "Kriswell will be your engineer, and Win Potter your copilot. Littlefield will ride with you."

"That's fine with me, Andy, except that Lucas makes lousy coffee."

"Both Hercs can go any time you're ready, since you're not going to establish any speed records," Wyatt said. "We're not filing any flight plans, and we're going to Northfield, Maine."

"Northfield? Is it on the map?" Jordan asked.

"I hope it's not very apparent," Wyatt said. "We're supposed to get all of the tanks topped off there, then the Hercs go first again."

"Are we allowed to know the next stop?" Demion asked.

"As long as we don't tell anyone else until we've departed CONUS. It's a little place in Algeria called Quallene."

"That's our staging base?" Gettman asked.

"No. It's just a filling station."

Wyatt spent the next twenty minutes going over routes, times, and frequencies. Everyone jotted notes in their little black books. He knew that they wanted to know more about the preparations and the routes in Africa, but he and Bucky had kept the full plan to themselves, relying on their military experience of providing only what information was necessary for each phase of the mission. The strategy avoided needless worrying and kept pilots focused on the immediate objective.

They ran a little late.

By three-forty-five, the C-130s took off. Wyatt and the others moved the Citation and the Jeeps into the hangar. Everyone made a call on the bathroom in the corner of the hangar, then dressed in flight suits and G suits. They took turns with the single start cart that had been left behind and started all of the turbojets. Wyatt carried the single ladder from airplane to airplane, assisting each pilot aboard his craft.

He hooked the ladder on the side of seven-seven, climbed up, checked the ejection seat safety pins, then slid inside. He disconnected the ladder and dropped it to the ground. His parachute harness was already in place, and he pulled it on, then strapped into the seat. Lifting his helmet from the floor, he settled it into place and hooked into the aircraft systems. He dialled his Tac One radio into the common frequency for Minneapolis—the local air control, just in case some air controller called him. The Tac Two radio was set for interplane communications.

"Yucca Flight."

"Two."

"Three."

"Four here."

"Five's reading five by five."

"And Six on the tail end."

"Let's go by twos," Wyatt told them.

He released the brakes and headed for the taxiway. Barr pulled up alongside him, grinning like a horsey maniac.

189

"How's your brakes, Bucky?" he asked.

"Who needs 'em? I'm not slowing down for anyone."

At the end of the taxiway, after checking for airborne aircraft, he rolled onto the runway.

Down by the airport office, a few people were gathering. They had probably noticed the C-130s taking off, and now they would be treated to a flight of six. The Noble Enterprises outfit had become something of an accepted fixture at the old bomber base, and the people down there probably also thought they were coming back.

Wyatt lowered his canopy.

A blue Pinto came racing around the office and headed toward Hangar 4.

"That'll be Julie," Barr said. "I didn't get a chance to say goodbye."

Wyatt couldn't see her face, but the car slowed, then stopped, when she saw the fighters sitting at the end of the runway.

He thought the whole thing was pretty forlorn.

"Damned if I'm not going to miss Nebraska," Barr said. "Some damned good people around here."

"Let's go," Wyatt said.

"Waiting on you, partner."

He slammed the throttles forward.

Kramer and Liz Jordan went to a Wendy's for dinner. Both of them were depressed, and their dinner conversation revolved around everything but what was on their minds.

Kramer hadn't told Liz or anyone about Wyatt's proposal. She thought she'd just wait.

With the way she was feeling about this operation, there might not be a wedding.

The thought depressed her further. She was torn by conflicting emotions.

They had worked late, and it was after eight when they walked out of Wendy's.

"I am going home," Jordan said, "and crawl into the spa and think good things about Cliff."

"I may call Sears and have them send up a spa."

"Not Sears, Jan. They don't have spas."

"So I've got to wait until tomorrow?"

"Unless you want to use ours."

"Thanks, but I'll just opt for bed."

They reached their cars in the lot and said good night. Kramer unlocked her Riviera, then remembered a chore.

"Hey, Liz. Did you feed Ace?"

"Oh, damn. I thought you had."

"That's okay. I'll run back and check on him."

"That cat's more trouble than he's worth," Jordan said.

"Have you seen any mice out there?"

"On second thought. . . ."

Kramer drove back out to the airport, passed the passenger terminal and the end of the runway, and pulled into Clark Carr Loop. She parked in front of the building.

Walking up to the front door, she retrieved her keys out of her purse.

Unlocked the door and pushed it open.

Reached out automatically to tap the security code into the keypad on the wall beside the door.

And saw the green light.

The alarm system wasn't armed.

She positively remembered setting it before she locked the door that evening.

Cautiously, she looked around the reception room. The light of the setting sun kept it from being dark, and it appeared normal.

The door to her office was closed, as it should be. Only she, Wyatt, Barr, and Liz Jordan had keys to it.

She looked at the base of the door.

Light peeked from under it.

And Ace the Wonder Cat was squatting next to it, rubbing up against the doorjamb.

She could hear a tap-tapping.

Kramer crossed the carpeted reception area and tested the door handle.

Ace nuzzled her ankle.

The door wasn't locked.

She turned the handle and shoved the door open.

A man's back was bent over her computer keyboard. There was blue lettering against a white background on the screen.

The man was suddenly alerted.

His head whipped around.

And Ace snarled, took two bounds and one leap, and landed right in the middle of the man's face.

Interment

Eleven

"Goddamn cat!"

The man's arms flailed wildly, and Ace dodged them, danced off his shoulder, and landed on the desk top. He spun around, sliding on a stack of loose paper, arched his back, and bared his tiny sharp teeth.

He hissed.

Ace left his mark. Half-a-dozen deep gouges began oozing blood from the man's temples and cheeks.

"Son of a bitchin' cat," Arnie Gering yelped as he bolted out of the chair.

"What in the hell are you doing in my office?" Kramer demanded.

"Goddamn cat!" Gering said again, backing away from the desk.

"You're screwing around with Ace's computer, Arnie. Tell me why, and tell me now."

Gering dug a handkerchief out of the back pocket of his jeans and began dabbing at his face. He spluttered some more when he saw the blood.

"Let's have it, Arnie."

Kramer stayed close to the door, ready to scream and run if he turned on her. She didn't know what he was up to, but she was damned proud of Ace the Wonder Cat.

Ace stopped hissing now that Gering had moved away, but he remained alert, his hind legs tensed for another launch.

She glanced quickly at the computer screen:

SPECIAL PROJECTS

CONFIDENTIAL FILES—ACCESS CODE REQUIRED

ENTER PASSWORD: BLUE DA–

Gering had been attempting to hack his way into the special projects files.

"What's going on?" she demanded again.

Gering was regaining some degree of composure. "I'm working late."

"Working on what?"

"Damn it! Can't you see I'm scratched up. Why don't you declaw that damned cat?"

The blood continued to seep from the cuts, obliterating the freckles on his sunburned face.

"I don't give a shit about your face, Arnie. How did you get in here?"

She checked the door and jamb, but couldn't see any scratches. Gering had a key to the building, but not to this door. Maybe he had used a credit card on the lock.

"It was open," he said.

"This door is never unlocked at night."

"It was open."

"What are you after?"

Gering cleared his throat. "I was just checking on that job we did in Nebraska."

"Why?"

"Well, shit. Lefty and I only got a lousy two grand apiece. We ought to get as much as the others are getting."

Kramer moved sideways across the room, facing him, and closing in on the desk. She reached out and gently stroked Ace's neck.

She could feel the bunched up muscles under his skin. Ace wasn't going to relax just yet.

"You're fortunate to have received a bonus at all."

"I'm entitled to more."

"How much more, do you think?"

"Well, I want to know what the others are getting."

"Forget the others," she said. "How much do you think you're worth?"

Gering grinned at her. "I ought to get another five thousand."

"Maybe you'll find a job somewhere that will pay you that much more."

His grin faded. "What? You can't fire me."

"I can't? Seems to me I'm the one who hired you. I've changed my mind."

"You fire me, and I go right to the newspapers," Gering said.

"With what?"

"There's something screwy about that deal. You just watch, Kramer. Some reporter will dig into it."

"And visit you in jail, too?"

"Jail?"

"Breaking and entering. Attempted theft of proprietary information." She picked up the phone and dialled a nine and a one.

"Hold on, damn it!"

Kramer kept her forefinger poised over the button. "Get out, Arnie."

With a face turning redder than normal, and still holding his handkerchief to his cheek, Gering spun around and stomped out. She waited until she heard the front door slam, then dropped the telephone back in its cradle and settled into her chair.

She took a deep breath. She was more rattled than she thought she had been.

Damn. Where are you, Andy?

Grabbing the phone, she dialled the number in Washington and got the answering machine, which simply said, "Yes?"

At the beep, she said, "This is Klondike. There's a problem with Icarus, and someone had better call me fast."

Twenty minutes later, which was pretty fast for Washington, the phone rang.

It was a male voice she had never heard before.

"Klondike, I'd like a password."

"Sugar time," she said.

"And I'll say, 'mustard.' "

"Who are you?"

"Um, I'm someone knowledgeable about all of Icarus. What's the problem?"

She told him about Gering.

"And you canned him?"

"Yes."

"Well, that may have been a little precipitous."

"I can't have someone working here that I can't trust," she said, jotting a note to have all the exterior locks changed in the morning. Also the security alarm codes.

"Yes. You're probably correct."

"I know I am."

"I'll check into it."

"And you call me back," she said. "I don't want to spend the rest of my life wondering."

"I'll do that."

She hung up. Ace the Wonder Cat promptly flopped on top of the phone.

"You deserve a medal, you know that?"

Ace got busy cleaning his claws.

The single airstrip in Northfield, Maine, was a tiny one, but long enough. The F-4s had used every available foot of its length without having to deploy the drag chutes, and as soon as the last Phantom—seven-seven, flown by Wyatt—was down, the runway lights had promptly been extinguished.

Parked in the weed-choked field off the edge of the runway were the six fighters, the two C-130s, and an unmarked Falcon business jet. Two dark blue tanker trucks without identification other than Maine license plates, manned by men in blue denims without insignia, moved among the aircraft, topping off the fuel tanks. Across the runway, a few civilian small aircraft were parked in an unlit area. The few buildings on that side of the field appeared to be deserted, and Wyatt could be assured that they were. Embry's people would have threatened or bribed anyone who wanted to hang around the airport at night.

Most of the Noble Enterprises crew were inside the Hercules transport, filling up quickly on MREs.

Wyatt and Barr sat with George Embry inside the Falcon's cabin. Embry had brought along coffee and club sandwiches, and every time he took a bite out of his, Wyatt felt guilty about the guys stuck with the military rations.

Embry lifted fourteen manila envelopes from the attaché case resting on the table between their seats.

"Documentation," he said.

"Is it any good, though?" Barr asked.

"The best. Social security cards, credit cards, flying and driving licenses, some nifty passports, the works. Before I leave, we'll collect all of the ID you guys have. I'll ship it back to Albuquerque for you."

Embry passed Wyatt a thicker envelope. "Operating cash, in case you run into any emergencies."

Wyatt opened the envelope and spilled the bills on the table. There were U.S. dollars in fifties and twenties and a few hundreds, French francs, Algerian dinars, CFA francs for Chad, and Libyan dinars.

"It adds up to around ninety thou, U.S.," Embry said.

"This getting charged against my contract, George?"

"Nah, this is a freebie. Just in case anyone has to hitchhike out of the ·country."

"Or the continent," Barr added.

Wyatt divided the rubber-banded stacks, kept about a fourth of it, and shoved the rest to Barr.

"Gee, thanks, Daddy."

"Split it up with the others, Bucky."

"My guys," Embry said, "are loading a couple cardboard boxes on the transport. That's the small arms you asked for, as well as the maps, radios, and other crap for the survival packs."

"We won't be needing those," Barr said.

"Thanks," Wyatt said.

"On the Nebraska end," Embry said, "I've arranged for a team that will hit there in the morning. By nine o'clock, there won't be any evidence that you were ever there."

"Except for eyewitnesses," Wyatt said.

"Can't avoid that, can we?"

"I don't think anyone will ever have to testify," Barr said. "And if they do, they'll only remember us as hard-working gentlemen who spread a few bucks around."

"Let's hope so," Embry said. "Okay, brief me on the mission."

"I thought we'd done that a couple months ago," Wyatt told him.

"There's not a doubt in my mind that you've made some changes in the tactics, and Church wants to be fully aware of every phase."

"There's just one, well maybe two, little alterations," Barr said.

Wyatt explained, point-by-point and chronologically, the plan he and Barr had prepared subsequent to the skeletal mission profile he had previously laid out for Church.

"Hot damn!" Embry said. "I like your changes. If the computers back at Langley knew about them, they'd up your chances a bit."

"You ran a game scenario on us?" Barr asked.

"Of course. Standard procedure."

"How did it come out?" Barr wanted to know.

"You don't want to know."

"Come on, George. You can count on me to over-come the odds anyway."

"The machine suggested a seventy-four percent success ratio."

"Before we made the changes," Wyatt said.

"Before you made the changes. I'll bet you upped it by ten or fifteen percent."

"Comforting," Barr said.

"Any time you're ready," Wyatt said, "we'd like to hear about this new and urgent deadline. You also mentioned some fatalities."

"Yeah, well, I've got a source inside the country, and she's gotten close to an army lieutenant colonel."

"Army?" Wyatt asked. "We aren't going up against the army, are we?"

"His name is al-Qati, and he heads up their special forces unit. They've been training with the bomber command that apparently will deploy CW weapons. The commander is a guy named Ibrahim Ramad, a full bird. They're doing coordinated air and ground attack exercises."

"Are these the Sukhois?" Wyatt asked.

"Su-24s, right. So, this is the major change I've got for your mission."

Damn. Jan was right about last-minute changes.

Embry unrolled a large reconnaissance map and spread it over the table.

"This is the base at Marada, or near Marada."

"You want us to hit an air base?" Barr said. "What the hell happened to the chemical plant?"

"You get to do both of them now."

"We're short about four aircraft, in that event," Wyatt said.

"It can't be helped, Andy. Hell, I didn't know about this until this morning, a couple hours before I called you, and we're flat out of time."

Wyatt studied the map, which was actually a blown-up recon photo. There wasn't much to be seen except for an antenna complex and a runway.

"It's underground," Barr said.

"Right. See these shadows here, look like wide lines?

Those are the entrance doors to the subsurface hangars. You can barely make them out, but there are six ramps, leading down to the doors, see here? The runways are painted in camouflage, but we've known about this base for years. You'll be able to locate it, as well as the chem plant, by geographical coordinates. They're listed right here."

"Those hangar doors will be blast doors," Wyatt said. "We'd have to catch them when they're open if we want to slip a couple heavyweights in there."

"Yeah, I know. This is the way it goes. Your primary objective is the chemical plant, which is about ten miles north of Marada Air Base. The secondary target is any Sukhoi you can catch on the ground. We'd like to put a dent in their long-range bombing capability. Third target, if the opportunity presents itself, is the base."

Wyatt looked at Barr.

"Why not?" Barr said. "I'm bound to have a couple bombs left over after I knock out the chemical plant."

"You sound like you're doing the whole damned thing alone," Embry said.

"I could, but these other hot-shit pilots wanted to come along."

"All right," Wyatt said. "The decision to target the planes and the air base means that there's a new development somebody in your building doesn't like."

"Ahmed al-Qati told my source that Ramad intends to hit three Ethiopian refugee camps with nerve, toxic, and psychological agents."

"Shit," Barr said.

"It's supposed to prove to outsiders what they can, and will, do, which is deliver CW over a long range. I guess they're also interested in evaluating the results of each agent."

"What camps?" Wyatt asked.

"Unknown."

"On August second. What time?"

"Also unknown. My agent will attempt to learn the takeoff time, but she can't probe too deeply without risking herself."

"Do you have independent corroboration?"

"No," Embry admitted. "We're trying, but my source is reliable, and we don't want to wait and risk having her be right and us be wrong."

"You going to the UN with it?"

"I don't play at those levels, Andy. My guess is that the time line is too tight for a round of high-level diplomatic discussions and less-than-veiled threats."

"We're not set up, not armed, for an interdiction mission," Wyatt said.

"I know, and we're not suggesting that you go play dogfighter with a bunch of MiGs and Sukhois. We figure if we can cause enough damage at the plant and the base, they're going to forget about Ethiopians, at least for a little while."

"That's good," Barr said, "because I'm not a dogfighter. Lover and wild horse rider, yes, but dogfighter, no."

Wyatt studied the map for awhile, then said, "I don't think we need to know the takeoff time. I'd hate to go in there and hit a bunch of them on the takeoff run, yet allow one or two bombers to escape and light out for Ethiopia. Or when they know they're under attack, they just might divert them to Tel Aviv. The best bet is to hit them early and hard enough to shake them out of the fantasy."

"I second that thought," Barr said.

Embry licked his lips. "Church thought it would be

good to catch them in the open, on the ground. You cause some secondary explosions of CW ordnance, and we'd have gas all over the area, maybe sucked into the underground ventilation system. Goodbye Marada Air Base."

Barr whistled through his teeth.

Wyatt sagged back in his chair. "That is an interesting thought, George."

"We knew we'd have casualties hitting the chemical plant," Embry reminded him.

"Yeah, but a whole air base? What's the composition?"

"The Sukhoi bomber wing and a fighter/interceptor/strike wing of four squadrons. MiG-23s and MiG-27s."

"That's a lot of people," Wyatt said.

"Look what they're planning, just for a test, Andy. And keep in mind that we're targeting military capacity, not poor, damned hungry people."

"You haven't confirmed it, yet," Wyatt said.

"Look, Wyatt. I don't think we'll find a confirmation. We just don't have enough assets in the area. And we're not here to debate the targets. You're the contractor; we pay the freight and you do the job."

"We're not backing out, George. But as the commander on site, I'm going to reserve judgement relative to the final attack profile. We'll buy the three targets, but we'll remain flexible about the approach. Let's not forget that we're the ones with our asses on the line and that time-over-target is going to be damned slim. Bucky?"

"I'll go with that."

"George?"

Embry took off his glasses and nodded slowly. His

eyes seemed redder, more fatigued, with the glasses removed.

"Yeah, all right, Andy. You call the final shots. I'll keep pushing my gal, and update you if we learn more about the H-hour."

"Anything else we need to know?"

Pursing his lips, Embry said, "Marty didn't want me to tell you this, so keep it to yourselves, huh?"

Wyatt and Barr both grunted.

"You may get there, and then we'll tell you to turn around and come home."

"What the hell?"

"It seems that Icarus isn't approved by all the higher-ups just yet."

"Well, goddamn it!" Wyatt said. "Stupid old me, I thought you people had your act together before you extended the contract."

"With the information we just got, the DCI is scrambling to touch bases with everyone who counts, and we'll know more in the morning."

"For Christ's sake!" Barr exclaimed. "You guys are living up to your negative publicity."

"You can punch me out, Bucky, but I swear I didn't know. I do believe, with what Mari . . . with what my asset has provided, that the DCI will have a stamp of approval by morning."

"This is pretty damned balled up," Wyatt said.

"I agree," Embry said. "I always plan for something to go wrong, but this one can't get much worse."

It did.

Just as Barr and Wyatt were deplaning, one of the Falcon's pilots stuck his head out of the cockpit. "Mr. Embry, scrambled call for you."

Wyatt waited while Embry picked up a phone. He mouthed the name, "Church."

Embry uh-huhed and huh-uhed a couple times, swore three times, and then said, "Yes, sir."

When he hooked the receiver back on its bulkhead cradle, Wyatt said, "What now?"

"Your man Gering?"

"Oh, shit!"

Embry told him about the confrontation between Gering and Kramer.

"She's all right?"

"She's fine. She fired the guy on the spot. Church is going to have some people take a close look at him."

"You just can't count on anyone, anymore," Barr said.

"Come on, Bucky, let's get this circus airborne before any more clowns show up."

Ferry flights were supposed to be boring, but Barr was enjoying himself. Not more than three months before, he believed he'd never again fly a hot fighter plane.

He loved the F-4, and this one was greater than ever with all of the new systems.

Settled comfortably in his seat, with the autopilot directing operations, he had reviewed his new passport and accompanying documentation. His name was Jack O. Milhauser, and he had a couple matchbooks from a New Jersey topless bar as well as a thin catalog of X-rated videos. He figured he knew what the "O." stood for, and he thought he would give Kramer hell about the persona she had set up for him. She had probably laughed all the way through it.

If she was still there when they got back. He was

going to have to prod Wyatt some more. Though they had been best friends for so long he had forgotten the starting date, he knew that Wyatt could be pretty damned obstinate about some things. His first marriage had soured him on the emotive aspects of life.

Barr also knew, based on his own experiences and the rotating roster of women he dated, that he wasn't particularly qualified as a matchmaker. Maybe Wyatt knew something he didn't know. Hell, he didn't know what to do.

He was sure that Kramer's problem involved frustrated love, but he couldn't just shove Wyatt into something he didn't want to do.

Life was a bitch sometimes.

Like for some Ethiopians he had never met, but knew he'd like if he ever did. He thought about that for awhile, to get his mind off Wyatt and Kramer.

Checked the skies around him. The lightening skies were cloudless, but were full of Phantoms, unarmed but with twin drop tanks slung beneath the wings. Wyatt and Gettman were ahead of, and a quarter-mile above, him. Zimmerman was riding his right wing, and Hackley and Jordan had paired off a half-mile to his left.

At thirty-two thousand feet, he could see the dawn coming at him, shooting spears of light off the Phantoms above. It was coming up on four A.M. local, which was just a solid expanse of darkened ocean. A glance at his fuel state told him that it was also time for an F-4 breakfast. They had taken off from Maine at eleven-fifteen Eastern Daylight Time, two hours behind the Hercs, and had just about reached their fuel limit.

The problem with this leg of the trip was that it was forty-two hundred miles long, and the F-4s, with a low-consumption cruise at 550 miles per hour, could plan on running out of fuel twice, at sixteen hundred miles and at thirty-two hundred miles. The C-130s, even with a maximum overload takeoff weight of 175,000 pounds, could extend themselves to five-thousand miles and complete their share of the journey with ease.

The Phantoms needed a couple refuelings apiece, but their tanker didn't have the capacity to meet that need.

Wyatt and Barr had figured it as closely as they could, poring over almanacs and meteorological studies for average prevailing winds at various altitudes. Without the drag of weapons and pylons, but with the drag of drop tanks, and with careful manipulations of the throttles, it was going to be possible. Each jet would get one full refueling and, later, another six-tenths refueling before the tanker's fuel bladders were drained. Depending on tail winds, they might have to do some coasting to make Quallene on fumes.

They would also have to hope that their penetration of the African shoreline went unnoticed. There wasn't much tolerance for wasting fuel in radar-dodging maneuvers. They would cross the coast low, wishfully below possible radar coverage, but those few minutes would consume fuel at high rates.

Barr hit the transmit button. "Hey, Big Yucca, you see Thirsty yet?

Only Wyatt was utilizing his radar occasionally, so as not to advertise six radars.

"About thirty miles ahead, Bucky. What's your state?"

"I can wait a while."

Wyatt asked each pilot for his fuel state, and, after

the replies, said, "Yucca Six, then Four, then Two, then Five, then Three."

A few minutes later, Ben Borman came up on the Tac Two channel.

"I count six still with us. You see me?"

Barr had already located the tanker, several miles ahead and a thousand feet above. She was clearly defined against a brightening sky.

He rogered the query when his turn came.

After Jordan and Gettman had had their chances, Barr took a sip of water from the baby bottle tucked into his harness, then eased in throttle and gently closed the gap between himself and the C-130F.

The refueling hose was fully extended from the port wing, seeming to float below the Hercules. The small airfoils near the tip allowed the operator to fly the tip within a short range, making the last maneuvers to dock the tip in the receiving aircraft's fuel receptacle. He could see Borman, though not clearly, in the Plexiglas bubble at the rear of the tanker.

"Atta way, Bucky, come on a tad more."

"What the hell's a 'tad more,' Ben?"

"Up ten feet. Speed's matched."

Barr was studying the end of the hose, which was just above him. He opened the refueling receptacle, which was located on the top of the fuselage, behind the canopy.

A bad spot of air, a misdirection with the stick or throttles, and that heavy tip could do devastating things to canopies and pilots.

He eased back the stick a notch.

The hose lowered on him.

"Don't go getting the hiccoughs, Denny," Barr cautioned Maal.

"Hiccough," Maal said.

"Easy, Bucky." From Borman.

Centered the stick.

"A tiny goose of the throttle; come to Thirsty," Borman said.

Nudge.

The hose slid overhead.

"You hang tight, right there," Borman said.

He centered the stick and watched the wings of the C-130, ready to match any change the tanker might make.

"Gotcha!"

He felt the hose connector make contact with the airframe, but he kept his eyes riveted on the airplane above him, taking quick glances at Borman behind his protective window.

"Do you want to catch the windshield while you're at it, Ben?"

"Sure thing. You using a credit card? I got a four percent discount for cash."

"Guy behind me is picking up the tab. Ask him."

It didn't take long. He flicked the rotary switch to check fuel loads on the main and external tanks.

"That'll do it, Ben."

"Roger. I'll be seeing you again soon."

Barr eased off the throttles and the C-130 pulled away. He closed the receptacle, did a half-wingover, and slid away from the tanker.

"Eighteen hundred and forty gallons doesn't go very far, does it, Bucky?" Zimmerman asked.

"Hell, man, we're getting almost a mile to a gallon."

"Don't tell the EPA," Gettman said. "They'll want us to change to four-cylinder engines."

* * *

As was typical, Martin Church arrived at his office at seven in the morning. He was barely into his third cup of coffee when the first call was passed through by his secretary at eight o'clock.

"Good morning, Mr. Director. This is Cal Norman at the Post."

"Good morning, Cal. How are you?"

"Fine, sir. I'm trying to get confirmation on an item that landed on my desk. Or my phone."

"What is that?"

"There's this guy out in New Mexico somewhere that. . . ."

"A guy? Does he have a name, Cal?"

"Uh, yeah, he gave me his name, but I'm supposed to keep it confidential."

"That's understandable," Church said. "So he gave you a hot tip?"

"That's what he says. Something about a clandestine air force operating out of Nebraska. His guess is that the CIA has to be involved."

"His guess?"

"Well, there's not too many groups have themselves six F-4 fighters," Norman said.

"F-4s? Those are all but obsolete, aren't they, Cal?" Church was fond of talking to reporters in question marks.

"I don't know. I haven't looked into this too far just yet."

"How about survivalists? Or white extremists? Those groups are building some fascinating armories, Cal."

"But airplanes?"

"Hell, I don't know. Maybe the FBI does. What does your informant have to do with it?"

"He said he worked on the planes."

"And did what with them?"

"Painted them, for one thing."

"What color?"

"Color? Cream with red stripes."

"Those aren't the colors I'd use on warplanes, Cal."

"That's a fact, Mr. Director."

"What kind of ordnance did he report?"

"Ordnance?"

"Weapons."

"Well, he didn't mention any weapons."

"I'm sure you're aware of this, Cal, but your informant seems to be a little short on facts. Did he say anything about a use for the planes? Have they got targets?"

"Well, a couple of my colleagues are checking with Nebraska and with some of the Middle East people in the city."

"Why Middle East, Cal?"

"Uh, given the current world conditions, that seemed the most obvious. Don't you have some ideas, Mr. Director?"

"I've been trying to give you some leads here, Cal. How about the DEA?"

"DEA?"

"The drug enforcement people might use airplanes like that for interdiction. Hell, I don't know. I'm just trying to help you out."

"Well, I appreciate it," Norman said.

"Maybe they tossed him out of the group, or something. Maybe he's got a grudge? If I were you, I'd call him back and ask about weapons. Or if he got himself blackballed from the group."

"Yeah, maybe I'll do that. Thanks, Mr. Church."

* * *

They took on the last of their fuel two hundred miles off the coast and two hundred miles south of the Canary Islands. Wyatt then ordered all of the aircraft into a tight formation, the C-130s flying nearly wingtip-to-wingtip, and the Phantoms flying in a compressed diamond beneath the transports. On any radar in the area, they would be picked up as one blip, a single airplane on its way to somewhere.

One unknown airplane is much less threatening than eight unknown airplanes.

Once they were grouped up, Wyatt ordered a gradual descent, conserving fuel as much as possible.

The formation crossed the coastline at one thousand feet of altitude, one hundred miles north of Dakhla, Western Sahara. The next northern city of relative importance, Laayoune, was nearly three hundred miles away.

The Western Sahara Desert, once they were past the tiny bit of green along the coast, was dismal and forbidding. At their low altitude, it seemed to go on forever. Millions of square miles of rolling, undulating, almost color-free blandness.

Wyatt had flown in North Africa before, but never in this region. He had studied the maps, but the maps were short of landmarks and population centers. No one wanted to live here, and he couldn't blame them.

He checked the chronometer. 0912 hours local.

He looked up. Jim Demion was holding the Hercules steady two hundred feet above him.

"Wizard, Yucca One."

They had agreed to use only call signs after violating the airspace of Western Sahara.

"Go, One."

"Give it about ten more miles, then start gaining al-

214

titude at a hundred feet per minute. We want to get up where the fuel consumption reads a little better."

"Roger, One. We'll do it."

They were at fifteen thousand feet, idling along at 350 knots to stay with the transports, an hour and forty minutes later. The landscape hadn't changed much at all, though the sun was higher. There wasn't a cloud in the sky, and though that generally was a positive sign for pilots, Wyatt missed the clouds.

"Yucca One, Four," Gettman said.

"Go."

"You suppose we're within fifty miles of where it is we want to be? At that time, I begin to go into my famous panic routine."

"Let me check on it, Four."

Wyatt spun in the frequency on his Tac One radio.

"Degas."

He waited for a count of ten, then tried again.

"Degas."

One thousand one, one thousand two, one thou. . . .

"That you, Yucca?"

"Roger that, Degas. I need a signal for my ADF."

His Automatic Direction Finder needed a radio trans-mitter emitting a signal in order to be useful.

"Yucca, I hate to get mean about it, but you're a couple days off schedule, you know that?"

"I know it," Wyatt said.

"This mean I have to get rid of my harem?"

"Just give me the damned signal."

"Ah, roger the signal, Yucca. Coming up."

Twelve

When he heard the first faint drone of airplane engines, Neil Formsby finished his glass of iced tea, donned the shirt he had prepared, rose from his cot, and left the tent.

There was a light breeze blowing out of the southwest, but it was not strong enough to raise a lot of dust or sand.

For some unfathomable reason, he had been enjoying his solitude. There was nothing like being by one's self a thousand kilometers from anywhere to enforce introspection. Jesus Christ in the wilderness. He felt as if he needed another thirty-five days, and he halfway resented Wyatt showing up early. And contrary to the careful planning, they had arrived during daylight; he would not be allowed to demonstrate his jury-rigged runway lights.

Formsby had known Wyatt for fifteen years. They had first met when Wyatt was detached to the Royal Air Force to learn to fly Harrier jumpjets with Formsby's squadron, and they had become good friends. Wyatt had made the arrangements which brought Formsby to the United States for a year-long course in air superiority tactics, and he had smoothed the way for Formsby to get time in F-15s and F-16s. That alone was worth a lifetime's friendship.

When RAF Captain Neil Formsby had lost power on his Harrier at a hovering thousand feet and jammed his foot through the firewall in the ensuing crash, he woke up in the hospital to find Wyatt in attendance. And after he was out of the hospital and in rehabilitation, Wyatt had been there with a job offer. Only for Wyatt would Formsby isolate himself in a hostile and foreign desert and come to enjoy it.

He was impressed when he first caught sight of the approaching aircraft. The two lumbering transports were flanked on each side by three fighters. They were a thousand feet off the ground when they passed over, the roar of twenty engines thundering with an impact he could feel right down through his toes.

One of the jets waggled his wings at him.

Formsby truly missed, and achingly longed for, the cockpit of a fighter aircraft.

As they went by toward the east, the C-130s fanned out wide and let the Phantoms have first chance at Formsby's crude runway. They turned back and made their approaches quickly enough that he supposed fuel was becoming critical.

It wasn't until the first aircraft touched down that he considered that his efforts at leveling ground could possibly be inadequate. Wyatt had told him that they would substitute softer tires for rough airfields, but the F-4 still managed five hops before it settled in.

His runway was almost too short.

Sand-covered hard earth did not offer the same friction as concrete or asphalt, and excessive pressure on the brakes induced skidding.

The first Phantom reached the end of the airstrip and had barely turned off when the next one touched down.

Formsby ran out to meet the first plane. His running gait was a trifle lopsided because of his ankle.

Its nose bobbled up and down in rapid little motions as it crossed the sand toward him. In the glare of the sun off the windscreen, he could not make out who was at the controls.

He spun around, revealing the back of his shirt to the pilot. In big black letters on the white shirt were the words: "FOLLOW ME."

Trotting toward the tanker trailers, he led the big jet to a spot near his tent, then turned and waved his hand in a horizontal circle.

The pilot raised his canopy as the Phantom turned ninety degrees, then braked to a stop.

Formsby gave him a cut-throat signal, and the turbojets spun down.

The pilot slipped his helmet off, and Formsby recognized Barr.

"Good morning, Nelson," he called.

"Who?"

"You."

"Oh, right. Sometimes, I forget who I am. G'day to you, mate."

"That's an atrocious accent, Nelson."

"We do what we can."

"You must have been lowest on fuel," Formsby said.

"I resent that, Neil. I've got two, maybe three liters left."

Formsby grinned at him, then trotted out to meet the next plane.

In twenty minutes, he had all of the planes parked,

the jets aligned with their tails toward the tank trailers, and the C-130s side by side in front of them.

Men spilled from the Hercules aircraft, produced ladders, and helped the pilots out of their cockpits.

He received at least a half-dozen compliments on the design of his shirt.

Crossing to the fourth interceptor, he greeted Wyatt as the man came down the ladder.

"Welcome to my humble air base, Andrew."

Wyatt threw out his hand, and they shook hands. "Outside of a demonstrated need for more practice with a bulldozer, Neil, you've done very well. It's good to see you."

"We are meeting earlier than expected, are we not? I would hate to think my calendar has been running slow."

"We're early, and I'll tell you why in a little while," Wyatt said. "First, we'll visit your latrine. . . ."

Formsby waved his hand at the vista around them.

". . . then, if you've got something to drink?"

"There's about nine thousand gallons of water. Or, your unexpected arrival has caught me with a few bottles of unconsumed ale and champagne. It's in the icebox."

"You always did know how to live in the desert," Barr said as he approached, his hand out. "What's for lunch, buddy?"

"We live off the land here, Nelson."

"Ecch."

Formsby shook hands also with Demion and Kriswell, both of whom he had met before, then Wyatt took him in tow and introduced him to the others.

The group scattered for the dunes to relieve themselves while Formsby popped the corks on his last four

219

bottles of champagne, put out the ale, and started stacking paper plates with ham-and-cheese sandwiches. He used Swiss cheese since Americans in general had no palate for more exotic cheeses.

Since they could not all fit inside the tent, they ate their lunch sitting on the hot earth in the shade created by a C-130 wing.

Wyatt brought him, and apparently most of the others, up to date on the reasons for the premature initiation of their mission.

Formsby was appalled by the callous disregard for human life. "Refugees? Women and children?"

"That's the word, Neil," Wyatt said.

"What kind of a bastard are we dealing with?" he asked.

"The worst kind, apparently." Wyatt briefed them on the commanders involved, referring to biographies provided by the CIA. It was always good to know one's adversaries, and Formsby memorized the names. Ramad, al-Qati, Salmi, Ghazi.

"And," Wyatt added, "the Langley people suspect there will be some deniability built in—such as rogue commanders acting on their own. However, they're also certain that the great Leader and his chief advisor, Kamal Amjab, have given a thumbs-up to the plan."

The heat was intense, and Formsby got up and crossed to his tent to get the last of the ale, a stack of paper cups, and a big jug of iced tea. He brought them back and walked around the group, pouring.

It was not high tea.

Wyatt spent forty minutes briefing the mission. Formsby could tell they had discussed it before, but Wyatt was now making some changes in timing and targeting.

220

"Questions, anyone?" Wyatt asked.

"The distance to target," Hackley asked, "is five hundred miles?"

"From the staging base," Wyatt said, "five hundred and six miles."

"And with this bird, we've got a full-load combat range of five-twenty."

"That's right, Norm. Time over target is going to be almost nil."

"All that means," Barr said, "is you got to be accurate. Hit what you aimed for and skedaddle."

"What the hell?" Gettman said. "If we run short of fuel, we've made plans for hitchhiking."

"That's doing it the hard way, Karl, but yeah, we've got backup," Wyatt said.

Cliff Jordan—Formsby was concentrating on attaching faces to the names of the people he had just met—pointed at the tanker trailers. "Neil, do those rusted, broken-down buckets actually have all the fuel we need?"

Fuel—its availability and transport—was probably the most crucial aspect of this mission. Lacking a sufficient quantity in the right location meant that the ordnance did not reach its targets. Formsby was quite content with his success at producing the required amount in the correct geographical location.

"But of course," Formsby said. "Andrew told me a minimum of thirty-one thousand gallons, forgetting that I must negotiate in liters, naturally. I have five five-thousand-gallon tankers and one eight-thousand-gallon tanker."

"The way we'll handle it," Wyatt said, "we'll refuel all of the aircraft here, which eats up twenty-five thousand gallons, and load the balance in the C-130F. After we fly to the staging base, the C-130 will top off all the fuel cells again."

"Neil," Barr said, "I have one little question. How'd you get all that junk here without tractors?"

Formsby explained his arrangement with the paranoid and greedy Jacque. "But that brings up a point I'd like to discuss, Nelson. Originally, I had planned to return to Rabat with Jacque and his fellow travellers. After considering the man's demeanor and my suspicion that he may well think I have more dollars than I have, I believe the better course would be for me to accompany you to Libya."

"Libya is safer than Jacque?" Barr asked.

"You haven't met Jacque."

"It's just as well, Neil," Tom Kriswell said. "I can use you as an assistant air controller."

"I would be pleased to serve," Formsby said.

"What about the fifty grand you owe Jacque?" Wyatt asked.

"Why, I'll leave it for him. It wouldn't do to skip out and have my reputation tarnished. And I might well have to do business with him again in the future. Especially if Andrew keeps lining up these contracts."

Wyatt looked at his wristwatch. "All right, guys. Anything else?"

The pressing matters appeared to have been met.

"Let's go to work," Wyatt said.

With a few groans and a few profane comments about the temperature, the men levered themselves from the ground and spread out to the aircraft. Formsby pitched in, helping to strip the red tape, logos, and N-numbers from all of the aircraft.

Two men went from plane to plane with a large roll of brown paper and masking tape and masked off canopies, air intakes, exhausts, and the lower side of the wings and fuselage. Two more men rolled compressors and gasoline generators from the cargo bay of the Hercules. Stepladders with broad plates on their legs, to prevent them from sinking into the earth, were carried out of the C-130, and the two men—Littlefield and Cavanaugh, Formsby thought—donned face masks and began to spray paint the first F-4.

Not much effort was given to precision and finish for this paint job. Random patterns of brown, tan, and beige were sprayed over the original cream, mixed with drops of perspiration from the two artists. With the low-visibility gray of the undersides, the new camouflage colors would make the F-4s hard to pinpoint from above or below. The C-130F would also get camouflage, but the transport was being left in its prim, unadorned aluminum finish.

Nelson Barr ran back and forth, supervising the spray job, claiming he was in charge of decorations. Littlefield tried to shoot him with a spray gun, but Barr dove beneath a wing just in time.

Two more teams of men laid out hoses between the fuel trailers and aircraft, powered up the pumps, and started refueling. The mixed aromas of JP-4 and catalyzed paint drifted on the breeze.

Jim Demion and two others hauled tools from one airplane to another, making adjustments and quick-fixes listed on a clipboard he carried.

Formsby gathered all of the red tape remnants and stacked them in a pile.

Then he went to help Wyatt and Ben Borman pull the tarpaulins from the ordnance pallets. With tin snips, they went around each pallet, cutting the steel strapping that held the crates and cradles in place.

Wyatt and Formsby used crowbars to pry the lids off crates while Borman climbed into the Hercules, then returned with a small tow tractor pulling a train of mobile bomb cradles and a small crane. He started transferring bombs from the pallets to the cradles with the crane.

As soon as all of the aircraft were masked off, those two men—Maal and Vrdla?—started hauling weapons pylons from the C-130, distributing them to the Phantoms.

Formsby was suitably impressed by the efficiency of Wyatt's team. No one complained, except good-naturedly, and generally the complaints were related to the heat. All had a job to do, or a series of jobs, and all took on their chores without orders from a superior.

As the crates came apart, revealing missiles, bombs, and countermeasures pods, Formsby carried the cast-off crates over to his pile of tape and stacked them on top. Just before they took off, he would set fire to the stack.

The pylons were mounted, including a pair each on the underside of the wings of both Hercules aircraft. Wyatt explained to him that the upgraded Phantoms had internal countermeasures derived from the F-15. The C-130s were each designated for a pair of countermeasures pods, and Kriswell and Vrdla dropped what they were doing to inspect and test the ALQ-72 countermeasures pods after they had been hoisted into place and fastened to the pylons.

By four o'clock, they had accomplished all they were going to accomplish in Algeria.

Each F-4, with paint barely dry to the touch, was outfitted with six five-hundred-pound bombs on the pylons and four Super Sidewinder missiles semi-recessed on the underside of the fuselage. With the external fuel tanks in place, they appeared almost too heavy for take-off.

All that was left on the pallets were ninety kilograms of plastic explosive and cotton-packed detonators, and they were carefully loaded aboard the transport by Borman, who had the experience with ordnance-handling.

Formsby had saved his best for last. At three o'clock he had wrapped big Idaho potatoes in tinfoil and shoved them into newly fired charcoal briquets. He served them at four-thirty with fresh butter, sour cream, and chives, alongside sixteen-ounce sirloin steaks, grilled to perfection.

He thought it was very American.

They got to wash it down with two cases of Coca-Cola that had been on ice for four hours.

"Neil," Barr asked, "how would you like to move to America?"

Colonel Ghazi, the army commander, arrived at Marada Air Base at five o'clock.

Ahmed al-Qati walked up the long ramp from the hangar to meet his airplane. He wanted a private discussion with his superior before the two of them met with Ramad.

The airstairs were lowered from the door of the Lockheed JetStar, and al-Qati climbed them quickly, before Ghazi could deplane.

He found the colonel still seated in one of the plushly cushioned swivelling chairs. His uniform shirt appeared freshly pressed, and it was pressed also from the inside-out by his large torso.

"Good, Ahmed. I am glad you came to meet me. Please take a seat."

Al-Qati sat across the aisle. "I thought perhaps we should have a few moments to talk between ourselves, Colonel."

"Yes, I had thought the same thing."

Al-Qati leapt right into what was bothering him. Bothering him? It was nearly killing him. Only Sophia helped him keep his sanity.

"This . . . this Test Strike is foolishness beyond comprehension. I fear the outcome will not be what is envisioned."

"The leadership feels otherwise, Ahmed. They firmly—very firmly—believe that the Israelis and Americans will view our country with heightened respect. Even with dread, which the Leader appears to desire more than respect."

"The world will damn us, Colonel Ghazi."

"I doubt the world will ever know. The Leader is certain that the Israelis will want to bury the incident. They are so beleaguered now, they will not want to admit publicly to another threat. And we know that the United States always goes along with them."

"But, the Ethiopians. . . ."

"Will say nothing. Theirs is a chaotic administration, and, if anything, they will be relieved that the draw on their food and medical resources will be lessened. I think you worry unduly," Ghazi said.

"In recent years, all countries run to the United Nations the minute they perceive a threat against them."

"So? Should it come out, we are only following orders."

"That excuse did not go over well at Nuremberg," al-Qati said.

"Nevertheless, we do have our orders, and we will follow them."

The army commander must be under a great deal of pressure to go along with this fantastic scheme, al-Qati thought. He had always respected Ghazi for his rationality under stress, but this was completely irrational.

"Colonel, I appeal to. . . ."

"In vain, I am afraid, Ahmed. We are committed."

Ghazi did not say that *he* was committed, but he had grouped himself with the powers that were.

"As you say, Colonel," al-Qati said. There was no other place to go, no other person to hear his argument.

"Now," Ghazi said, "let us proceed to what I wished to discuss with you. The People's Bureau,"—which was what the Leader had re-termed all of the embassies and consulates—"in Athens has forwarded to the intelligence bureau an interesting item."

Al-Qati waited with the appearance of attention, even though his stomach churned.

"The Bureau has several agents in Washington, of course, and one, a student at Georgetown University, collected a rumor that may concern us. There are several reporters from different newspapers, and from the Cable News Network, dashing around the city asking questions about a group of F-4 Phantom fighter aircraft."

"F-4 fighter airplanes?" al-Qati asked, just to be asking something.

"Indeed. Apparently, some men have prepared six of the airplanes for a special mission. The reporters appear to be grasping at straws, asking their sources what possible use the fighters could be put to. One theory in circulation concerns the chemical plant north of Marada."

"That is speculation."

"Very probably, Ahmed. And yes, rumors of other

targets abound—Syria, the Bekaa Valley, some in China. Still, it is interesting that our fertilizer factory is mentioned prominently, is it not?"

Al-Qati did not think it interesting. He thought it irrelevant.

"What is of greater interest, Ahmed, is that these airplanes disappeared from wherever they were being held shortly after the Leader took his decision on Test Strike."

Now, it was relevant. In al-Qati's world, timing was everything.

"Do you think, Colonel, that news of the strike plan has leaked?"

"It is possible, Ahmed. More and more people have acquired knowledge since the decision was taken."

"And the Americans will intervene?"

"I think not. Not as they did before. If it is to happen, it will be a covert operation, and that makes this rumor of unaffiliated fighter aircraft all the more suspicious."

"What do you wish me to do, Colonel?"

"Ramad listens primarily to himself. When I bring up the matter in our meeting, I would like to have your support."

"Of course. My support of you, or of my country, has never been in question."

Al-Qati meant that sincerely, but he was beginning to question just how blindly he was to follow the instructions issued in Tripoli.

At one o'clock in the morning, Janice Kramer parked her Riviera in the parking lot of the Four Seasons Motel, locked it, and entered the lobby. She was wearing

Levi's and a red, low-cut Mexican peasant blouse, and three guys in the lobby, who had struck out earlier in the evening, instantly started to get out of their chairs. She chilled them with an icy glare of her green eyes.

What she ought to be, she thought, is home, curled up on her couch with a brandy snifter, reveling in her future prospects as Mrs. Andrew Wyatt. Her elation, so far, had been curtailed by her worry.

What she ought not to be doing was running Martin Church's errands for him. He didn't even pay her. Except indirectly, maybe.

She damned sure wouldn't be here if the outcome wouldn't help Andy.

She crossed to the lounge, which wasn't being heavily utilized, and stood in the doorway for a few seconds, looking around.

"Hey, Jan!"

Arnie Gering raised his hand high from a booth on the sidewall.

She walked over to it, waving off the waitress, and sat across from him.

He eyed her blouse.

"Good to see you, Jan. I was sure glad you called."

"I have a proposal for you, Arnie."

"Yeah?"

"First, I need to know who you've talked to."

"About the Nebraska thing?"

God, he was dense.

"Yes, Arnie. About the Nebraska thing."

"Well, you know, I got hold of a reporter."

"Just one?"

"A couple, maybe."

"How many, Arnie?"

"Three."

"Newspaper reporters?"

"Oh, and one guy from CNN."

"Tell me what they said."

He squirmed on his bench seat. "Well, they were, I guess, skeptical."

"I can see why they would be."

"They wanted documentation. With documentation, they said, I could get some big bucks."

"How big?"

"Well, we haven't gotten to that stage yet. You know, you could print out some stuff from the computer for me, Jan. We could split it, like, sixty-forty."

"I get the sixty?"

"Well, I'm the one who made the calls, after all."

"What else did they say?"

"Just that they'd look into it. Ask around."

Church had told her that they were, indeed, asking around, but that they weren't finding anything substantial enough to go to print with. Unless they got curious enough to give Gering a first-class ticket to Washington.

Kramer pulled the stack of bills from her purse. They were bound with a rubber band, and she had been so angry with Church's suggestion that she didn't even put the sheaf in an envelope. He had called it "damage control," but she called it bribery. She laid it on the table and kept her hand on top of it.

Gering's eyes left her breasts and landed on the bills.

"That's ten thousand," she said.

"It's damned good-looking. Can I count it?"

"Trust me. You can have it."

Immediate suspicion crossed his face. "Yeah, but what's it cost me?"

"Your signature."

From her purse, she took the single sheet of paper and passed it across to him.

He struggled with it for a while, then said, "This is all legalese. What's it really say?"

"That you go to jail for fifteen to twenty years if you say one more word about . . . the Nebraska thing. It has to do with national security, Arnie."

He looked up at her then, and she saw the worry in his eyes. That made her feel better.

"Uh, they wouldn't . . ."

"They might pick you up any day and hold you for arraignment. What they're suggesting here is that it might be simpler to just make a deal."

She made liberal use of that magic "they." Everybody always worried about "them."

"I sign this, and I get the ten thou?"

"That's right. Then, if you say word one to anyone, you go right to Leavenworth. There won't be any trial involved."

She had written the agreement, following Church's suggestions, and used as much gobbledygook language as she could. It wouldn't stand up for more than thirty seconds in any courtroom in the land.

"And if any of those reporters call you back, you say you were having a bad dream or you were drunk."

Gering eyed the letter of agreement, then the stack of green.

"Got a pen?" he asked.

She found one, and he signed the agreement with a flourish. She took the paper, folded it, and put it in her purse. "This will be kept in Washington, in the Department of Justice probably."

In their trash can.

"Yeah. Can I have the money now?"

Kramer pushed the stack across the table to him, then stood up.

"Goodbye, Arnie."

"See you in the morning."

"No, you won't. You don't work for us, anymore. Remember that far back?"

He looked crestfallen.

"You sure?"

"I'm sure."

She turned and walked away from him.

He called after her, "Well, hey! Do I get a letter of recommendation?"

The briefing again included all wing and squadron commanders as well as Colonel Ghazi who had come to Marada to observe Test Strike. He sat now at one side of the room with al-Qati, Major Shummari, Captain Rahman of the First Special Forces Company, and Lieutenant Hakim, the Strike Platoon commander.

Ramad was appreciative of the deference he had been shown by Ghazi. The army commander had apparently been put in his place by Farouk Salmi and others close to the Leader.

After reports by the meteorological officer in regard to conditions expected on the day of the attack and the maintenance officer as to the readiness of all aircraft consigned to the exercise, Ramad had reviewed in detail the elements of the planned strike. In flights of three aircraft, three squadrons of Su-24s would strike the three identified targets at five o'clock on the morning of August 2. Three squadrons of MiG-23s would fly combat air patrol (CAP) for the bombers and the personnel transports. After being transported to a secret staging base in the Sudan by C-130s, Shummari's helicopters would insert the ground troops ten minutes after the initial bombardment. The villages were located in the province of Wallaga, near the border with Sudan. The troops would remain on the ground, establishing a defensive perimeter, for three hours, then be extracted. Three of the MiG-23s in the combat air patrol would be equipped with reconnaissance cameras and would shoot videotape of the entire mission, to supplement the photographs taken from the helicopters and from cameramen on the ground. The Leader wanted a complete photographic history of the exercise, perhaps in the event that American satellites overlooked the escapade.

"We will have at our disposal," Ramad continued, "four aerial tankers. It is important to note that our targets are twenty-two hundred kilometers away. A successful strike at that distance will certainly raise eyebrows in the right defense departments."

Al-Qati asked, "Have we secured the permission of the Sudanese to overfly, and to land, in Sudan?"

The man kept pestering over the most niggardly details. "Of course, Colonel al-Qati. They have approved a long-range training and refueling operation."

The Sudanese had not approved landing, establishing a staging base, or carrying live weapons over their territory, but Ramad knew that his combat elements would be down, into Ethiopia, and then out before the Sudanese military suspected and/or could react.

"We have promised to keep all aircraft well clear of Khartoum, which we will do," Ramad added, to increase his credibility.

Al-Qati sat back, but he did not appear particularly satisfied. Ramad would prefer to have him replaced, but part of the Leader's approval had been based upon utilizing his elite troop, and that meant al-Qati.

"At one o'clock on the morning of August second, I will release the appropriate chemical weapons to squadron commanders," Ramad said. "Each squadron leader will be accountable for all weapons assigned to him, and must provide a detailed report on their deployment."

Those reports would subsequently be destroyed. There would be no written record of this mission.

There would be only the photographs.

Captain Gamal Harisah of the first squadron sat up and raised his hand.

"Yes, Captain?"

"What will the ordnance load consist of, Colonel?"

"Two weapons per aircraft, six per target. We think that should be sufficient. Your wing commander will brief you before takeoff on wind conditions at the target sites so that we can strive for the best possible dispersal of the agents."

After several more mundane and routine questions, Ramad turned toward Ghazi. "Colonel Ghazi, you wished to speak to the group?"

"Yes, Colonel Ramad. Thank you."

Ghazi did not come to the podium, but rose from his chair and stood against the wall, careful to not get chalk from the blackboard on his uniform.

"Libyan Intelligence," he said, "has obtained information which, to be truthful, I rate as about twenty percent reliable. However, you should know that the potential exists for a strike against you, or this base, or the chemical plant, by clandestine aircraft."

Ramad cleared his throat. "Why was I not informed of this threat?"

"I am informing you now, Colonel. It is the primary reason I am here."

"These are American airplanes?" Ramad asked.

"Yes."

"And pilots?"

"That is unknown. It seems certain that the aircraft were prepared in the United States, but the operators are unknown."

"What type of aircraft?" Ramad demanded.

"The source says they are McDonnell Douglas F-4 Phantoms. That alone suggests that the operators could be of any nationality."

"F-4 fighters?" Ramad said. "Do we know how many are involved?"

"The source says six."

Ramad almost laughed aloud. "In its day, the F-4 was formidable. If this remote possibility proves itself out, Colonel, my MiG-23s will obliterate the threat quickly."

"Perhaps," Ghazi said. "All I am suggesting is that, as part of your planning, you might prepare a defensive contingency plan."

It was ridiculous. Ghazi's people spooked at the mere sight of a rumor on the horizon.

Al-Qati stood up. "That seems sensible to me. It would be a shame to have the glory of Test Strike overcome by world media reports that an antiquated airplane shot down another of our aircraft, even if only one."

The army man was playing with his pride of ownership of Test Strike, and Ramad was about to reject the game when he noted that his commanders were almost nodding in syncopation with al-Qati's speech.

"Very well," he said. "Captain Harisah, would you prepare a scenario and a reaction plan for me."

"Right away, Colonel Ramad."

Ramad then decided that he was not being forced into anything. If Ghazi were pleased, then others at the top would also be pleased. And if Ghazi were crying wolf at the door, and the wolf did not show up, then that was Ghazi's problem.

Wyatt sat in seven-seven, with the throttles at idle. The sweat was pouring from his forehead into his eyes, and he frequently used the back of his hand to sluice it to one side or the other.

He looked down the line in time to see Cliff Jordan raise his hand above his cockpit in triumph. The start cart was quickly disconnected from his F-4 and trundled back aboard the C-130.

Demion started turning the props on the Herc, and all four of them came on line.

Dennis Maal had taken off with the C-130F ten minutes before.

Wyatt hit the transmit stud. "Yuccas."

One after the other, they all checked in.

"Secure weapons," he said.

Again, they all checked in with affirmative responses. Wyatt made sure his own panel was secured. The safety pins were still inserted in the missiles and bombs, but it never hurt to be extra certain.

He leaned to the right and looked back toward the fuel trailers. Formsby emerged from his tent with a duffel bag, a bedroll, and a three-gallon can of gasoline. He crossed to the stack of crates and decorative tape, doused it thoroughly with gasoline, then struck a match.

The stack caught fire with a poof!

Formsby ran for the Hercules in his off-gaited ramble, went up the ramp, and then waved at the Phantoms before the ramp closed.

"Yucca, Wizard," Demion said.

"After you, Wizard."

The transport rolled slowly away, the props raising a cloud of fine dust, and Wyatt closed his canopy. The heat was intense, and his air-conditioning wasn't very effective at idle, on the ground.

He called off the numbers, and the F-4s swung into line behind the Hercules. Wyatt went last.

They got off the ground in better fashion than they had in landing, though it seemed to take longer even in afterburner. The takeoff roll was rough, bouncy, and long with the full load of ordnance. He was relieved when he felt the lift take over, and he pulled in his landing gear less than twenty feet off the ground.

He looked back once to see the bonfire raging next to the empty fuel tankers. If that fire got out of control, the fumes in those tanks would create a lot of shrapnel.

Jacque's fifty grand, resting on Formsby's cot, would go up in green smoke.

For Formsby's reputation among the scum of the earth, Wyatt hoped the money didn't burn.

He settled the Phantom in at a steady rate of climb of 150-feet-per-minute, and the whole formation ascended to twenty thousand feet. Aboard the Hercules, Kriswell and Formsby would be monitoring the threat receivers, but it was unlikely that there was a hostile, or friendly, radar set within a hundred miles of them.

Within twenty minutes, they caught up with Maal and the tanker. Wyatt eased the stick back, added power, and climbed to twenty-five thousand feet.

Looking down, he was pleased with the way the F-4s and the tanker blended into the landscape. They were damned hard to see, and if he hadn't known they were there, he would probably have missed them.

By contrast, the transport stuck out like a hitchhiker's thumb. The aluminum skin reflected the sun in piercing glints that hurt the eyes.

"You're pretty obvious, Wizard," he said.

"Not my fault," Demion replied. "We could have used a water-based paint."

"Shall we go back and get some?" Barr cut in.

"And miss the party?" Gettman asked.

"Okay," Wyatt interrupted. "I'm sorry I got this started. Let's can the chatter."

Their transmissions were scrambled, but a listener who happened to catch their frequency while it was in use, though he wouldn't understand the words, would certainly understand that there was something strange going on in the area.

Drifting along at 370 miles per hour, to stay with the C-130s at cruise, it took them an hour and a half to reach the border with Niger.

Formsby reported it. "That's Niger down there, if you didn't catch the change in landscape."

In fact, the government of Niger really needed to draw a big black line on its borders. The slowly undulating, barren scrub land didn't change at all.

"Yuccas," Wyatt radioed, "I'm going to take a look ahead."

He eased his throttles forward and gradually pulled out of the formation. Fifteen minutes later, the formation was out of sight behind him.

Wyatt used the NavStar Global Positioning System

to establish his position, then checked it against the co-ordinates he had written in his notebook.

He eased into a left turn, taking up a heading of eighty-four degrees.

He also reduced the power setting and started a slow descent.

He was over Chad.

Directly south of him was the village of Wour. Farther south was the depressing and devastated area of the Bodele Depression.

The earth ahead of him didn't look all that grand, either. The vegetation was almost nonexistent, and as far as he could tell, there wasn't one solid landmark that he would rely on. As soon as he locked his eyes on what he considered a hilltop, it dissolved into flatness.

He trusted to the readouts on his screen, and continued on course while he lost altitude. Libya, he was certain, was careful about patrolling its borders. The flights might be infrequent, but they would occur.

As he came within twenty miles of the Libyan border, he was flying at three hundred feet AGL, hopefully below any airborne radar coverage.

He almost missed it.

Blinking his eyes against the sunset glare off the desert, he picked it up again.

A single short airstrip.

It had been built, then later abandoned, by the French, who often found themselves assisting Chad in putting down aggression by its neighbors. There were two buildings, old hangars, but their roofs had caved in.

He flew low down the runway, noting the cracks in the asphalt and a few chuckholes along the right side.

Midway down, there were a couple of gaping holes on the left side.

Incongruously, the remnants of an old wind sock still fluttered from a pole at the corner of one hangar. It hung dead still.

Wyatt leaned into a right turn.

"Wizard, Yucca One."

"Go, One."

"We don't have a welcoming committee; we don't have anything worth noting. We're in business."

"What kind of business?"

"Somewhat perilous. You'll need to put down at oh-one-oh, and keep it tight to the left side of the strip. There's a few holes on the right. Halfway down, veer slightly to the right, so you can miss the holes on the left side. Like the satellite snapshots told us, it's short. We'll be using the drag chutes."

"You mind if I take a look for myself, before I try it?" Demion asked.

"Chicken," Barr put in.

"Don't waste fuel," Wyatt said.

Formsby interrupted. "I happen to be on this bird, and I second your motion, James. That's why I brought along a couple thousand extra gallons."

Thirteen

Barr was the fourth one on final approach.

Far ahead he could see Gettman turn off the runway, dragging his arresting chute behind him.

With the sun low, the shadows were tricky. Black splotches on the earth, or on the runway, could be two inches deep or two feet deep.

He touched rudder and stick lightly and danced to the left, lining up on the left side of the runway.

Inched the throttles back and felt the fighter sag.

Selected full flaps.

The Phantom bounced upward with the added lift, but not excessively. She was carrying a full complement of weaponry, plus the drop tanks, and she was heavy. Under normal circumstances, the idea was to lose the bombs and missiles before landing.

Barr remembered an extended exercise he had taken part in when he was still an active military pilot. His squadron of Phantoms had moved to a hastily assembled training base in Panama to practice working out of a forward area airfield. The strip was short, utilizing PSP—Pierced Steel Planking—for a surface, and the landings were arrested, taking advantage of the F-4's arresting hook. They did it like the Navy boys did it, except that the runway didn't shift directions unexpectedly or act like a yo-yo.

On a day when they were using live ordnance—bombing a bunch of floating oil barrels chained together in the Pacific Ocean, he had a bomb hang-up. The nose of the bomb dropped, pulling the tethered cable, and allowing the small propeller on the nose to rotate and arm the bomb. The bomb's rear hanger didn't release from the pylon, however. His wingman told him the bomb was locked in place, with the nose at a forty-five-degree angle to the wing.

He tried everything to shake it loose. Jiggling the plane, going into negative Gs, a barrel roll. It stayed right where it was.

The wing commander got involved, telling him to ditch the plane, but Barr thought it was a pretty good airplane. He was offered one of the Army's runways in the Canal Zone, but thought about having that bomb come loose and hit something populated. He took it into the short field which was at least isolated in the jungle.

With gear, flaps, wing slats, and arresting hook down, he floated that Phantom in toward the three sets of arresting cables. It felt featherlight to him, floating, floating. He missed the first cable, caught the second, came to an abrupt and jarring halt, and slammed the airplane on the ground. He scrambled out of the cockpit, slid to the ground, and ran about a half-mile away.

The bomb was still hanging on the pylon, but the Bomb Disposal Unit had only to lift the nose six inches to have the rear hanger release.

It felt the same way this time.

Barr floated the F-4 toward the darkening runway,

felt the main gear touch down, then chopped the throttles.

Punched out the drag chute.

The chuckholes on the right side—black irregular ebony voids—whisked by in his peripheral vision.

Nose gear down.

There was sand and dirt and clods on the runway. The wheels kicked it up, and he heard the clunks against the skin of the fuselage and wings.

Easing in the brakes.

Halfway down the strip?

Started slewing the nose to the right.

The right brake pedal went soft.

A black spot leapt out at him.

Thunked into it.

The airplane tried to leap to the left.

Rocked sideways.

Keep the right wing up.

Easy now.

What the hell?

Blown left tire.

Again moving to the right.

The left gear back down on the ground.

Screeching.

Tearing up the wheel rim.

Fighting the pull to the left.

Slowing.

The aircraft bucked and fought his control, then finally slid to a stop.

"Yucca Two?" asked Wyatt from the sky above.

"Blown tire," Barr radioed back as he opened the canopy. "Hold everyone off until I see if I can get it off the runway."

"Roger, Two."

"Yucca Four, Two," Barr radioed.

"Four," Gettman replied.

"You want to get out of your bird and run over and drop a flare in that first pothole?"

"Roger, Two. I'll see what I can do."

Jockeying the throttles, Barr spun the plane to the left, dragging on the wheel rim. He figured all of the rubber of the tire had shredded off. He used three-quarter throttle on the left turbojet, and the Phantom edged its way forward, then off the runway. The wheel dug a deep rut in the earth and bogged down. The tail of the F-4 was still protruding over ten feet of the runway.

He killed the engines.

"Yucca One, Two."

"Go, Two."

"Let's get Wizard down next. I need a tractor and a spare tire. And Wizard, please be advised my ass-end is still on the runway."

He turned on his navigation lights to give Demion a clear indicator of where the F-4 was located.

Just to be certain, Barr released himself from his couplings, jammed the safety pin in the ejection seat, and slipped over the coaming of the cockpit. He lowered himself down the fuselage side until he was hanging by his fingers, then released his hold. He hit the ground hard enough to sting his ankle.

He hobbled a couple hundred feet away to watch the Herc come in.

Gettman's flare, in the bottom of the chuckhole, provided the warning Demion needed without blinding him. The big transport glided in, burned a little rubber, then veered toward the right side of the strip. When he had slowed enough, he turned left and came toward

Barr, rumbling past the wounded Phantom and off the runway.

Minutes later, Win Potter drove the tractor down the ramp, hooked a tow bar to the nose gear of the F-4, and dragged it twenty feet from the strip.

Wyatt began landing the rest of the planes.

It was almost nine o'clock before they had the wheel and tire changed and the fighters and C-130s lined up near the wreckage of the two old hangars.

Wyatt forbid the use of any major lights, not wanting to attract the attention of any possible airborne border patrol. Pilots and technicians used penlights to perform their postflight checks. They made certain that bombs and missiles had not been damaged by rock debris on the runway.

From the two drums of water they had brought along, Formsby passed out rations in small cardboard pails. That was for bathing, getting the sweat and dirt out of the pores. Hank Cavanaugh issued MREs, but few of them were very interested in eating.

It was too hot.

It stayed that way long after the sun went down and a billion brilliant stars came out. Wyatt allowed a single red light to be illuminated in the cargo bay of the Hercules, where everyone gathered, some to try and sleep. A chess game got underway, as did a four-handed game of poker.

Barr and Formsby walked up the ramp, passed through the cargo bay, and joined Wyatt in the crew compartment. A dim glow of cerise light spilled through the hatchway.

Since the bunks had been removed, they sat on the floor, leaning against the bulkheads.

"You handled that landing well, Bucky," Wyatt said.

Barr shrugged. "Part of the territory we walk."

"I admit to being somewhat concerned about the ordnance load you were carrying," Formsby said.

"I thought about it some myself," Barr said.

He really hadn't considered it deeply, though. The reflexes and the instinct assumed command in times of crisis, and the mind kind of followed along. His responses with the stick, rudder, throttles, and brakes had been automatic; he hadn't thought about what action to take at all.

"Did you guys have time to think about what Church wants us to do?" Wyatt asked. "About catching Ramad's aircraft on the ground on the morning of the second?"

"I did think about it," Formsby said. "Being an air controller with nothing to control allows a certain flexibility of time. I think he's right."

"Ditto," Barr said. "If we go up against those blast doors with five-hundred-pounders, we're only going to leave dents behind."

"All right, then. That means we sit here through the day tomorrow and hope no stray Mirage spots us."

"With no appreciable amount of time over target, however," Barr said, "it would be helpful to know Ramad's thoughts on a takeoff time."

"Dawn is likely," Formsby said. "I don't think many Libyan pilots like to fly at night."

"If all we had to do was intercept the flight, we could hide out over the Sudan and pounce on them," Wyatt said. "But half our mission is delivering HE against the chem plant. We're a little short of aircraft and ordnance type for what we're facing."

"Do you want to change the roles for the C and D

246

models, Andy?" Barr asked. "We could load bombs on the centerline and move their missiles to the E models."

"It's a thought, Bucky. Let's keep it on the desk for the time being."

"The crucial point," Formsby said, "is still Ramad's takeoff time. Do you suppose your spies have determined anything more?"

"Not my spies. But we can call 'em and find out," Barr said. "With all of the risks currently involved, I think we can add the risk of a short radio call. I should think they've got their satellites still in position unless they've given up on us."

"They received my transmission a couple days ago without apparent trouble," Formsby said.

"Hokay," Wyatt said and got his feet under him. "It's still afternoon in D.C."

He went to the console and powered up the radios. Selecting the Tac One set, he punched in the frequency numbers that Embry had given him.

Barr got up and went to stand beside him.

Wyatt depressed the transmit button and said, "Paper Doll, this is Yucca Flight."

The response was immediate. The NSA people were monitoring them closely.

"Yucca, this is Doll."

"I need to talk to Paper Doll One or Two."

That was Church or Embry.

"Stand by, Yucca, I'll see what we can do."

It was twenty minutes later before they heard Church's voice.

"Yucca Flight, Paper Doll One."

"I've been waiting for this," Barr said. "Can I talk to him?"

Wyatt waved him toward the desk microphone.

Barr picked it up and said, "Hello, Dolly."

Formsby laughed.

A very sober Church said, "I trust you're in place."

"Righto," Barr said. "We have a need for data."

"What data?"

"The Test Strike launch time."

"We haven't gotten anything yet, but I'm hopeful. I'll call as soon as I know anything, but at least by 4:00 A.M. your time."

"0400 on the first of August?" Barr asked. "It's almost that, now."

"0400 on the first," Church confirmed.

"Yucca out," Barr said, dropping the mike back on the console. "Hell, I might as well go find an oasis."

"See if they've got take-out, will you, Bucky?" Formsby said.

For the duration of the exercise, Lieutenant Colonel Ahmed al-Qati had established the encampment for the First Special Forces Company one kilometer east of the Marada Air Base. Major Khalil Shummari's helicopter crews were also stationed at the cantonment area.

The tents were aligned in neat rows, and many of his enterprising soldiers had suspended parachute canopies inside the tents, to trap a layer of insulating air between the canopy and the tent roof. The construction detracted several degrees from the forty degree Celsius temperatures that were being achieved during the day.

The first tent in the first row was utilized as the headquarters tent, and al-Qati met there with Shummari and Captain Rahman late at night.

"With the information leakage that takes place in

Tripoli," he told them, "I would not be at all surprised if Test Strike is common knowledge in the West."

Shummari nodded.

"And since I prefer to be prepared for all contingencies, I am going to assume that an air assault by—it doesn't matter by whom, is an imminent possibility."

"That would fall to the province of the air defense organization, would it not?" Rahman asked.

"It should, yes, Ibn. However, I am also concerned that Colonel Ramad does not take the threat seriously. His staff and pilots are preparing a plan, but I believe that their hearts are not in it."

"We must work from assumptions," Shummari said.

"Yes, we must. First, I assume that the attack would be launched as preemptive of Test Strike, and therefore, must come prior to the morning of August second.

"Second, I assume that aircraft of the American Sixth Fleet will not be utilized, as being too obvious. This assumption is partially supported by the intelligence report of F-4 aircraft being prepared."

"Not by the Israelis?" Rahman asked.

"That is possible, but I think no one will want to point fingers at the Americans or the Israelis—that is, to the sea, or to the east. The attack will come from the west or from the south."

"It may not happen," Shummari said.

"It may not, and we will be all the happier. However, in the event that it does, what can we do?"

"I will keep my SA-7 air defense missiles on alert," Rahman said.

"And I can load air-to-air missiles aboard the four Mi-28s," Shummari added.

"Good. And I am afraid that is the extent of our air defense capability. But I want to think beyond that.

With Ramad's MiG-23 interceptors ranged against the F-4s, it is likely that one, or perhaps two, of the intruders will be shot down. Ibn, I want your Strike Platoon ready to take off at any moment. Khalil, we will need to assign two of your Mi-8s to them. We want to be the first on the scene of a downed aircraft, to gather evidence, hopefully to capture a pilot alive."

"I see where you are going with this," Shummari said.

"Yes. If the attack occurs prior to Test Strike's launch time, perhaps we can prove to our superiors that knowledge of the exercise is widespread."

"You would like them to call it off?" Rahman asked.

"Absolutely."

"I would like that, also," the captain said.

Al-Qati looked to Shummari.

The aviation company commander nodded his approval.

The two officers left him alone with his thoughts, which was not particularly good for him. His mind was divided along two paths lately, and he was never certain which path he would travel.

He was extremely tired of worrying about Ramad's ambitious designs.

He preferred wandering the path of Sophia.

And he looked to the back of the tent, where the radio set was located on a spindly-legged table.

Rising from the camp stool he sat on, he carried it back to the radio.

He called his battalion headquarters in El Bardi and had the radio operator dial the telephone number for him, then connect him with the landline.

She was waiting, as she always was. Al-Qati thought

that a statement in itself. Any time he called, she was waiting. It elated him.

"Yes?"

"Sophia, it is Ahmed."

"Wonderful! You are here?"

"Alas, no. I just have a few minutes, and I wished to fill them with your voice."

"Ahmed, you are too charming."

"That is not the image I have of myself," he admitted.

"Nonsense. When will I see you again?"

"As soon as this exercise is completed. I think that it should be soon."

"When does it begin? So that I might count the hours."

He almost told her, but then remembered he was on an open radio link.

Also, a little question mark popped into his mind.

It was on the path labeled, "Sophia."

Wyatt had difficulty getting to sleep. The interior of the Hercules had become stifling, and he had moved his sleeping bag outside, under the transport, and sprawled out on top of it, draping his mosquito net over his head. The heat of the earth seeped through. There wasn't a whisper of a breeze.

All around him, others had also unrolled their sleeping bags and wrapped their mosquito netting around them. They had brought tents with them, but no one was eager to erect one.

Night in the desert brought with it creeping, crawling animation, and several times, he felt, or thought he felt, something walking on his legs. He shook it off, real or imagined.

He wasn't alone. Occasionally, he heard someone slapping at clothing.

A few had given up and gone back into the Hercules, preferring heat to insects.

The only real positive was that, with no pollution to taint the air, the starscape was a dazzler. He could see infinity, and he could believe in it.

He was worried about the air strike and all of the things that could go wrong. He was halfway amazed that they had made it to the staging base with only the loss of one tire.

Though he felt relatively confident in the upgraded F-4s, he didn't want to become overconfident. The MiG-23 was still a worthy adversary. Barr had made some sense in suggesting they turn the C and D models into strict bombers and use the F-4Es as air superiority fighters, rather than try to accomplish both missions with one platform.

But he still thought his strategy would work against the MiGs, and that would be their salvation. Zimmerman's F-4C and Jordan's F-4D were expendable and would remain that way.

He rolled over onto his side and pillowed his head on his forearm.

On the faraway horizon, in the stars, he saw Jan's face.

He was glad he had been forced into finally admitting his love to her. He had known it for some time, of course, but he had had as much difficulty making the realization known to himself as he had had in making it known to her.

If he had a regret, it was that this mission interfered

with his emotional awakening. It didn't help him, and it certainly wouldn't help her if his Phantom went out from under him. He hated raising false hopes for her.

He had almost closed his eyes when a bulky shadow crawled across the sand toward him.

"Andy, you asleep?"

He whispered back, "Wouldn't it be better to ask if I were awake, Bucky?"

"Same coin," Barr said, scooting around to sit back on his broad buttocks. "Got a question for you."

"Is it answerable?"

"Maybe not."

"Shoot."

"I've been worrying about Kramer."

"Don't. Worry about Ibrahim Ramad."

"Go to hell. I know what her problem is."

"Do you?"

"Yeah. I think you're screwing her over."

"Why is that, Bucky?"

"I mean, everybody knows you two have a thing for each other."

"Do they?"

"No secrets around our place. Now, goddamn it, I want you to treat her right. Either marry her or break it off."

"I haven't heard your question yet, Bucky."

"You going to do what I say?"

"You want to be best man?"

Barr pored over that one for a full second. "Good night, Andy."

"Night, Bucky."

Despite his skepticism over the rumor of some silly

253

effort to interfere with his plans by antiquated fighter aircraft, the report had chaffed at Ibrahim Ramad all day long.

He conceded to himself that it was possible.

His proposal had been making the rounds of the military and political hierarchy for three months. Someone may have slipped, a loosened tongue dropping hints that analysts loved to manipulate and decode. Perhaps a People's Bureau minister in some foreign city. He did not know all of those to whom the Leader may have confided the plan.

It was possible.

He sat in his office most of the evening, worrying about the possibility and the possible outcomes if it were true. It did not matter who the opposition was. If they knew the date and time, and if he were them, he would certainly attack before Ramad's aircraft took to the air.

That meant tomorrow.

Early in the morning, he would place the interceptors on twenty-four hour alert.

Or, if they knew the time, and he were them, he would attack while the bombers were on the ground, out of the hardened hangars.

Six F-4s?

His pilots would down six F-4s in a matter of minutes. What was he worried about?

He would order his personal MiG-23 prepared, and he would lead the counterattack. It could not hurt his career aspirations.

But what if one of the attackers got through and destroyed an Su-24 on the ground, detonating chemical warheads? The gas would permeate Marada Air Base, sucked into the ventilators. He would be remembered, not for developing a successful strategy and forcing the Israelis to cower in their corner of the world, but for his culpability in the deaths of Libyan airmen and base personnel.

Allow this thought: some clandestine fighter-bombers would attack Marada Air Base between, say, four o'clock in the morning and eight o'clock on the morning of August 2.

It could happen.

It might not happen.

But even the possibility could be circumvented.

Ramad smiled to himself.

Then called the sergeant at the duty desk. "I want all wing and squadron commanders in the briefing room immediately. Notify Colonel Ghazi of the meeting. Send a truck to the encampment for Colonel al-Qati and Major Shummari."

He made some other calls.

It was eleven-twenty at night before they were all assembled in the briefing room next to his office.

Ramad stood at the podium and smiled.

"I have put my mind to the problem raised by Colonel Ghazi, and I have determined the solution."

Some of his subordinates smiled their appreciation. Ghazi and al-Qati waited stoically.

"This base is now on full-alert. I have ordered tanker aircraft from Tripoli. We will put the first defensive cover squadron into the air within the hour. Given the possibility of information leaks, I have shut down the telephone system. No phone calls may be made from here, or accepted from elsewhere, for the next forty-eight hours.

"Test Strike is moved up one day. We will launch the C-130s with Colonel al-Qati's company and Major

Shummari's helicopters at precisely,"—he glanced at his watch—"four-twenty-seven. The bombers will depart at five-forty.

"I would advise all commanders to leave here now and prepare your units.

"Are there any questions?"

There were quite a few.

Martin Church accepted the call on his secure line. It was the DCI.

"Martin, I'm afraid I have bad news."

"What is that, sir?"

"We just don't have enough to go on, and I can't convince the right people. Icarus is cancelled."

"But, sir. . . ."

"Get hold of your team and turn them back."

Fourteen

George Embry's office was not as large as Church's, and it was made even smaller by the dominant, double-sized poster of Madonna in a classic Marilyn Monroe pose on one wall.

"Jesus, George. Why did you put that up there?"

"To remind me of the love of my life."

"Not Madonna?"

"No, Marty. Women."

Church skirted the corner of the square conference table, which had been shoved against the wall opposite Madonna, and sat in a chair next to Embry.

"Welcome to the high-tech African desk, Marty."

"I see."

There were two high-resolution monitors on the table, along with a blue telephone and a green telephone.

"I want you to understand that this stuff isn't in my budget, Marty. I cajoled them out of the NSA's rent-to-own program."

"We could have just driven out to Fort Meade."

The National Security Agency, which was responsible for the monitoring and interception of electronic communications, was located at Fort George G. Meade,

Maryland. It was the largest agency in the intelligence community, and, though it was an agency of the Department of Defense, worked closely with the CIA on the development of foreign intelligence.

"I've got other irons in the fire, too, Marty. I don't want to sit around out there for two days. Look, the blue phone is a direct link to NSA, so Cummings can reach me."

Marianne Cummings had a tiny transceiver concealed somewhere in her hotel room. It had a range of only a mile but a relay and satellite up-link was emplaced in one of Tobruk's derelict buildings within that range.

"The green phone is hooked into the Air Force's CRITICOM satellite communications system, which we're borrowing for our link with Wyatt." He pointed to a blank monitor. "That one is decorative, I think. They tell me I can get maps and the like if I ask for them, but I haven't asked. The other monitor is giving us a live, near real-time shot of the region from a KH-11 they've moved into geo-stationary orbit."

"I can't tell shit from that," Church said.

"Well, the orbit is over the equator, some twenty-two hundred miles south of Wyatt's position. Then, too, you're seeing light-enhanced, night-vision video. Plus, the lens is at the limit of its telescopic ability, and the angle and the distance make things a little fuzzy. See this dark blue stuff at the top of the screen? That's the Med."

"I picked right up on that, George."

"Then, down here, where they've superimposed a red circle? That's Marada. The runway is painted in camouflage colors, but the high-tech tinkerers have outlined it for us with white lines. They're great guys over there."

"And the yellow circle is Wyatt?"

"You've got it, Marty. Go to the head of the photo analysis class. One other thing, they can get us infrared, also."

"For what?"

"Live video of camouflaged aircraft against the desert may not show us anything. If it doesn't, we can pick up on their heat trails."

"All right. So what are they doing?"

"Nothing. Same thing they've been doing for lo, these many hours. Actually, I can call and have them put up earlier tapes on the other monitor, if you want to see a flight of MiGs take off from Marada or Wyatt's people landing at the staging base. They all look like the little airplanes you see on computer games."

"I'll pass. What were the MiGs doing?"

"Normal recon or air defense patrol, I think. They flew the border with Egypt, then returned to base."

Church leaned back in his chair, and Embry got up to refill his mug from a drip coffee maker on the credenza behind his desk.

"Want some, Marty?"

"No, I'm coffeed out. Did you get anything from Cummings on a time line?"

"Not yet. I have to wait until she calls. Won't do to ring her up, if someone's in the room with her, you know."

"I promised to contact Wyatt at four his time with any new data. That'll be eight o'clock tonight our time."

"I can count, Marty."

"You don't want to break policy and call her?"

"No. I want her to live through this. Oops."

"What?" Church asked.

"Look here," Embry said, pointing to the red circle on the screen.

Two aircraft had appeared, as if out of nowhere. Church understood that they had been underground. They rolled onto the outlined runway and paused.

The two men waited.

The jets began moving, gathering speed quickly, then rising from the runway and moving out of the red circle.

"MiG-23s I think," Embry said.

"They make many night flights, George?"

"Not very many."

"So this is unusual."

"Yes."

"I don't like unusual, George. Or surprises."

"Am I going to get a surprise?" Embry asked.

"Yes. You can send all this stuff back to Meade. Call Wyatt and tell him his vacation is over."

"Bullshit."

"No. The DCI can't get sign-off."

"I am going to call the son of a bitch," Embry said.

"No, you're not."

Embry's eyes burned hot. "Marty, get on that fucking phone and stand your ground. If I recall this mission, I walk."

Church studied him for a full two minutes, then walked his castered chair over to the desk, picked up the phone, and asked Embry's secretary to locate the Director.

When somebody found him, he said, "Yes, Martin?"

"Mr. Director, the time for politicking is over. I want an executive order for Icarus, and I want it on my desk in the next two hours."

"Martin? What the hell?"

260

"You started this shit, and you'd better damn well finish it. We're not playing one-upsmanship in this room. You go, you beg, you borrow, you spend your favors, you do what you have to do to back up what you started."

"Martin. . . ."

Church hung up.

He felt good.

He also felt unemployed.

Ahmed al-Qati and Khalil Shummari drove directly back to their cantonment area from Ramad's briefing. The whining roar of a second pair of MiG fighters taking off from the base deferred any talk. Shummari got out of the truck beside one of his Mi-28 assault helicopters.

He leaned back into the cab. "Well, Ahmed?"

"There is no choice to be made, Khalil. I will give my men another hour's sleep, then wake them and have them prepare their gear."

The major nodded. "I will begin moving my helicopters to the base soon. We will need to fuel them, fold the rotors, and load them aboard the transports."

"Go with God, Khalil. And be prepared for the devil to strike."

Al-Qati drove on to the headquarters tent, shut off the ignition, and walked inside. An older sergeant manned the duty desk, which was composed simply of a folding table and a telephone.

"Sergeant, take a few minutes' break, then, at one-thirty, awaken the officers. At two o'clock, begin waking the rest of the company."

"Yes, Colonel."

The sergeant left the tent, and al-Qati went to sit on the camp stool behind the desk.

He thought Ramad's decision precipitous and foolish. Accelerating the launch time would only heighten the problems. There would be mistakes made, and they would be costly mistakes. As far as it went, the exercise was well-planned, but throw in a few unexpected developments, and many things would go wrong. The cost could be counted in lives.

Al-Qati thought that Ramad was exchanging lives for his own advancement.

Worse, he was certain that Colonel Ghazi was also aware of Ramad's self-interest, but Ghazi was apparently powerless. He would not speak up against the sycophants surrounding the Leader, Salmi and Amjab.

It would be far better, in al-Qati's view, to delay Test Strike for a week and see if the suspected incursion took place first. The country would best be served by devoting her resources to defense at this moment, rather than to boasting her offensive capabilities.

And far worse, he thought, could be the international consequences of the folly to be executed in Ethiopia. The demonstration of offensive strength might well have gone as Ramad envisioned—unattributed, yet faintly identifiable—had the information not leaked from some source in Tripoli.

Or from Tobruk, as he had come to suspect.

Sophia.

Al-Qati called Ramad foolish, and even Ghazi, but he knew in his heart that the most foolish of all was himself. He had disgorged everything, or almost everything, he knew to the gorgeous creature in the Seaside Hotel.

And he loved her. He knew that he did.

But she used him, abused him, probed in catlike ways for the secrets he held.

And he coughed them up so willingly!

How she must laugh at him.

He was heartsick and humiliated.

And responsible for the deaths that would come.

He heard the whine of helicopter turbines starting. Shummari was moving his company to Marada.

The gases would writhe like maddened snakes across the barrenness of Ethiopia.

But he need not be the root of that evil, of innocents sent to the slaughter.

Rising from the stool, he walked back to the radio, dialled the frequency for the battalion radio, and asked for a connection with the telephone system.

She was always there, of course, and at one-twenty in the morning, likely sound asleep. The telephone rang three times before she answered.

"Yes?"

"I am sorry to awaken you, Sophia." His voice sounded flat and dead, even to himself.

"Ahmed! Where are you?"

"I call only to tell you that you may start counting the hours from four-thirty this morning."

"What?"

"Are you awake? Did you understand me? Four-thirty this morning."

"Ahmed. . . ."

He broke the connection.

He could not know whether or not she would believe either him or his information.

She now knew that he knew.

And that was that.

Ibrahim Ramad walked slowly through the underground hangars, moving from one to another as the preparations continued. The ground crews were slowly coming awake after being jarred out of sound sleep. The ordnance men worked as if they walked on eggs, and perhaps they did.

Ramad had released the chemical warheads earlier. He had not signed for them, since no record was to exist of their deployment. Even the fuel requisitioned for the aircraft involved was to remain unaccounted for and charged to evaporation.

In two of the hangars, nine of the Su-24 bombers were being fitted with the bombs on the inboard pylons. The outboard pylons, on the pivoting wings, would carry four AA-8 air-to-air missiles in the event of an attack on the bombers. Ramad thought the missiles would go unused.

The nine planes were formed into three squadrons, to be called Red, Green, and Purple for this mission. Each squadron carried one type of chemical bomb, toxin, psychological, or nerve agent. The advance party in the C-130s was codenamed Black, and the escort for the bombers, composed of eight MiG-23s, was to be called Orange.

Before the infantry company left, Ramad would personally select one man in each platoon to carry and use the sealed still and video cameras. The photographic record was to be complete and close to the action.

Ramad's nine MiG-23s would stay in-country, securing Marada Air Base with round-the-clock patrols of four aircraft each, two patrolling to the west and two to the south. Four MiG-23s would stay on full alert at the end of the runway, prepared for instantaneous launch.

He stopped to watch the loading of AA-6 and AA-7 missiles on the pylons of a MiG-23, part of the Orange air cover. These, too, would not be used, he was certain.

His personal MiG-23 was already outfitted with AA-8 missiles and a full magazine for the twin-barreled 23 millimeter cannon. It would be moved up to the runway, with the avionics warmed up, and be instantly available the moment he decided to leave. He stopped beside it and gazed at his name stenciled below the cockpit canopy.

Ramad almost hoped that the rumor proved to be grounded in fact and was not simply a scare tactic. The Americans frequently did that—leak threats that never came to fruition.

An F-4 did not frighten him. His J-band radar, which NATO called "Jay Bird," had a search range of twenty-five kilometers and was nearly the equivalent of that in the F-4. With radar range comparisons nullified, he was confident that the MiG-23 could outfly and out-maneuver the F-4.

He saw Gamal Harisah preflighting his aircraft and crossed the hangar to join him.

"Good morning, Colonel."

"Good morning, Captain. What do you think?"

"They do not even look like bombs, Colonel."

The cannisters were almost blunt-nosed, and they were three hundred millimeters in diameter, perhaps two meters long. They were finished in a matte gray. It was almost ludicrous how such unassuming cans could contain such a fatal substance.

The ordnance specialist moved with careful precision as he connected the arming tether between the bomb and the pylon. Once the bomb dropped, the arming pin would be extracted, starting the internal clock. After the clock registered ten seconds, the bomb would be fully armed. Its barometric altimeter was set for two thousand meters, six hundred meters above ground level at the target site for the Purple Squadron. When the bomb reached that altitude, a one-kilogram explosive charge would detonate, destroying the cannister and releasing the nerve agent to the winds.

"The meteorologist," Harisah said, "told me to expect ten-knot winds along the foothills near the target. With a half-kilometer spacing between airplanes, we are going to release four kilometers upwind from the village. The dispersal should achieve a wide range from that point."

"Good, good," Ramad said.

Purple Target, an unnamed village, was not even a village. The camp was a collection of tin and fabric tents, goats, camels, dogs, and at last count, thirty-two hundred emaciated and diseased people. The last photographs, taken two weeks before, showed several white United Nations trucks parked near the camp, so there might be some UN workers there. Then again, there might not be. Ramad was not going to worry unduly about it at this point.

He crossed the hangar to the back, entered the tunnel, and double-checked that the doors to the chemical weapons stores were locked before walking back to his office.

He was getting impatient.

Test Strike was going to be a huge success, insuring his participation in the policy development group that surrounded the Leader.

In fact, he was so confident of the exercise that he

found himself daydreaming about Americans or Israelis insane enough to attack Marada Air Base.

He wanted so much for it to be true. He needed the diversion.

He was still daydreaming when Colonel Ghazi appeared in his doorway.

Startled, he looked up. "Oh. Colonel Ghazi. Please come in."

"There was just one thought I wished to share with you, Ibrahim."

"Certainly."

"What defensive precautions have you taken for the chemical plant?"

"The chemical plant? They have their own air defense system of antiaircraft guns and missiles."

"Do you suppose that is sufficient?"

"It does not matter, Colonel. It is not my jurisdiction."

"It is now," Ghazi told him.

At six-fifteen in the evening, Martin Church was thinking seriously of going home early and crawling in bed. Tomorrow night was going to be a long one, and he wanted to be as fresh as possible.

He got up and took his suit jacket from its hanger on the hall tree behind the door.

He was shrugging his way into it when the phone in the outer office rang.

He called through the doorway, "I don't want to take that, Sally."

"Right, boss." She answered, then called back to him, "It's for you."

"I just said. . . ."

Through the doorway, she mouthed, "The Director."

Church crossed to his desk and picked up.

"Martin, you've got your go-ahead."

His sigh of relief was almost audible. "Thank you, sir."

"Your information had better be accurate. This cost me two years' worth of political points."

"I believe in it."

"Good. I'll try."

The Director hung up.

The man might even earn Church's respect, if he kept this pace up.

He dialled Embry's office.

"You've got your go-signal, George."

"It's about damned time."

"You can cancel the abort."

"I never bothered to abort. I trusted you, Marty."

"Oh, Jesus."

"Come on down here," Embry said.

"What now, George?"

"Come on down here. Quick!"

With that much urgency in Embry's voice, Church just slapped the phone down and headed for the elevator.

When he got there, he found a disheveled Embry hunched over his table before the monitors, scribbling notes on a yellow legal pad.

The scene on the screen didn't seem to have changed much until he looked closer. There were large aircraft on the runways at Marada Air Base.

"What's going on?"

"Those are C-130s, Marty. Right now, they're loading helicopters."

"Whose helicopters?"

Embry pointed at the blue phone. "NSA tells me they go with al-Qati's First Special Forces Company."

"So they're moving them somewhere?"

"Apparently. Sit down, Marty."

Church dropped into one of the straight-backed chairs at the table.

"I got a signal from Cummings."

"Okay, good."

"They're going at 0430 hours."

"That soon?"

"Today. Today in Libya, anyway."

"Shit."

"You want to call Wyatt, or should I?"

"I'd better do it."

Ben Borman woke Wyatt.

"What?"

Borman turned the penlight on his own face.

"Hey, Ben, what time is it?"

"0223 hours, Andy. You're wanted on the radio."

"Damn. He wasn't going to call until four."

Wyatt rolled over, pushed himself onto his knees, and slipped out from under the Hercules. Now, it was cold. Either that, or he couldn't adapt to the range of temperature change in this desert.

He followed Borman through the hatchway into the crew compartment and picked up the desk microphone on the console. A red light for night work had been rigged above the unit.

"Yucca One."

"Paper Doll One, Yucca. I've got some new and hot data for you."

"How hot?"

"This is just off the wire. They're jumping off at 0430 hours."

"Okay, we'll be ready."

"That's 0430, one August."

"Goddamn it!" Wyatt said, involuntarily checking his wristwatch. "What happened?"

"They may have tumbled to you, and moved up the deadline to get a jump on you."

"That's nice to know."

"Also, our source thinks she's been uncovered. She's going to get on the first plane out of the country."

"This only gives us a couple hours," Wyatt said.

"Maybe more. The analysts think, because of the distance involved, the transports will leave with the infantry first. As a matter of fact, we can see them loading choppers now. Paper Doll Two has made some calculations here, if I can interpret his handwriting. He thinks the transports have to have about an hour-and-a-half lead over the bomber force, in order to set down somewhere and deploy the choppers."

"Hell," Wyatt said, "they could leave two days early, if they wanted to."

"The source thinks not."

"Okay, so that puts the bombers on the runway at 0600 in the morning."

"At the latest."

"If we leave here at 0500 and hit them an hour later, we miss the bombers if they go half an hour early."

"I know, Yucca. It's a judgement call."

"They need tankers. Are they coming out of Marada?"

"We don't think so. It'll probably be Tripoli, but we don't have an eye in the area."

"I'm stretching it to get five minutes on-target," Wyatt said. "I can't hang around longer than that."

"Your call, Yucca. Suggest something."

"Hell, we'll split the difference. We'll hit the target at 0545 hours."

"Go with it," Church said. "Anything else?"

"I've got as much as I'm going to get, I think."

"Hold on. Two wants a word."

Embry took over on the other end. "Yucca, I've got a request from my asset."

"You allow that in your business?"

"She's special."

"What's she want?"

"Don't shoot al-Qati."

Jesus Christ.

"Don't shoot him. Damn it, I don't even know what he looks like."

"I'm just passing it on, Yucca."

Wyatt signed off.

Borman said, "You want me to ring the chow bell?"

"Yeah, Ben, let's get them up and around. We're about to go visiting."

Fifteen

One of the effects of Church's last-minute alteration of their timing, Wyatt thought, was that it circumvented a buildup of anxiety. If they had had to wait around in the heat for another twenty-four hours, thinking about the coming fight, their nerves would have achieved jangled status.

Everyone rolled out of their sleeping bags, bitching in expected ways, and dove into the chores that had been originally scheduled for later in the afternoon.

"Flashlights, Andy?" Win Potter asked.

"Why not? If a roving patrol hasn't spotted us by now, maybe our luck will hold."

Kriswell and Vrdla made a circuit of the aircraft, performing final checks on the avionics, especially the critical data-links and the video-links between aircraft.

Potter and Littlefield topped off the fighter and transport fuel cells to within a quarter-inch of the caps.

Borman, with Dave Zimmerman's reluctant help, retrieved the C-4 plastic explosive from the Hercules and started cutting it into smaller blocks and shaping it into small cones. They carried the small charges from plane to plane, attaching it to the super-secret electronic black boxes, to instrument panels, and to fuel cells. All eight aircraft received a liberal dose of *plastique*. Then Borman, without a very relieved Zimmerman's assistance, inserted detonators in each charge and wired them into already installed wiring harnesses according to a schematic he had designed. Two switches were part of the harness. One, controlled by the pilot, initiated either a thirty-second or a forty-five-second timer, hopefully giving the pilot time to eject after he closed the circuit or to get a long way away from the plane if he was on the ground. In the event that a pilot was unable to flip the toggle on his own, an impact switch—requiring five-hundred footpounds of force—was installed in the nose.

If any F-4, or either of the C-130s, was hit or went down, there wouldn't be enough left of it for salvagers to reconstruct key components.

The downside of the self-destruct precaution was that flying the aircraft was like piloting a volatile fuel cell while smoking half-a-dozen Havanas. Borman had been thorough in his design, however. All of the charges were in protected spots, behind titanium panels or in structural members, so that a few rounds from a hostile gun was unlikely to set off the sensitive detonators. The *plastique* itself, Borman liked to say when he was juggling balls of the stuff, was completely harmless.

Jim Demion and Cliff Jordan spent their time removing the plunger-type impact fuses from the twenty-four Mark 84 bombs slung beneath the E-model Phantoms. There were three bombs on each pylon, six per plane. The bombs on the C and D models would remain in their factory configuration.

In place of the impact fuses, they installed the nose cones that Kriswell, Vrdla, and Borman had modified in Nebraska and brought with them. The cones contained the avionic heads from the HOBOS two thousand-pound guided bomb. Though the three designers had not had a MK 84 available as a model, the cones slipped into place perfectly, substituting an electronic impact fuse, and giving the bomb eyes. The nose cone and trailing antennas were taped into place with duct tape. The additional wiring harness plugged directly into a receptacle already installed in the pylon.

Wyatt, Gettman, Hackley, and Barr preflighted each airplane, paying particular attention to weapons hardware connectors and firing up the computers and radars for software checks.

Dennis Maal and Hank Cavanaugh installed the final linkages and examined and tested all of the new solenoid-activated controls. They tested the electronic consoles built into the transport and into the backseat areas of Yucca Three and Yucca Four.

They had completed four dry runs of the procedures while still in Ainsworth, and the live exercise came off without a hitch. They were finished by 0410 hours.

Formsby, who had not had an assignment, contented himself with tending the radio and positioning the two start carts before Borman rigged them with plastic explosive.

Then, whether they wanted them or not, they dug into their stash of MREs, heated whatever they drew over flaming Sterno cans, and chased it down with mugs of the hot coffee Formsby had brewed.

Barr, in standard form, consumed the contents of four of the MRE packages.

Sitting on the ramp of the transport, Barr said, "You know, I don't think Yucca Two has more than five or six brake cycles left."

"You really think you're going to need brakes Bucky?" Jordan asked. "You want brakes, I'll trade you airplanes."

"No way, man. Yours flies like a Navy hog."

"You haven't even flown it."

"I can tell by looking at it," Barr insisted.

Wyatt forced down the last of his biscuit, swigged some coffee, then climbed into the Hercules to find a mirror and a paper cup of water. He discovered his razor in his duffel bag—someone had straightened out all of the personal belongings en route to Africa. The soft rubber seal of his oxygen mask chafed his face red if he had a stubble, and he quickly cut it down.

Formsby stood next to him, with his own cup of water, sharing the mirror. He probably shaved out of habit, Wyatt figured.

"Are you expecting to have to impress someone, Andy?" Formsby asked.

"Not today, unless it's my Maker, and I'm not planning on that."

"Amen."

With the chores completed, many of the men were thinking about their future. Or lack of it.

He shed his jeans, dressed in his dove gray Noble Enterprises flight suit, and went back to the cargo bay to sit on the ramp.

Cavanaugh, Littlefield, Vrdla, and Potter had started a card game.

The temperature was starting to come up.

Ben Borman had collected the drag chutes from yesterday's landings and stacked them on top of the start carts, weighting them in place with pieces of broken two-by-fours from the ruined hangars. When the start carts went up in flames, so would the parachutes.

275

Barr emerged from the cargo bay, also dressed in his flight suit, and sat down beside him.

"Going to miss this place," Barr said.

"For how long?"

"Maybe twenty seconds."

"How you doing, Bucky?"

"Good, I think." Barr held out both hands, steady as granite. "I hope to hell they stay that way, come bomb delivery time."

"I hope to hell the technology substitutes for practice," Wyatt said.

None of them had dropped a bomb in years. Their flight skills were still honed by their daily work, but civilian chores didn't always involve placing MK 84s in tender spots. Kriswell had argued that the guidance system was all they would need. He had run them through some simulations in Nebraska, connecting the HOBOS heads to the aircraft computers.

"My fear," Barr said, "is that the technology is soon going to substitute for humans in the cockpit. Hell, it already has. Where am I going to get a job?"

"Maybe they'll make you president of Yale?"

"They should. Look how I turned out. How many of my classmates can be found sitting in the sand of Chad, waiting for some jerk in Washington to say go?"

"I don't know. How big was your graduating class?"

"I didn't pay attention. I think most of them are lawyers by now. Either that or cat burglars."

Dawn was pinking the horizon now. The drab topsides of the fighters took on a glow, their silhouettes slowly becoming defined.

"I like that airplane," Wyatt said.

"Me, too, buddy. There'll never be another like her, or one that acted so many roles."

The F-4 had been used as a fighter, a bomber, a Wild Weasel—attracting SAM launches in order to strike the SAM radars, a photographic reconnaissance platform. She had taken to the air in 1958, and she was still flying combat missions in reconnaissance form during Desert Storm in 1991.

After the work they had put into them, Wyatt was almost reluctant to force them into their next roles.

"Andy?"

"Yeah?"

"You mean what you said last night?"

"Probably. What'd I say?"

"You going to ask Janner?"

"She already said yes."

"Damn. I knew I should have called earlier."

They sat and waited for the sun to come up or for something else to happen.

There was not enough space in the subterranean hangars for the C-130 transports, and the six of them were lined up next to the runway. The first four contained Shummari's helicopters, and the last two were now loading the First Special Forces Company. Al-Qati divided the company evenly between the two transports. If one went down, he didn't want to lose all of his fighting capability.

He stood with Shummari near the last airplane, and listened as, one by one, they began to start their engines. The crescendo grew steadily.

"I do not feel as confident as I should about this mission," Shummari said.

"You are in good company, Khalil."

Al-Qati had a sudden inspiration relating to his survival. "We should have a contingency plan."

"Such as, Ahmed?"

"Give me a codename."

Shummari had to speak louder, as the roar of engines increased. "Moonglow."

The colonel grinned. "I am surprised, Khalil. You are a romantic."

"I wish that I were."

"I will be Sundown. This is in the event that we need to change the plans made for us."

"We do not control the transports, Ahmed, and that bothers me. I prefer having my helicopters free to roam."

"Is your side arm loaded, Khalil?"

Shummari patted his holster. "Yes, of course."

"That is all the command you need."

"But, Ahmed. . . ."

"Very likely, it will not be necessary. Still, we must think ahead. I will be in the fifth aircraft, with the first and second platoons. I think you should fly with the two Mi-8s."

"As you wish, Ahmed."

Al-Qati regretted that the mission did not allow for him to bring along any of the armored personnel carriers. He would hate to be stranded in the Sudan or in Ethiopia without motorized transport.

Shrugging his shoulders in the web gear, he patted Shummari on the back, then trudged slowly across the tarmac toward the transport.

Embry yelped, "They're moving!"

Church was reclined in Embry's high-backed desk

chair, his shoeless feet propped on the desk, and his head lolling from side to side as he drifted in and out of sleep.

He sat up abruptly, slid his feet off the desk, and stood up. He nearly fell down when he determined that his left leg had gone to sleep without him.

Rounding the desk, he reached the table and leaned on it, shaking his leg to get the circulation going again.

With a ballpoint pen, Embry pointed out a silver airplane on the screen. "That's the first one airborne. The others are moving into takeoff position."

"Let's keep track of them."

Embry grabbed the blue phone, and someone on the other end answered immediately.

"We want a fix on their course, speed, and altitude," he told the desk person on the NSA end of the line. "Don't lose them."

Church picked up the green phone.

"Captain Murphy, sir," the man at the Pentagon said.

"Captain, hook me into Yucca, please."

"Right away, sir."

Several minutes went by before a voice with a British accent came on the air. Church figured it was Formsby, though he had never met the man.

"This is Paper Doll One. Who is this?"

"Yucca . . . oh, I must be about Fifteen. Give or take a digit or two."

"The transports are taking off now, Yucca."

"Roger that," Formsby said. "We will be going shortly, then."

"Give me a rundown, please."

"Time to target at selected cruise is fifty-seven minutes, and we need eleven minutes from engine start to takeoff. We plan to reach the target at 0545 hours."

"You've got it calculated that closely?" Church asked.

"Who in the world knows? The boss feels good if we use odd numbers."

Formsby came through the hatchway from the crew compartment into the cargo bay and yelled, "Andy!"

Wyatt turned to look back.

"The C-130s are off."

Wyatt climbed to his feet. "Anything else, Neil?"

"That's all the man gave me."

The pilots and technicians began to stir out of their resting positions on the ramp and in the bay.

"Okay, guys, we're on," Wyatt said. "Let's do it like we drilled it."

Demion said to Kriswell, "Come on, Tom. You can play with the throttles while I see if this big mother will start."

The two of them headed forward to the flight deck with Kriswell saying, "I want to see if I can retract the wheels this time. Would that be okay?"

"I'll tell you what, Tom," Demion said, "I'll think about it."

Dennis Maal and Hank Cavanaugh headed for the Hercules tanker.

Wyatt walked out to Yucca One with Win Potter, who carried a ladder. When they reached the plane, Wyatt slipped into his G suit, then checked his survival pack. The survival packs had been specifically provisioned for this mission, and he took out the most important item, the radio, and checked it for operation. He made certain he had extra batteries for it. Uncomfortable under his left arm was the holster for his Browning 9-millimeter automatic. He didn't plan on using it.

"Good luck, Andy."

"Thanks, Win. I'll be seeing you soon."

"Maybe we can have lunch," Potter grinned.

"Plan on it."

Wyatt went up the ladder and into the cockpit. He strapped into his parachute, then into the seat. Potter came up and helped out with the umbilicals.

Lifting his helmet from the floor, he slipped it on and fastened the chin strap. Potter grabbed the comm cord and snapped it in place.

Wyatt gave him a raised thumb, and Potter went down the ladder.

Borman was ready with the start cart, and, in three minutes the twin turbojets were turning.

They waved at him, and moved the start cart over to crank Gettman's F-4.

In a short time, the turboprops of both Hercules aircraft were idling, as were all twelve turbojets.

"Formation lights," Wyatt said.

The dim wingtip lights started popping on.

Wyatt sat in his cockpit watching the ballet.

After extending flaps to the full-down position and synchronizing the engines, Maal and Cavanaugh climbed out of the tanker and ran for the transport scrambling up the ramp.

Dave Zimmerman and Cliff Jordan slid out of their F-4s, Yuccas Five and Six—the C and D models, and scampered up the ladders and into the backseats of Yuccas Three and Four. They left their jets idling with the flaps down.

Grabbing ladders and a few scattered tools, the remaining mechanics sprinted for the Hercules.

Ben Borman was last. He set the timers on the start cart explosives, then rambled his way to the transport.

As soon as he was aboard, Wyatt touched the transmit stud. "Okay, Wizard, you're gone."

Demion said, "I may be slow, but I'm ahead of you."

While raising its ramp, the big Hercules released its brakes and headed for the end of the runway.

Because of the way they had been lined up, Barr was the last one off the ground. He took off in the same direction he had landed, dodging holes with a drift to the right as he shot down the runway in afterburner, necessary because of the short field and the takeoff weight.

Ahead of him, the twin exhausts of Hackley's Phantom burned bright, like two flares in the false dawn, slowly climbing away to the right.

As soon as the wheels quit rumbling, and the wonder of flight took over, Barr retracted his gear, keeping an eye on the airspeed indicator. He eased into a right turn, behind Yucca Three, got the speed up, and pulled the throttles out of afterburner.

The F-4s all had their formation lights on in the hopes of avoiding a collision with anyone except the Libyans. He continued to circle right, gradually gaining altitude to one thousand feet AGL.

He leaned right and looked down at the field.

The C-130F was on the move, headed for the end of the runway. As he watched, Yucca Five began rolling away from Yucca Six, then turned jerkily and followed the tanker.

"Be tender, guys," Wyatt said, "we don't want to pile them up right there."

"Trust Thirsty, Yucca," Dennis Maal said. "I've done this before."

"With a C-130?" Barr asked.

"Well, no. But it did have a forty-five-inch wingspan and a top end of sixty miles an hour."

"I'm impressed, Thirsty," Formsby said. Formsby had taken Cavanaugh's seat as copilot of the Hercules.

Utilizing the data down-link, the ex-E-2 AWACS console aboard the transport had some control over its subordinate aircraft through the autopilot. Kriswell and Vrdla had added some functions—full throttle arc, landing gear and flap retraction—in order to enhance the remote control. In addition, some data feedback—altitude, attitude, heading, speed—was displayed on the controllers' screens.

In the past, Barr had had an AWACS controller, with more powerful down-looking radar available, actually do his flying for him, taking him up through cloud formations that had blinded Barr but appeared perfectly clear to the high-flying AWACS.

Remotely Piloted Vehicles (RPVs) had been used for a long time, as target drones and as reconnaissance platforms, but they weren't generally as large as F-4s or C-130s.

From the backseat of Yucca Three, Zimmerman would attempt to fly Yucca Five, and Cliff Jordan had control of Yucca Six from the backseat of Gettman's Yucca Four. Additionally, Zimmerman and Jordan had a view. Cameras in the noses of the remote-controlled Phantoms transmitted their images to the instrument panel screens of the backseaters. That feature had not been incorporated into the tanker.

If they got the F-4 RPVs as far as Marada, Wyatt wanted Zimmerman and Jordan to be able to target well enough, through the camera lens, to fly the planes right into the targets. Modern day electronic kamikazes without the benefit of cultural and spiritual upbringing.

Barr and Wyatt, when they had developed the concept, had discussed M.E. Morris's intriguing novel, *The Last Kamikaze,* but they couldn't figure out a way to program the computers with the same dedication demonstrated by Hirohito's pilots.

In any event, Barr didn't think the RPVs were going to make it to the target. Crashing them into the chemical plant had become the second of their priorities.

Gettman came on the air. "Hey, Thirsty, if you're going to dump that big toy, dump it off the runway, will you? I still want a chance to get airborne."

"Shut up, Four," Maal said.

Wyatt wasn't killing the banter this morning, and Barr figured it was because they were only a few minutes away from being discovered anyway.

He continued his circle, staying behind Hackley's formation lights. On the far side of the field, he could see Wyatt's and Gettman's Phantoms, but he couldn't tell which was which. The Hercules was higher, coming in from the south, directly above the runway so Formsby or Demion could coach Maal on the ICS, the Internal Communications System.

The C-130F was now on the runway, lined up. In the gathering dawn, Barr could see the exhaust from her four engines building.

She began to roll, picked up speed quickly since her fuel load was now confined to what was in the wing tanks. Barr passed the south end of the runway as the tanker began swerving to the right, too hard.

Maal corrected, she straightened out, achieved lift, and rose slowly from the airstrip. Maal, with his experience with flying models, had tutored all of the pilots—since any of them might end up flying the RPVs—to not make abrupt moves with the remote controls. It could rapidly translate into stalls, lost lift, and pancaked airplanes. A radio controller didn't *feel* the attitudinal changes made by RPVs. Maal had admitted crashing six or seven models while learning to fly radio control, and he was a pilot. The revelation was not a morale builder.

There were a few cheers on Tac Two as the C-130 gained altitude.

Maal reported, "The data feedback says I've got gear up and airspeed. I'm taking it cool, and we're out of here."

"Nice job, Thirsty," Wyatt said. "Wizard, we'll see you on the other side."

The two C-130s would join up, climb for altitude, and head north.

By the time Barr had reached the northern end of his circle, Yucca Five was on the runway.

"I've got a nice picture on the screen," Zimmerman said. "That is, the resolution is nice. The view is dismal."

"Any time you're ready, Five," Wyatt said.

"Going to afterburner."

The end of the runway lit up, and the F-4C leapt away. She built momentum quickly, missed the chuckholes, and rotated.

The F-4D was off the airstrip, retracting gear and flaps, by the time Barr completed his next circle.

"All right, Yuccas, let's form up," Wyatt said.

Barr ran in some throttle and closed on Hackley as they eased into a heading of 010. Seconds later, the two of them joined with Wyatt and Gettman in a finger formation. They climbed for two thousand feet AGL, providing enough control-correction tolerance for the RPVs, and staying low enough to avoid radar for awhile.

"Let's kill the formation lights, Yuccas. Heading zero-one-three, speed four-zero-zero knots."

Barr reached out and flipped the toggle on his lighting panel. The wingtip lights blinked out. As they gained altitude, however, the day brightened. He could make out the silhouettes of the Phantoms ahead on his left.

Somewhere, fifty miles ahead, and at the same altitude, were the Hercs.

Somewhere, a half-mile ahead of them, were Yuccas Five and Six, flying point for the combat formation. The two RPVs were supposed to be flying about two miles apart to prevent an accidental collision.

The red-lit chronometer on his instrument panel read: 0454.

"You notice, One," Barr said, "that we're six minutes off schedule. Pretty sloppy, that."

Formsby asked, "Does the CIA give out demerits?"

"Only for spending Uncle's money on champagne," Barr told him.

"Does this parachute work?" Formsby asked.

Sixteen

Janice Kramer was zapping burritos in the microwave at seven o'clock in the evening.

The telephone rang.

She gave up watching the burritos to step to the opposite counter and pick up the phone. Through the window, she could see the shadows lengthening, slowly overcoming the day.

"Yes."

"Miss Kramer, this is your friend on the East Coast, returning your call."

She thought it was Church's voice, and she wouldn't yet, if ever, describe him as a friend. At least, he had called after she left her message on the machine.

"What can I do for you?" he asked.

"I want a status report."

"Miss Kramer, we can't. . . ."

"Those are my people" she said. "I want to know if they landed safely."

Church, sighed, hesitated, then said, "It's underway."

"What! But it. . . ."

"Yes. There's been a change. At any rate, it'll be over in a couple of hours."

Her stomach clenched up on her. "Will you call me as soon as you know?"

"I will."

He hung up, and she carefully placed the receiver in its cradle.

She wasn't hungry.

Canceling the microwave's timer, she went into the living room and curled up on the couch.

She curled up in a fetal position. Her stomach hurt.

God. She had thought it was five days away.

Another change.

Another chance for error.

Turn back, Andy. Come home to me.

"You want to take her for awhile, Neil?" Demion asked.

"Marvelous, James! I would like that."

Outside of a few small aircraft he rented on weekends, Formsby did not often get a chance to fly. He especially did not get a chance to fly military aircraft, even the lumbering, four-engined Hercules.

"Would a barrel roll be appropriate?" he asked.

"I think you'd get some complaints," Demion said, crawling out of the pilot's seat.

"Some people just have no sense of adventure."

Demion descended from the flight deck, found the pot of coffee Littlefield had made, and brought two mugs back to the cockpit.

"You might have thought about me," Kriswell said.

He was seated in the flight engineer's position, leaning forward to peer out the windscreen at the C-130F. The tanker was a half-mile ahead of them, at the same flight level of two thousand feet AGL.

288

"You're too busy, Tom," Demion said, "and my hands are too full."

"I haven't told Denny to make a correction in thirty or forty seconds," Kriswell said.

Maal, seated at the joystick controls down at the console, was flying the tanker with the telemetry feedback plus oral instructions from Kriswell over the ICS.

Demion gave him one of the mugs, then went back down to the crew compartment for another.

Sam Vrdla, also at the console, was in charge of the radar, and he asked, "Command pilot, can I have a radar check?"

Demion told him, "Two sweeps, Sam. But keep the power down."

"Roger."

A few seconds later, when Demion was back in his seat, Vrdla reported over the intercom, "All systems check out, Jim. We should get our one-ninety-mile scan at thirty-five thousand."

Aboard the original E-2, with its massive radar antenna enclosed in the radome, the search area could be extended to 250 miles. With the modified antenna protected by a fiberglass bulge on the C-130's fuselage top, they had managed only 190 miles. It was not quite what they had hoped for, but Wyatt felt that it was adequate.

The MiGs they were going up against had a radar range of twenty-two miles, less than that of a production F-4. The modified radar in the fighter, Kriswell had told him, gave them a hundred-mile edge. That ability to say, "I see you" first might be all that was necessary to insure success. Even though, for weight and range considerations, the Phantoms were carrying short-range missiles, the radar superiority would increase the preparation time or the evasion advantage.

Formsby felt, rather than saw, a shadow on his right, and he glanced out the side window to see the F-4s pulling alongside. Wyatt was in the lead plane, with the three others in echelon off his right wing. He looked up and saw the two RPVs several hundred feet above and spread far apart.

"Actually, James, this is rather exciting. I am glad I decided to come along."

"Actually, Neil I'm amazed that we've got all eight planes in the right configuration at this point in time. My better instincts and a few laws of probability say we should have lost at least one to equipment failure by now."

"Speaks worlds for the design team," Formsby said.

"It does, doesn't it?"

The intercom chatter died down as they flew on through a brightening day. Tension was building within the Hercules crew, Formsby knew, even though this aircraft would not approach within 220 kilometers (175 miles) of the targets. That was an exceptionally short distance for a MiG-23. Especially when their defenses would be limited to what the countermeasures pods could provide. They would soon lose their fighter-bomber protection.

Thirty minutes later, Wyatt came on the air. "Wizard Three, Yucca One."

"Go One," Vrdla, who was Wizard Three, said.

"I'm showing two-two-zero from the IP."

The Initial Point for the bomb run was seventeen miles west of Marada Air Base and the chemical factory.

"Roger that, One. We match up."

"All right." Wyatt said. "Wizard, Thirsty, go to your stations. Yuccas Five and Six, initiate your run."

Demion said, "Wizard, wilco."

From the console below, Maal called, "Thirsty's on her climbout."

Zimmerman replied, "Five."

And Jordan said, "Six moving out."

"I'll take her back now, Neil."

"Just when I was getting to know her better," Formsby said. "Story of my life."

When he felt Demion's touch on the yoke, Formsby released his grip and took his feet off the rudder pedals. His ankle was aching some, but it was not something with which he could not live.

"Let's take the power to ninety percent," Demion said to him.

"Nine-zero coming up."

Formsby worked the throttles, keeping an eye on the tachometers so as to not get too far out of synchronization. When he had them adjusted, he fumbled for his oxygen mask, slipped the straps over his head, and let it hang around his neck. At thirty-five thousand feet, a stray missile could result in a sudden decompression, if not total annihilation.

"You've got to move a little faster than that, Denny," Kriswell said over the ICS.

The tanker had fallen well below them, and Maal added more power from his remote controls in order to increase the rate of climb.

"That better, Tom?"

"Much better," Kriswell said. "How about the rest of the crew? You all have your oxy handy?"

Potter, Borman, Cavanaugh, and Littlefield all checked in with affirmative responses.

They left the tanker at twenty-five thousand feet, its autopilot circling it in a three-mile-diameter circle. Maal was finally able to give up the joysticks and relax.

Depending upon one's definition of relaxation, Formsby reminded himself.

The Hercules kept climbing toward the north.

Ibrahim Ramad stood with Colonel Ghazi in his control center watching the grease-painted blips change position on the Plexiglas wall. Al-Qati's C-130s, Black Squadron, were over the Kufra Oasis, in southeastern Libya. They were about three hundred kilometers away from penetrating Sudan airspace. Orange Squadron, the air cover for the transports, was ranged above and ahead of them. The tankers were moving into position.

"It will not be long now, Colonel Ghazi."

"No." Ghazi seemed to be quite withdrawn this morning. His face reflected morose thoughts within.

"Are you certain you would not like to accompany the mission?" Ramad offered. "We could find you a seat in one of the bombers."

"I will see everything I need to see from right here," Ghazi said.

On the secondary tactical channel monitor, they could hear the eight MiG-23s conversing with the tankers out of Tripoli. They would have to refuel in about forty minutes. Then they would begin their descent to one thousand meters, staying ahead and above the transports, which would transit the Sudan at five hundred meters of altitude, simulating a low-profile, radar-avoidance attack.

Two MiG-23s—Alif Flight—were six hundred kilometers to the west. They were supposed to be patrolling against any incursion of hostile aircraft from that direction, but he had listened to their radio conversations and was certain they were playing games with a flight out of Tripoli. He had issued a stern order against that nonsense.

The MiG-23s flying under the call sign of Bā that had flown surveillance along the southern border were now in their landing approach. They would land for refueling.

Four MiG-23s, call sign Tā, were about to take off. They would patrol the region around the base until the bombers were well under way, then join the bombers. By then, Bā Flight would be refueled and again be in the air. The bombers and Jā squadron would meet the tankers over Sudan.

It was all proceeding so smoothly.

Alongside the see-through map, the status board showed him that the nine Su-24s were now being towed from the hangars. From the overhead speaker, he heard the ground controller telling them to line up on the taxiway behind the MiG-23.

Several minutes later the controller said, "Tā Lead, Marada. Incoming craft are now down and clear of the runway. You have clearance for takeoff."

"Tā Lead, with a flight of four, proceeding."

Ramad crossed the room to stand behind the radar operator. The supervisor, in contact with the aircraft through his headset, also stood behind the corporal. On the radar screen, Ramad saw the first two aircraft make their takeoff runs toward the north, then start into a right turn. Shortly thereafter, the second pair followed.

He was about to turn away from the radar scope when he noticed two small blips near the bottom edge of the screen, about 150 kilometers away. They had to have been there for some time because the radar was set for a 220-kilometer scan.

"What are those, Corporal?" he demanded.

"Uh, where, Colonel? Oh. They just appeared."

"Idiot! Identify them!"

"I, uh, we don't have an aircraft in that region right now, Colonel."

The supervisor was already on the radio, demanding identification from the pair on the primary frequencies. Airplanes flying in pairs were not accidental tourists.

"They are not transmitting IFF, Colonel," the corporal said.

"Get me a position, you pig!"

"They are bearing almost directly on us, Colonel. One-four-eight kilometers, altitude two-thousand meters."

Merciful Allah! Ghazi could be correct! But no, he could not be!

"How fast?" he demanded.

"Ah, closing at nine hundred knots, Colonel."

Supersonic!

Ramad glanced over at Ghazi, who was watching the activity at the radar with passive disenchantment.

The incoming airplanes suddenly began to emanate radar emissions, the pulses showing up vividly on the screen. Every eye in the vicinity of the radar set was drawn to them.

"Radiating," the corporal said.

"I can see that!"

Ramad's mind immediately went into a defensive posture. He ripped the headset from the supervisor and spoke into it.

"Tā Leader, Marada."

"This is Tā Leader."

"You have a flight of two unknowns at your heading one-nine-two, altitude two-zero-thousand, distance one-four-zero, speed nine-zero-zero. Take them!"

"Uh, Marada, do you want us to identify them?"

"Tā Leader, I want you to shoot them down!"

Ramad dropped the headset and ran for the door, yelling, "Tell my crew to have my airplane ready!"

Ghazi stopped his flight with one raised hand. "Are you notifying Tripoli, Colonel?"

"I will take care of this, Ghazi."

"Yes. I am certain that you will."

"Keep me apprised, Yucca Five," Barr heard Wyatt demand of Zimmerman.

"The RPVs are sixty miles ahead of us," Zimmerman said, "and seven-five out. My feedback says five is being hit with search radar."

"Won't be long now," Jordan said.

"Hell, even by long-distance, I'll give 'em a run for their money," Zimmerman promised.

Barr scanned his instrument panel and HUD. All nice readings. He was itching to fire up the radar and find something to track.

"Yucca One, Two," Barr said, "I think it's time."

"It's close enough," Wyatt agreed. "Let's lock open the channel."

Barr flipped the toggle on the communications panel which kept his transmit mode open. It made for easier interplane conversation during hectic maneuvering.

"Four, you with me?" Barr asked.

"Roger, Two. Lead the way."

Barr made a slight correction with his stick and rudders, dropped out of the formation, and veered off on a more northerly route. Gettman, with Zimmerman in the backseat, followed and fell in on his right wing.

He could imagine the intensity of concentration Zimmerman and Jordan were having to maintain. They would have to ignore attitudinal changes made by the aircraft they were in and keep their minds attuned to what was happening in the RPVs.

The desert below was now fully, though hazily, lit. It appeared no less forbidding. He saw a few lights off about ten miles to the west and pinpointed them as the village of Zella. It was not, he thought, a tourist attraction.

They were way the hell into it now. The southern border was so far behind, it could have been in another atlas. Barr wondered why they hadn't considered hightailing it for the Med, ditching the aircraft, and getting picked up by someone's luxury yacht.

Then remembered that yachts were slow, and someone might catch them.

And learn some true names.

Which wasn't supposed to happen.

He glanced to his right. Wyatt and Hackley had disappeared. They were probably less than two miles away, but the camouflage blended them right into the desert below.

He was still holding two thousand AGL, and he was pretty certain the bad guys hadn't spotted him yet.

"One," he said, "can we have an AWACS check?"

"Go, Wizard Three," Wyatt said.

"Going."

Two seconds.

Three.

"I'm showing four bandits, bearing zero-four-three,

coming hot on the RPVs. Four-five miles on them, and closing."

"Roger," Wyatt said. "Keep Five and Six alerted from here on in."

Five and Six were emitting radar energy to attract attention only. Their radars could not be read by Zimmerman and Jordan.

"Yucca Five and Six are five-eight from target," Vrdla said. "Can you guys see anything?"

Zimmerman reported, "I've got a nice, clear picture on the camera, but I can't see anything but dirt."

"All Yuccas, One. Weapons are free. Arm 'em up."

Barr reached for his armaments panel and switched off the safety. He no longer had a backseater, and he selected "Pilot" for triggering. Just to be prepared for an airborne attack, he selected a Super Sidewinder for the time being.

The Ford Aerospace/Raytheon AIM-9L missile had an eleven-mile range at a cruising speed of Mach 3. Compared to the sixty-two-mile maximum range Sparrow, with which the F-4 was normally equipped, it was like using a knife in a street fight rather than a sniper rifle. Wyatt and Barr had elected to switch to the Sidewinder, however, for two reasons. For targeting, it utilized infrared homing, rather than semi-active radar guidance, and lacking backseaters, the infrared was preferable to them. Additionally, they saved twelve hundred pounds per plane in weight, which boosted their crucial performance data: speed and/or fuel consumption.

With its twenty-five-pound warhead, instead of the Sparrow's eighty-eight-pound warhead, the Sidewinder could still destroy enough of an enemy aircraft to temper its aggressiveness. As an infrared-seeker, the missile usually found a hot exhaust pipe to home on, and when that was the case, that was all it took.

"One and Three jumping off," Wyatt said. "Go afterburner, Three."

"Sure you don't want some help?" Barr asked.

"Hell, Bucky. there's only four of them," Hackley came back. "Andy can wait here if he wants to, and I'll be right back."

"Two and Four going hot-shit for the coast," Barr said. "Can we pick you up a hotdog or a girl in a bikini?"

"I rather doubt," Formsby said, "that you're going to find either."

"What a downer," Barr said as he kicked in the afterburners.

Checking his right side, he saw Gettman accelerating with him, grinning widely.

Ramad was in his cockpit, performing his final preflight checks. The wings were extended and locked in their sixteen-degree configuration. The armaments panel showed him the availability of three hundred rounds of 23 millimeter cannon shells, two AA-7 missiles, and four AA-8 missiles. The AA-7 missiles, called Apex by NATO, were good at medium ranges, sixteen to thirty-two kilometers. The AA-8 missiles were designed for high-maneuverability targets at close range. They had only a seven-kilometer effective kill range, but they were very accurate. All of his missiles were infrared-homing.

He looked to the east, where the sun had now ascended just above the horizon. There were a lot of men standing around on the ramp, trying to figure out what was happening. To the west, the Su-24s were stretched along the taxiway, awaiting their orders.

"Marada Ground Control, Vulture," he said.

"Proceed, Vulture."

"I am ready for takeoff."

"Vulture, the bombers are now in position for take-off."

"Move them. I am going first."

He waved away his ground crew and released the brakes, heading quickly for the taxiway and closing his canopy as he went.

As he approached them, he saw the Su-24s sidling ahead and easing to the right, to allow him passage along the left side of the taxiway.

He had barely turned onto the runway when he heard Tā flight on the tactical radio.

"Tās, Tā Leader. Targets two-five kilometers. I have a lock-on."

"Tā Two, lock-on."

"Tā Three. I also have a target."

"Tā Four, target on the screen. Now, lock-on."

"Two missiles each, Tās," Tā Leader said.

Ramad shoved his throttles forward and sagged into the seat as the gravitational force mounted.

Save one for me.

As he rotated and retracted his landing gear, he found himself becoming excited by the prospects.

If Ghazi's reports were correct, there were another four hostile aircraft somewhere, and he was going to get one of them for himself.

"Yucca Six. Missile lock-on," Jordan said easily. It

299

was easier to say when he wasn't sitting inside the target.

"Ditto with Five. They're infrared seekers. I'm still shutting down radar."

"Six shutting down."

Wyatt checked his HUD. He was making 1040 knots, over the barrier, consuming fuel like it was hot chocolate on a wintry Nome night.

"Back off a little, Three."

"Wilco," Hackley said.

He worked the throttles back a little. They were still at two thousand feet AGL.

He tried to imagine what was happening with the RPVs. They had initiated their radar to make them attractive targets, and they had been fired on by infrared-homing missiles. Switching the radars to passive mode didn't make a lot of difference.

"Five and Six," he said. "Go ahead and launch all of your missiles."

"Five, roger."

"Six."

They couldn't actually aim the missiles, but it was a shame to waste them. If nothing else the eight missiles would scatter the Libyan formation.

"Wiz Three, here. I got missiles all over the damned sky. The homeboys are breaking up. No hits yet on either side."

"Sitrep, Five?"

"I'm doing things I can't believe I'm doing without being there, Andy," Zimmerman said. "Loops and rolls. Showed 'em my tail for a few seconds without planning it. The image on the screen is crazy. I don't know if I'm up or down. I lost feedback on the airspeed indic . . . ."

"Five?"

"I think I'm dead. Everything went blank and zero."

"Six?"

Jordan reported. "I'm inverted at five hundred AGL. I think I've dodged about six hundred missiles. Upright, now, pulling for altitude. Oh, shit! Threat warning on IR missiles. Maybe two of them. Rolling."

"Wizard Three, report!" Wyatt ordered.

"Three," Vrdla said from the Herc. "All my blips have gone crazy. I think that's Five spinning in. Gone. Okay, showing five bogies. That must be Yucca Six near the ground. Missiles all over hell, but they're blinking out. Yeah, Six go hard right and climb."

"Going hard right," Jordan called. "Hell, I'm losing airspeed bad. Got to put the nose down."

"Hard left."

"Left. Stalling out."

"Their formation is a shambles." Vrdla reported. "They're all over the sky. I see you at two-zero from contact, Yucca One."

"I got it back, I think," Jordan said. "Airspeed coming up."

Wyatt said, "Three, lose the drop tanks."

"Roger."

He hit the external tank jettison and felt the slight rise of lift through the stick as the tanks fell away.

Wyatt pulled back on the stick and the nose leapt upward. He shoved in the throttles, checked to his right.

Hackley was right with him.

The adrenaline was pumping. His eyesight seemed sharper. The clarity of everything, in and out of the cockpit, was amazing. The airplane moved with his thoughts. They were one being, and he hadn't felt that in a long time.

"Yucca One, Wizard Three. I've got another bandit just off the runway at Marada, and I'm reading eleven aircraft on the ground."

"Those are the ones we want," Wyatt said.

"Should we take these out first?" Hackley asked.

"Why not?"

Wyatt felt like anything was possible.

Ramad monitored the action of Tā Flight on the radio as he rolled out on a heading of 194 and urged the MiG into supersonic flight with the afterburners.

He switched in his search radar and found five blips immediately. Four of them were converging on one from different angles.

He attempted to shove the throttles forward, but they were already end-stopped. He had broken the sonic barrier, and the airspeed indicator revealed Mach 1.8.

"One unknown destroyed," Tā Leader reported.

Ramad thought that atrocious. One airplane downed after firing eight missiles, all of them AA-7s judging by the distance involved when they were ignited.

One of Tā Flight's pilots shouted, "Son of a goat!" as his missile apparently missed its target.

Ramad was fifty kilometers from the engagement. He armed his AA-7 missiles.

Then glanced again at the screen.

There were suddenly two new targets to be seen, coming from the southwest and vectoring on the dogfight. They had been flying low and were now gaining altitude rapidly.

He was about to alert Tā Lead when Marada Air Base broke in. "Vulture, Marada. We have radar contact with an unknown aircraft emitting radar energy two-

302

two-zero kilometers, your bearing 178 degrees, altitude ten thousand meters."

Involuntarily, he looked at the screen, but the target would be beyond his radar range.

He would ignore it for the moment.

"Tā Flight, Vulture. You have two unknowns attacking from your bearing two-six-zero," he reported. "Disengage and meet the threat. I will assume your present target."

"But . . ." Tā Leader complained.

"Now!" Ramad ordered.

He was closing fast on the target, and his radar screen showed him Tā Flight peeling away from it. He selected an AA-7, armed it, then rolled right to center the target on the screen.

The missile's warhead began to hum in his earphones as the infrared seeker attempted to lock-on to the target. He was approaching it broadside, and was not yet close enough to obtain a strong heat source.

And then he noted two more blips appear on his screen. They were to the north heading almost directly east.

Toward the chemical factory.

Almighty Allah! They come from everywhere!

In the back of his mind, he was counting. There were now seven unidentified aircraft.

Where Ghazi had said there would be six.

Something was wrong.

This was a massive invasion. There would be more, appearing from all points of the compass.

Switching to the secondary tactical channel, he called the squadron overflying the transports. "Orange Squadron, Vulture. Return to base immediately!"

"Uh, Vulture, we cannot. We must first refuel."

Ramad cursed under his breath. "Refuel en route. Do it now!"

Back on the tactical one channel, he told Marada Air Control, "Recall Alif Flight."

"At once, Vulture."

The high-toned pitch in his earphones told him the missile had locked-on to the target.

He triggered it, and the missile leapt from its rails, a bright, hot exhaust almost blinding him.

He pulled the nose up and began to climb, so as to avoid the debris when his missile struck.

"Yucca One, eight miles to target," Vrdla said. "They're at angels seven and climbing."

"Roger, Wizard."

Wyatt cut in his search radar and scanned the HUD. Altitude 12,500 feet AGL. Speed Mach 1.1. Heading 086.

He put the nose down.

The desert rolled through his HUD, speeding quickly beneath him. He could see six targets in the immediate path of his search radar. Four, in apparent disarray, were closing on him from widely scattered positions. The fifth was apparently Yucca Six on an eastern course, attempting to gain altitude. The sixth was streaking across the screen on a perpendicular course to the north at almost double Mach. He saw the missile launch.

"One coming at you, Six."

"Roger," Jordan said. "I'm cutting throttle."

Jordan would attempt to fool the missile attacking the RPV by reducing the heat source, then turning into the missile to get his hot tail pipe out of its infrared vision.

"Jesus!" Jordan said. "I can see the damned thing on camera."

Wyatt blanked out Jordan's voice as he concentrated on the four targets coming at them.

"I've got the left two, Yucca Three."

"Roger, One. Taking the two on the right."

He expected to hear his missile threat warning sound off at any moment. The MiGs were two thousand feet below them, climbing, six miles away.

He guessed they had used their medium-range Apexs on the RPVs and were now left with the short-range Aphids.

Which meant that his and Barr's tactics were paying off. The RPVs' primary role was to draw the long- and medium-range weapons. Beyond that, if they survived, anything they accomplished was icing.

He had a solid lock-on tone from the first Sidewinder. The words "LOCK-ON" appeared on the HUD.

And now the targets were visual, black dots against the terrain.

"Tally ho, Three!"

"I see 'em," Hackley said.

They were taking on the enemy aircraft head-on, which wasn't the most effective configuration for heat-seeking missiles, which preferred a hotter energy source. The Super Sidewinders, though, were being operated at a longer wavelength of 10.6 microns, and they "saw" whole targets whose skin was heated by the friction generated from passing through the atmosphere.

Depressing the release stud, Wyatt closed his eyes for an instant, to avoid the exhaust glare as the missile dropped from its semi-recess in the fuselage, ignited, and shot away.

Kicked in a little left rudder.

Selected the second Sidewinder.

Heard an immediate lock-on tone, and fired.

Checked back to the right.

Eased in some rudder and aileron.

Closing so fast, the seconds screamed by.

His missile was streaming vapor toward the target, which he could clearly identify as a MiG now.

The MiG pilot knew he was in jeopardy. Even in his firing sequence, he hauled the nose up to dodge the Sidewinder.

Wyatt selected his third missile.

The MiG pilot evaded the Sidewinder, but his two missiles launched on a crazy angle and headed for no-where.

"LOCK-ON."

Wyatt fired number three.

Number two impacted the MiG on his far left.

A bright yellow-orange blossom burst into bloom, spewing segments of shrapnel out of its center.

One mile away.

Wyatt hauled back on the throttles, kicked in left rudder and aileron, and slid across the sky to avoid the head-on rush of his first MiG. With its ton-and-a-half of bombs still on the pylons, the Phantom felt heavy. He hoped the bombs stayed with him. The G-meter numbers ascended toward eight.

The Sidewinder slammed into the MiG's air intake, detonated, and the MiG lost its entire right side and wing. What was left went immediately into a spiraling, tumbling descent.

"Dodged my missile attack," Jordan yelled on the air. "Six's going to original heading. Wizard, help me out."

Vrdla gave him some headings.

"Got two of the bastards," Hackley said with a great deal of jubilation and adrenaline in his voice.

"I count four down," Vrdla said.

"Roger, four down," Wyatt said.

His vision had dimmed with the high-G turn, but was coming back.

He rolled out to the right, checked his position against the programmed coordinates for Marada Air Base on his HUD, and settled into a heading of 095. They had drifted northward during the engagement.

The fuel state wasn't impressive.

His altitude of nine thousand feet AGL was sufficient. He wouldn't waste fuel trying for more.

The speed had dropped to 660 knots. That would do, also.

Hackley moved in next to him.

"Very nice," Formsby said from the Hercules. "I wish I were with you."

"Let us not forget," Vrdla said, "that you've got another bogie out there. Plus, the aircraft on the base are starting to move."

Seventeen

Ramad could not believe his poor luck.

It had to be luck that allowed that perfect pigeon in his sights to go unharmed.

He eased back the stick, turning and bleeding off speed. Perhaps he had been going too fast.

As he turned back to the south, he became aware that the excited chatter of pilots on the tactical channel had ceased.

He searched his radar screen.

They were gone.

His four MiGs were gone.

All that remained was the low, fast blip of the airplane he had targeted—he had seen that it was indeed an F-4—headed for the base.

And it was followed by an additional two blips some twenty kilometers behind.

He was alone against them.

"Vulture! Vulture!" cried an anguished controller.

"Marada this is Vulture. Order the bombers to take off immediately. Bā Flight is to follow them."

Ghazi's voice came on the air. "Vulture, you have made a most regrettable mistake."

He did not need an army man to tell him that.

Ghazi continued, "I have ordered the defensive batteries to full alert. We will be able to stop the intruders."

The way the pilot of that first F-4 flew, Ramad was not certain, but he was also running short of alternatives.

"More important," Ghazi said, "is the chemical factory. They do not have an equal number of surface-to-air missiles. You must stop the attackers."

Without realizing he was accepting an order from an army man, Ramad lifted his left wing and went into a tight turn to the right. Seconds later, his radar picked up the two fighters moving almost directly east toward the chemical factory. He estimated that they were making nearly nine hundred knots at three thousand meters of altitude, and they were but seventy kilometers from their target.

He was thirty-five kilometers southeast of their flight path.

Ramming the throttles into afterburner, he selected his last AA-7 missile. That would do for the first target, but he would have to get closer for the second.

And the timing was going to be critical.

Ahmed al-Qati rested against the bulkhead in the flight compartment, standing behind the pilot and next to the flight engineer. His helmet was clipped to his web belt, and he wore a headset.

The pilot had just reported to his superiors, the airlift command in Tripoli, that their MiG-23 air cover had just turned back, along with the tankers.

That seemed to be creating some consternation in the military headquarters in Tripoli.

Al-Qati had listened to the clipped, low-descriptive dialogue on the primary tactical channel since the attack had begun. It was confusing, but he had deduced that four MiGs had been shot down, that their air cover was racing to the rescue, and that the bombers were only now taking off.

And Tripoli was just now waking up to the crisis.

He tried not to think that Sophia had been successful. He longed to talk to her. If he used the airplane's radio, he could reach her through his headquarters in El Bardi, but that would endanger her as well as himself. He would point no one in her direction.

"What am I to do?" the pilot asked for perhaps the third time. "We will be crossing the Sudan border in minutes."

After a moment's dead air, the controller from Tripoli radioed, "You are to continue your mission."

Sophia had been successful, but not successful enough. The idiots were still going to go through with the farce.

But not all of them were idiots.

Al-Qati unsnapped his holster, slipped the automatic from its sheath, and laid the barrel almost gently on the pilot's shoulder.

Startled, the man whipped his head around, saw the muzzle of the gun, and looked up at al-Qati, his mouth agape, and his eyes twice as large as they should be.

He said to the copilot, "Switch the radio to the secondary channel."

The man hesitated until al-Qati rubbed the pilot's throat with the automatic.

He glanced at the engineer, but that man had backed up as far as he could in his seat.

Reaching up to depress the transmit button on his cantilevered microphone, al-Qati said, "Moonglow."

"Sundown," came back to him.

"I am going."

"And I will follow," Shummari said.

Over the roar of the engines, al-Qati said, "No one will touch the radios. Copilot, return to the primary channel so that we may listen to Marada."

The man reluctantly changed the switch position.

"Pilot, drop out of the formation, then turn west. I want a heading of two-eight-zero degrees."

Al-Qati had a pretty fair picture of where he was geographically. If the raiders returned to the south, he might be in a position to intercept them.

He was even prepared to ram their airplanes, which would likely be unarmed by the time of their return leg, with this C-130. Al-Qati might not relish the chemical bombing of civilians, but he was a patriot, and he would not let this incursion into his national territory go unchallenged.

It took a nudge of the pistol against the pilot's ear to urge him into compliance. He eased the yoke forward, and the transport fell away from its place in the formation, then rolled into a right turn.

When he bent over and peered through the side window, he saw Shummari's transport following along.

Within a minute of their departure from the group, a battery of queries rained upon them from the other transports.

As long as he held the gun, no one was going to respond.

Belatedly, Barr tightened his harness.

He had heard the elated reports of downed MiGs on the open channel, but had refrained from entering the repartee. He might need a clear channel soon.

He decided to use it now.

"Four, let go the tanks."

"Roger," Gettman said.

He had switched to his main tanks earlier, when the drop tanks had coughed up the last of their precious liquid, and he abandoned them now without regret.

"Four, you have the lead."

"Roger."

Yucca Four drew alongside, then eased into the lead. Zimmerman, having lost his RPV, had reverted to his Air Force role of backseater, and he would guide both Phantoms onto the target.

Barr selected two of his three bombs from each pylon. He wanted to save two of the five-hundred-pounders for a second pass if it was necessary, or for a drop on the air base on their outbound run.

"IP on my mark," Zimmerman said.

The Initial Point was an abandoned township some seventeen miles west of Marada Air Base, but south of their line of flight toward the factory. Zimmerman was making his bomb run based on navigational extensions.

"Mark."

Seventeen miles out.

Air speed 845 knots.

They had to start reducing speed soon. The optimum speed for the bomb release was 450 knots in order to improve the accuracy.

"Let's everybody come right to zero-nine-three," Zimmerman ordered.

Barr eased into the turn, then locked-on the heading.

"Hate to mention this," Zimmerman said, "but I've got a bogey twelve miles south, on intercept."

"He's mine," Barr said.

He reselected a Sidewinder as he brought the nose up, then boosted the throttles. He was no longer thinking about fuel conservation.

The bogey was clear on the radar screen, and after he turned a few degrees to the right, appeared on the HUD.

Thirteen miles to target.

The bogey turned toward him.

At their combined rates of speed, they would meet in about thirty seconds.

The Sidewinder began to moan.

The MiG released a missile. Barr guessed it was an Apex.

Threat warning howl.

"MISSILE LOCK-ON" blinking on the HUD.

He ignored it.

Ten miles to target.

Sidewinder screaming happily.

He punched the stud.

The missile dropped and whisked away.

Barr tugged the stick back and right, kicked in the right rudder, pulled up, then rolled inverted.

He launched two infrared countermeasures flares.

Yanked the stick back again, and shot for the earth.

The Apex chasing him lunged upward toward the flares, changed its simple mind, reversed itself, and went down for him, but too late.

It sailed over his tail, detonating a quarter-mile beyond him.

He came back up, looping, and rolled out at the top, back on course for the factory.

The MiG had veered off toward the north and was dancing a ballet, attempting to evade the Sidewinder.

And he saw another missile coming at him. A short-range job this time, he supposed.

He rolled hard to the left.

Brought the nose down.

"Missile off!" Gettman called. He had fired on the defender also.

Rolled upright.

The missile was swerving toward him.

He turned into it.

Fired two flares.

Then turned past it.

The missile missed a direct impact with the Phantom. But its proximity fuse detonated it off his wingtip.

The F-4 shuddered at the concussion.

And immediately rolled to the right.

Barr caught it, forced his way upright, and looked out at his left wing.

What was left of it.

About three feet of the wingtip was shredded.

"You okay, Bucky?" Gettman asked.

"We're supposed to use call signs," he said.

"Fuck that. What's your status?"

"Flying. These old buckets are tougher than grandpa."

"Goddamn it! Give me a sitrep." That call was from Formsby.

"I've lost some wingtip," Barr reported. "I can still unload my ordnance, provided the bogey stays away."

He balanced his throttles, putting more power on the right engine to match the drag created by having more wing on that side.

"The bandit's gone north," Gettman reported.

"Wizard Three here," Vrdla said. "Your bogey outran both Sidewinders, but he's out of the plan for about fifteen seconds. Do your stuff."

"Call it, Yucca Five," Barr said.

Zimmerman said, "We're right on course. Two, come left three degrees. Let's get the speed down."

"Forget the speed," Vrdla said. "Your bogey will catch you."

"Maintain eight-zero-zero knots," Zimmerman said.

Maintain eight hundred? Barr was down to 670. He worked the throttles up, keeping more power on the right engine.

The landscape ahead was still barren. If there was a chemical factory out there, it had been painted to match Barr's color scheme for the Phantoms.

The plant's geographical coordinates had been pre-programmed into the computer, and Barr called them up.

He got exactly nothing.

"This is Two. My adding machine went on strike."

"Stay with me," Gettman said.

Yucca Four had pulled ahead of him as he fought to regain airspeed and he could see her a quarter-mile to his left.

He forced in some more turn. The extra drag on the right made all of his maneuvers tougher.

Considering that he might not make it as far back as the air base, and considering that he needed to be as light as possible, as soon as possible, Barr selected all of his bombs. He switched on the electro-optical targeting system. It seemed to be working because a target reticule immediately appeared on the HUD.

"Targeting computer is still earning a paycheck," Barr reported.

"That's the American work ethic in action," Formsby told him.

He checked the chronometer, urged it to greater speed. The seconds seemed to be dragging.

He looked ahead and maybe saw a few blockish shapes forming on the horizon.

"There 'tis!" Zimmerman said.

They had been losing altitude without his realizing it since he had been following Gettman's lead. The radar altimeter reported thirty-five hundred feet AGL.

Barr found the plant a few seconds later, sighting through the HUD. The computer wasn't generating a target for him, but he saw the plant live. It was a complex of eight or nine buildings, and he suspected from the construction style that there were several subterranean levels below the single story showing above ground.

He used the joystick to center the reticule on the structure second from the right, then locked it on. He pressed the pickle button to commit the drop.

From that point on, the computer—if it was working—would accept what it was seeing from the bomb's point of view, add to that the altitude and speed factors, and release the load at the proper moment.

No matter what Barr did with the airplane.

Maybe.

"I've got four miles to target," Zimmerman said. "Four's committed."

"Two's committed."

"Your bogey's on your ass," Vrdla added.

"SAMs coming!" Gettman yelled.

Barr saw three surface-to-air missile launches, but they were too late. The Phantoms were moving low at nearly twice their bombing speed, and the SAMs whistled harmlessly by them to the rear.

Closer to the target, five or six antiaircraft guns opened up, their high-explosive shells erupting in gray-black blossoms all around them.

They would just tough out the AAA.

The image of the chemical plant grew quickly in the windscreen.

A set of Lego toys.

A playhouse in the backyard.

A white vapor floated on the air above it.

And there it was, just disappearing under the nose.

The Phantom leapt a little as the bombs dropped away.

And then the plant was gone, and he was flying over desolation once again.

Ramad could not believe it.

He had almost reached firing range of his last three AA-8s when the bombs dropped from the airplanes ahead of him.

The clock stood still while he counted the hits. Ten of the twelve bombs struck the second, third, and fifth buildings. It seemed as if the bombs holed the roofs, counted to ten, then erupted.

A visible concussion ring rose from the buildings, followed by great geysers spewing blackened vapor and debris. The walls bulged outward, the roofs collapsed, and the walls caved in on them. The first, fourth, sixth, and eighth buildings began to buckle also.

The bombs that entered building five must have gone through the first floor into the subsurface level, where the warheads were constructed, for a secondary blast gushed red-orange flames chased by a yellow fireball.

He had to swerve to the left to avoid the detritus filling the air.

He wondered if the fire would consume all of the released chemicals before they invaded the nerves and minds of his countrymen.

And he became furious at the destruction. Libya's future, in his hands, had become shaky. He must kill the infidels, any of them.

All of them.

And he realized that the still unidentified radar blip to the south would be their airborne control.

One of the two Phantoms ahead of him was damaged badly. From what he knew of their range, he did not think either of them would reach the borders of Libya. The pilots could be captured at will.

He would strike down the damnable commanders.

"Marada Base, Vulture."

"Vulture, they are attacking!"

"Give me a vector for the southern target, Marada."

"But Vulture . . . uh, take a heading of one-nine-six."

Neil Formsby was feeling antsy, listening to the chatter on the radio, and trying not to put his two cents worth in. He had dozens of extremely positive suggestions, but he wasn't on the scene.

"Damn, damn, damn," Demion said. "Come on, somebody! Report something!"

"Wizard, Two," Barr called. "One chem plant down in the dirt."

"Damage estimate?" Formsby asked.

"Call it ninety percent, Neil. There's still two smaller buildings standing, but I don't think they're part of the main plant."

"Good show, Bucky."

"Hell, Karl got two buildings. I only got one."

"How's your structural damage?" Formsby asked.

"The damage is all right. I don't know about the plane. In any event, I've elected to head south. I believe I'll skip the party at Marada."

"Stay with him, Four," Demion ordered.

"Tight as ticks on a hound," Gettman said.

"This is Wizard Three," Vrdla broke in. "Your bogey's going to leave you alone, Two."

"Good news," Barr said.

"Not so good. He's coming after us."

"I've been hit!" Jordan yelped.

The report startled Wyatt for a moment, until he remembered Jordan wasn't in Yucca Six. The RPV operators tended to think of themselves as being in their craft.

Wyatt and Hackley were eleven miles from the target, past their IP, and catching up with Yucca Six, which should have been about two miles from the target.

His radar screen was going crazy, reporting SAM radars lighting up all around the base. When he checked the windscreen, in the distance he could see antiaircraft guns opening up on Yucca Six.

In the back of his mind, he worried about Bucky Barr. He had heard the exchanges with Wizard.

"How bad, Six?" Formsby asked.

"Hold a sec. I think I'm under control. I don't think I've got a right aileron. Shaky as hell."

319

"Please tell me what you see, Clifford," Formsby said. "I'm not getting much out of my role as a vicarious kibitzer."

Wyatt selected all of his bombs, as well as the electro-optical targeting system. All of the correct green LEDs came to life.

"I think I'm about five hundred AGL," Jordan said. "The altimeter's fucked up, but my picture is clear. I've got the base in view."

"Bombs are armed?" Formsby asked.

"I don't know. I hit the switches, but I'm not getting feedback. I think I took shrapnel through the fuselage. I can't tell about distance. Coming up fast. Oops. She tried to roll right. Oh, Christ!"

"What! What do you see?" Formsby yelled.

"Su-24s. Two of them are on roll out. I'm pulling left. She doesn't want to go. There. Closing. Nose down. Two bombers on my screen. I. . . ."

"What's up, Six?" Wyatt called.

"It all disappeared, Andy. I probably took a SAM."

"You're a backseater again. Start calling it."

It took a few seconds for Jordan to reorient himself, then he said, "Three, come right two degrees. One, back off a few hundred yards."

"Roger," Wyatt answered and quickly reduced his throttle setting.

Through the windscreen, he saw a column of dark gray smoke rising in the distance, ascending from a ball of reddish flame. That would be the wreckage of Yucca Six.

"That's a formidable fucking array of SAMS," Jordan said. "Take it down five hundred feet. Let's go to six hundred knots."

Wyatt backed off on the throttles some more. The altimeter read three thousand feet AGL.

Six miles to target.

"Yucca One, how many missiles do you have left?" Jordan asked.

"One lonely Sidewinder."

"We've got three. Let's launch them all, and see if we can screw up some SAM radars."

"Give me the word," Wyatt said, resetting the armaments panel.

At four miles out, with antiaircraft flak beginning to burst around them, Jordan said, "Now!"

Wyatt launched his Sidewinder straight ahead and reselected his bomb load, taking four bombs for the first release and two for the second.

Gettman's missiles zipped off right behind his own.

A few of the SAM radar operators were apparently alarmed by the sudden new echoes on their screens and half-a-dozen missiles whipped off their launchers. Missile vapor trails crisscrossed in the skies ahead. The Sidewinders swirled around, looking for the best heat sources, then dove toward the earth. Wyatt lost track of them and didn't know where they hit.

Wyatt worked the stick gently, jigging back and forth to the sides to put the AAA gunners off-stride. Ahead of him, Hackley was doing the same.

"Goddamn!" Jordan called. "Look at that!"

Wyatt rotated the thumbwheel and zoomed his video lens in on the base.

The magnified view on the HUD showed him a single runway that appeared to be in utter chaos.

Yucca Six must have impacted the runway right on top of the two Su-24s taking off. The whole north end of the runway was a carpet of burning chunks of fuselages and wings and engines. Rubble was spread everywhere. The separate fires contributed dark smoke to the single funnel climbing to the sky. A whitish haze was spreading quickly from the wreckage, dissipating in all directions except upward.

He wondered what kind of gas it was.

On the south end of the runway were another seven bombers, all lined up nicely on the runway and the taxiway. A couple hundred yards away from the taxiway were two MiG-23s being tended by fuel trucks. They were also being abandoned as figures ran away from them.

The bombers' route to freedom and the skyways was blocked by the destroyed aircraft on the runway.

If the ant-like things he could see scurrying about on the screen were men, they were leaving the bomber aircraft where they sat, taking off in panicked flight for the desert, probably upwind. More ants were streaming up the ramps from the underground hangars.

Wyatt centered the reticule on the first three bombers in the lineup and pickled the bombs off.

The HUD reported, "BOMBS COMMITTED."

There was suddenly a hangar opening on the screen. He quickly locked the reticule in place, then clicked the release button again.

"BOMBS COMMITTED," blinked twice.

Waited two seconds.

Wheeled the magnification down to normal.

Closing on the target.

The ants became terrified men, running at top speed for the open desert.

"Bombs away," Jordan reported.

The tail pipes of the Phantom ahead of him suddenly

turned white-hot as Gettman went to afterburner and turned the nose skyward.

Another second.

Tha-WHUMP!

The F-4 lurched sideways as an antiaircraft shell burst right alongside him.

Despite his tightened harness, Wyatt was thrown hard against the right side of the cockpit.

The first stick of bombs released.

The Phantom tried to go over on its left side, and he fought the control stick back to the right.

The second stick of bombs released.

Wyatt's ears rang from the concussion of the antiaircraft shell.

The airplane danced a jig.

A terrible rending noise erupted behind him on the right side.

He glanced down at the instrument panel. His vision seemed dimmer than normal.

The right turbojet was coming apart, spitting up turbine blades like a newborn. He had a whole bank of red lights blinking at him.

He shut it down.

The Phantom steadied.

He checked the rearview mirror.

Marada Air Base, what was left of it, was several miles behind him. Dozens of fires raged now.

He eased into a right turn.

His speed was coming down drastically.

"My God, Andy," Gettman said, "you must have gotten a couple inside the hangar. There's secondary explosions just rocking the ground. The desert floor is caving in in about a hundred places."

"How about the bombers, Karl?" Wyatt was forgetting his own fiat regarding call signs.

His head felt thick and sluggish.

Concussion. Mild concussion. That was all.

"What bombers? They got a scrap heap there. We can count eleven kills on the surface and take a wild-assed guess as to what was below ground."

"They'll rename it Ramad's Salvage and Recycling Center," Gettman said.

Wyatt tried to assess the damage he had sustained. The fuselage skin on the right side was shoved into the cockpit by five or six inches.

Down near his feet, he could see three rips in the skin. The wind shrieked through them.

He seemed to have all of his flight controls. He carefully tested each.

The engine monitors for the left turbojet were still operating, as was the engine. His airspeed indicator was gone, however, and he had to estimate that he was maybe holding three hundred knots.

That wouldn't last for long.

No altimeter either.

Looking through the right side of the canopy, which had a major and expanding crack in it, he saw that the leading edge of the right wing was peppered with holes. One hole, maybe two feet in diameter, went clear through the wing. The camouflage paint blended nicely with what he could see through the hole.

He wondered if he was thinking irrationally.

The right side of his face felt numb. The hearing in his right ear seemed to be gone.

He unclipped the oxygen mask and felt his right cheek. There was no blood, but he had definitely just left the dentist's chair.

"Hey One, Three."

"One."

"You coming up here with me?"

"I don't think so," Wyatt said.

Martin Church was still in Embry's office.

He had tired of studying Madonna.

Embry had sent out for a large pizza, but each of them had only had one slice out of it.

After number six, he had lost count of the cups of coffee he had poured down.

"If I'd been thinking ahead," Embry said, "I'd have put a descrambler into our satellite circuits so we could listen to what was going on."

"You think there's much going on, now?"

"All you have to do is look at that," Embry said, pointing to the monitor.

The heavy smoke over the chemical plant and Marada Air Base was very apparent in the satellite picture. After careful scrutiny of the screen and checks with the analysts at NSA, both Church and Embry were certain that none of the bombers had gotten off the ground.

The satellite lens couldn't capture the camouflaged aircraft in near real time, actual imagery, so they weren't sure which airplanes were still aloft. Embry had called the NSA and had them switch to infrared tracking for a few moments, and they had been able to count five infrared tracks, all headed south. In addition, the camera angle gave them the infrared tracks of the two C-130s circling about two hundred miles south of the target zone.

There were three alarming aspects, as far as Church was concerned.

First, there were two apparently heavy aircraft approaching from the east.

Second, a flight of eight aircraft, identified by their infrared signatures as probable MiG-23s, had turned back from original courses, though they were apparently headed directly for Marada Air Base.

Third, he was deeply saddened by the loss of two of Wyatt's airplanes.

"George, do you suppose we can do something for the families of those pilots? Quietly, of course."

Embry's eyes narrowed, then he said, "Oh, I forgot to tell you, Marty. There weren't any pilots in those planes."

"You son of a bitch!"

Embry grinned. "I've got to have one card up my sleeve when I'm dealing with you, Marty."

Eighteen

Nelson Barr found that his Phantom still had almost six hundred knots left in her. He used all of them, found a heading of 210 degrees, and climbed to fifteen thousand feet.

The F-4 seemed to prefer flying in a slewed fashion, canted to the right, and he used practically all of the left rudder trim available to counter the drag of the extra three feet of wing on the right side.

Karl Gettman moved in on his left wing and surveyed the damage.

"What do you think, Karl?"

"You'll dance again, Bucky. You're dangling some cabling and what looks like the hydraulic jack for the leading edge slat. Where the slat used to be."

Barr tried his navigational computer.

Negative.

But he had all the basics, and that was what he had learned to fly with.

"Where's that MiG, Dave?"

"About sixty miles south, burning fuel like he's got his own oil well," Zimmerman said.

"You guys go on ahead. The Herc may need help."

"You sure?" Gettman asked.

"Go."

Formsby had been listening. He said, "We're quite all right, you know."

"So am I," Barr said. "Take off, Four."

Gettman climbed upward, got away from Barr's Phantom, and kicked in the afterburners. He wasn't worrying about fuel at this stage, either.

Barr was beginning to worry about it.

"One," he said, "I haven't heard from you."

"We're plugging along," Wyatt came back. "Three's joined up with me."

"How plugged are you?" Barr asked.

"There have been better days. I've lost the starboard turbojet, but I'm managing what, Three?"

Hackley said, "Two-seven-oh knots. Right now."

"You drop all your ordnance?" Barr asked.

"I've thrown away everything I can throw away."

"Give me some coordinates, Norm. I'll find you."

"To hell with that," Wyatt said. "You go where you're supposed to go."

Barr shut up.

He was passing south of the air base, and he wished he had brought a camera along. The damage was spectacular. There was burning wreckage all over the runway and taxiway. The ground had sagged deeply in a half-dozen spots over the subterranean hangars, and smoke and flames had broken through in several spots. A ground fog of white mist hung over everything. He saw men grouped together in clusters out in the desert away from the complex, and more people were still running, attempting to get away from the base.

There were a number of bodies spread around also, and he tried to skip over those.

But he couldn't.

Wyatt had full power on his remaining turbojet and he was watching the temperatures closely. He had trimmed the controls out as far as he could to balance the aircraft, but he still had to maintain pressure on the left rudder. The calf of his left leg was going to know about it soon, he thought.

Hackley had told him he was holding thirty-two hundred feet AGL, and he was beginning to believe he could maintain that for awhile. Fuel wasn't a problem at the moment; he had lost half of his consumption end.

"Can you come right a bit more?" Hackley asked.

"Sure."

Wyatt released pressure on the left rudder, and the Phantom obediently swung right.

"There you go, Andy. That puts you on two-one-five."

"Take off, Norm."

"Not on your life, which is what we're talking about, right? When you go down, I want your coordinates, and you don't have anything left to tell you what they are."

That point was difficult to argue.

"Wizard Three," Wyatt said.

"Go, One."

"What are you showing in the area? Anything coming out of Tripoli or Benghazi?"

"If they are, I haven't seen them. We're showing that MiG about a hundred out, and that's all."

"You guys skedaddle."

"We've got this one covered," Demion said. "You just pay attention to what you're doing."

Wyatt concentrated on his flying.

Ramad tried calling Marada Air Base, but no one answered his call. The fools were probably hiding under the tables. He thought about diverting Orange Squadron from its Return to Base command, but knew he would not need them for an attack on a slow-moving target.

He thought about tuning in the Tripoli command frequency, and decided against that. He didn't want to talk to anyone from the staff until after he had finished this.

The altimeter read ten thousand meters.

His airspeed was Mach 1.7.

Abruptly, a target appeared on the top edge of his radar screen. It was thirty-five kilometers away, and it appeared to be flying in a large circle.

It was definitely their command plane, and he would blow it out of the sky.

He checked his armaments panel. His three remaining AA-8s were indicating availability.

Reducing his throttle settings, he remembered someone with whom he should talk. He used the secondary tactical channel.

Ahmed al-Qati heard Ramad calling.

After the fourth try, he responded. "Vulture, this is Colonel al-Qati."

Ramad ignored the use of his name. "What is your position?"

"Colonel, the C-130s have been recalled and are returning to El Bardi. Some of the MiGs are still refueling. Tripoli has recalled the entire operation."

Al-Qati did not mention that the transports he and

Shummari now commanded were no longer part of the group of C-130s retreating to the coast. They were now one hundred kilometers west of the border, heading west-south-west.

"That is impossible! I have not called off Test Strike."

"There is no more Test Strike, Colonel. Your bombers are destroyed on the runway. Your air base is destroyed. The casualties are high. The last report said seventy dead and many more than that wounded. Colonel Ghazi has been killed."

Al-Qati realized he was talking to no one. Ramad had given up listening.

But then, he had done that many months before.

"You won't be needing me here, will you, James?"

"Go ahead, Neil," Demion said.

Formsby removed his headset and disconnected his oxygen mask, then pushed himself up out of the copilot's seat.

Demion had already taken the Hercules out of its programmed circle and was on a heading of 190 degrees. The four turbine engines were churning out one hundred percent power.

Formsby was no more out of the seat than Kriswell was into it.

Kriswell said, "I've always wanted to fly a combat mission."

"You can fly it, Tom. Just don't touch anything," Demion told him.

Sliding down the ladder to the crew compartment, he found a crowd. Potter, Borman, Cavanaugh, and Littlefield had not been able to wait it out, sitting in the cargo bay. They were ranged around Maal and Vrdla, who were seated next to each other at the console.

Potter had rigged up an oxygen distribution hose for all of the extra people, and Formsby plugged into it. Borman handed him an extra headset. They were all conversing over the aircraft's internal communications system.

"Thank you, Benjamin." He was still trying to remember everyone's names.

He peered over Vrdla's shoulder at the screen.

"Tell me, please, Samuel."

Vrdla used a stubby forefinger to point to each blip on the screen. They were not using the Identify Friend or Foe equipment, so none of the blips was automatically tagged by the computer.

"This is Andy and Norm. They're making two-seven-zero, and they're a hundred-and-forty-five miles north of us. Over here,"—about forty miles west of Wyatt—"is Bucky. He's doing all right, and he's a hundred-and-twenty out. Ahead of him, here, is Karl and Dave. They're a hundred out. This fucker here is the MiG. He's slowing some, but he's still hauling ass. He's twenty-one away. Here, south of us, is the tanker."

"No chance that Gettman will catch the MiG, is there?" Formsby asked.

"Not in this world," Vrdla said.

"What do you think, Neil?" Maal asked.

"I think it is time. Perhaps past time."

"Jim?" Maal asked.

"Let's go with Neil's timing, Denny," Demion said.

Maal sat up straighter in his seat, worked his shoulders, then placed his hands on the twin joysticks in front of him. The right one controlled ailerons and elevators. The left controlled rudders and throttles. A small

332

Bakelite box in front of the joysticks had several toggle switches identified with black labeling tape——LNDG GEAR, FLAPS, AUTOPIL, FUEL SEL. There were a couple of additional controls for setting the autopilot.

Set into the console was a cathode ray tube that displayed the C-130F's pertinent data via a radio feedback. Airspeed, heading, altitude, attitude (turn-and-bank indicator), and rate-of-climb were the primary readouts, but engine tachometers and oil pressure relays were also shown.

A similar setup had been used to control the RPV F-4s with the addition of the video relay.

Maal reached forward and flipped off the autopilot. Using the sticks, he kept the RPV in its turn.

"Where do we want to go, Neil?"

Formsby glanced at the aircraft positions on the radar screen. "I think about oh-five-oh should do it, Dennis."

Maal eased out of his turn as the heading came up. "Five-zero, right on."

Formsby checked the tanker's altitude. Twenty-five thousand feet.

"Then, I'd like to see you put it in a slightly nose-down altitude."

"We want speed, right?"

"Exactly."

"I think I can get about four hundred knots out of her," Maal said.

He eased the nose down until the rate-of-climb indicator showed a negative twenty-five-feet-per-minute. Then he pushed the left stick full forward.

"We're not getting the same revs out of each engine," he said. "She's probably shaking pretty good."

Formsby looked at the tachometer readouts and found

them differing by as much as a couple of hundred revolutions.

"If it gets to be a problem," he said, "go ahead and back off."

The five men standing in the compartment behind the console operators remained quiet staring at the readouts and the radar screen.

"What's it look like, Sam?" Demion asked from his pilot's station.

"Denny's got her up to three-nine-zero knots," Vrdla said. "I'm showing her six miles away, closing fast. She's ten thousand below us."

"And the MiG?"

"One-seven."

"From my reading of the combat action," Formsby said "I believe the MiG will only have Aphids left. He's got to position himself within five miles of us."

"I think he can do that," Kriswell said.

"Tanker's three miles away," Vrdla said.

"I'm going now," Demion said. "Grab onto something solid."

The men standing in the compartment reached for grab bars. Formsby gripped the back of Maal's seat, which was bolted to the deck.

Abruptly, Demion put the nose down and began a steep dive.

"He saw that," Vrdla reported. "And I don't think he liked it. He's coming on a little faster. I read him at Mach one-point-five. One-two out."

"Lucas, you ready?" Demion asked.

"Ready, boss," Littlefield said.

He held a cable with a handgrip and two thumb switches on the end of it. The switches controlled the chaff and flare dispensers on the countermeasures pods.

"I do not think he has radar-guided missiles," Formsby said, "but it wouldn't hurt to be cautious."

"Jam him," Demion said.

Vrdla clicked on the radar-jamming transmitters in both countermeasures pods.

"The tanker just went under us, Jim," Vrdla said. "We had about a two-thousand-foot clearance."

"Glad to hear it," Demion said.

"I've got the tanker up to four-hundred-and-six knots," Maal said. "But the jamming is interfering with my control."

"Let's not worry about control at this very minute," Formsby said.

"Four-oh-six knots? Hell," Demion said, "I can beat that."

He did not pull out of his dive.

Ibrahim Ramad had picked up the second blip on his radar screen a few minutes before. Again, he was amazed. The raiders had at least eight aircraft. Ghazi's information had been entirely incorrect.

The newest aircraft was also a slow mover, and he estimated it for a transport.

They would not actually attempt to land troops at Marada Air Base and attempt to capture it intact, would they?

Then again, he was landing troops in Ethiopia.

Anything was possible.

Distance to target: twenty kilometers.

His target was running, but slowly. It was also losing altitude.

The new target was advancing on him at a much lower altitude.

The blips merged as they passed each other, and the newest target kept coming.

A foolish, foolish pilot, he thought.

Altitude seventy-five hundred meters.

The target was now ten kilometers away.

He began easing off the throttles.

The primary target continued to dive.

The second target continued toward him.

A verifiable idiot.

He would take his original target first, then come back for the second.

Speed down to Mach 1.1. He needed to be much slower to make his turn back.

Distance to target eight kilometers.

Back on the throttles.

A burble as he passed down through the sonic barrier.

Seven kilometers. The second target had now passed below him and was behind.

His primary target began to level off at three thousand meters of altitude, then to zigzag. He knew what was coming.

Ramad grinned his pleasure.

Six kilometers.

Soon.

Airspeed six hundred knots.

Five kilometers.

Ahead, against the desert floor, he saw it. A bright and shiny C-130, banking left and right as it attempted to foil his shot.

He held the MiG steady, and when the transport slipped through his sight, triggered off two AA-8s.

He knew, deep in his heart and soul, that it was a perfect shot against an unarmed C-130. The commanders of this treacherous incursion against Ramad's personal empire would pay dearly. They would burn in hell forever.

And he would collect the evidence which would prove their treachery, and it would exonerate him with those in Tripoli.

Exonerate?

He required no exoneration.

His duties were performed only in the advancement of his native land.

For the first time, however, he allowed the possibility that there had been some damage at Marada Air Base. Perhaps even at the chemical plant. He did not think it would be extensive, and when he showed the Leader that he had saved the day, had destroyed the commanders, he would be received in honor.

Ramad rolled to the right and pulled the control stick hard toward his crotch.

The MiG responded aggressively, turning hard back to the north.

He concentrated on finding the other transport on his radar screen.

There.

It also was diving, but at a shallow rate. It was twenty-five kilometers ahead of him, to the north, but he would catch it easily.

He glanced up at his rearview mirror in time to catch the twin white-yellow flashes as his missiles disintegrated the C-130.

The sheer pleasure of it coursed through his veins and made him proud, a true warrior supporting the cause of Allah.

Fifteen kilometers.

Checking the armaments panel, he made certain that his final AA-8 was selected.

His thumb caressed the firing stud without setting it off.

It was most sensual.

WHOOF!

The MiG jumped slightly sideways.

The shudder in the airframe brought him out of his reverie. His head jerked back and forth as he sought the explanation from his instruments.

The left turbojet had ceased to operate. The RPMs were spinning quickly down.

WHOOF!

The right turbojet flamed out.

Ramad's eyes darted to the fuel state indicator.

It read: 0 KILOGRAMS.

Impossible! He could not be out of fuel!

But he was.

He had utilized the afterburners for most of, too much of, his flight.

Quickly, he looked at the screen.

The target was pulling ahead, sixteen kilometers from him.

Furious, he thumbed-off the missile.

It screamed from its rail, but it was mindless, and it swirled the skies ahead of him, seeking a target, but not finding one, detonating itself harmlessly.

It could not happen to him!

The speed began to drop drastically, and he put the nose down to restore it.

Still, he was down to four hundred knots very quickly. Ignoring the automatic operation of the computer, he extended the wings from their swept-back configuration to increase his lift.

Altitude two thousand meters.

Looking frantically around, he tried to orient himself. There was nothing. Not a road nor a hill nor a wadi for a landmark.

He checked the radar screen.

His target was now far ahead, but worse, another blip had appeared on the screen, coming at him very rapidly. It would be one of the escaping F-4s.

His glide was steep, but he could not take many evasive maneuvers without losing lift and altitude.

Turning slightly to the right, moving toward the east, he attempted to widen the gap between himself and the approaching F-4.

Seconds later, he saw the aircraft as it neared him, slowing, and turning to match his direction.

His speed was down to 330 knots.

The F-4 descended, pulling in behind him.

He waited for the missile.

It should not have come to this, Merciful Allah. I only sought to do your bidding.

The F-4 suddenly accelerated and moved up along his left wing.

Ramad looked over at them.

There was a black face in the front seat and a white face in the rear.

The black man held up the middle finger of his right hand, then abruptly climbed away, increasing speed, performed a wing-over directly over Ramad's cockpit, then was gone.

Ramad's relief was so great that, for precious moments he did not realize how close to the ground he was.

When he saw the dunes ahead of him, without one

flat spot available, he looked at the altimeter: 635 meters above ground level.

No more time.

He tucked his elbows in, grabbed the ejection handle between his legs, and jerked.

The ejection seat crunched his spine as it fired.

Nineteen

"I just didn't have the heart to shoot the son of a bitch down," Gettman said.

"Karl did give him the finger," Zimmerman added, "so that probably got to his ego."

"Did you see a chute?" Formsby asked.

"Yeah, he made it out," Gettman said, "but if he walks sixty miles in any direction, he still ain't going to find anything. That sucker better have a good radio and a hell of a lot of water with him."

"Any asshole that can't figure out he's running out of gas deserves the walk," Zimmerman said.

"What is your fuel state?" Formsby asked.

"Well," Gettman said, "uh, come to think of it, we may be joining him shortly."

"Conserve as well as you can," Demion said.

"How are you guys doing?" Gettman asked.

"He blew the hell out of a bunch of flares," Formsby said. "Lucas did us proud."

He looked over to Littlefield, who gave him a big, wide grin and held up his flare launching control.

Demion said, "We're going to reduce speed now, so

everyone else can catch up with us. I'll hold it around two-two-zero knots."

"Damn, Jim, you don't have to do that," Barr broke in. "I can catch you any day of the week. Wings or no wings."

Maal waved Formsby close and spoke over the intercom, "Let her go now?"

"I believe she has done her job well, don't you, Dennis? I firmly believe she diverted his attention from a thorough attack against us."

"I hate to do this, Neil."

"If we simply let her go, and they do not shoot her down farther north, she could reach the Mediterranean," Formsby said. "But she might not hit hard enough to detonate the plastic explosive."

Maal shoved his elevator stick forward and watched the readouts. At a rate-of-climb of negative five hundred-feet-per-minute, he centered the stick.

They did not have to wait long.

After a few minutes, all of the feedback readouts went blank.

Barr came up on the radio. "I saw her go in. I offered up a prayer."

"Did the plastic detonate, Nelson?" Formsby asked.

"It must have, along with the fuel tanks. She's an inferno."

Maal climbed out of the seat he had occupied for so long and said, "Lucas, you have any of that rotten coffee left."

"I don't think so, Denny, but I'll make more. How rotten do you want it?"

"Just as bad as you can get it."

Most of the others settled to the deck to sit, and Formsby climbed the ladder back to the flight deck and took the engineer/navigator's seat. He pulled on the headset but did not bother connecting the oxygen mask. They were flying at three thousand feet now.

It was pretty much quiet on the intercom and the tactical channel.

He supposed most of them were thinking about Wyatt.

Until Vrdla spoke up. "We may have a minor problem, Jim."

"What's that?" Demion asked.

"I just picked up two targets to our east. Range two-one-five and closing. They're slow moving. I give 'em three-five-oh knots."

"That's an unexpected development," Demion said. "I thought we'd planned it out for every contingency."

"It has to be two of those troop transports that took off earlier," Formsby said. "They will not be armed."

"That's right," Kriswell said. "What the hell can they do?"

Martin Church had gone down the hallway to the men's room. When he got back, he found that Embry had contacted the NSA and asked for an infrared image again.

He sat down at the table and stared at the blue-green-orange-red splotches on the monitor.

"Where are we now, George?"

Embry pressed a finger against the screen. "See that bright red spot. The tanker went in."

"Jesus!"

"It wasn't manned, Marty."

"Goddamn it! George, will you quit springing this shit on me? Are any of them manned?"

"The rest of them. Everyone's still airborne. The last hostile plane in the region went down. I don't know whether it was shot down or not, but it didn't burn."

"So all these hot spots are our planes?"

"Except these two down here to the east. I've been watching them."

"That's wonderful. Can you watch them into oblivion?"

"Doubt it, Marty."

The telephone rang, startling him. His concentration on the screen had been so intense for so long—it didn't seem like only an hour and forty minutes—that he had blanked out the rest of the world.

Embry scooted back in his castered chair and grabbed the phone from the desk.

"Yeah, put her through."

He handed the phone to Church.

"You get to talk to her, Marty."

"Who is it?"

"Kramer."

Church took the phone and pressed it to his ear.

"Yes."

"Tell me what's happening," she said. The anxiety in her voice was palpable.

"There's really not much to report just yet," he said. Just the destruction of an air base, a chemical factory, a bomber squadron, and an interceptor squadron. Of course, none of that would ever be reported outside of Agency channels.

"You've got to be watching it," she said. "You have all your secret devices."

"Indirectly," he admitted.

"Tell me, goddamn it!"

"Everyone with whom we are concerned is still airborne," he said, "but that's all I can say right now."

"Thank you," Kramer said and hung up.

Church looked at the screen, at the relative positions of the hot spots. Two of them were lagging far behind, but he didn't know who was flying them, and he certainly wouldn't pass speculation on to her.

They had scrambled defense fighters out of Tripoli and Benghazi, but from what al-Qati was hearing on the radio, those defensive forces were gathering along the coast and moving toward the Egyptian border. The three companies of his battalion left at El Bardi had also been alerted.

The Leader was expecting additional attacks from the Israelis, he supposed. That was a knee-jerk reaction and was an action al-Qati did not believe would occur. Not unless it was Israelis who were behind the attack on Marada Air Base.

That was possible.

But unlikely, given his suspicions of Sophia. He knew she spoke Italian fluently, as well as English. She was about his equal in French, which was rudimentary. Her Arabic was spartan, and the two of them had usually conversed in English. She might well speak Hebrew, but somehow, he doubted it.

He wished he could step outside of himself, outside of his body, and kick himself.

He would kick himself right in the testicles, which were what had led him to be so asinine.

But he had loved her.

Had?

He still loved her.

And she had used him.

He had used her also, to attempt to prevent the senseless attack in Ethiopia.

He had succeeded brilliantly.

So brilliantly that his nation had lost a staggering amount of her military resources and personnel. He was chagrined to think of the many that had died at the base and at the chemical plant.

His countrymen.

He knew, of course, that in war one must expect that any given situation would be infinitely worse than anticipated. But the miscalculations that had occurred this morning were inexcusable.

He could lay the blame for inadequate defense at Ramad's door, but he could not place it all there. He should have admitted to Ghazi his involvement with the spy and accepted the death sentence he would have received.

He had not. And he would not.

All he could do was what he could do.

Fortunately, they had not heard from Ibrahim Ramad for some time.

"Where are we now?" he asked the pilot.

Al-Qati no longer held his pistol to the man's head. The pilot and his crew appeared to have accepted their lot, especially after additional news of the attack on Marada Air Base had been disseminated.

"It is difficult, with our limited radar, Colonel. On dead reckoning, I believe we are some three hundred kilometers from where we estimated the AWACS aircraft to be. And remember, that was based on information we overheard from Marada Air Control. I suspect that the AWACS has left the region."

"How soon until we are in radar range?"

"Perhaps another half hour, Colonel."

"Very well. Thank you."

Instead of threatening the copilot with a pistol he reached for the selector on the bulkhead next to him and switched from the intercom to the secondary tactical channel. The first channel was jumbled with orders and counterorders emanating from Tripoli. Among the government and the military bureaus, chaos reigned.

"Moonglow, Sundown."

"Proceed, Sundown."

"What is your status?"

"Quite relaxed," Shummari reported. "The errors of many ways have been seen."

"And your helicopter crews?"

"We can be off the transports and airborne within fifteen minutes. The assistance of your soldiers would probably improve that time."

"Very good. You may expect assistance."

Al-Qati still did not know what he would find when they got to where they were going.

He could only hope that the intruders were utilizing a staging base which he could cut off.

After what had taken place at Marada, the raiders deserved to be slaughtered, and given the chance his duty was to slaughter them.

Barr heard Wyatt's voice for the first time in fifteen minutes.

"Let me have a status check," Wyatt said.

All of the planes read off their fuel states. Except for the Hercules, none of the numbers were encouraging.

"Positions?" Wyatt asked.

"Four's alongside Wizard," Gettman replied.

"And Two's got both of them in sight," Barr said. He had had the bright skin of the C-130 visually for several minutes. He estimated that he was six or seven miles behind them. "We're a bit more interested in you, Andy."

"I'm down to under two hundred knots and fifteen hundred feet of ground clearance. I'm sending Norm on now."

"The hell you are," Hackley said.

"You know the course I'm on. Scoot!"

"Shit. Roger."

"Jim," Barr asked. "What have you got for terrain?"

"Not too bad, Bucky. I saw a flat spot a couple of miles back. I can't tell how soft it is."

"Well, we're sure as hell not going to make it back to Chad. You circle the wagons where you are, and I'll tell you how soft it is. Andy?"

"Your call," Wyatt said. "You're the lowest on fuel."

"Let me," Gettman said. "I lied. I've got the short straw on fuel."

"You've also got a passenger," Barr said.

"Nelson," Formsby said "why don't you simply punch out? You could test the surface with your feet."

"I get airsick in a parachute," Barr said.

"I understand. I happen to feel the same way myself."

Ahead of him, he saw the transport enter into a circular pattern. A few seconds later, as he closed up on them, he saw Gettman's Phantom tucked in tight with the transport. They stayed at around seven thousand feet as Barr began to drain off speed and altitude.

"Two, Wizard Three."

"Come on, Sam."

"You'll want to take it left five degrees."

"Going."

After several seconds on that course, Vrdla said, "Now, Two, come to one-nine-eight."

Barr banked into the new heading, still letting down.

When he was at fifteen hundred feet AGL, Vrdla said, "That's it."

Barr surveyed the surface of the ground as he swept across it at 250 knots.

"Jesus, Jim! You think that's flat?"

"I wanted to use the dune on the west as a launch ramp," Demion said.

"You've got any number of dunes to choose from," Barr told him.

The landscape, like most all of the landscape he had seen in the last couple of days, was barren and desolate. It undulated here by several feet along a two-mile stretch. If he stopped to count, he might be able to calculate a half-dozen scrubby bushes along the whole length.

What was more important, however, the surface didn't appear to have a totally sand composition. It seemed to be composed of crusted earth, and his job was to see how hard the lack of moisture and the heat of the sun had made the crust.

He circled back to the east.

"What do you think, Nelson?"

"Absolutely worth a try."

He took the Phantom five miles east, then turned back to the west, deploying his flaps. With his missing wingtip, he wasn't going to have leading edge slats for increased lift, and his landing speed would be a trifle higher than he liked.

Maybe he wouldn't get airsick in a parachute this time?

"Nah."

"What did you say, Bucky?" Demion asked.

"I yawned, Jim. This is a yawner."

Demion's flat spot was about a quarter-mile wide, bounded on the north and south by dunes that were higher than the average dune. He selected the right side of the area. If he screwed it up, he wanted the others to have room to get down.

He debated bellying it in. It would be preferable as far as he was concerned, but it wouldn't tell the others anything about the surface's ability to support tires.

Punching the landing gear switch, he saw three green lights.

Eased back on the throttles.

Felt the tail sag and let it.

He wanted as much flare as he could get, using his lift until the last possible moment.

The F-4 floated in.

"Like a feather," he said.

"What?" somebody asked.

He didn't answer.

Nose down a little.

Little dunes hopping at him.

Long, smooth, downward slope coming up.

Chopped the throttles.

The Phantom touched ever so lightly.

He was a damned choreographer.

The tires began spinning against the surface of the earth.

Then digging in.

The nosewheel touched down.

Speed well down.

The airplane rose and fell with the terrain, but the unevenness wasn't particularly drastic.

Slowing.

He tapped the brakes.

There weren't any.

"Fuck."

"What?"

The F-4 dragged to a stop after maybe a mile-and-a-half.

Barr let his breath out.

Killed the turbojets.

"That was nice, Bucky," Demion said.

He opened the canopy and felt the heat swirl inside. "Hey, Karl."

"Yo."

"You want to ditch the rest of your missiles before you try it? I forgot to."

"You got to think about these things, Bucky."

"And Jim, your goddamned brakes didn't work."

"You told me you didn't need them."

"Oh. Right."

"So what do you recommend, Nelson?" Formsby asked.

"Drag the tails on the fighters on approach and keep the nose gear up as long as possible. Once the nose tire's down, you aren't going to do much steering. Also, once the Phantoms are down, they're not taking off again."

"What about the Herc?" Demion asked.

"Let me get unhitched and jump down there, then I'll tell you."

Barr unclipped his mask and chin strap, slipped off his helmet, and hooked it over the HUD.

He worked his way out of his harness, saved his sur-

351

vival kit by tossing it out of the cockpit, slipped ove
the coaming, and slid to the ground.

It felt pretty solid under his feet.

He checked the ruts behind the main gear.

And then had a hell of a time climbing back up ont
the wing, over the intakes, and into the cockpit.

When he finally reached it, he pulled the helme
close and spoke into the mike. "Two, here. My calcu
lations say you'll make it, Jim."

"How good are your calculations?"

"I'm the best damned consultant in a five- or six
mile radius."

"That's all I need."

Barr disconnected his helmet. The United States Ai
Force had issued it to him, and he was damned wel
taking it home with him.

Within twelve minutes, they had Gettman, then th
C-130 on the ground. The Hercules, with its rough-fiel
design and big, soft tires, had less trouble than he ha
expected, but the low ground clearance of the fuselag
managed to level a few small hillocks. As soon as i
slowed enough, Demion turned it around and headed i
back toward the east.

Seven minutes later, Hackley appeared low out of the
east and made one pass over the strip.

He made a circuit, then his approach. The touchdown
was perfect, but as soon as the nosewheel settled, it hit
a soft spot, and the Phantom lurched right, put its right
wing down, caught the earth, and cartwheeled.

It spun laterally, ripping off a wing and the vertical
stabilizer, dug its nose into the ground, and slithered to
a stop.

Upright, fortunately.

Barr was already running by the time she had stopped,

and mercifully, he heard the turbojets winding down. Hackley had killed them the instant he lost control.

The rear canopy was gone, but the forward canopy slowly raised as he approached.

He slid to a stop next to the fuselage which, buried in the dirt, gave him a clear view inside the cockpit.

Cliff Jordan said, "See if I ever ride with you again, Norm."

Both men were shaken up, and Hackley had a big bruise on his forehead, but nothing was apparently broken. Barr and Formsby got them out of their seats, and Littlefield and Potter led them away toward the Herc.

Barr sighed.

"I'd say," Formsby agreed.

"I hope my suitcase and civvies are still aboard the Herc," Barr said. "I'm giving up the Noble Enterprises job."

He stripped out of his G suit and the dove gray Noble Enterprises flight suit, then tossed them both into the cockpit of the F-4.

In his shorts, he leaned over the coaming of the cockpit, found the timer, and set it.

On their walk back to the Hercules, Formsby set the timers in the other two fighters. Barr didn't want to destroy his own bird.

Twenty

Wyatt had been sorry to see Hackley go.

In the immense wasteland surrounding him, he felt terribly alone.

Ah, Jan. I wish I hadn't given you anything to hope for.

He didn't think he was a particularly pessimistic man, but it didn't look good from where he sat.

He sat about eight hundred feet above an earth churned up by some earlier sandstorm. He figured his speed was down to around 180 knots because the F-4 was struggling. He had deployed his flaps and slats earlier in the effort to increase his lift. The flaps had moved only a third of the way into position before they grated to a stop.

He also figured he was sixty or seventy miles behind the others.

That was a long way in any desert, but particularly in this one, when there might be pursuit. He was worried about the transports Vrdla had been tracking.

On the other hand, he was relieved to know that the others had landed successfully, even if a little unconventionally on Hackley's part. No doubt, Kriswell would give Hackley a constant ribbing from this day on.

Peering as far ahead as he could see, he could find nothing that looked promising in terms of putting the airplane on the ground in a fashion that even came close to Hackley's performance.

A quarter-mile to his right was a wadi that appeared as if it hadn't seen water in two or three decades. It was, however, the only depression in miles, and he would feel better if he had a depression to hop into. To the south of it was a line of dunes that might serve as a secondary hiding place.

Just in case.

She wanted to go down some more, and he couldn't afford to lose much more altitude.

"Andy?"

"Right here, Bucky."

"How you doing?"

"Bopping along the same course I was on. I think."

"We're all down."

"I heard Sam reading it off. Everybody okay? Cliff and Norm?"

"Damn betcha. You going to make it?"

"As a matter of fact, Bucky, I'm going to punch out in about five seconds."

"Don't go wandering far from where you put down, okay?"

"Plan on it."

The aircraft was humping now, wanting to drag her tail, slowing, struggling for lift. The air intakes were at full depression, attempting to maintain a clean airflow into the operating turbojet.

Wyatt reached down into the crevice next to the seat,

lifted the flap on the box, and flipped the toggle on the timer.

"Sorry, honey," he said. "You've been a fine lady."

He made sure the safety pins were out of the seat, pulled his heels back as far as they would go, let go of the stick, and pulled the ejection handle.

For a quarter-second, he didn't think the seat was going anywhere.

Then the explosion blew him out of the cockpit, numbing his spine.

The wind blast caught him in the face and slapped his oxygen mask against his jaw.

The seat went over backwards, the sky flashing through his vision. He started counting, but knew he was counting fast, urging the release.

After a couple of eternities, the seat fell away, and the drogue chute spilled from his parachute pack, dragging the main canopy behind it.

It cracked open, abruptly slowing him, when he was less than a hundred feet above the surface. The canopy went concave for a few seconds, then filled.

The ground below appeared rough, and he grabbed the toggles and steered himself toward the wadi.

He didn't reach it, but touched down lightly, running, then tripped on a rut, and tumbled to the earth, rolling onto his left shoulder. The Browning automatic stung his ribs. The canopy settled around him, and he rolled onto his back and lay there, feeling exhausted. Keeping the airplane in the air had been more wearing than he had thought.

The Phantom didn't wait for the timer. When she hit the earth, the impact switch closed the circuit between the batteries and the detonators.

The explosion rumbled through the earth, gently shaking him.

He sat up and looked to the south. He couldn't see the crash site, but a column of smoke a mile away showed him her burial place.

It saddened him immensely.

Wyatt struggled to his feet, shrugged out of the parachute harness, and spread the canopy over the ground, securing it with piles of dirt he scooped by hand from the earth. It would give the Hercules a homing landmark.

He hoped.

Slipping the helmet off, he looped the chin strap through his web belt and let it hang off his right hip.

The sun felt particularly intense. The heat increased his rate of perspiration, and his damp forehead turned muddy with the dust already on it.

He retained his survival kit and rehooked it on his web belt.

Pulling the automatic from its holster, he ejected the magazine and checked the load. Wyatt wasn't sure why he did that; he didn't plan on using it.

Habit.

The military taught all kinds of habits.

The survival kit had a canteen of water, and he dug it out and took one sip, just enough to wet his mouth.

Until he saw the Herc, he wouldn't waste water.

He walked over to the edge of the wadi and looked down into it. It was about seven feet deep, he judged.

He sat down on its edge and dangled his legs over the side.

Slow day at the office, he thought.

And then thought about Jan Kramer.

He supposed she wasn't having a great day, either, and he was sorry for that.

Kriswell lost both of his seats.

Maal took the copilot's seat and Barr, now in jeans and a blue golf shirt, but still wearing his flight boots took the engineer's seat.

Jordan had wanted to fly the transport, but Demion told him he was suffering from shock, which may have been true, Formsby thought. Demion had consigned both Jordan and Hackley to sleeping bags in the cargo bay.

Formsby elected to hold onto a grab bar on the flight deck, so he could see through the windshield.

"You ought to tie yourself up, Neil," Demion said.

"I have an inordinate amount of faith in you, James."

He leaned over so he could see through the windscreen. They had something of a narrow alley to traverse between the two F-4s on the left and Hackley's crashed Phantom on the right.

Barr looked at his watch, and Formsby knew he was thinking about the timers on the explosives.

He checked his own watch. Thirty-two minutes before the three F-4s transformed themselves into shrapnel.

Demion advanced the throttles.

The turboprops increased their pitch.

The Hercules began to move.

Rolled twenty feet, picking up speed.

And the nose settled.

The nose gear sank into a soft spot, and the transport lugged down, slowed, stopped.

Demion goosed the throttles.

Nothing.

Demion tugged the throttles back.

"Shit!" Barr said. "Okay, everybody grab a shovel and get outside."

* * *

Kramer called again.

Church took it on Embry's phone. He was glad his ife didn't sit by a telephone with an automatic dialer rough every crisis in his office.

"There's nothing to report yet," he said.

"I can count minutes," she said. "Fuel states are itical."

Church looked over at the monitor, which was now ack on real time, since the infrared returns had disppeared. The small silver shape of the C-130 sitting the ground was visible, though the camouflaged F-4s ere not. The transport had started moving, then opped. Embry was trying to figure out why. It hadn't oved in fifteen minutes.

Also visible were two C-130s approaching from the east.

"They're all on the ground," he told her reluctantly. He dn't mention that the NSA had reported that one Phanm had crashed seventy-three miles north of the others.

"Where?"

"In the host country."

"But that's not right!"

"Fuel may have been a factor. But it appears that ey're changing aircraft now."

"Call me," she said and hung up.

Church wasn't certain he wanted to make the next ll.

The column of smoke grew larger as the C-130 lost ltitude and centered its nose on the funnel. Ahmed -Qati stood behind the pilot's seat and studied the round.

When they finally came into range, their radar ha
tracked this airplane until its demise. Captain Rahma
had yelled triumphantly the second it went off th
screen.

The radar had also followed another aircraft whic
had been flying with this one. It had split off and flow
farther to the south and then also went off the screen
Al-Qati had elected to examine this one before chasin
after the other.

"There!" the copilot exclaimed.

Switching quickly to the windows on the other side
al-Qati peered downward and saw the parachute canop
spread on the ground.

"He got out of the airplane before it crashed," th
copilot needlessly explained.

They passed over the burning wreckage. Al-Qat
thought that the pilot was a very lucky man. He ha
not seen an aircraft that had suffered so much de
struction in a crash. There were thousands of smal
pieces spread over a half-kilometer diameter. It wa
impossible to tell from here what kind of airplane i
had been.

"Land the airplane, Lieutenant," he told the pilot.

"I cannot, not here."

"Find the best place."

The transport rolled to the right, and al-Qati wa
forced to brace his feet.

"Sundown?"

Pushing himself back to the opposite bulkhead, al
Qati switched to the tactical radio channel.

"Moonglow, we are going to land now and deploy
the helicopters."

"Acknowledged."

They had to fly almost fifteen kilometers north before they found a place where the pilot would attempt to land. The landing was quite rough and could have been better, al-Qati thought, but it was certainly superior to that made by the intruder's fighter aircraft.

When the transport finally came to a stop, he, Rahman, and the Strike Platoon's commander, Lieutenant Hakim, were the first to deplane, exiting the crew compartment hatchway. The ramp was lowered next, and the soldiers of his First Special Forces poured out. Many of them appeared relieved.

Shummari's transport touched down two minutes later, and almost before it stopped, the ramp started to lower. His crews were already unfastening the cables holding down their helicopters. The Strike Platoon soldiers loped over to help disembark the Mi-8s.

The officers met in the space between the two airplanes. The dust raised by the landings hung in the air, coating their faces, but not protecting them from the heat.

"Khalil, we will want one helicopter for Lieutenant Hakim and the Strike Platoon. I will go with them to find the pilot of this airplane. The rest will go with Captain Rahman in the other helicopter and search for the other bomber."

Shummari said, "I will fly this one myself, Ahmed."

Within ten minutes, the first Mi-8 had rolled down the ramp, unfolded and locked its rotors, and the platoon embarked. Al-Qati tossed his CW gear aside, checked the magazine of his pistol, found a canteen, and climbed aboard.

Major Shummari strapped himself into the pilot's seat

and went through the sequence of starting the turbine engines.

They lifted off in a swirling cloud of hazy dust, and the nose swung around and dipped toward the south.

They would find the pilot, and al-Qati would soon know the names and nationalities of the people who had created so much havoc in his homeland.

He could be brutal when it was necessary.

Wyatt had first heard the welcome sound of C-130 engines, stood up, and turned to face the direction from which they came, the east.

The smoke from the burning Phantom was beacon enough, he had decided, and he had left the survival radio and the locater beacon in his survival pack.

He had then heard the blended roar of additional turboprops and considered that discretion might be in order. Slipping to the ground again, he eased his legs over the lip of the wadi, rolled onto his stomach, pushed backward, and let himself slide downward.

Pressing himself tightly against the side of the crevice, he waited. His back ached from the ejection. His face felt burned by the sun. He was getting thirsty again.

The thunder out of the east approached quickly, then washed over him.

Two Hercs, and both of them carried Arabic ID.

Not good, he thought.

They flew over the wreckage a mile away then banked toward the north.

They didn't come back.

But surely they had seen his parachute canopy.

The sound of their engines died away, and he didn't know whether to be relieved or not.

He did think that it might be better to make up his mind in another place.

Not closer to the wreck.

He turned to his left, stepped out to the middle of the wadi, and headed east, trotting even though the concussive jarring of his heels hitting ground was transmitted directly to his lower back.

The bottom of the wadi was irregular, catching his heels at odd moments, and forcing him to stumble. Its width varied, as he ran, from ten to fifteen feet wide. Dried-out armatures of old shrubbery clung to the sides of the trench. It was deep enough that he couldn't quite see over it.

He couldn't help remembering one of the first movies he had seen as a child. *The Bridges at Toko Ri.* William Holden and Mickey Rooney in a ditch, fighting off Chinese Communist soldiers.

There hadn't been a happy ending.

And then he heard the thrupp-thrupp of rotors.

And picked up his pace.

The pilot placed the Mi-8 on the ground near the parachute canopy, and al-Qati and his first platoon spilled out of it.

They spread out in a loose circle, moving warily away from the helicopter, sensitive to some sniper in the wadi or the hills to the south.

Nothing moved in that barren landscape.

Al-Qati examined the canopy. Fresh dirt had been

piled on it to hold it down. This pilot was expecting a rescue. The prospect held promise.

They might just greet the rescue party with open and tracer-spitting arms.

He went back to lean in the pilot's side window and yell over the roar of the engines.

"Khalil, they might attempt a rescue. Go back to the transports and wait."

Shummari nodded, and after al-Qati bent his head and trotted out of the rotor's arc, lifted off. The helicopter was soon gone.

"Lieutenant Hakim, take the first and second squads and work your way toward the wreckage. Notify me immediately if you find anyone. He is to be taken alive."

The platoon commander nodded, signalled his men into a skirmish line, and started toward the west.

The earth here was hardened into a surface that did not often leave the imprint of passage. In spots, however, there was a softness that gave way to heavy boots. In the area where the parachutist had landed, for instance. The ground was trampled there from the landing impact and, apparently, from where the man had fallen to the ground.

The wadi was, naturally, suspect. It offered the most cover in the near proximity. The man could have run for the low hills to the south, but if he had, he would still be there when the search teams reached the hills.

Al-Qati walked to the rim of the wadi, then along it until he found a place where the earth had crumbled and clods had fallen to the bottom. He saw no footprints, but he did not think they were necessary.

"Sergeant," he said to the first squad leader, "take your men to the other side of the wadi. We will walk both sides of it to the east."

"Right away, Colonel."

He ordered three men from the remaining squad to walk the bottom of the dry streambed, and spread the remaining four out to his right.

They moved out at double time, assault rifles at the ready, with purpose, and with some urgency.

This intruder was not going anywhere very far or very soon.

They used the broken vertical tail plane from Hackley's F-4 to lodge under the pair of nosewheels and form a ramp back to the level of the desert. It took quite a bit of digging under the wide fuselage in order to get it in place. They couldn't dig a wide hole without endangering the track of the main gear.

Barr was getting anxious about the timers in the F-4s. Being thorough professionals, they had designed them so they couldn't be shut off and so that, if someone messed with them, a premature detonation occurred. The closest Phantom, his own, was less than thirty feet from the left wing of the Hercules. If it went up, the debris would slice through the wing fuel cells, and it would be all over.

Winfield Potter said, "We aren't going to get it better than that, Bucky."

"Okay. Let's go."

As the men scrambled back aboard, Bucky asked Demion, "Jim, would you take it as a personal insult if I wanted to take the controls?"

Demion stopped with his right foot inside the hatch. "What are you getting at, Bucky?"

"No criticism. This is a mission I want to fly. Need to fly."

Demion shrugged. "No sweat. You want me in the second seat?"

"Damned right."

They climbed inside and Borman was there to close the hatchway. As he passed behind Vrdla, Barr said, "Sam, as soon as I get a generator going, fire up the radar and see what we've been missing."

"Roger that, Bucky."

He climbed to the flight deck, eased around the control pedestal, and lowered himself into the left seat. Dennis Maal gave up the right seat in favor of Demion.

"Neil," Barr said, "I know you like to look through the windows, but I want everyone down in the crew compartment, on the deck, backed up against the bulkhead, until after I get this mother off the deck."

Formsby didn't argue. He and Kriswell dropped down the ladder. Maal took the flight engineer's position.

They went through the start-up procedure as fast as they had ever done before.

Barr checked his watch.

Nine minutes to detonation.

Hackley's plane would go first. That was on his right, a quarter-mile down the makeshift airstrip. If the Herc was going to bog down again, he had to make damned sure he got way beyond Hackley's crashed Phantom.

"You've got nice power," Maal said over the ICS.

"How much can I have, Denny?"

"You can have it all, Bucky. Don't sweat it. Take an even strain, as Cliff would say."

"Jim, run 'em up."

Demion set the pitch on the Hamilton Standard propellers, then took hold of the bank of throttles and moved them smoothly forward.

Barr stood on the brakes as the power came up. He watched the tachometers. He felt the airframe shuddering, the wings vibrating, the brakes struggling to hold.

Eighty percent.

Ninety percent.

"That's a hundred," Demion said.

He released the brakes.

The Hercules hesitated at her new freedom, lurched forward, and the nose came up.

A few hollers rose from the men in the compartment behind him.

Lunging forward, the nose threatened several times to dip again.

The whole airplane leaned to the left as the left main gear crunched through the surface. The outboard prop came dangerously close to touching down.

The airplane bounced over a rise.

Leveled out.

"Twenty-fucking-miles-per-hour!" Maal yelled.

And forty.

And eighty.

"That's one-ten," Demion said.

He was getting enough lift to take the pressure off the landing gear.

The speed came up quickly then, though the plane was rising and falling with the uneven terrain.

"Rotate," Demion said.

Barr eased back on the yoke, and the nose gear broke free. The main gear followed.

When he had ten feet of clearance, the airspeed still building, Barr said, "Pull the gear, Jim."

Demion retracted the landing gear.

At three hundred feet, he started a left turn.

"Una problema," Vrdla said.

"What's that, Sam?"

"We've got a UFO on our ass."

"Shit."

"No shit. It's a slow-mover. Put some knots on her, Bucky."

The throttles were already at their forward stops. Barr lowered the nose a trifle to increase his rate of acceleration, then went into a shallow right turn.

He waited for the missile.

But none came.

They came around 180 degrees, and Demion, watching through his window, said, "It's a goddamned helicopter! Where'd that come from?"

"Can you tell if he's armed, Jim?" Barr asked.

"I don't think so. It's a Hip."

Mi-8. If they were armed, they carried rocket pods on fuselage pylons.

"Make your circle wider, Bucky," Maal said. "We can outrun this bastard."

Barr leveled off from the turn, then eased the yoke back again, searching for altitude.

"He's turning inside us, but he's losing ground," Demion reported.

"Damn," Maal said, "who expected that?"

"I'll tell you, maybe," Vrdla said. "Those transports from the east disappeared off my screen. I'll bet he came off one of those."

"If there's one," Barr said, "there's more. What do you see around Andy's location? And give me a damned course, Sam!"

"Go three-four-five. Nothing flying up there. Wait. I've got some faint return, but it's in the ground clutter. I'm guessing when I say the transports are on the ground near Andy. Give me a couple minutes and some more altitude, and maybe I can tell you more."

"All right," Barr said. "We've got to keep our eyes open. Everyone take up stations. Neil, get on the direction finder and see if Andy's transmitting a locater signal. Give me a time line, Sam."

Vrdla said, "Twelve minutes to the zone."

They had to take him alive.

If they wanted to learn from him.

That was some consolation.

But not much.

Alive, he'd scream more.

Wyatt's mind bounced a linked thought with each slap of his boots on the earth.

He tripped and went down, his face scraping the hard, gritty soil. His back was aching fiercely, his right ear still felt numbed from the antiaircraft shell. His breath came in sobbing gasps.

He sat up. Blood oozed from a laceration in his cheek, forming drops, and dripping from his jaw.

Got to his feet.

Started trotting again.

He had heard the helicopter put down, but then it had left immediately. He didn't think they were giving up; he thought they had a ground search underway.

His mouth was dry, and still running, he levered the canteen from his survival pack, twisted the cap off, and splashed a couple ounces in his mouth.

He slowed to a stop, catching his breath.

They would follow the wadi. There was just no other cover for him, and no other trail to follow for them.

Unless he could make a break for the hills to the south. He estimated that they were a couple thousand yards away. Fine at night, but not during the day.

Then again, he could sit down and shoot the first one or two who showed up.

He'd get two for their one.

At the moment, he didn't think his chances were much better than that.

About to take off running again, he heard the pounding of feet behind him.

A couple of muted yells in a language that was not English.

They were breathing heavily.

Or was he imagining that?

They were getting very close.

He looked around for a depression in the side of the trench, in the bottom, anything he could fold himself inside.

There was nothing.

Wyatt pulled the Browning from its holster and slipped the safety.

In the far distance, he heard turboprops.

Were they bringing in more troops?

Thought about the radio. It had a range of a couple of miles. If the others were near, they should know.

He slipped the survival pack off his webbing and unzipped it. Pulling the harness out and tossing it aside, he found the radio.

Flicking the on switch, he immediately heard, ". . . back to me, Yucca One."

Wyatt turned the volume down, then pressed the transmit.

"One."

"Gotcha!" Vrdla said. "Saddle up! We're coming!"

Dropping the radio, Wyatt shoved the pistol into his belt, picked up the harness, and stepped into it. He pulled it up, snugged it into his crotch, then hooked the shoulder strap fasteners. From a yoke at the top of the shoulder straps, a coiled line of cable was suspended, held in place by a plastic tie. On the other end of the one-hundred-foot line was a small pouch.

The pounding feet were coming closer.

He picked up the pouch, pulled it free of the balloon, jerked the lanyard on the aluminum cartridge, and heard the helium escaping into the bright orange balloon. It filled rapidly, rose from his hands, and trailed the thin cable behind it after he broke the plastic tie.

He was watching it rise and listening to the oncoming turboprops when the pounding boots stopped pounding.

He looked up to the top of the wadi.

A soldier, an officer, stood there, panting slightly and aiming his pistol up at the balloon.

He felt the tug when the balloon reached the end of its tether.

It was, however, a bit too late.

Al-Qati yelled to his soldiers in Arabic, "Do not shoot! We want him alive!"

The soldiers fanned out on both rims of the depression, keeping the muzzles of their AK-74s trained on the man who was wearing a soft gray flight suit. His helmet was attached to his webbing belt and looked out of place.

The three soldiers in the wadi went to their stomachs, rifles extended before them.

The pilot was holding his own pistol, aiming it directly at al-Qati.

Without letting his own aim waver from the balloon, al-Qati said in French, "Who are you?"

Al-Qati was well-versed in military strategies. He knew what the balloon meant, and he knew what the approaching airplane engines meant.

He also knew that if he shot the balloon, he would die seconds later.

The man did not answer.

He tried again, in English. "Who are you?"

"You speak English? That's nice."

"Give me your name, or I will shoot."

"Your last shot," the pilot said.

He seemed very determined, standing with his legs spread wide, the pistol aimed at al-Qati's heart.

"Perhaps. It would be yours, also."

"I'm not too handy in Arabic," the man said, "but does your name tag read, 'al-Qati?'"

"It does."

The airplane engines were becoming louder. They raised their voices in compensation.

"I'm not sure I believe this."

"What are you talking about?" al-Qati asked.

Unbelievably, the pilot lowered his pistol, then shoved it into the holster under his arm.

"She loves you, you know," he said.

"What! Who?"

"She specifically asked me not to shoot you. So I won't."

Ahmed al-Qati was stunned.

And also hopeful.

He lowered his own pistol.

And stood there as the massive C-130 came roaring down the wadi, its four propellers scattering sunlight, a hundred feet off the ground, trailing a big wire loop from its lowered ramp.

The loop snatched the balloon.

The pilot was there one second.

And gone the next.

Reincarnation

Twenty-one

The sun had gone down hours before, leaving North-field, Maine, wrapped in blackness. There were no runway lights, and there was no traffic.

At the side of the runway, the C-130 was parked next to Church's Falcon business jet.

With the aid of flashlights and stepladders, a half-dozen men were taping blue stripes to the side of the Hercules and changing her N-numbers.

Inside the Falcon, Wyatt lounged in one of the soft seats, sipping from a squat glass of Chivas Regal.

Barr, who had grabbed the bottle and was pouring his second glass, said, "Your budget must have improved, Marty. This is real Scotch."

"I bought that out of my own pocket, Bucky," George Embry said. "But it's only because I thought you deserved it."

"You have nice taste," Barr said. "Send me a case for Christmas."

"This can't be what you people call a debriefing," Jan Kramer said.

She had flown to Washington right after Church had called her to say they were out of Libya, and she had demanded that Church bring her along to this meeting. Barr was riding back to Washington with Church, to catch a plane to Lincoln. He planned to personally deliver one of his scholarships to Julie Jorgenson.

Kramer was sitting in the chair next to Wyatt, and he reached over and took her hand.

"We work slowly up to it," he said.

"Get on with it, will you?" Her voice was hard, but her hand was soft when she squeezed his own.

Barr did the honors, uncharacteristically skipping the frills and condensing the substantial points. ". . . and then we made one last stop," he said, glancing at Kramer, "picked up Andy, and came on home."

Wyatt set his glass down in the armrest holder and scratched the beard on his face. The numbness had gone, and his hearing was coming back in the right ear, but his left cheek was scabbed over. He wouldn't be shaving for awhile.

He hoped he wouldn't be doing any more ejections or ground retrievals ever again. His back was going to be sore for weeks.

Embry looked over at him and said, "Ahhhh, that more or less corresponds to your first reports. You did meet al-Qati?"

"For one extremely brief moment," Wyatt said.

"My gal says to thank you. She has, by the by, resigned from the Agency and is living in Rome."

"And al-Qati?"

Embry shrugged. "Who knows? We haven't heard about him. Perhaps one day, he'll show up in Rome."

"What are the first reactions?" Wyatt asked.

Church answered that one. "The Leader has appealed to the UN for assistance in locating the perpetrators. Remember, this is the man who doesn't like UN interference in his affairs. This was a few hours after he insisted that the explosions at the factory were simply an industrial accident. I think he changed his mind after overflying the area.

"On specifics, the chemical factory is out of business. Our people estimate that the gases have already dissolved, and they may go back in and try to rebuild. The same holds true for Marada Air Base. It's hard to keep these people down."

"Ramad?"

"I don't know. He seems to have disappeared, but then again, he's disappeared on us before. He may be on the run, if the shortcomings at Marada are placed on his head."

"They're determined people," Wyatt said. "They'll probably rebuild."

"I hate to think we might have to go back and do it all over again in a couple of years."

Church smiled while saying that.

"If it's necessary, Marty," Kramer said, "give me a call and we'll talk about it."

Church stopped smiling.

Kramer smiled and ran her forefinger along Wyatt's palm. "There was a board meeting of the only available board member of Aeroconsultants yesterday, and there's been some restructuring. I'm now in charge of contracts."

Wyatt grinned at her. "What else was reorganized? Am I still president?"

"Of course."

"And me?" Barr asked.

"You don't do much, Bucky, so you're still just right for vice president."

"That's a relief," Barr said. "I'd hate to have to go to work."

"There's just one other change," she said. "The new chief of security is Ace the Wonder Cat."

William H. Lovejoy is a successful author of techno thrillers, espionage novels, and mysteries. He lives with his wife in the Rocky Mountains of northern Colorado.

FOLLOW THE SEVENTH CARRIER

TRIAL OF THE SEVENTH CARRIER   (3213, $3.95)
The enemies of freedom are on the verge of dominating the world with oil blackmail and the threat of poison gas attack. *Yonaga*'s officers lay desperate plans to strike back. Leading a ragtag fleet of revamped destroyers and a single antique WWII submarine, the great carrier must charge into a sea of blood and death in what becomes the greatest trial of the Seventh Carrier.

REVENGE OF THE SEVENTH CARRIER   (3631, $3.99)
With the help of an American carrier, *Yonaga* sails vast distances to launch a desperate surprise attack on the enemy's poison gas works. But a spy is at work. The enemy seems to know too much and a bloody battle is fought. Filled with murderous rage, *Yonaga*'s officers exact a terrible revenge.

ORDEAL OF THE SEVENTH CARRIER   (3932, $3.99)
Even as the Libyan madman calls for peaceful negotiations, an Arab battle group steams toward the shores of Japan. With good men from all over the world flocking to her colors, *Yonaga* prepares to give battle. The two forces clash off the island of Iwo Jima where it is carrier against carrier in a duel to the death—and *Yonaga,* sustaining severe damage, endures its bloodiest ordeal in the fight for freedom's cause.

*

Other Zebra Books by Peter Albano

THE YOUNG DRAGONS   (3904, $4.99)
It is June 25, 1944. American forces attack the island of Saipan. Two young fighting men on opposite sides, Michael Carpelli and Takeo Nakamura, meet in the flaming hell of battle that will inevitably bring them face-to-face in a final fight to the death. Here is the epic battle that decided the war against Japan as told by a man who was there.

THE WINGMAN SERIES